UNCONSCIOUS

UNCONSCIOUS

A collection of short stories

by

GERALD ARTHUR WINTER

Adelaide Books
New York / Lisbon
2021

UNCONSCIOUS
A collection of short stories
By Gerald Arthur Winter

Published by Adelaide Books, New York / Lisbon
adelaidebooks.org

Editor-in-Chief
Stevan V. Nikolic

For any information, please address Adelaide Books
at info@adelaidebooks.org

or write to:

Adelaide Books
244 Fifth Ave. Suite D27
New York, NY, 10001

ISBN: 978-1-955196-22-2

Printed in the United States of America

For my Sophia, with love forever

Contents

The Catch **9**

Afterglow **15**

Hand to Hand **27**

River Rats **39**

The Jogger **62**

Menagerie **84**

A Free Sampling **103**

Jetsam **111**

Fractured Frontier **124**

Vermilion **137**

Priceless **143**

Star Struck **158**

Buried Treasure **178**

Treadmill **204**

Unconscious **210**

Jersey Gal **222**

The Last Gulag **232**

A 30% Chance of Tomorrow **245**

Flowers on the Wall **256**

The Aviary **265**

Vaccine Nation **276**

Acknowledgements **325**

Visuals **327**

About the Author **329**

Many thanks to . . . **331**

The Catch

The young boy had been casting his kudzu net into the shallows for several hours with no luck. The minnows were too small for the hook on his make-do bamboo pole. He hoped for a catch that day to match his appetite with a burn in his gut for several days after ingesting only onion grass, dandelion greens, and one Tiger Lily blossom he'd snatched from an iguana's sharp teeth. Without a larger bait fish on his hook cast beyond the shallows before sunset, he'd go to sleep hungry for the fifth day in a row. Uncle Tuatoo had warned him last week that five days would be the limit for a fifty-pound boy under four feet tall before he'd begin to imagine people and things that aren't real, but which nevertheless could still physically harm him.

"You will meet your spirits before your time is right," Tuatoo told his nephew, Zumbata. "We all will meet our spirits sooner or later, but the later the better, hopefully when we are so old that endless sleep is more comforting than a life of aches and pains and deep sorrows from missing those we'd loved."

"I would like to introduce myself to my spirits now, when I'm alert and agile," Zumbata told Tuatoo , the most respected elder of their village. "Then, after I've lived a full life, I'll have wisdom to share with my ancestors to make their afterlife a blessing of endless delights."

"You have an upside down view of the universe," Tuatoo cautioned him. "Time goes clockwise while *your* mind spins counterclockwise. You'd best take care that your unbridled thoughts don't make the world spin off its axis and take us all with you into a fiery pit of hell for angering the gods."

"Kind uncle, I'm thankful for your concern for my well-being, but I can't live this life without challenging these rules governing our thoughts. They're laws imposed by *man*, not by Nature. And even if some should turn out to be true, they have no hope of real truth unless they are tested. All laws must be pulled and stretched like my mother's dough in preparation for baking bread. How else can we affirm their justification? How can yeast make dough rise, like my father from the dead, without my tugging at these hard-fast conclusions written in stone? Bread is life, but stone is death."

"Stubborn nephew, you will be the death of your mother, my beloved sister, if you don't quell these rebellious feelings. Since your father was lost at sea, she depends on you to fill the void left by your father's absence. He had the same unruly spirit that now draws you away from our sad village."

"What if my father, Chakotah, is merely lost? Perhaps he still lives waiting for his brave son to bring him home to his waiting family. Shouldn't I, his only son, attempt to find him? Wouldn't my effort to do so make my mother, Saluz, rejoice over my bravery? If I found my father and brought him back to her, wouldn't my parents tell the world they have the best son ever born?"

"Not if you are their *dead* son, Zumbata. That would break my sister's heart long before her scheduled time to leave us. Her mourning wails for her only son would make her moans for her husband fade into a solemn grief, so hardened that it could never be penetrated or soothed, even by the infinite expanse of Time. Even the gods would whimper for Saluz's losses."

"True, wise uncle, but just the same, I must try to find him. I have my whittled scrimshaw hook, a bamboo pole, and fishing line tough and resilient that I've fashioned from my mother's coarse black hair. I shall live by my daily catch until I find my father. But don't look so sad, Uncle Tuatoo. If I remained in our village just to comfort my mother in her grief, there would be no hope for my father's return. If I'm lost, too, and never return, at least the village will carve my likeness for the Shaman's alter to honor my memory for my mother. Even in my failure to bring back my father, I shall be hailed by our village just for trying, and my mother will be glorified among us for all time."

Zumbata's own words from three days prior echoed in his head and curdled in his stomach pained by his hunger as he continued to cast his net when the sun descended with half its orange glow behind the sea's distant horizon. The orange turned crimson dissipating on the sea into vermillion sparkles that turned violet then were gone. Gentle waves lapped against the shore, then the warm surf around his ankles made his bare, calloused feet sink into the wet sand.

He thought he heard a water bird's trill. but it was different from any he'd ever heard. There was the whoosh of the surf followed by the trill, then a sudden tug on his kudzu fish net.

Perhaps a school of larger bait fish, he thought, or even a huge fish to stifle his starvation for several days.

Just when he thought he'd lost his catch, a jolt from the net almost pulled him over face-first into the surf, but his feet had sunk so deep into the sand that, even in his weakened state of hunger, he could brace himself against the force threatening to drag him out to sea. In total darkness of a moonless night, he couldn't see what was in his net, but its strength alarmed him as he resisted against it with all his might.

"I've got you!" he shouted, but only a trill responded.

He reached deep into his heart for his greatest strength to land the bulk trapped in his net, but the exertion made him faint from hunger . . .

"Zumbata . . . wake up, Zumbata. It's your father, Chakotah."

Zumbata's eyelids fluttered, but the sun was rising behind the backlit head of the figure leaning over him so he couldn't distinguish the face. The voice, however, was surely his father's.

"Are you speaking to me from the dead, or are you among the living?" Zumbata asked, but he was answered only by the trill. "I need to know the truth!" he demanded.

He heard heavy swishing beside him and turned to see a long scaly tail thrashing about trying to get free from the net. He took a deep breath filling his head with an intoxicating scent of jasmine. He turned back to speak to his father, but the figure was gone. The trill drew him back to the tail now swirling around his thin bony limbs. Attached to the tail was the naked torso of a young woman with a concave navel where a ruby the size of a Brazil nut was pinned. Above were two pert, pink-nippled breasts, long thin arms, and a neck upon which rested a sweet, rosy-cheeked face. Her thin eyebrows were raised above her long-lashed, green eyes that shimmered at sunrise. Her pink lips were pursed and from them came the same trill.

"Where is my father?" Zumbata asked her. "Do you speak *Mandobaba?*"

"I speak any language that is spoken to me," she said. "I thought you were a blue heron, the way you were standing with your feet so deep in the sand." She trilled. "See. I was speaking *Squeesquakas*, the international language of waterfowl."

"I don't know it," he said.

"Of course not," she tittered. "You're not a mermaid."

"Oh? I see . . . *That's* what you are?"

"Well, I'm not a shark or a dolphin, but perhaps a combination of both. I'm a predator like sharks and crocodiles, but I have a warm heart and breast-feed my young for a year until they are strong enough to survive on their own."

"That's very interesting, but where is my father? He was here just a moment ago."

"He joined me some time ago beneath the sea and we have a new family together. Chakotah is a survivor, adaptable to any new environment. You have three half-brothers and only one sister now. The other sister was caught in a kudzu net much like yours."

"She's dead?"

"Mermaids don't die, like your father, we adapt. But she's only half-mermaid, so she's mortal, but resourceful. If she takes after me, she'll be around for the next millennium."

"My mother loves my father. He must return with me. I owe it to her to bring him home safely."

"I'm sorry for her loss, but it's been my gain. I can't let him go. He belongs to me now. The only way to free him, would be to kill me, but I'm the predator, you see, and you a starving child are my pray. And you're not much of a meal either. I'll be hungry again soon. Have you no brothers or sisters who've tagged along behind you, upon whom I might feast later?"

Zumbata grinned sweetly at her, which touched her tender heart as if he were one of her litter.

"Perhaps I should fatten you up and make a better meal of you for another day," she said, pulling him close and offering him breast milk.

But as her hardened nipple touched his lips, he reached into his pocket for his scrim-shaw fishhook and forced it between her ribs into her heart. He was glad she seemed to suffer no pain. There was no outcry, just a single tear down her rosy cheek quickly turning pale. Lifeless, her eyes instantly dilated with a thin ooze of blood from her pursed lips.

"Good job, my son," Chakotah's deep voice came from behind with a pat of his hand on Zumbata's bony shoulder before all faded into a deep abyss of muted darkness . . .

The morning sun hurt Zumbata's eyes and made his head ache as he sat up to see his father Chakotah, his mother Saluz, and his uncle Tuatoo seated on the ground around a fire roasting a great fish on a spit.

"Once you've had a good filling of this tender fish you've caught," Saluz said to him. "Uncle Tuatoo says your wild imaginations from lack of nourishment for five days will bring you back to normal."

"Your mother is right, Zumbata," Tuatoo said. "I can tell from the glare in your hollow eyes that you've experienced things of which I'd warned you. But don't be afraid, even if you still have occasional nightmares about it when you've become a young man with children of your own. None of it was real, or at least not of this world, the world we respect for its rules and order."

His father, Chakotah, said nothing, but gave him a wink, which he found comforting until he bit into a piece of the huge fish he'd caught in the net when he'd found his father washed up on shore. He chewed around the hard bit of grit concealed under his tongue then waited till he was alone in bed at night before spitting it into the palm of his hand.

The moon shown bright that night as Zumbata held his palm close to his face. He saw his own wide-eyed expression reflected in the mermaid's ruby. It was red like her blood and the crystallized remnant of his father Chakotah's unfaithfulness to his future children's grandmother, Saluz. She was the most honored sister of their village elder, Tuatoo, whose empathy for his wronged sibling was greater than her husband's passion to stray.

Afterglow

He was startled by the knock at the front door. Then the doorknob jiggled for a moment before he heard the key inserted and the deadbolt click open. The metal door creaked on its hinges as it swung open. The bright, rectangular light from the open door hurt his eyes from twenty feet across the hardwood floor to the sofa where he'd been anticipating . . . anticipating . . . anticipating . . . something—anything to help him regain what he'd lost.

A backlit figure, obviously of a woman with her graceful, dance-like strides, came toward him. With the setting sun at her back, her lithe figure cast a long shadow, a narrow black path that cut straight to his doubts. She turned to close the door behind her, but he objected.

"No! Leave it open . . . I need fresh air."

"Fresh air?" she questioned with a thin taint of mockery in her tone. "I think you may have had too much of that already,"

"How so?"

"I've been calling you for the past—" She looked at her pink smart phone's screen. "Jesus, Jared. It's been eighteen hours."

He frowned then gave her a blank stare. The time hadn't registered. She sat beside him and put her cool palm to his fevered forehead. "Are you ill?" she asked. "Should I take you to your doctor?"

"It's Sunday, Bethany."

"Then to the ER."

"No . . . I just need rest . . . to gather my thoughts."

"Thoughts about what? About us?"

"Everything doesn't have to be about *us*."

"Maybe not, Jared, but lately it seems everything has *nothing* to do with us."

He grimaced and shook his head. "I just needed time to complete my novel. I'd promised delivery of my final draft by . . . shit! By tomorrow."

"That's why I've been calling. This three month separation has been hard on me . . . I've missed you, Jared."

Without response, he just stared blankly at her.

"Damn you! Kiss me," she implored with a puckered closed-eyed lean toward him.

"Hmm," he responded in her embrace, as her lips searched for his tongue, like an anaconda unhinging its jaws to swallow a capybara along the Amazon, but he resisted.

"Jared! What's with you? Is there someone else? You slept with her last night and now you're done with me?"

"You're being ridiculous, Bethany. I'll never be done with you, but . . . I may be done with *me*."

"What are you talking about, Baby?" she asked nuzzling his neck, but before he could answer, she pulled back with a start. "Jared! What happened to your shoulder? My God!"

She pulled his bathrobe off his shoulder, bruised deep purple. As she kept pulling the bathrobe lower, she saw that his entire arm was the same lavender hematoma hue.

"I'd better get you to the ER right now," she said.

"No ER . . . I'll be fine. It doesn't hurt. I saw it when I took a shower. It goes down my back on the left side and—" he pulled open his bathrobe to reveal his total nakedness, no surprises there after three years as lovers. "My left hip and down my thigh past my knee to my lower calf." He raised his left leg and rotated his foot. "The ankle's fine."

"How can it not hurt?" she asked. "It looks dreadful. It hurts just to look at it."

"Because compared to my inner hurt, these exterior bruises are insignificant."

"Don't go literary on me at this crucial moment. This looks fucking serious! Do you think anything's broken?"

He grinned with the corner of his mouth, creasing a dimple that had first attracted her to him. "Not any bones," he sighed. "Just my spirit."

"Okay. Let's start from the beginning," she said as if she were prepared to take dictation. She occasionally had when the only way he could create a short story was verbally because his fingers couldn't keep pace with his mental narrative.

Jared struck a pose in Lord Olivier, Shakespearian fashion, "It was a dark and stormy night as Jared emerged from his mother's womb."

She punched his right shoulder. "Damn you, Jared! I'm serious!"

He pulled the robe off his right shoulder. "I'll give it an hour, but you may have hit me hard enough to have matching purple shoulders. Jeez. Where'd you learn to punch like that?"

"I grew up in Philly. My best defense against the mean girls."

"Well just control yourself. I had a pampered childhood."

"Yeah, right. Ozone Park, Queens? That couldn't have been a church social either."

"Guilty as charged," he huffed, but slipped back into the dregs of his morose. "What have you been doing these past eighteen hours to have ended up such a fucking mess?"

"Blank . . ."

"What do you mean?"

"A total blank."

"You mean you don't remember?"

"Not a damn thing—zero."

"Wow! Okay. Go back in your mind to the last thing you can remember."

"I'd been working eight or more hours a day since the end of June till—what day is it?"

He'd already had his wall calendar out on the coffee table before Bethany arrived, so he leaned forward from the sofa and pointed to the day Bethany had said it was.

"It's Sunday. We just talked about that. Remember, your doctor's office is closed today."

He nodded and pointed. "Hmm, today is Sunday, June twenty-fourth. Yesterday, I had the last scene in my novel to write, only a couple of pages left to go. I used Hemingway's advice by not writing the last scene, even though I'd already worked it out in my mind. Papa said it was best to stop writing near the peak of a climax and sleep on it so all the creative juices could percolate overnight. It's supposed to give a writer greater insight to write what had been concluded in the subconscious, a much purer environment for creating effective fiction."

"You mean that Dr. Butler *Dreamscape* shit?"

"Precisely. Intending to sleep on it, I'd been living like a monk these past ninety days to meet my publisher's deadline tomorrow, so I'd gone to *a clean well-lighted place* for cocktails and dinner before coming home to sleep on it. The plan was to wake early this morning to complete the novel and submit it tomorrow for my agent to deliver."

"And so?"

"So I don't remember leaving Adaggio's where I had two glasses of Merlot with my veal chops marinara."

"How could you not remember leaving?"

"That's the million-dollar question."

"We should go to Adaggio's and inquire."

"I called an hour ago. Spoke directly to Anton, the owner. He said I seemed fine when I left with the woman?"

"Woman? What woman?"

"I went alone. I ate alone. I don't remember leaving, with or without a woman."

"Anton couldn't tell you anything about her? How about a description?"

"He'd never seen her before, but she was a blonde, wore sunglasses as I did, because I was seated on the exterior balcony facing the sunset, much like tonight's. It was about twenty-four hours ago when I was finishing my dinner."

"Did you finish, then have dessert or coffee?"

"I don't think so . . . I remember looking down at my empty plate expecting the waiter to clear the table, but then—"

"Then what?"

"There was a crashing sound, I felt jolted, then I . . . then I . . . jeez, I can't remember, not a thing till less than an hour ago. It's all a blank."

"Jesus."

"Jesus, Mary, and Joseph—a fucking blank. I've been trying to write those last few pages of my novel and none of it makes any sense. Each time I think I'm done, I realize the last three pages are the same—the same! Over and over, the same goddamn pages, paragraphs, sentences, and words. It's as if I'm not writing them, but they're writing themselves . . . They have a life of their own."

"Show me," she said.

As she read the pages, Jared stared at the widescreen TV left on mute. It was the local news. A boy had been run over and left for dead in a hit-and-run incident with no witnesses. It happened in a rural section of town where there were no security cameras to view a video of the apparent vehicular homicide.

Bethany read aloud: "He felt like an angel, his feet not touching the ground as he descended the balcony stairs to the parking lot. In his mind, he seemed to float across the parking lot to his car. It looked like a good chance of rain with dark clouds hovering on the horizon above the sun setting atop the distant trees. He opened the hatchback of his SUV and took out a cheap umbrella, the kind sold for three bucks on city street corners in a sudden downpour, but not meant to survive more than a single squall. Much as he felt about himself regarding his longevity in the nameless shit storm that his writing career had recently become—"

He interrupted her narrative from the manuscript on his laptop. "Stop. Please, quick run downstairs to the garage and bring me my umbrella."

"What the hell for?" she balked.

"Uh, I want to see if it's wet from using it in the rain last night. It might help my memory."

"You've been lying around till almost dinner time, Jared. Can't you get it yourself?"

He lowered the shoulder of his robe to reveal the purple bruise and fawned for sympathy. "Christ, you're such a baby."

He opened his robe like a flasher. "That's no baby—Baby."

She huffed, "I liked you better when you had no memory of what an asshole you can be."

"Sorry. You've been so kind in my hour—make that eighteen hours—of need."

"You sound like John Barrymore in an old Thirties flick that I wish had remained silent.

Okay. I'll get the umbrella, but I think I should take you to the ER for a look at those wounds—and to check for a concussion, too. Which may explain your memory loss."

When she closed the door where she'd entered minutes ago, he waited until he heard her footsteps descending on the exterior wooden stairs from the balcony to the garage. Then he turned up the TV's volume and heard: "The police have been going door to door in the neighborhood surrounding the alleged scene of the hit-and-run. The boy was pronounced dead at the scene when found at eight o'clock this morning by another boy on a bicycle. The coroner put the time of death at no later than nine o'clock last night. Apparently the body had been left alongside the light-trafficked country road for about twelve hours before discovered. If you know anything, anything at all, please call the hotline shown on your TV screen. The boy's parents have been distraught since he hadn't return home last night from his job at McDonald's. He was expected by 10 p.m. but never showed."

Jared heard Bethany shriek from the garage. He turned off the TV and heard her rapid ascent on the stairs. The door swung open just as before, still startling him even though this time he was anticipating her entry.

"What?" he asked as she approached him.

"When did you have an accident with your car?" she asked.

"Accident?"

"Your left front fender is totally crunched."

"Oh . . . when you said 'accident' I thought you meant with another car. I hit a deer a week ago. Poor thing never had a chance. I was going to report it, but with my novel's deadline, you know how it is."

"Where did this happen?"

"Hmm, let's see. It was when I took a short-cut off Ulmerton Road. That country road that winds around the horse farms and saves you fifteen minutes with no traffic lights. You know how bad the traffic can be on a weekend."

"Weekend?" she asked. "Which weekend? Not last night?"

"Last night?" he hesitated staring into space for a moment. "Oh, no. It happened the weekend before." He began repeating himself in Trumpian fashion, hammering details into the solid metal of the listener's brain until his truth became hers by amalgamation. "I'd just bought a book I'd wanted to read for a long time. I went to Barnes and Noble in town, got the book on discount with my membership then drove home."

He reached for his wallet lying on the coffee table beside the calendar. From between the loose bills, mostly twenties, he pulled out a receipt from the book purchase. He unfolded it and squinted at it closely then handed it to her as if it were a Special Delivery of fact: Exhibit A.

She squinted at the receipt as well and said, "Hmm. September sixteenth. Then the car is drivable, right? Since you hit the deer?"

"Well . . . I drove it home that night but . . . I guess I haven't tried to drive it since."

"Why not?" she asked.

"I figured I'd just call and have it towed by the body shop when I was ready to make the insurance claim."

"Don't you have to make a claim within limited time, like twenty-four hours, maybe forty-eight at most?

"The novel . . . the deadline . . . it's consumed me," he rationalized. "The dent isn't important compared to that . . . it's my living. The dent is nothing but an unfortunate reminder of an animal that didn't have the good sense to look before it leaped."

She said, "You're forgetting one important fact, Jared."

His mind raced. *Fact? Fact? Forgot a fact. Forgot a fucking fact?*

She took a deep breath then spoke in high C, like air slowly released from a balloon. "You must have driven your car to and from Adaggio's last night when you had dinner . . . with that damn mystery woman."

"The blonde?"

"The same . . . with the sunglasses . . . who Anton never saw before."

"It's coming back to me now . . ." he said as if visualizing a scene.

"Oh, really?"

"Yes."

"Who is she, Jared?"

"My Uber driver."

"You can't expect me to—"

"No. Really, Bethany. Her name was Lilly."

"Like short for Lillian?

"No . . . no. She was very unusual. She introduced herself to me, as Lilly when she picked me up here to go to Adaggio's last night at six. But her name on her posted ID said "Lilith.""

"Oh, boy! That's a good one, Jared. So some psycho Uber driver with satanic genes beat the crap out of you and gave you all these bruises. Maybe you didn't tip her enough after she drove you home, so she threw your ass down that twenty-foot flight of stairs from your balcony to your garage?"

"It's a thought," he said with a shrug, but she wasn't buying it.

Obviously pissed, she waved an arm at him with dismissal and said, "Have it your way, Jared. But I'm going to call Uber and find out who this psycho bitch is who threw you down the stairs. Not like I haven't wanted to do the same to you often enough."

As he heard her footsteps in decent on the exterior stairs, each clunk on the wooden steps reminded him of his drunken tumble down the stairs last night. Was it 9:45 p.m. or 10:15

p.m.? The numbers had been blurred on his SUV's digital clock right after the impact, enough from the side along the dark road's shoulder to collapse his fender, but not enough to inflate the airbag. He swore he'd seen a deer, an eight-point buck writhing with its muscles in his rearview mirror. Nothing else, so he'd kept driving with only a mile left to his home.

He'd fumbled with the remote garage opener, but entered without a scratch. He'd gotten out of his car, beeped the car lock with his keys, then closed the door and headed up the stairs to have that last night's sleep for the closing scene of his novel to congeal the action in his grey matter.

He undressed and put on his robe and sat on the sofa, gathering his thoughts as he flipped on the eleven o'clock news. As he'd drifted off in slumber, he felt at peace with himself, in a smooth transcendence from what is and what might be . . .

He felt like an angel, his feet not touching the ground as he descended the balcony stairs to the parking lot. In his mind, he seemed to float across the parking lot to his car. It looked like a good chance of rain with dark clouds hovering on the horizon above the sun setting atop the distant trees. He opened the hatchback of his SUV and took out a cheap umbrella, the kind sold for three bucks on city street corners in a sudden downpour, and not meant to survive more than a single squall. Much as he felt about himself regarding his longevity in the nameless shit storm that his writing career had recently become. He was feeling lightheaded from his two glasses of wine at dinner. Anton knew his car, so it wouldn't be towed if he left it overnight and took a cab home. He dialed Uber.

Within two minutes, the Uber driver showed up, lowered her window and said, "Hi, Mr. Smythe, I'm your ride."

When he sat in the passenger seat beside her, he read her ID card on the dash and made a muffled *hmm* sound.

"Problem?" the driver asked.

"Oh, no," he said with a shrug.

"What then?" she asked.

"I used to date a woman with the same name."

"No shit."

"Yes, shit," he said, grinning. That dimple crease in his cheek held her attention.

"You're my last fare tonight," she said. "I started at 6 a.m."

"Whew! Sixteen hours? Is that legal?"

"No . . . but I am."

There was a minute of silence. Ten minutes from Adaggio's she was already pulling into his driveway.

Nice to meet you, Mr. Smythe," she said. "Here's my card. I'm local so you can always call me direct when you're in a hurry."

"You want to come up?" he nodded to the stairs leading to his second-floor balcony.

"You mean for a drink?" she asked, totally blasé and not offended by such an open, male predatory gesture.

"Or for the night . . . but only if you want to," he said, showing all his cards.

"Didn't I see you with a woman in the parking lot just before I arrived to pick you up?" she asked.

"The blonde?"

"The blonde."

"Business associate," he said.

"What's your business?"

"I'm a writer?"

"What do you write?" she asked.

"The jury's still out on that."

"Can I be your jury-of-one tonight?"

"Why not? Come on in, *Bethany.*"

She followed him up the stairs and they entered his condo. She went to the guest bathroom to freshen up and he did the same in his. In his bathrobe, he came to the living room and poured two glasses of Merlot then waited for her to join him. He was startled by the knock at the front door. Then the doorknob jiggled for a moment before he heard the key inserted and the deadbolt click open. The metal door creaked on its hinges as it swung open. The bright, rectangular light from the open door hurt his eyes from twenty feet across the hardwood floor to the sofa where he'd been anticipating . . . anticipating . . . anticipating . . . something— anything to help him regain what he'd lost.

A backlit figure, obviously of a woman with her graceful, dance-like strides, came toward him. With the setting sun at her back, her lithe figure cast a long shadow, a narrow black path that cut straight to his doubts. She turned to the open door behind her, where two other figures followed her.

"Jared Smythe?" one of the men asked.

"Yes," he said with resigned calm as the blonde took off her sunglasses.

"Sorry, Jared," she said. "They've seen your car in the garage. The dented fender. There's blood. It's a match."

"Bethany!" He called to the bathroom. "Come out and tell these people where I've been these past eighteen hours."

He thought he still heard the shower running, but it turned out like most of the past eighteen hours, that it was all just the afterglow of his imagination . . . music of the night that spun a tune to suit its composer, but echoed untruths, perhaps lies, even to himself.

Hand to Hand

Chet never thought his study of fine art in college could provide him with a life of luxury for a decade on Madison Avenue. Michel Angelo's (1475 –1564) and Leonardo Di Vinci 's (1452 – 1519) works reviewed in his elective course, Art History 101, planted the first seeds of his fascination with human anatomy.

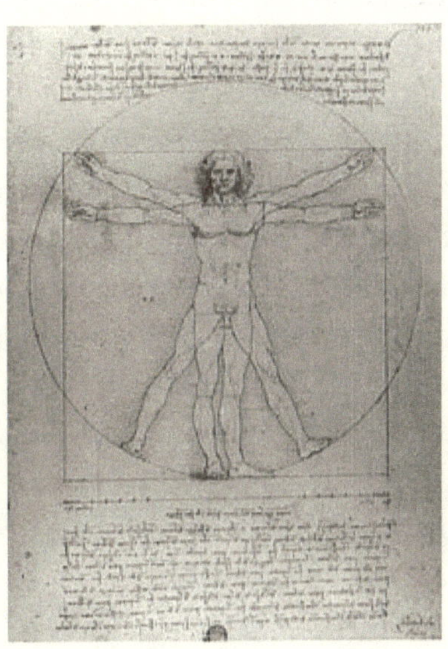

With three mouths to feed and another on the way, Chet got a Draft exemption in 1942 by working for the Department of Defense using his draftsman skills rather than bearing arms against the Axis powers of Italy, Germany, and Japan in ascending order of strength by 1945. Though Chet never gave much thought to his drawing skills, something that just came naturally, when World War II ended, the late '40s provided a window of opportunity. Though photography was the media of the future as demonstrated by the black-and-white photo covers of *Life* magazine, illustrated renderings would become the mainstream medium of advertising through the next decade.

Chet had taken his father's advice after college—"If you want to get ahead in this world, start by marrying a redhead. They can light the fire in a man to make him succeed."

Chet's wife Lilly may not have been the Lucille Ball flaring redhead that Chet's dad had in mind, but her auburn coif ignited a passion in Chet to make her proud of him. Work was hard to find with so many veterans returning from war, so Lilly checked the want ads for Chet while she kept her three-year-old son out of mischief and nursed her newborn daughter.

At his drawing table in their small apartment in Queens, Chet worked on his portfolio of illustrations from appliances to food, drink, clothing, and cigarettes. His rendering of a pack of Lucky Strikes ® was his pièce de résistance featuring his understanding of perspective, color, and lettering. But it wasn't until an art director at Grey Advertising looked at his portfolio presentation and posed a question that sparked Chet's brilliant future.

"Where have you been working?" the art director asked Chet. "Your work is as close to photographic as I've ever seen. How come I've never heard of you?"

"I've been doing catalog work from home the past year," Chet said.

"Catalogue work?"

"You know, in Sears Roebuck, refrigerators, dishwashers, and the like. But I prefer the bras and panties section," Chet said with a wink that made the art director grin.

"Do you prefer to freelance or are you looking for a salaried position, Chet?"

"If I were single, freelance would suit me better. I'm married with two kids, so a salary appeals to my wife to provide more certainty for our future."

"I need someone in our art department as soon as possible. Can you start now?"

"Well, I—" he started to stall, but Lilly's face hovered in his mind. "I haven't had lunch yet."

"We'll order out on me. Does pastrami on rye with mustard sound good?"

"That would be swell. Thanks—?"

"I'm Hal. What're drinking?"

"Coffee's good. Black—keeps me sharp."

Hal escorted Chet through the "Creative Department" and introduced him to the guys in the bullpen who made mechanicals for engraving guidelines and used a photo stat machine the size of a Chevy coup to make quick cheap copies of illustrations or photographs or art directors' rough visuals for print ads. TV hadn't made its mark for advertising yet with less than ten percent of homes having a television. There were no women in the bullpen. The only women Chet had seen were receptionists on each floor as you came off the elevator and as personal secretaries for the main department heads of Sales, Copy writing, and Art.

"We have a Pall Mall ad coming up this week and the copy-writer wants to show a man's hand lighting a woman's cigarette with a Zippo lighter. Time to show America that the war's over and it's safe to have kids—lots of kids—ya know, like a Baby Boom."

Chet gave Hal a *no sweat* shrug of confidence.

"Problem is, I need finished art by tomorrow noon for client approval and the deadline to get to the engraver without paying overtime is five o'clock tomorrow night."

Chet gave Hal a look of confusion.

"What? No can do?" Hal asked.

"Can do. But I was just wondering why you've got so many other men reading the funny papers at their drawing boards? Why do you need me if you've got a deep bullpen with guys lounging around with their thumbs up their butts."

Hal laughed giving Chet a pat on the back. "I knew I was gonna like you when you made that crack about preferring to draw panties and bras. No BS, just straight to the point, which is how I promise to be with you. These guys all lack one talent that only you've demonstrated in your portfolio. You can draw hands, men and women's, that have expression."

"Can't any of these other artists draw hands?"

"None like you can, Chet, so get to work and ask for anything you need."

Chet went to his cubby hole and arranged his palette. Within the next hour he had a rough pencil sketch of the woman's hand holding the cigarette between her index and middle finger. There was a subtle profile of the woman's pursed lips at one end of the cigarette and the Zippo lighter's flame at the other. The man's hand holding the lighter with the expertise of a WW II vet showed a rugged masculine assuredness compared to the slender grace of the woman's smooth hand with long, but unobtrusive fingernails.

Within two hours Chet was knocking on Hal's open door that said "CREATIVE DIRECTOR."

"I'd like you to approve the direction I've taken in my preliminary sketch," Chet said.

Hal was on the phone and waved him closer and nodded for Chet to angle his sketch toward the afternoon light from the window facing Madison Avenue from the 7th Floor.

"Hold on a minute," Hal told his caller then his mouth dropped open. "Jesus, Chet! That's fantastic. I wouldn't change a goddamn thing, but now I need the finish in color for tomorrow."

Chet nodded then as he went out the door he heard Hal say to the party on the phone, "You're gonna love this fuckin' ad. I just hired a guy who nailed it."

* * *

From 1948 to 1958, Chet's commercial illustrations for top advertising print ads made him a fortune with his special talent to render expressive hands. He didn't stay on salary more than a year before demand for his expertise made freelance work more profitable than ad agency bullpen assignments, even for clients paying $100,000 for a full-page color ad in top magazines.

"You could eliminate the middleman, Chet," Lilly said. "Sure, this has been a great year for us, over fifty thousand dollars and two weeks paid vacation, but if you worked as a freelancer for hire, you could name your price, maybe earn as much as the Yankees pay Joe DiMaggio."

"Joltin' Joe?" Chet said with a laugh. "He makes as much as President Truman."

"Chet, honey, with your talent you could draw Harry Truman's hand giving the middle finger to Governor Dewey and everyone would know it was your creation."

"I doubt that," Chet said.

"I made a call this morning, Chet. The Democrats are willing to come up with five thousand dollars if you give them finished art for mass production by Friday—five grand! Enough to pay for Chet Junior's college education. Maybe Carol's, too."

"Carol's? You mean nursing school, or secretarial school?"

"No! I mean a four-year college degree for our daughter."

Lilly flashed her green eyes and fluffed her shoulder-length coif recently died as bright orange as Lucille Ball's. She could afford a weekly manicure as well with Chet's current salary but she wanted more. Chet realized his father was right about marrying a redhead.

Though Chet made the deadline for the Democratic Party, better judgment blocked releasing the artwork into circulation. Even though it was a perfect expression of the Truman legacy that followed, censorship demanded that it be destroyed with any rough sketches Chet made in preparation for the finished art. The perfect negotiator, Lilly told Chet to demand $10,000 if his work was destroyed. He got $12,000 when the GOP started sniffing around over rumors of Chet's artwork's existence. It was Chet's first freelance contract, but to protect the paper trail from scrutiny, Lilly did the billing simply referring to the artwork on Chet's invoice as "Hand Job."

When President Truman went to sleep on Election Day in 1948, Thomas E. Dewey had been declared the victor. When he woke the next morning, Truman learned as the rest of the nation had, that he had four more years as President.

Chet was later approached by GOP ancillaries to reproduce duplicate art so they could say it was the original to discredit President Truman for his vulgarity during his next term. Despite their offer of $10,000, Lilly declined in Chet's behalf because, now as his agent, she said he'd be too busy for the next four years working out of their Connecticut home to meet illustration demands of five Madison Avenue advertising agencies paying a combined total of a million dollars. Chet, Jr. and his sister Carol would be going to Ivy League colleges.

With Lilly arranging Chet's schedule and handling his billing, they rode the gravy train between New Canaan and Grand Central Terminal for the next ten years, but by the late 1950s photography had become more cost effective with advanced means of reproduction. Eastman Kodak took advantage of leadership in photo technology reproduction that challenged commercial illustrators to lower their charges to ad agencies who were employing staffs of a new breed of artists—photo retouchers.

Chet was among a few fortunate artists who'd had a wife like Lilly to discipline him by putting aside ten percent of his earnings into savings and investments so that when demand for his talent declined and was replaced by a new breed of photographers and retouchers, he and Lilly could still continue their lifestyle after their children had families of their own.

The unexpected often catches us short in life as was the case for Chet when Lilly died in her sixties, cutting short their dreams of exotic travel. Widowed at age seventy, Chet had no one to come home to from Manhattan to Connecticut at night, so he sold their home for twenty times what they'd paid for it in 1950, and rented a one-bedroom apartment on the eastside of mid-town Manhattan where most of his working adult life had been spent with great demand for his talent.

I ran into Chet in Manhattan on my way to The Studio Bar on Second Ave near the adjoining corner of 44th Street near McCarthy's Steakhouse and The Palm, which were too rich for my blood as a photo retoucher in a sweatshop studio typical of the 1960s. I was taking a sandwich my wife had made for me that morning to have my lunch at the United Nations Plaza where I could watch the East River water traffic from the park filled with flowers and a bright patch of green grass to offset all the concrete and steel of New York City.

I'd just come through Grand Central Terminal toward Lexington Avenue but took the short cut through the lobby of The Graybar Building so that, as instructed by my elderly friend Chet's wife to him a decade ago, "People will assume you're working for J. Walter Thompson in that building, so you can raise the price of your artwork."

So far, that hadn't worked for me, but I was only in my twenties that day when I saw Chet coming out of Schrafft's restaurant. He'd had his two martinis up and the fish platter.

He'd stopped eating red meat on doctor's orders the year before, but had said to me at the time, "Without Lilly, life is still worth living, but only if I can still have my two martini's at lunch. If not, I'd prefer the dirt nap six-feet under."

Chet provided a wealth of wisdom for me in my early years working in Manhattan with a commute from north Jersey. I was just an apprentice photo retoucher at Rialto Studio at the time I met Chet with his bowties and suspenders and metal clips on his forearms to keep the watercolors from getting on his crisp white dress shirts. He also wore a full denim apron to protect his chest and lap from paint spatters so he'd always look his best in Schrafft's. I'd kidded him once, asking, "Do you think you might meet another redhead at Shrafft's?"

I'd felt bad about the question when he got teary-eyed and said, "Lily was my one and only everything, not just a redhead."

I'd never kidded him about anything personal again, but he did have a sense of humor about the profession that had made him rich.

"If I was asked by my relatives or highbrow Connecticut friends in the bar car heading home about what I did for a living, I gave them the honest answer—*I play the piano in a whore house.*"

He also taught me to never sell my talent short.

"The best way to get a raise if the bastards won't give you one, is go work for the competition for a year, do your best there, then come back and the pricks will pay you twice what you were making before you left. Ya know, a rolling stone gather's no moss. Who the hell wants god damn moss when you can get cash!"

Chet learned a lot from Lilly over the years. As an artist for detail he was a keen observer. He didn't just have his nose to the drawing board all day. He negotiated his own deal with Rialto Studio for a four-day work week, unheard of at the time. Although he couldn't earn the kind of income he had in his prime, nothing close that, on an hourly basis, he was the highest paid artist on staff because his work looked as realistic as a photograph, which was in great demand at the time approaching the 1970s.

"The world has a way of stealing from you over time," he'd told me. "What's the *in-thing* today is tomorrow's trash."

Chet was right because the photography technology brought with it the demand to work with chemicals rather than with watercolors on photographs. The Kodak dyetransfer era of 1980s required "bleach-and-dye" application on photos. Chet called it the "bleach *or* dye" movement in photographic illustration. The need for his painterly talent rapidly diminished.

"I'm like a silent film star after 1927," Chet said. "Obsolete."

The last time I saw Chet was 1988. In his nineties, he was just a shadow of the man I'd known. I was in my professional prime as a bleach-and-dye photo retoucher with a full-page ad in THE CREATIVE BLACK BOOK and a penthouse apartment to work from off First Avenue. My studio was a nine-iron chip shot from the United Nations Plaza where I used to have a sandwich from home for lunch in the park. Now I could entertain my own ad agency clients at The Palm for lunch or The Billy Munk Pub around the corner for my lesser clientele. The food was great there, too, but the ambiance included Irish waifs with bedroom eyes that beckoned for more than a tip. There were always a few choice redheads in the mix.

I'd called him just to chat during a slow spell and he came up to my studio to meet the seven other photo retouchers who worked for me. He brought a package under his arm in a large, flat envelope the size of a 20" x 24" dye transfer photo.

I showed him some of our recent work and he just nodded silently with his chin resting on his fist. He said nothing about the package he was carrying so I finally asked, "Whatcha got there, Chet? You back to freelancing? If we get busy again soon I'll give you a call. I can always find a job for someone with your gift."

"Thanks, but I'm done with working. Before I show you what's in the package, you ought to read this article in *The New York Times* from yesterday." He took a crumpled page of newsprint from his suit jacket, handed me the article, then straighten his bowtie.

The article was about a computer called the Sci-tech machine, which could retouch photos by the use of pixels, computer units that can create image details and color variations.

The claim of the article was that this technology would replace both photographers and retouchers who didn't adapt and learn the new process.

I just shrugged then handed it off to be shared by my staff. "You don't really think we can ever be replaced by computers . . . do you?" I asked Chet.

"You could be in the same position I was thirty years ago—a silent movie star," Chet warned, then motioned for me to open the large envelope he'd brought with him.

As I unwrapped it and set the artwork on our presentation table where art directors viewed finished photos ready for engraving, Chet took me aside and told me the story behind the artwork.

"I want you to have this as a reminder to you a few years from now that nothing lasts forever. The world is in a constant flow of change, sometimes for the better, sometimes not, but change just the same. It's yours to do with as you wish, but I've kept it hidden for over seventy years and now I'm ninety-five. The most I was ever paid for my talent was *not* to reproduce this illustration, so I trust you won't either, but will remember the story I've told you about it. Think of my gift to you as hand to hand, one hand washing the other."

"So you didn't destroy the original after all?"

"I had to give them the destroyed art to get paid, but Lilly thought it would be wise for me to paint another one from scratch for insurance—redheads—go figure."

I nodded in agreement as he departed. I never saw Chet again other than reading his obituary in *The New York Times*. He'd survived his wife and both children and his commercial illustrations had been compared to Norman Rockwell's work. What I think of most when I remember Chet, is that my bigger than life-size portrait of Harry Truman's hand flipping the bird to Thomas E. Dewey will be imbedded in my mind forever.

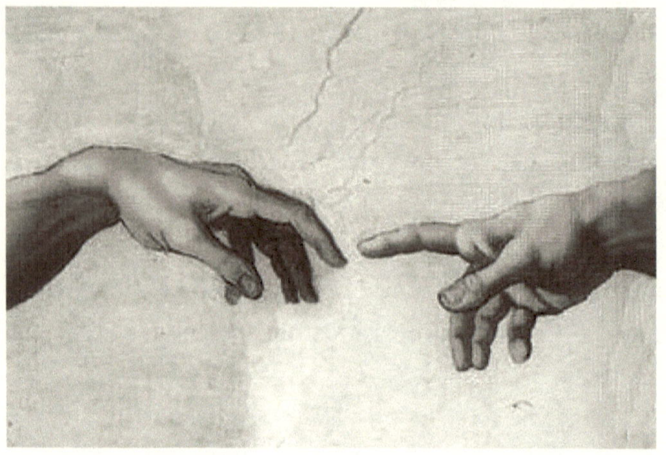

River Rats

Oakdale, Florida was more like a movie set than a real town. You had to drive ten miles to I-75 just for a junk burger. If I didn't want to spend the next forty years at *The Banner* writing obituaries, I'd have to return with a news story that rang true about the monster flood that nearly wiped out a town nobody but its residents had ever heard of.

Heading to the flood site, I sat beside Sheriff Davis seated at the wheel in his patrol car. He drove at five miles an hour like a Disney World tour guide, but there wouldn't be much to see till we reached the edge of the raging river.

I couldn't wait to get out of this lazy-ass town and back to Ocala where hard news was at my fingertips every day without driving an hour in my old Toyota crap-mobile with a piss-paint refinish and holes in the driver's seat cushion. OK, so it was a hand-me-down from my mom, my graduation present from USF last May. The sheriff's patrol car was a pleasurable change from my rattletrap. His red convertible looked like it belonged in a NASCAR series—hot and fast— yet we continued to crawl toward the town's lowland swamps where the flood presumably had caused the most damage.

"Nothing moves *fast* in Oakdale, accept the river when it's flooding," the sheriff said.

He was six-four, well over two hundred fifty pounds with a beer paunch pressed against the steering wheel. His wrinkled face showed a man who enjoyed life with a sparkle in his blue eyes when he wasn't wearing his wrap-around sunglasses. His tan uniform already had dark sweat stains at the armpits and it was only 9 a.m. in steamy September. Rather than cooling things off, the heavy rain that had caused the flood was like throwing ice water on sauna stones—*psst, sizzle,* burn.

On his short-sleeve shirt, the sheriff's gold badge sparkled from his barrel chest. His Stetson, with a tilt to his right ear, sat on his short-cropped, greying head with both ears flat against sideburns cut level slightly above a his earlobes.

It must have been the same hat he'd worn for over twenty-five years, because it fit his square-jawed face like a comfortable, old slipper long overdue for the trash. His straight teeth were coffee stained, but he didn't smoke. His hands, tanned and veined, were like bear claws grasping the steering wheel, and his fingernails were squarely manicured, but with oil grit under them from working on the patrol car, a red 2020 Camaro, the town council's gift to celebrate his twenty-five years of service that cost more than Oakdale's annual budget.

"How far are we from the river?" I asked.

"A mile from here," he said with a sleepy expression. "Nothin' to see but debris floatin' downstream. Same flood, different year. Nothin' newsworthy."

"Where'd you get that fancy gear shift?" The Camaro's shift knob was a Budweiser draft spigot.

"Do someone a favor, they do you back."

"I'm going to take some photos of the damage with my iPhone. Where we heading?"

"Only one place to go—homes along the river. Curious to see how my old house held up."

"Your family still lives there?"

"Nah. In the Heights on the ridge, but I've got boyhood memories from the low ground along the river. The more floods you survive, the tougher you get."

I jotted down some questions to ask him about the town's history, but before I could ask him about the flood zone, his car phone buzzed.

"Damn! Just when I thought we'd take a short cruise through the flood zone," he said. "Can't be important. Nothing exciting has ever happened since I've been sheriff."

"Maybe someone drowned."

He shook his head. "No one's ever drowned here . . . Hi, Bobby," he said into the speaker phone noting the caller I.D.

"Hi, Sheriff," a man's voice came over the static speaker. "Coupla bodies just washed up on the west rim of the Apopka Reservoir."

"Don't touch nothin', Bobby."

"I ain't touchin' nothin' . . . they're wrapped in a hug."

"A hug?"

"That's right."

"Men or women?"

"Can't tell—just bones. But not too big, maybe kids—teenagers."

"On my way," he said, turning to me with a wink. "Finally, a chance to blow my siren and flash my lights. Ya takin' this all down, son?"

* * *

The sheriff hit his siren and flashed his lights. "Never took her over fifty before. Hold on!"

The highest speed in Oakdale was thirty-five. The Camaro hit seventy on the straightaway toward the reservoir. With the convertible top down, my hair and tie blew in the wind's rush. Before he could slow down, a wave from the rampant river came over the hood, and the patrol car was stuck in three feet of rushing water.

The sheriff turned off his siren, kept his lights flashing, and cursed. We were surrounded by two gushing streams. Flotsam and jetsam slammed against his precious Camaro. He took off his Stetson and fanned himself as perspiration trickled down his face. He panted like a hound after a chase.

"We gonna be OK, Sheriff?"

The flashing lights died and the engine stalled. He turned the key, but the Camaro just shuttered. He tried again with just a clicking sound, then zip.

"Got a stay put." He pointed where the river was channeling around a house and coming at us from two different angles. "If the river expands any more we're screwed. Can ya swim."

My stomach curdled. "Doggie paddle." I felt the grits I ate that morning backing up to my throat with a burn. "How can we get out?"

"Current's too strong. Forget the car. We'll need a chopper to lift us out."

He removed his sunglasses, revealing a crooked nose bent to his right as if he'd been in a few brawls. Despite his tough physical appearance, his smooth, deep tone was an endearing trait that I grasped onto as the voice of experience that might get us out of this jam.

Please God, I thought, recalling the Gideon Bible in the drawer of my Motel 6 Room up river on higher ground.

***

The sheriff called Deputy Mike on his flip-model, dumb-phone. "I got a situation here. I was on my way to meet Bobby at the reservoir, where a couple of bodies washed up, but I'm stuck in the flood and sure as hell can't drive out a here. I got that kid reporter with me."

I bristled at the word kid. I was twenty three.

"Call the Troopers and put out a call to Flood Rescue for a chopper . . . Tell Bobby where I'm at. He's expecting me to meet 'm, but I can't get there till they lift us out. If you can't reach me, it means this phone went dead and we're just hanging on. We can't keep the water out of the car once it comes in over the doors, but at least that weight will give us some drag, so we won't move as fast downriver or flip over."

Taking a deep breath, he must have thought I was scared, but I was pumped with adrenaline, knowing if we survived, my inside story on the flood could be my break to reporting hard news fulltime.

"You said no one ever drowned here."

"Not *yet*."

"And *no* crime here since you've been sheriff?"

He shook his head.

"How about when you were a kid growing up in the flood zone? Anything you can give me for my article on this monster flood about local history?"

The sheriff swiped flecks of grit with his index finger from the corners of his azure eyes. He ran his finger over the bridge of his crooked nose, as if that hard bump held some secret from his past. He looked me straight in the eye and spoke with a calming resonance, maybe just to dissuade me from fear of our immediate peril. He tried to distract me with a story about when he was a boy as we waited for help. The rampant river was too dangerous to attempt to swim away from the car. I'd probably drown and take the sheriff with me if he tried to save me.

The sheriff began his distraction: "There were three of them, ages fourteen, fifteen, and sixteen. Always up to no good, they weren't much for schoolin' neither. No intent to go to high school, and the two oldest left back so many times, the three of them ended up in eighth grade together. Two of them did time in Reform School. The youngest was the only one with a spec of good in him, but he was a scrapper, known to kick the crap out a boys five years older. From youngest to oldest, their names were Tommy, Ricky, and Andy."

I jotted down every word, but before the sheriff finished his story, a log a yard long and a foot wide came downriver and shot over the trunk of the Camaro and shattered the inside windshield.

"Damn!" he hollered, standing up on the bucket seat and dusting glass shards from the windshield off his lap and chest. He used a handkerchief to pat his face where it bled.

I jumped up, too. Astonished by his story, I asked, "What ever happened to those boys?"

Davis turned to me and plopped his hat on his head at an angle. He said the two older boys had been known for not coming home for days at a time. But after three days, their mothers had finally called the sheriff. Most in town had assumed they'd run off together, as they'd often threatened they would. When they hadn't shown up for a month general opinion had been that they were either jailed felons or dead. They'd vanished leaving no clue.

Their younger friend had told the sheriff that they planned to hitchhike to West Palm. Except for their mothers, no one had missed them, and the town had forgotten about them for the past forty years.

"What about Tommy?" I asked, but before he could tell me, the fluttering of a helicopter turned our attention skyward as the rescue crew hovered thirty feet above us and dropped a line with a harness to lift us to safety.

"You first," the sheriff shouted over the roar of the chopper as it blew off his Stetson. The wide-brimmed hat bobbed out of sight in the river's strong current. From the look of loss on his face, I could see he would never be comfortable wearing another hat.

We stood, then the sheriff helped me with the harness. I fumbled with my notebook trying to tuck it in my belt, but the sheriff shook his head.

"Your life is more important than that old wives' tale," he said. "Keep it to yourself in your head." He tapped his finger against his temple. That's where I've kept it all these years."

He waved to the crew to pull me up. But just as I lifted off, the river gushed over the Camaro's doors. My weight made the difference. As they pulled me up into the chopper, I watched the sheriff fall backwards with the jerk of the car, then the car surged forward downstream. The sheriff held onto the steering wheel, but the brown, river current pulled the car under. The red Camaro suddenly leaped out of the river like a whale before submerging again beneath the muddy current.

The chopper followed in the direction where the patrol car was last seen and headed downriver for two miles before we saw the Camaro, upside down wedged beneath a train trestle with no sign of the sheriff.

✳ ✳ ✳

Within half an hour the helicopter brought me to safety on high ground in Oakdale, I planned to recompose what I'd written in my lost notebook about the no-name storm that washed away most of an entire town.

My car was still on dry land upriver where I'd parked it at "Katie's Place" for breakfast with the sheriff earlier that morning. I went into Sadie's and ordered two large coffees with cream and sugar, like I knew the sheriff drank his. Sadie put them in a cardboard holder, assuming they were for me and the sheriff, as I asked her how to get to the Apopka Reservoir.

"Don't drive too close to the shore," she warned. "We get sinkholes in these parts that could swallow an eighteen-wheeler."

I took the two coffees in the box and placed them on the floor in the backseat of my '96 pea-green Toyota heap. Then I drove out to the reservoir, hoping my reporter's instincts were right. As I rounded the swollen reservoir, I listened to the radio reporting the storm's devastation. The river had caused mud slides in "The Heights" area of town. Erosion had washed away the Miller's home that the sheriff had referred to in his tale about the three boys from forty years ago.

I found Deputy Bob standing on the shore with his cell phone to his ear, trying to reach the sheriff and wondering why he hadn't shown up. Though I had a brief moment of ethical conscience and moral doubt, I decided not to tell the deputy that the sheriff had died in the flood, not yet.

I called to him from a distance and walked toward him. I carried my spare microphone from the car since my own got washed away in the sheriff's car. It wasn't plugged into anything, because I wasn't interested in anything the deputy had to tell me. The sheriff had said it all, but I needed to confirm what I suspected.

"The sheriff said you'd be here with two bodies that washed up this morning. He's got more than he can handle down river."

"Where's he at?" the deputy asked, squinting as if he was looking for the red Camaro to come to a screeching halt behind me to relieve him from his watch.

"He's down by the train trestle," I said with a quiver in my voice. At least I had some solace that it wasn't an outright lie. I pointed to a lump on the shore that looked like a pile of fish nets knotted together. "Sheriff Davis said you should let me have a close look . . . for my news story about the flood."

He cocked his head. "Ya gonna put my name in the paper? I'm the one who found 'm."

"Absolutely . . . Deputy Bobby, right?"

"That's right. How'd ya know?"

"Sheriff Davis told me," I said and waved the dead microphone. "Sheriff wants me to confirm in writing what you'd told him earlier."

"Wha's 'at?"

"That the corpus delicti is two skeletons wrapped together in a hug, that they might be teenagers."

"That's right. But they must've drowned," Deputy Bob said with a confused expression and a shake of his head. "It prob'ly ain't one a them *corpus* thingies. Looks like an accident—not a crime."

Crap, I thought, side-stepping toward the skeletons, *Bubba might've read a law book or two at the Police Academy.* "The sheriff is waiting for my confirmation," I said.

"Don't he believe me?" Bobby said with hurt in his tone and expression.

"Sure, but he has to confirm it for the records with all the news stations swarming around. Got to look good if the FBI steps in."

That convinced him, but he sidled up beside me step-for-step right to the bodies with flies buzzing around them. With my pen clenched between my teeth, I swatted at the flies with both hands. I couldn't tell what gender the bodies were, and in their embrace with their knees bent toward their chests, I couldn't tell how tall they were. A DNA test from Ocala CSI would determine those details. I couldn't wait. The smell of the rotting bones in the heat nauseated me, but made me wonder how long they've been dead. If they'd just drowned, why was their flesh so decomposed? Were they already dead before the flood. Had they been washed into the raging river days ago? Had vermin consumed their flesh first? Maybe a mud slide had washed away a cemetery and their embrace was merely coincidental.

Then something caught my eye. I almost reached out to touch it with my pen, but Bobby was hovering over me and said, "Damnedest thing, huh?"

"I've got some hot coffee for us in my backseat over there," I said, pointing to my car, which made him turn his head. "Would you bring the coffees here, while I give this mess a closer look?"

He nodded and looked back once over his shoulder, heading toward my car, and said, "Don't touch nothin'."

I called back, "Just looking!"

When he opened my car and bent to pick up the coffee, I looped what I found with my pen and slid it into my shirt pocket. Bobby was already heading toward me at a quick gait, so I couldn't examine what I'd found.

"The sheriff will be pleased to know that your observations were correct," I said, as he handed a coffee to me and sipped his own. "You got a coroner in this little town?"

"That'd be Doc O'Grady. He's the only doctor we got. He writes the death certificates when somebody dies."

"Call him. With those flies and the stink, it's a health hazard," I said.

As I got in my car and pulled away, I saw Deputy Bob talking to someone on his cell, hopefully, to Doc O'Grady. I drove my car back toward Main Street and parked outside Sadie's. I waited several minutes before I felt in my pocket for what I'd taken from one of the bodies. I held it in my tight fist then turned it over in my palm. I held it close between my thumb and forefinger with one eye squinting to read the name etched inside the cheap ring.

I was exhausted and couldn't do what I needed to do until the sheriff's body was found, so I went to my motel room ten miles away on I-75 and spent the restless night, dreaming about people the sheriff had told me about, but was more troubled over the terrible news the sheriff's family must have received by now. But during that fitful night in my motel, the story he'd shared came to life in my mind as if I'd seen it all happen myself.

* * *

In the morning, I went to the address Sadie had given me when I came to Oakdale yesterday looking for the sheriff. But Sheriff Davis had found me first, so I'd had no reason to go to his office or home. I drove slowly down a dirt road for half a mile before it opened up to a two-lane paved road then brown fields of shriveled corn stalks gave way to green sod and a large white house in the distance. With my windows open, I heard dogs barking and soon saw two black Labs running alongside my car, not aggressively, but more like a welcoming committee. The paved road came to a gate at a white fence where a sign on the gate said: "Welcome to the Davis Homestead."

Though the dogs seemed friendly, I hesitated to get out of the car, so I beeped my horn. An attractive, strawberry blonde, probably in her fifties like the sheriff, but looking more like early forties, came out of the house and called to me, "They're harmless! I'll open the gate!"

I wondered if Sadie was a close friend and might have called ahead to Mrs. Davis to tell her that the reporter from *The Banner* was heading out to see her. I figured the news must be out about her husband's drowning, so I wondered why she seemed so bubbly.

I drove through the open gate and parked. The two dogs sniffed at me with curiosity, but were quickly disinterested and plopped down on the porch. I followed Mrs. Davis through the screened door into the house. She told me to sit on the sofa and she offered me a glass of sweet iced tea. My throat was parched in anticipation of what I would say to her, but her big smile with perfect teeth took me off guard. She did all the talking with a stream of excited drawl that my mind couldn't keep up with.

She punctuated her incredible story with, "There he was, still hanging onto the Camaro by that damn Budweiser gear shift."

Ironically, her voice sounded muffled, as if we were both underwater. But by the Grace of God or some force of nature, we weren't, and neither was Sheriff Davis.

"He'll be glad to see you," she said. "He needed rest after that ordeal. Broke a couple of ribs when the Camaro slammed into the trestle, but he's a tough ole boy."

That he was. As I came into his bedroom, he was propped up with pillows on a king-size bed with a view out a circular window where horses were running in a pasture behind his house.

"How ya doin', son?" he asked, extending a big hand that smothered mine with a vice-like grip. I heard one of my knuckles crack, but felt no pain, just so glad to see him alive.

I laughed. "How am *I* feeling?"

"I was worried, because I left you in the lurch when the chopper came for us. If you got hit in the head getting' into the chopper, you might've had amnesia and forgot about the story I'd told ya."

Mrs. Davis came in and chortled, "I think my sheriff has had too much OxyContin for his broken ribs. No hooch for you tonight, baby."

"How bout some *kooch* instead, darlin'?"

"Time to holster yer pistol and take a nap," she said to her injured bull of a man.

She put a gentle hand against his rough cheek, and he closed his eyes.

When I followed Mrs. Davis out of the bedroom, the sheriff said in a deep growl, "Ya can take the rat out of the river, but ya can't take the river out of the rat."

I wasn't sure what he meant. I thought about it all the way back to the motel. I was exhausted just from thinking, let alone the physical duress of being in that patrol car moments before the river swallow it, then spit it out. I couldn't drive back to Ocala. I needed more time to consider what I should do about the ring I'd found. I'd need the sheriff's reaction, then I'd know.

I'd already written a draft for Sheriff Davis's obituary in *The Banner*. I'd said Davis was a fine upstanding peace officer who'd raised himself out of poverty in Oakdale. He'd graduated from Ocala High School where Oakdale kids had been bussed. He'd been the star fullback on the football team, had served four years in the U.S. Navy, then he'd graduated from the Orlando Police Academy. Over twenty-five years ago he'd been elected Sheriff of Oakdale and now was just weeks from retirement. He'd planned to teach his grandsons how to fish in the local swamp. Since I wouldn't be submitting his obituary, I spent that night piecing together the sheriff's story from forty years ago.

* * *

Three Oakdale boys, Tommy, Ricky, and Andy, often hung out in a deserted bear cave on the mountain ridge after school, where they smoked cigarettes and told dirty jokes and tall tales, mostly about local girls. Their families lived in the cheap cottages along the riverbank, so their bragging was about skanky river girls they'd French-kissed, or stuck-up Heights girls they wished they had.

"What was Reform School like, Andy?" Tommy asked.

"They shanked me once, but when I told them my dad was a lifer for killin' a Florida Trooper, they backed off."

Ricky said, "If it wasn't summer vacation, they would've expelled me for stealin' the sheriff's patrol car. I made it to the Ocala Mall, but they caught me shopliftin' blue jeans. My stepfather beat me with his belt, but I still told 'm to go screw himself. The son of a bitch took it out on my mom again."

"Nice goin' at the movies, Tommy," Andy said, grinning.

"Yeah, man," Ricky said. "I wish I'd seen it. I heard when ya popped that high school senior from the Heights, his nose bled all over his white varsity sweater."

Tommy laughed. "He said his friends would get me that afternoon, but I just gave him the finger and asked if they were bringin' tire irons or chains? Pussies."

For these three boys, hopping onto a moving freight train was a thrill in third grade, but by their teens, even a dive roll at 30 mph from a boxcar into a field of slithering cottonmouths just drew a yawn. Tommy dared the other two to jump off the train from the middle of the railroad trestle, a thirty-foot drop into the slime of the stagnant river below, green with algae in the summer drought. Laced with toxic waste that had killed the gators, the river's surface looked like a putting green, concealing any jagged junk that lay at the rocky bottom.

Being the oldest, Andy led the way. Always the middleman, Ricky followed. Tommy came right behind before Ricky even hit the water. When the three surfaced, Andy and Tommy laughed, but Ricky crawled up the riverbank with his shirt bloodied and torn.

Tommy and Andy swore not to tell anyone, because Ricky feared his stepfather would do even worse to him if he found out. Washing Ricky's clothes, his mom saw the blood and took him to the ER in Clermont for a tetanus shot and fifty stitches. Just missed his spleen.

When they became teenagers they raised the bar on their misadventures.

Tommy told Andy and Ricky about his victory, "The jerk said, 'Shut your mouth, *River Rat*, or I'll shut it for you!' I told 'm to take his best shot. He did, but I didn't go down. Then with one punch, I dropped him like a sack of potatoes."

"River Rats, forever!" Andy shouted, his voice echoing in the cave.

"River Rats, forever!" Tommy and Ricky toasted, passing a pint of cheap wine and dragging on Marlboros.

"What're ya gonna do in June if ya don't graduate, Andy?" Tommy asked.

"My mom said she'd sign the papers that could get me into the Navy. Screw that! I'm tired of people telling me what to do. I'll hitchhike to West Palm and steal from fat, old rich people— easy pickin's. I'll get me a midnight special, take their diamonds and gold, and if they're good lookin' women, I'll screw 'm, too."

"Girls there are half-naked in bikinis," Ricky added. "Let's go now!"

Tommy admitted that he couldn't go because he'd be graduating and going on to high school.

"What the hell for?" Andy asked. "River Rats *never* finish high school."

"A girl from the Heights told me that, with my grades, I could graduate from high school, then even go to college."

"The Heights?" Andy balked. "You kiddin'? What're ya listenin' to some stuckup Heights bitch for?"

Ricky grumbled and spit. "Yer just screwin' with us—right?"

"I didn't do much homework, but I got A's on few tests, so I got a B-plus average."

The other boy's mouths fell open, then Tommy told them about how he'd recently followed Wendy Miller home from school.

The principal had expelled Andy that week for throwing food in the cafeteria, so he hitchhiked to a pool hall in the colored section to buy a pint of Night Train for fifty cents. The old janitor from grammar school would get him cigarettes, booze, and even weed to share with Ricky and Tommy in the cave.

Ricky had gotten detention for using foul language in class. So with his pals unavailable, Tommy held his own, taunting Wendy Miller as she waited on the playground for her school bus to the Heights section of Oakdale. He sidled up to her as she gossiped with two girlfriends. The girls ignored him, but he clung.

"What do *you* want?" Wendy said with a scowl.

"You know," Tommy said, rolling his eyes.

She shook her long, red ponytail, pursed her lips, and pointed her nose in the air.

"I'm riding *your* bus home with ya?" he said.

"You don't scare me," she huffed. "See if I care."

When the bus pulled up and the kids boarded, Tommy headed toward the back of the bus and slid into the seat beside Wendy. She cringed as the other kids looked away, leery of any confrontation with a cornered River Rat out of his habitat—the fetid swamp along the river.

Wendy's house sat two hundred feet above the river against the hillside, which rose another hundred feet from her backyard to the crest. Her nearest neighbor was a quarter-mile away and out of sight.

Tommy got off the bus with Wendy and followed her up her winding driveway. Wendy's mom was a nurse and usually came home at dinnertime. Her dad commuted to Orlando and never got home before seven o'clock. Giving Tommy that information, Wendy's tone was more of a threat than encouragement, but he made the best of a rare opportunity to run solo without Andy and Ricky.

"You can't come in my house," she said.

"Then where?"

"You think you're so tough. Did you really break Jim's nose?"

"He asked for it."

"Are you crazy?" she said. "The high school football team will kick your ass when you're a freshman next year."

"I'm not scared of them. Besides, I'm not going to high school."

"That's stupid. Your grades are OK, and you don't even do the work. If you tried, you could go to college."

"College? Now, who's stupid?"

"Why do you hang out with those two creeps? They're going to jail someday.

Is that what you want?"

"You know what I want."

"You and a hundred other boys, but they're *all* going to college."

"Jeez. You're so damn stuck up."

She grabbed his hand. "C'mon. I want a cigarette. We have a shed out back." She led him around the house to the backyard.

With grammar-school intimacy they passed a Marlboro back and forth for a few minutes. Sharing a cigarette was as close to sex as either had experienced.

"You better leave now," she said, taking the final drag.

Before she could stop him, Tommy pulled her close and kissed her. They pulled and grabbed at each other until they heard a car coming up the driveway.

"My mom!" Wendy straightened her blouse. "Come back tomorrow when it's dark," she said, shuffling back to the house and waving him toward the woods. "My mom will be on the late shift at the hospital. I'll be alone until seven o'clock when my dad gets home. Bring cigarettes."

Tommy hid in the woods up the mountainside and waited until dark. He felt chilled as the sun went down, but he didn't leave. Thinking about Wendy's encouragement to finish school, with frustration, he picked up a fist-sized rock and lobbed it. He expected the rock to roll downhill toward Wendy's house, but the leaves on the ground seemed to gobble it up.

Moonlight illuminated the woods as he sat on a log and continued tossing rocks. Each time, the rock rolled and vanished. He dropped another rock near where the others had disappeared. Seconds later, in the hush of night, he heard an echoing splash come from below the surface where he stood. With another rock tossed then swallowed by the earth, he heard the same delayed splash. He took note of the trees around him. With caution, he backed away, then headed home, thinking all night about kissing Wendy tomorrow after school.

Next morning, Tommy met Ricky in the schoolyard.

"Andy's coming back to school today," Ricky said. "When I got out of detention yesterday I couldn't find ya. Where were ya?"

"I took the Heights bus."

"No way!"

"I kissed a Heights chick and copped a feel."

Ricky nodded toward Wendy in a circle with her friends. "Was it that hot one over there, the redhead with the ponytail and big boobs. Was she the one who told ya to go to college?"

"Yeah. So?"

"Whew! Some creampuff. Did ya stick it to her?"

Tommy shrugged as Ricky's attention wandered past him, and he shouted, "Hey, Andy! Wait'll ya hear this!"

Tommy turned to see Andy looming behind him.

"Tommy followed that cute redhead home," Ricky taunted, "but I think he came up empty."

"The redhead?" Andy nodded toward the circle of Heights girls. "Great boobs. I know, cause I seen 'em—naked."

Tommy stammered. "N-naked? N-no way!"

"Sure. I was hitchhikin' through the Heights one night on my way to play pool when I seen her pull in the driveway with' er mom. I snuck behind her house and got a great view of her bedroom window. Man, I watched her for half an hour, taking off her bra and checkin' herself out in the mirror. I seen everything."

"Ah! Yer bull shittin' us," Ricky huffed.

"If it's true, why didn't you tell us before?" Tommy asked.

"I figured you guys were too young to appreciate a fine piece a tail." Ricky said, "Let's check her out tonight."

"The three of us will go," Andy said. "I'll bring weed, Ricky booze, and Tommy . . . just bring whatever you got down there to make her squeal."

If only Tommy had convinced the other two to stay in the woods and not go into the house . . . but once Wendy opened the door for Tommy, there was no turning back.

Wendy unlocked the chain on the door and asked Tommy, "Where were you?

I hope you weren't hanging out with those two river rat freaks?"

He distracted her with a kiss. "I'm here, now. What're you gonna do about it?"

"Come to my room."

As she led Tommy through the kitchen toward the hallway, he glanced over his shoulder and saw the chain unlatched and the knob button still open just as he'd promised to leave them for Andy and Ricky to come in behind him.

Tommy saw a clock on Wendy's dresser and noted the time. He kissed and petted her, but saw that five minutes had quickly passed. As he was about to help Wendy pull her sweater over her head, the phone rang.

"I have to get it—my mom's checking up on me." She picked up her phone. "Hi, Mom. I'm fine . . . just doing homework. Yeah, I'll have supper ready for Dad."

Seconds closed in on ten minutes. Wendy hung up. His eyes were on her, but his ears anticipated sounds from the kitchen, Andy and Ricky crashing through the bedroom door, but only silence . . . more silence . . . unending silence.

Wendy anticipated her father's return home and Tommy remained on edge, regretting his pact with Andy and Ricky. With no intrusion on their forbidden romance, at quarter to seven, Wendy led Tommy from the bedroom through the kitchen to the backdoor.

"Be my steady girl," he said, pulling off his eighth-grade ring, a cheap memento engraved with his name inside it. He handed it to her.

"Not until high school," she said, dropping the ring back into his shirt pocket. "Our secret till then," she said, stopping him with a lingering kiss. She opened the door. "See you at school." She latched the chain and waved to him from the window as he left.

Tommy headed up the mountainside and let his eyes adjust to the dark. He heard a low groaning sound nearby. He walked toward the rasping whisper coming from the dark, "Tommy . . . help."

Tommy came within a few feet of the voice. He lit his lighter and saw Andy's wide eyes peering from the ground. His muffled voice strained and his hands clutched at the loose soil around him.

With caution on one knee beside him, Tommy asked, "Where's Ricky?"

Andy hissed like a cornered gator, "He fell through first. Damn it! Pull me up!"

Andy flinched, losing his grip, but lurched with one hand and clutched Tommy's shirt pocket. Tommy stood with a quick jerk, and his pocket ripped away, but he couldn't grab Andy's tight fist quick enough. Without enough air left in his lungs to cry out, Andy slipped through the earth followed moments later by an echoing splash from below.

***

Though the storm with no name was somewhere in Greenland by now, gradually receding, the muddy river's stench carried all the way to my motel room. I started my Toyota's belabored engine and headed back to Oakdale in the morning mist.

The haze stayed with me along the dirt road through the fallow cornfields, then green sod flanked me up to the gate at the white fence. Oddly, I heard no barking. The dogs were nowhere in sight.

I got out of the car and opened the gate. A dim light glowed at one window through the fog. I rapped on the front door. I thought I heard a murmured response, but no one came to the door, so I knocked harder. The door opened with a long creaking sound that cut through the morning fog. Mrs. Davis stood there with no makeup and her hair askew. Her burgundy, terrycloth robe clung to her midriff. Her red eyes told me she'd been crying and still was with tissues left in a trail on the floor.

"What happened?" I asked, but she just embraced me and wept against my shoulder with a shudder, gasping for breath.

"He's gone," she said. "Not an hour after you left. Doc O'Grady had warned him about his heart, telling him to retire and let a younger man take over. He was stubborn and wouldn't listen." She sniffled and wiped the back of her hand under her nose, then backed into the kitchen and plopped into a hard wooden chair.

"I found something that washed up in the flood," I said. She asked with a tremor, "What is it?"

I placed the ring gently in the palm of her cupped hand. She stared at it closely for a moment then laughed.

"I'm sorry for your loss, Mrs. Davis. I'll come back for the service. Please, let me know the arrangements."

"I heard from his deputies yesterday that two bodies washed up after all these years," she said with a shudder. "Who have you told?"

"No one."

"Who you gonna tell?"

I tried to inhale but couldn't. My breath was sucked from my lungs making my voice pitch an octave higher, "Not a soul."

She forced a smile. "Tom was a good man."

I nodded and turned, closing the front door behind me as I left. The two black labs lay on the porch huddled as if they were one. Going down the porch steps, then walking to my car,

I couldn't feel my feet touching the ground, as if I were merely a spirit floating through this town. It no longer felt like a movie set. Though no one else would know them, folks had lived and died here. Two had been lost, but now, including me, *four* were found.

The Jogger

It's minus 10 degrees at 6 a.m. for the fifth day in a row, so I skip my morning run again and sleep another hour. I'll feel empty all day without my run. I have all week. The morning shower makes me tingle, not how I'd feel if I'd had a five-mile jog. The power-spray from the showerhead pounds against my skin, but my blood doesn't come to the surface the way it would if I'd had my aerobic rush. Drying with a fluffy towel, I see a drop of blood trickling down my chest. Must've nicked my chin shaving. Watching the slow, red trail trickling to my bare feet and circling the drain like Janet Leigh in *Psycho,* makes me feel morbid—dead.

Scraping my frozen windshield with the heat blasting inside my Jeep, I wonder how others might've missed my jog after five days of neglect. I anticipate phone calls, but the agreement holds—never call—not me, not them, not ever . . .

Last Monday

Twelve minutes on foot from the apron of my driveway is Sharon's house, a '50s Cape. I see her porchlight a block ahead so I increase my pace. I don't have to knock or ring her bell. The door has been left open. I close it behind me and smell coffee brewing and muffins baking. I turned forty-two last fall and Sharon's fifteen years younger. The lit porchlight means I'm welcome.

"Bring your coffee and muffin in here!" she shouts from her bedroom.

"You want some, too?"

"I've already had mine."

"I might spill the coffee and leave crumbs on your silk sheets." I'm standing in her bedroom doorway with hot coffee and a buttered muffin in hand.

Sharon is a grad student at Rutgers, but she's on Winter Break before exams. She'll get her MBA in May, but works for a financial firm. She does my taxes, but we share an intellectual ilk. I've often said she should be a writer. A corporate job would never make her happy. We both have a carefree outlook on life, but share nothing outside her bedroom.

"I don't need a job to make me happy," she says. "I have my jogger."

"I doubt I make you happy . . . just satisfied . . . until the next time."

"This *is* the next time—and the next and the next . . ."

That was the last time I saw her, five mornings ago. I don't know if her porchlight is on this morning because I'm not jogging today—too damn cold. I'm tempted to drive by, just to see if her porchlight's lit, but don't. I sense she's been watching for me. Hate to disappoint, but maybe this deep freeze will thaw soon. I can jumpstart the cycle on Monday.

Last Tuesday

Four blocks from Sharon there's a long winding driveway. The porchlight has a motionsensor and doesn't light until I come to the door. I've repeated this ritual enough to count to ten before the door opens without knocking on it or ringing the bell.

Celia's husband, Rocco, is a contractor, usually gone by 5 a.m. on weekdays. Celia remotely opens the three-car garage to let me see that Rocco's Escalade is gone.

Celia comes to the door, looks up and down the block, then pulls me with both hands by my collar into the house.

Celia is ten years younger than Rocco. Their three kids are away at college. They have a black Lab, but he's confined to the back porch before I arrive. I'd usually hear him whimpering in the background. Celia and I went to high school together. We'd never dated as teens, but now in our forties, we've skipped a generation as friends—now, twenty years later, with benefits.

Celia's older brother, Sonny, is rumored to be *connected*, giving Rocco a jump on city contracts in Bergen County. Maybe that's why he's had to get up a 4 a.m. His loss—my gain.

"Rocky's been a pain in the ass this week," Celia says. "He's got a goddamn assistant. He said he wouldn't have to leave until eight this morning. I told him Sonny called, said he had to be on site by five o'clock for an inspection."

"What if he comes back home when he finds out you lied?"

"Maybe he will," she says. "So we'd better get started."

Celia likes to play it close to the edge. She was a cheerleader in high school. Have to give her credit for keeping in shape. She likes to take out her cheering uniform from the attic just to prove it still fits. She can still do a split.

Had we dated in school, I often wonder what might have come of it. I've reconsidered with the adage: No wine before its time. Celia is ripe, low-hanging fruit for harvest. Unlike Sharon, Celia has nostalgia to share with me. Tuesdays feel like stolen watermelon on a hot summer day, though it's still dark and minus-something Fahrenheit.

Last Wednesday

Ten minutes down the road from Celia, I go to the back-door. Danielle thinks I'm out of breath from jogging, but Celia's gymnastics from yesterday still has my lungs bursting. I have to cross the main drag in town, but it's too early for heavy traffic. "Danny," as she likes me to call her, comes naked to the back-door. Her tattoos swirl artistically from left shoulder to right ankle with several strategic vignettes in between. Her erogenous zones are pierced to heighten our sensations.

She pulls me through the doorway, not by my collar. She prefers an oral exchange without words. No words could give justice to the next ten minutes. Danny's a vice cop in Hackensack's Bergen County Division. Takes one to know one.

"You've been a naughty fellow," she says, locking me in handcuffs and pretending to swallow the key. Her platinum blond coif is spiked with a lavender streak. She's undercover.

Among her arrests, high-level politicians and businessmen are listed as johns in the *Bergen Record*. She's literally empowered by her convictions. Danny's appearance is never the same, so she can't be tracked. Higher-ups who've tried to thwart her arrests have failed. Her imagination is ingenious. She's thirty-five and has been divorced three times.

"A-holes, all of them," she'd told me the first time I'd stopped by on my jog.

I'm a target for all of Danny's frustrations. Her lust empowers me despite being bound. In weak moments, I've considered making her my only pleasure-pause of the week, because I'd never become bored. She's a different woman each time I stop by. There are no husbands, boyfriends, children or pets to intrude, but that's the deal-breaker for any solitary union—less adrenaline from Danny's predictable unpredictability. I admit that I'm spoiled.

Last Thursday

On the bend heading back toward home lives Sally, Super-intendent of Schools. She just turned fifty. I've tried to console her about that milestone. With menopause on the horizon, her hormones have gone ballistic. She'd graduated from college when I'd graduated from eighth grade. She rose through the teaching ranks to her coveted, highly-paid position. Her success was grief driven. Widowed five years ago, Sally's childless with no plans to remarry—an ideal date.

Though merely rumors—girls will talk—Sally knowns better than to push me about what others have inferred concerning my morning jogs. Sounds paranoid, but I sense glares at checkout in Whole Foods—curiosity with a taint of envy from other hungry women. I'm neither a Svengali nor hung like a horse, but cuddly and quite frankly, just fucking lucky.

Sally's race against the biological clock enhances her performance, fearing that her well might soon run dry. Though she'd lost her husband tragically in the first Iraq War, she's never been one to seek pity. For that, I admire and respect her, but she enjoys being *disrespected.*

"You've got a domination complex," I often tell her, but she pays little heed since my analysis is off the books.

I'm a professional psychologist but, for the past five years, I've made a good living writing books and giving seminars—more leisure for the same pay without the cost of an office. Less liability, too, with no malpractice suits. Well, I don't count that incident when I was twentyfour, right out of grad school, and worked as a high school guidance counselor. My lawyer, Izzy Cornfeld, had that fallacious fellatio charge expunged—done deal. His bill was ten grand, but it beat having my name listed in this exclusive neighborhood as a child sex-offender.

Can't remember her name, but she was seventeen going on thirty—a textbook nympho—end of story.

Whenever I arrive, Sally is always fully dressed in a business suit for work. I've never seen her fully undressed, which gives our passions a boost with an aura of mystery. I call her my "mermaid," because often times she's topless with her snug skirt like a fish tail—no trespassing below her waist.

"I had my annual mammogram yesterday and I'm still tender," she said one time.

I figured I'd have to be a gentleman and take a pass, but she guided me south of the border.

She has an office that used to be her husband's den, with a high-back leather swivel chair and a huge oak desk. In that environ, she is Superintendent, never removes her glasses, and always makes me undress her slowly, never letting me know when she'll say, "Stop!" Her commands set the limits.

Sally has taught me to savor small portions. I've never appreciated a navel, a nipple, or the utter softness of an inner thigh as much as when they were each, at separate times, the only item on the menu.

I've told Sally that the best part about teachers is making you do it, again and again, until you do it right. That was the first time I'd seen her unbridled laughter. It seemed better than a climax—at least to her it did.

Last Friday

Janine's condo comes at the ten-minute stretch back to my house to complete my jog and also my weekday routine. Yesterday was the first time I hadn't shown up, so she must be wondering why I haven't. Would she consider breaking our no-call rule?

She's a top real estate agent with her photo on every FOR SALE sign in town. Her bright smile greets me several times during my morning runs from her signs planted curbside. We celebrated her fortieth birthday last month with a candle wax ritual. The exchange gave new meaning to waxing and waning—along with some whining. She can be a brat.

Janine likes women as much as men. I may be the oddity on her weekly menu, a dash of salt to offset the sweets. She takes off Friday's because she works weekends. At least she's my last stop. I'll have two days rest before starting my weekly routine again on Monday with Sharon. What goes around *cums a*round.

"I waited to shower with you," Janine says. "I had my workout, too."

"I'll show you mine if you show me yours."

"Of course, but up close and personal, baby," she says.

With the whole day ahead of her free, Janine doesn't want me to leave. It's Friday and I have to go—speech engagements and publisher's galleys to proofread on my latest book, *Why Women Prefer Bad Boys in Bed.*

Janine sold me my house five years ago, and I've given her many referrals. She's a wealthy, independent woman, demanding of me in only one respect, total attention to her when we're together. Otherwise—out of sight out of mind—or so it had been. Till yesterday, I hadn't missed a Friday morning since we'd started five years ago.

Saturday

My cell buzzes on my dashboard. My Jeep's hands-free screen says:

CALLER IDENTITY WITHHELD.

I have an unlisted number, so I wonder who it could be. Guilt over missing my rounds last week troubles me. I pick up the *Bergen Record* at the local Krausser's and drop it on the passenger seat beside me. Peripherally I see a front page headline:

Oakdale Women Murdered
Believed to be the Work of a Serial Killer

My brakes screech and I pull over onto the shoulder. I shuffle to back pages looking for names and photos of the victims. There's a tap on my driver-side window. I turn with a start to see a Bergen County cop.

"License, registration, and insurance," he says. When I reach to my glove compartment, he says, "Slowly."

"Was I speeding?"

"Are you licensed to carry a weapon?" he asks.

"A w-what?"

"A gun," he says.

"No."

"I'd like you to come down to Hackensack to answer a few questions."

"Questions about what?"

"Where you've been this past week."

"Except to go to the store, the bank, and the post office, I've been at home. It's been the coldest week on record."

"I see you have this morning's paper," he says. "The weather's not half as cold as the serial killer on the loose in town."

"Who were the victims?"

"That's what we want to talk to you about," he says. "We believe you knew them—all of them."

"Do I need a lawyer?"

"Not if you're innocent—just routine."

I know I'm innocent, so my headstrong certainty flaws my logic.

"OK."

I follow him to Hackensack on Rte. 4 East until we turn off by Riverside Square. I try to leaf through the newspaper with my right hand and steer with my left. My mind is racing, pulse pounding, even without my morning jog.

***

Seated alone within a tight space for fifteen minutes, I sense that I'm being observed. Must have a video camera concealed inside the air duct in the ceiling. A plain clothes detective enters carrying a folder. He puts a bottle of water on the desk and slides a legal pad and pencil to me.

"Do you have any objection to my recording our conversation, just for the record?" he asks.

"No. Sure. Go ahead."

"Do you recognize this woman?"

I feel my breakfast coming up, but fight the urge to puke. It's Sharon with a noose around her neck. Her milky eyes stare at nothing.

"My god! Who did this?"

"That's what we're trying to determine, Mr. Shea," he says with eyes like zoom lenses recording my reaction to the carnage in the photo. "You are David Shea, correct? You're the same man on your driver's license and passport?"

"Passport? I haven't renewed my passport. It expired two months ago and I haven't had time."

From the folder, he unfastens my driver's license from a passport book and opens it for me to see. "That's you, isn't it?" he asks.

Short of breath, my passport photo, one I've never seen, shows the issue date—last week.

"When exactly were you planning to leave the country?"

"Leave? No plans—never seen this passport before."

He smirks and hands me a United Airlines boarding pass for this Monday's flight to Costa Rica from Newark. The flight leaves tomorrow morning. I vomit into the waste can beside the desk. An "everything" bagel with cream cheese and a medium hazelnut coffee with cream have formed a brown pudding-like glob at the bottom of the waste can.

The detective hands me a paper towel from a roll beneath the desk. I wipe my mouth with it. When I sit upright, I see a photo with Janine holding her realtor lawn sign. Her bright smile mimics her photo on the sign. One eye winks closed, the other glazed milky white. My head ends up in the waste can again until I feel I'll cough up my heart.

"Do you have anything to say, Mr. Shea?"

"You've got to find the person who did this."

"Perhaps we have," he says. "We found your DNA at all four crime scenes."

Visions of my last meetings with Sharon, Celia, Sally, and Janine flash through my mind—Olympic splooge fests. With Sally it was always different. Only a coroner would find *internal* evidence. Her photo is less violent, as if the killer had a soft spot for the school superintendent posed at her desk, wearing her glasses as if she'd just looked up from reading a book.

Then it hits me. "You don't have DNA except at the scenes so how can you match it to mine?"

He takes out a long Q-tip. "Will you provide us with your DNA to prove your innocence?"

"On what grounds?"

"Are you refusing, Mr. Shea."

"Yes. You have no grounds."

He seems to glance at the air-duct with a smirk. "It doesn't matter, Mr. Shea. We have your fingerprints from the crime scenes which match yours taken at Oakdale's school system when you'd been a guidance counselor. They also match those taken at your home."

"My home? You had no right to enter my home without a warrant."

He places a warrant in front of me. It was issued this morning. My head spins. "On what grounds was this warrant issued?"

"We'll get to that later, Mr. Shea," he says, standing and placing another photo in front of me. "You knew *her*, too. Right?"

Celia is wearing her cheerleading outfit. She's bent over a stack of pillows on her bed in a pool of blood. Her skirt is flipped over her lower back to reveal she's naked. Her black Lab, also dead, has his front paws placed on Celia's shoulders posed doggy style.

"We could probably just let you walk out of here if you'd like," the detective tells me. "Then members of this woman's family might save taxpayers the cost of your trial and future incarceration. Her brother is connected—the FBI has confirmed."

"I want a lawyer."

"Do you have one?"

I shuffle through my wallet and find my lawyer's card.

"Lawyer up, Mr. Shea. We'll put you in a holding cell until he gets here. Meantime, you have the right to remain silent . . ."

My lawyer, Izzy Cornfeld, is a high school friend. I used him to close on my home purchase five years ago . . .

"I'm a *trial* lawyer, Davey," Izzy had balked.

"We're buddies, Izz. I'll need legal advice on my next book, and many more after that. Just don't hit me for ten grand on this one. You should be paying me. You've probably never been close enough to a woman like Janine to smell her perfume. I'll pay you a grand just for a sniff of my realtor."

Izzy's wife, Fran, was a *five* on the one-to-ten scale, but only in heals and since her makeover, so he was pruriently grateful for that brief exposure to Janine. To Janine it was community service.

All the boys in school had known who Celia was, but she and the other cheerleaders had hung out with jocks. Izzy was a nerd and I was a poet with radical hair who provided weed. But according to Izzy's grim expression today, I'm about to become a member of *The Dead Poet's Society*.

"I could try to get the warrant thrown out for a mistrial," Izzy says. "But someone had given the cops a tip about your jogging schedule. They didn't have to look far to get prime DNA. They found a tissue with blood on it in your bathroom's waste can."

"I cut myself shaving this morning."

"Why were you leaving the country, Davey?"

I glare at him.

"The passport? The ticket to Costa Rica?" he queries.

"It's a frame."

Izzy grins and shrugs. "By whom?"

My mind flutters like the images pulled on a slot machine. "Rocco De Grazzio. He found out Celia was having an affair with me. He's got the underground resources to make a fake passport and buy an online boarding pass. His people must have stolen my ID from a credit card swipe."

Izzy humors me with nods of his head as if he's buying my reasoning, then hits me with, "What about Sharon? Your DNA was found like a Boy Scouts' circle-jerk in her bedroom."

I'm stymied for a moment. "They knew my routine and Sharon was their most vulnerable target—young, innocent, living alone. Sharon was just collateral damage to steer guilt away from Rocco to me."

"That's a tough connection to make," Izzy says. "A real stretch."

"Wait a minute—what if Sharon had a jealous boyfriend? Maybe he found out she was seeing me, became enraged with jealousy, and killed her."

"Ceila, too?" he asks with doubt.

"Separate incidents, one having nothing to do with the other, except bad timing."

"How about Janine?" Izzy challenges.

I see the realtor sign with her bright smile in my mind. "Someone's trying to frame me."

"What's the motive?" Izzy asks, sipping a cup of Starbucks takeout. I burst with pent-up anxiety. "Because someone's fucking crazy!"

"That might be your best defense—insanity," Izzy says with all seriousness. "Take a guilty plea and be out in time to collect Medicare."

"I didn't do it—none of it."

"OK. Then if you stay in custody, maybe there'll be another murder with the same MO. That might free you on bail."

"I'm not going to jail. I want bail now."

"No you don't," Izzy says. "For the reason I just gave you, for one, and with the plane ticket to Costa Rica, you're a flight risk. I've already inquired. Bail would be set at a million. You'll be in solitary except for visitations. I'll see you at least every other day until we set a date for your hearing."

"That's it? That's all you can do for me?"

"I can also tell you that the photo you saw of Janine, the realtor, was all that was found, Davey. Just a photo, no body. They're excavating your yard. Do you want me to call your lawn service to cancel your next scheduled cutting? Could save you a few bucks toward my fee."

As he leaves my holding cell, I hear Izzy grumble under his breath. "Fucking asshole, how could you kill that beautiful woman. A goddamn house closing for a lousy grand . . . now I've got ya, you fucking piker."

Monday

Two days later, Izzy returns.

"I can probably make a deal with the prosecutor on one condition," he says. "What?"

"Give us the names and addresses of any other women you were intimate with who might already be dead or that we might save before they are."

The cops have to be thinking of me as a Blackbeard-type serial killer when all I am is a writer and psychologist fortunate enough to have been intimate with several beautiful women within close proximity of one another. I'm sure I'll wake up from this nightmare soon. Maybe the frigid mornings and not jogging this week are playing tricks with my brain.

I decide to keep any details of my other affairs to myself, to be used more efficiently, if needed later in my plea.

Tuesday

"You have a visitor," a prison guard tells me. "Empty your pockets."

I pull my pockets out from my trousers to show him they're already empty. "Remove your shoes and give them to me," the guard says. "I'll return them after your visitor leaves. "Your belt, too," he gestures with impatience. "C-mon, c'mon."

I do as I'm told, but resent the guard's attitude. What happened to—innocent, until proven effing guilty?

I stand from my chair as my visitor enters the cell. So many emotions run through my mind from joy to gratitude—suspicion—anger—fury.

"Have a seat, Davey," she says. "Having a bad day?"

In many ways she's a stranger to me this morning, dressed conservatively in a gray business pants-suit with a pristine white ruffled blouse. Her coif is a mousey-brown shag and her only visible piercings are her earlobes with non-dangling diamonds that I'd given her on her last birthday. It's the first time I've seen her wear them. The earrings were misfits for our wild encounters in the not-so-distant past—a week ago from last Wednesday to be exact— "Hump Day" she'd called it.

"What the hell's going on?"

"That's my question, lover-boy," Danielle says. "My, my, you've been a busy fella."

"You know me, Danny. I'm not capable of violence."

"I think I'm a good judge of what you're capable of, but tangible, admissible evidence tells the prosecutor different." She shrugs with arms folded, tapping one high-heeled shoe.

"I'm being framed."

"Really?" she huffs. "From what I've seen on paper, I'd have been the next victim on your weekly jog. Seems like you decided to shut down your pipeline—no pun intended."

"I'd never have hurt any of those women, certainly not you. You know that!"

"I'm not sure what I know anymore, Davey," she paces with arms folded tightly against her breasts. "I feel rather lucky to still be alive. How would you have killed me? Kinky style or just a quick snuff?"

"You *are* lucky to be alive, because with me in jail, the killer won't come for you. The prosecutor will know I couldn't have killed you from jail. The killer will wait for my release. Then you'll need protection, certainly not from me, but from the one who committed these murders."

"I hope your attorney has told you to cut that nonchalant attitude about your claimed innocence," she warns. "It's not going over well with me. The prosecutor is lining up a woman judge for your hearing. Unless, she's another one on your weekly bed-hopping excursion, she's sure to be tough on you, *death penalty* tough. Ironically your lawyer is seeking another judicial venue to avoid local prejudice, but to a death-penalty state for first-degree multiple murders."

"You can help me, Danny. Track the leads on your own. There must be a trail the homicide detectives are missing. A set-up is always vulnerable to slips. You can get all the details on the investigation and report back to me."

"Oh, sure. My days are so filled with leisure time putting under-age prostitutes out of harms way."

"OK-OK, but I can give you detailed information about the four victims, stuff only I know about."

"Why should I help you?" she asks. "You sure as hell look guilty to me."

"I'm not, Danny. I swear I'm not."

"Show me you're not," she says. "Convince me."

"How?"

She stands on one leg and pushes the other high-heel into my crotch with a painful grind. She checks her watch. "Hmm. Not enough time this visit. Maybe next time."

She turns for the door and calls for the guard down the hall to let her out of the holding cell. She doesn't look back. The guard nods to her then eyeballs me with disgust.

Wednesday

Izzy comes into my holding cell at 10 a.m. He sits at the table between us and looks up to see my expression of contempt.

"What?" he asks.

"It's a frame, Izzy. I'm sure there won't be more killings while I'm incarcerated, just to make certain I'm convicted. I'm screwed."

"From my experience, a serial killer can hold out only so long," Izzy says. "They can't abstain from killing. It's an urge they can't resist. That's why I want to delay your hearing as long as possible until those urges bring the killer back to the surface."

"He must have been spying on me when I was jogging every morning."

"Jogging? If that's what you want to call it, Davey."

"It has to be someone who's up at 5 a.m. I'm still stuck on Rocco's motive. He must have people who take care of business. But why would he kill the other three women?"

"Like you said—to make it look like a serial killer and direct the blame to you by association with the other women. So was that it, Davey? Just the four?"

I don't trust anyone, so I keep Danielle's visit to myself. Izzy could inquire about any of my other visitors, but he's too befuddled over my hearing to consider it.

"That's all she wrote, Izzy."

"Not quite. The warranted search found your bags packed to travel. Another frame?"

Despite his penetrating glare, I show no emotion, no revelation. I'm screwed.

Thursday

Danielle shows up in my cell at 8 a.m. She's dressed completely in white from a pearl necklace to white stiletto heels in a two-piece outfit with her hem a foot above her knees and a smart jacket with a tight fit to accent her fine-tuned, athletic physique. The bow-neck sweater reveals tanned cleavage.

"Dressed for work?" I quip. "You must be going after high-rollers at the casinos."

"Jealous?" she asks with a flush to her long neck.

I shake my head. "That was rule number two. If you can't be with the one you love, than love the one you're with."

She blows a strand of her bangs from one eye. Her hair is dyed auburn in a pixie cut or maybe it's a wig. Looks natural enough to have matching cuffs at her hot-waxed landing strip. If I weren't in jail I'd be anticipating a gander at what lies beneath the surface of her seductive display.

"Rules were made to be broken," she says, sliding her firm buttocks onto the table. "Do you have something we can discuss about who's framing me?"

"No," she says. "But I have good news and bad news."

I take a deep breath and exhale slowly. "Normally I'd want to get the bad news over with so I could look forward to the good news, but I haven't had any good news since my arrest."

"So you want the goodies first?"

"Sure . . . I hope they've brought in Rocco for questioning."

"That's not good news, just routine," she says, taking off her white jacket and hanging it over the folding chair on her side of the table. A warm fragrance wafts to my flaring nostrils. "Rocco has a solid alibi for the coroner's ETD—he was at a construction site with a hundred witnesses."

"A hundred *well-compensated* witnesses."

"Only needed three," she says. "Security cameras with timers."

"A goddamn fix."

"Not likely. I think you're pointing your finger in the wrong direction."

I flip her the bird, because it suits her. "I thought you were going to give me the good news first, not the bad news."

"You're looking at it," she says. "The guard owes me. We've got only twenty minutes, So let's make the best of it before you start suffering negative effects of SBU."

"You're joking. Right?"

"Oh, my. You have missed me, Davey," she says spinning her butt on the tabletop and wrapping both legs around my upper arms so tightly I can't free myself.

"This is your first and last conjugal visit. We can't have you constricted for the trial."

I'm quickly exhausted, but feel the anvil of frustration lifted from my heaving chest.

"OK, so that was the good news, Danny."

She nods, fastening her bra and tucking her blouse into her tight skirt.

"I hope the bad news isn't as bad as the good news was good."

"You attorney will be here in ten minutes," she says. "I don't want to be the bearer of bad news—I'll let Izzy break it to you."

"But—" I start to say, but Danielle is gone, as if she'd never been here.

By the time I put on my shoes returned by the stone-face guard, Izzy enters my cell with shoulders slumped.

"I've got bad news," he says.

"Let's have it."

"It's Janine . . ."

"But that's great news. If the coroner determines Janine's ETD was while I was in jail, I'll be home free."

"Janine's not dead," Izzy says.

"Even better! Was she able to say who kidnapped her and tried to kill her?"

"Yes."

"Wow! I thought this would be bad news, Izzy. You've made my day."

"I have a copy of her statement for your hearing." Izzy takes a folder from his briefcase. "With her statement, your hearing has been moved up to tomorrow."

"Oh, man. I don't know how I can ever thank you enough, Izz."

"Read her statement. You'll see why I had no trouble moving up your hearing with Judge Simmons, known by defenders as "the hanging judge," not because we have a death penalty—we don't—but it refers to male defendants' genitalia."

I read the first sentence of Janine's statement: "Dave bound and gagged me and said he'd be back the next morning to kill me. Thankfully, the detectives found me in his basement before he returned . . ."

After the Hearing

"I don't get it, Izzy. Maybe Rocco paid Janine to finger me. Check her bank accounts to see if they've paid her off to frame me. Did she suffer any bodily injuries?"

Izzy doesn't look at me. He keeps his face buried in his files. "Superficial bruises," he says. "If you read further you'll see she said you told her you were saving the best for when you returned." He pauses making two tight fists and slams one on the table. "Damn you, Davey! You introduced me to her at your closing. How could you?"

"I'll swear by anything you ask me to, Izzy. I'm innocent. There's a killer out there."

"The best I could've done was a reduced sentence had you told me where you'd left Janine," he says. "I'll play the insanity card to have you confined in a mental institution for life. But that's the best I can do."

The Plea

Seated beside Izzy, I appear dazed by my insanity as he makes his plea in my behalf. "They'll bring back the chair or hanging if I let you make your own plea," Izzy told me earlier that morning.

When the judge passes sentence after accepting my plea, I turn to see Janine seated in the back row of the courtroom. Sunglasses cover her black eye and she's wearing one of my favorite business suits, the gray tweed with its rough texture that contrasts with the softness of her skin on Fridays. I understood why other women would find her so attractive.

I want to speak to her, to ask her why she lied, but Izzy nods for me to follow the police officer out of the courtroom to my holding cell. I pause and turn my head sharply in her direction again. I don't recognize her at first because she's dressed drably in a woolen coat. She's sitting beside Janine. Her black hair flows from under a purple beret to her slumped shoulders. She's holding Janine's hand.

It can't be, I think, trying to look back again, but I'm jerked forward by the bailiff.

Six months later

I have plenty of time to put the pieces together. The food at The Breezy Palms mental facility isn't half bad. The ankle bracelet with the tracker is annoying at shower time, but I've found a chess partner for after the dinner hour. He rarely speaks—an idiot savant with an IQ of 90 who always beats me. It seems the only word he knows is—"Checkmate."

He just stares into space when I tell him of my innocence, but my nurse told me he'd hacked up his family with an axe. I suppose the staff thinks we have more in common than just a game of chess. Neither of us are ever left alone.

"There's a package for you, David," my nurse says. "It's been X-rayed so you can open it, but if I find that it contains anything dangerous, I'll have to turn it over to the Proctor."

It's a six-by-nine-inch envelope, postmarked from Costa Rica. I open it under watchful eyes.

My chess partner adds two new words to his limited repertoire, "A . . . book."

It's Kafka's *The Trial* with an old photo of a girl I recognize, but she was only seventeen then when I'd kissed the top of her head in my counselor's office and whispered—"My sweet Danielle."

My partner across the chessboard yells what I am thinking, "Checkmate!"

Menagerie

"I want you to find my father. I don't know who he was or is—if he's still alive."

Matt Pershing took the young woman's statement as she sat facing him stiffly in a hard wooden chair. He sat slumped back casually at his desk.

Through the blinds, sunlight made a harsh, cage-like grid of shadows across her plain, expressionless face. She fidgeted in her ill-fitted, grey pants-suit, leaning forward to sip from a plastic bottle of water.

Her broad shoulders made Matt feel like an NFL quarter-back facing a defensive center ready to blitz. She was neither mannish nor butch, but taking notes on a legal pad, the best euphemism Matt could doodle was *big-boned*. With her satchel, she looked like a kid masquerading on Halloween— *trick or treat*.

"*The New York Post* said: 'Matt Pershing will go where angels fear to tread.'" Matt grinned and said with a shrug, "A blind search could be costly."

"I'm a millionaire, but I don't feel rich without a family."

"I require a five-thousand-dollar retainer and a grand a week plus expenses."

She didn't even blink.

"My secretary will send you a monthly itemized statement. I accept money orders, certified checks, and cash—no credit."

"Frankly, I thought it would cost more, Mr. Pershing."

He didn't blink either, and without revealing his regret that he hadn't asked for more.

Shuffling through her bag, "I don't expect you to find my father quickly. Consider this an advance." She handed him a crumpled, certified check from her trust account.

"I'll take your case, but do you have anything other than names to get started?"

"I was born April 7, 1987," she said. "My mother's name was Beatrice Cartwright, but I have no documentation that she ever married. My birth certificate says I was born at this address in Florida, but it doesn't say if it's a hospital—perhaps it was a clinic. I don't know if it still exists."

"Where did you get this information?"

"I wasn't supposed to know anything about my mother, but the Trustee of my mother's estate was an attorney in Florida. When he died last month, a carton arrived at my condo with information about my mother—nothing about my father."

"Tell me about your Trustee?"

"The only contact I ever had with him was by phone and from the checks he'd sent." She scratched her left shoulder then the back of her head. "The return address on the checks was a Miami P.O. box."

She handed him an envelope postmarked a week ago from Miami with the address she described and its contents inside.

The check from the trust was signed, "Guenther Wolf, Esq. Trustee."

"Will this be your last check?" Matt asked.

"The benefit from the trust will outlive me," she said, raising her round chin, pouting with a roll of her bottom lip, and emphasizing her under bite.

Leaning closer, Matt detected a musky scent, nothing from a bottle. He noticed fine wisps of facial hair running along her jaw to her full bottom lip.

"May I hold onto your birth certificate?" he asked.

"Certainly."

Her physical appearance posed a conundrum. Who was Denise Cartwright— as her birth certificate read—and why didn't her mother want her to know her father?

She handed him a photo of a young woman. "That's my mother— dated on the back—August 21, 1986."

Beatrice Cartwright looked about twenty with a pretty face and an upturned nose, unlike her daughter's—wide and nearly bridgeless. From the thinness of her mother's arms, legs, and neck, he assumed she was normally slender. From her abdominal swell, she was surely pregnant with big-boned Denise.

"I don't look like her. Do I?"

He shook his head slowly with subtle agreement.

"Maybe someone will recognize her from that photo and link her with some man to give you a lead."

"Where have you been living the past thirty years?"

"Foster homes," she said. "There were three different families before I turned eighteen."

"Do you have a job?"

"Ocean County Library—Exit 81. Breaks up the boredom. I have no social life."

He gave her a receipt then examined the birth certificate. From the Bureau of Records, Department of Health, Miami-Dade County, the document said "Denise B. Cartwright." SEX marked "F." DOB was "2 A.M. April 7, 1987."

The box marked RACE was blank. The PLACE OF BIRTH said "Miami-Dade County." Name of Hospital or Institution, was just an address—"595 West Rte. 41 W."

All of the boxes had been left blank regarding the name and information about the father. The same boxes indicating the mother's information gave her name as "Beatrice Anne Cartwright." The Usual Residence of Mother said "132 Weeping Willow Lane, Sweetwater, Florida" Occupation—"STUDENT."

A statement for witness had two choices: M.D. and MIDWIFE. Respectively, the signatures read: *Heinrich Schmidt, M.D.* and *Angela Buenavitas.* Matt noticed two boxes at the bottom of the document.

"I'm surprised you haven't mentioned *this,*" he said turning the document around and pointing to the information.

"What does it mean?"

"Total number of children BORN ALIVE PREVIOUS to this pregnancy . . . the answer is ONE. The last box asks for Number of children born PREVIOUS to this pregnancy and NOW LIVING—the answer—ONE."

She gave Matt a vacant expression, like a prime-evil death mask.

"You have an older sibling . . . please, drink some water," he cautioned, thinking she might faint.

She finished the bottle and crushed it with a toss into a waste can. "I had no idea, but if you can find my sibling, I'll *double* your fee. Where will you begin?"

"I'll follow the money. I'll fly to Miami first thing in the morning, Ms. Cartwright."

"Please, call me *Dee?*"

"If you recall anything else, Dee, you have my number."

He led her to the door and watched her walk toward the elevator down the hall.

Something wasn't right about her, but her check still clung to his hand.

***

Matt studied the photo of Beatrice, pretty and serene, but her expression, like *Mona Lisa*'s, put a wall between him and the truth. He wondered if her expression concealed the story of her untimely passing in Florida over thirty years ago.

Along Rte. 41 West, he stopped for lunch at an eatery with the weathered façade of a popular truck stop called ERNIE'S EATS. Battered pick-ups in the dirt lot surrounded by the Everglades told him locals might know about the occupants at the address he sought.

"Where's my effin' club on whole wheat, Ernie?" shouted the sultry counter waitress, a Cuban-Seminole mix with a mouth that snapped like a gator's.

Ernie popped his head out from the kitchen's swinging doors. A deep scar traversed his craggy face from his left temple across the bridge of his sharp nose and down to his right jawline.

Ernie rasped, "That club's past history. I put it out myself. Stop your damn flirtin', Chika, or take a hike!"

Ernie caught Matt staring at him with a grin. "Somethin' funny?" he snapped, coming toward Matt.

"Hard to get good help these days. Huh, Ernie."

Ernie looked him over, taking measure of his chances to toss Matt's wise ass out the door without adding another major highway across his well-traveled face. Since Matt's shoulders were broad and angled straight to his earlobes with an eighteen-inch neck, Ernie decided to talk first and fight later, maybe with a little help from the gruff looking yokels chowing down before their night fishing excursions into the Glades.

"What's it to ya, stranger?" Ernie snapped.

"My mom used to work as a nurse at this address down the road." As Matt handed him the address from Dee's birth certificate, he recognized a tattoo from Vietnam on Ernie's forearm. "I was a just a kid fighting in Nam when my Mom died, but she saved enough money to put me through college when I returned Stateside. I'm headed west to see where she used to work. Do you know the place down the road at 595 West?"

"That place closed a while back—some kind of clinic. I figured they were doing abortions for illegal Cubans, but I heard it was more of an experimental lab testing cancer drugs. Didn't your mom tell you?"

"I never got the chance to ask her before she died." Matt took the photo from his jacket. "Does she look familiar?"

Ernie squinted. "You liar, that's not your mom. It's Bea-bee!" Ernie reached for a long carving knife.

"Whoa, before anyone gets hurt for no reason." Matt waved his pistol. "I represent Bea Cartwright's daughter. Her mother died during childbirth over thirty years ago. She hired me to find her father. I could use your help, Ernie."

"Were you in Nam or was that bullshit, too?"

"101st Airborne Rangers. After my first nine months, I was picked to go Stateside for Recondo School, but I shattered my knee on my last patrol. Never made it to Frisco for LRRP training. By the time I could walk, I was fluent in Korean after a year's PT in Seoul." He gestured to Ernie's tattoo. "You?"

"25th Infantry, Air Cavalry, Cu Chi."

"Centaur?"

"Gunner on a Huey, but trained to fly choppers."

"Still fly?"

"Got a Glades custom job out back. My amphibious dragonfly takes me to my secret fishing holes. I assist fire rangers in the Glades."

"You called the woman in this photo *Bea-bee*."

"You ought to take that photo to Chief Dillon in Sweet-water. Bea went missing over thirty years ago . . . never found. They closed the case in '93. Dillon's first year as Police Chief was the year she vanished in '86. He's retired."

"This photo was taken in 1986, just before she gave birth. What was the name of the clinic down the road?"

"Odd name . . . Scientific Institute of . . . Mind Illumination and . . . Nature."

"How did you know Bea?"

"Bea-bee was my first waitress . . . spoiled me." He frowned at Chika glaring at him from the end of the counter. "She was a smart college girl, no Miss Universe, but cute. You know—the-girl-next-door."

"Was she pregnant when she was working here?"

"If she was, it didn't show. She never said nothin'."

"I guess she needed the job to pay for college."

"Nah. Her family was well-off, but she wanted her independence. She was a nice girl—respectful." He glared at Chika. "No foul language from Bea-bee."

"Was she still working here when she went missing?"

"No. She said she got a job—some kind of intern for the next school year."

"Doing what?"

"Mm . . . anthropology? Animal science? Something like that."

"Do you think she might've taken a job at that clinic down the road?"

"I never thought of that. But if she did, I would've thought she'd stop by."

"Did Chief Dillon follow that lead?"

"Couldn't say."

"When did Bea-bee stop working here?"

"Hmm . . . July 1985."

"I'll pay Chief Dillon a visit on my way back to Miami, but first I'll check out 595 up the road. They might have information about the former occupants." Matt put a fifty on the counter. "Do you have Dillon's home address?"

"Sorry, no. Check at the station."

***

The former clinic displayed a yellow sign with red lettering—MIKE'S USED AUTOS. Matt spotted a burly man coming toward him through the maze of inventory. The aroma from the man's illegal Cuban cigar stopped Matt in his tracks as he braced for a haggle assault.

"Not a lemon on the lot!" he called out to Matt. His white dress shirt was still crisp in 95 degrees. "Mike Flynn, at your service. I'll pay seventy-five percent of Blue Book Value, cash for your trade—as is."

"I'm a private investigator willing to pay for information. How much is an hour's worth of your time to walk with me around the premises?"

The armpits of Flynn's white shirt dampened under the heat of Matt's questions. "Here's two hundred for now. I'd like to look inside." He nodded for Flynn to head to the air-conditioned showroom away from the inventory baking on the gravel lot like muffins fresh out of the oven, but not so appetizing with the pungent smell of burnt rubber and oil. "Tell me about the previous occupants?"

"Nature nuts from what the realtor said. Sold through a testamentary trust and represented by a shyster named Guenther Wolf—weird bastard."

"The Trustee. He died."

"He was anxious to unload the property so its sale could pay out to the beneficiaries."

"Beneficiaries?"

"Two minors, Wolf said."

"Names?"

"Adam and Denise Cartwright."

"Did you level the old building and start from scratch?"

"I kept the original superstructure to get a tax break. I'd wanted to use the basement to store my records, but it's too creepy down there."

"Show me."

"I couldn't take out the bars without the building collapsing."

"Bars?"

"Floor-to-ceiling, to cage animals."

Flynn led Matt down dim stairs to a musty basement. Mice scattered. It felt cool with overhead fluorescent lighting from the high ceiling. There were four cages along one wall and sinks with water spigots beside four gurneys and two operating tables that might have been used for surgery or to deliver a baby—*or two*.

Matt's nose twitched from the pungent stench of the cages.

"Gives me the creeps," Flynn said. "Like a mid-evil dungeon for torture."

"Did Chief Dillon ever come here during your reconstruction?"

"Patty Dillon?" Mike squinted. "I've done nothin' illegal, so why would he?"

"Curiosity?"

"He's retired now, but if anyone tried to push a stolen vehicle on me, he'd have been the first to know."

"I need to talk to Dillon about the clinic. Mind if I take forensics?"

Flynn shrugged. "No problem. That lawyer was creepy, maybe a white slaver."

"Whatever they were doing, it's connected to my client."

Matt entered the first cage where he found dried stool. He took out a forensic toolkit and with a flat spoon, put the small dung sample into a Ziploc baggie he marked "1-A." In the opposite corner he spooned loose sand into another baggie marking it "1-B," hoping for a urine specimen. He followed the same procedure in the other three cages—maybe cells—depending on what they contained.

He figured if he found enough forensic evidence linked to Dee's mother, CSI could be more thorough later. He'd done reciprocal favors with Miami-Dade CSI in the past. He'd cash in his marker to run the samples through their lab.

Matt shut the dungeon behind him and the bright afternoon sun made his head ache until he put on his sunglasses and walked across the lot to his rental.

Flynn waved.

"Dillon bought a boat and lives on it at the Sea Horse Marina in Coral Gables. His skiff is called the *Sea Bea*. When Dillon retired earlier this year he bought a used car from me, an old bug to save on gas since he only drives to the food store and goes everywhere else by boat."

* * *

Matt dropped off the forensic samples at CSI. He had assisted Lt. Rush a few years ago pursuing a drug dealer suspected of kidnapping and hiding out at Key Largo.

"We're overloaded, could take a couple of days, Matt," Lt. Rush said.

"No problem. If I have to go back to New York beforehand, we can talk about the results by phone."

With that kettle of soup simmering, Matt drove to Coral Gables. At the Sea Horse Marina he found a maze of yachts docked along a long bulkhead.

Matt stopped a few slips short of Dillon's mooring and parked. He opened the car window and heard a dog barking. He took off his sports jacket and carried it over his left shoulder as he approached the *Sea Bea*'s slip. A spotted pit bull barked from the deck.

A gruff voice shouted from the cabin, "Shut up, Corky!"

The dog wouldn't stop. Dillon emerged, wearing a Marlins baseball cap, a greasestained, grey wife-beater, and khaki shorts riddled with holes. He squinted then grabbed the dog by the collar and pulled him back to the cabin. The dog yelped once, before Dillon latched the cabin doors shut.

"Hi, Chief. I'm Matt Pershing, PI from New York. I'd like to ask you some questions about the missing person's case from thirty years ago—Bea Cartwright."

No response.

Matt took out Dee's birth certificate and the photo of her mother. He held out each with hands spread in surrender and slowly approached.

"Bea wasn't murdered. She died giving birth. Her daughter hired me to find her father. Will you answer a few questions about your 1986 investigation?"

Matt stepped onto the boat.

"Did you search the basement at the Scientific Institute of Mind Illumination and Nature? Her daughter's birth certificate gives that address as her place of birth. Someone may've held her captive there while you were searching elsewhere."

"I'm *reti-i-ired*," Dillon drawled, staring at the deck and not looking Matt in the eye.

"I have Bea's photo taken days before she gave birth. You could help me reopen the cold case to find more answers about her disappearance."

"Ya deaf? I said I'm *reti-i-ired*,"

"You named your boat the *Sea Bea*. Were you the father of her child?"

"Nope. Her name's just a reminder to keep me from getting lazy, force me to remember how I'd screwed up in my prime. Now you show up with this crap."

"Are her parents still living at the same address in Sweetwater?"

"Her dad died. Her mom, Amy, wasn't the same after Bea wasn't found. She still lives there, but rarely leaves the house. Her husband's insurance and pension left her comfortable, but she's still tormented by her loss. I'd pay my respects, but I'm afraid I might drag up bad memories. You leave her the hell alone, Pershing."

Dillon's advice was more of a threat, but Matt knew that once the pieces to the puzzle of her daughter's disappearance led him to the identity of Dee's father, he'd have to reunite Denise with her grandmother to provide closure.

"You haven't answered my question about the clinic. The birth certificate connects Bea to that location. Her daughter was delivered while you were still searching for her."

"Sure, but we had no evidence for a warrant. No one had ever witnessed Bea near that location, so all I did was ask the Director for a walk-through and showed Bea's photo to the staff. They were accommodating, so I had no reason to go back."

"Ernie out at Ernie's Eats told me Bea had left her job at his place to work as an intern in her professional field. Did you think she went to work at the clinic?"

"Ernie was on my short list of *prime* suspects. From what folks told me, Ernie was sweet on Bea, so I wondered more about something he'd done to her after work one night. I figured he might've killed her when she turned him down, then used her for chum at one of his secret fishing spots in the Glades."

"There were four cages in the basement. Bea might have been held captive there."

"They were monkey cages," Dillon said. "They had a chimpanzee, a smaller monkey, and a young gorilla. Their permits and licenses were in order."

"There were *four* cages."

"They were expecting a delivery, so I figured I was wasting my time and concentrated on other suspects. I came up empty." He slapped the back of his hand at her photo. "Now you show me *this*."

"The lab is gone, but the cages are still intact in the basement. I've got forensics to find any leads to who my client's father was."

"You put on quite a road show, Pershing."

"The delivering physician was Heinrich Schmidt, and his assistant was Angela Buenavitas. Ring a bell?"

Dillon seemed exhausted by the burden he'd been carrying for thirty years.

"I interviewed them both. She called him Dr. Schmidt. I asked if he was a PhD. and what was his field? He was a medical doctor, his specialty was research. I asked what he was researching. He said he had a grant to study genetics searching for a cancer cure. He showed me the grants and offered me the tour. I found nothing suspicious."

"What did he say about the primates in the cages?"

"He showed me licenses to house the animals."

"Who was the Director?"

"Another squirrely German with an accent out of *Hogan's Heroes*."

"Guenther Wolf?"

"That's it," Dillon said. "He was an attorney and handled all the legalities so the doctor could concentrate on his research.

He was accommodating and seemed relaxed about my questions, so I didn't push it."

"He was the Trustee of Bea's estate. Her daughter, Denise, got a bundle of money to make the rest of her life comfortable. What about Angela Buenavitas?"

"A Cuban illegal, but that wasn't my purpose. I had no reason to return. They closed and sold the property to Mike Flynn's used car dealership."

"Mike gave me the tour of the basement. I have friends at Miami CSI running forensics. Take my card in case anything else pops into your head."

He took Matt's card and signaled that their meeting was over by heading to the cabin to let Corky out. Matt quickly debarked from the *Sea Bea* and walked briskly to his car. He thought a drive-by in Sweetwater might quell his curiosity. On his way, he called his secretary in New York.

"Last night my client drank from a water bottle at the office. It's in my waste can.

Pack it for forensics and overnight it to Lt. Rush at Miami-Dade CSI." Then Matt called Rush. "Got any results on the other forensics?"

"Three different male DNA confirmations, all simian primates." Matt pictured the monkey, chimpanzee, and gorilla described by Dillon.

"That's three."

"The fourth's a puzzle."

"How so?"

"The sample in D is an 80% match to C, which means they're related by blood.

The sample is male, but . . . that other 20% of his DNA is a mystery."

"I need answers, not mysteries."

"Some kind of hybrid or mutation, nothing seen before. "Can you determine age from those samples?"

"The Rhesus monkey was about seven years old, the chimp ten, and the gorilla five. The age on the hybrid is about thirty."

"Does that mean the hybrid was around long before the others?"

"No. The samples you gave us from the first three are decades old. Given their life expectancies, those simians are dead. The hybrid is from a few months ago."

"I have one more sample on a water bottle coming to you overnight from New York. I need it cross-referenced with all four. One small favor, I'm going to 132 Weeping Willow Lane in Sweetwater. If you don't get a call from me tonight by 10 PM, call me at this number. If I don't call you back in five minutes, send your boys—I'll be in trouble."

"I've covered your marker, but I'm not you're backup, shamus." Rush hung up.

* * *

She stared at her granddaughter's birth certificate. "My daughter didn't want us to know she was pregnant—found a doctor to deliver her baby for adoption. Bea died giving birth—baby died, too. This person Denise must be a con artist after my money?"

"She doesn't need your money," Matt told Dee's grandmother. "Bea's estate made her rich. She just wants to find her father. Do you know who and where he is?"

Coming through the backdoor, Sheriff Dillon pointed a .38 revolver at Matt.

"I warned you to leave her alone. Don't worry, Amy. The Glades will make him disappear."

"What *did* they do to your daughter?" Matt asked.

"Studying evolution at college was sinful," Grandma said. "But she kept pursuing it."

"We're taking a boat ride, Pershing."

Dillon cuffed Matt's wrists in front—no blindfold—a one-way trip.

***

Dillon lowered Matt into a dinghy with an outboard and they headed toward Alligator Alley down a narrow tributary with tall swamp grass scraping both sides of the boat. Ahead, red lights darted—gator eyes, jaws snapping with guttural growls and hisses as they passed.

Matt challenged Dillon with, "You're Denise Cartwright's father."

Dillon grinned. "You're not half as smart as you think, shamus."

"Why get rid of me? I just need to prove you're Denise's father and my job is done. As long as Bea died of natural causes during the delivery, I have no reason to contact the police—case closed."

"Bea was *my* daughter, but I could never see her. I promised I wouldn't. Amy Cartwright is a good woman, but we had an affair. I had to keep our secret to protect her reputation. Her husband thought Bea was theirs."

"So when Bea went missing, it was personal. You had to find Bea for Amy, and yourself."

"Amy confided in me that Bea was volunteering in a scientific experiment. I'm a God-fearing man. When Amy told me what Bea had agreed to do, I had to stop her."

"From what?"

"Last thing you'll ever see, Pershing. For Amy's sake, no one must ever know."

Dillon headed toward the light through tall swamp grass and slowed down to pull up to a dock in front of a log cabin. Something in the backroom screeched and panted, thumping wildly about. Matt used the distraction to head-butt Dillon, knocking him off balance and the gun from his grasp.

Though handcuffed, Matt got the gun. "Hands high! Back up slowly."

Dillon's eyes darted as he backed into the cabin dimly lit with kerosene lanterns. Matt saw that someone has lived a minimal existence here. "Where's Dr. Schmidt? Is he hiding out here?"

Dillon grinned. "He over extended his doctor-patient privileges. *Nature* got the best of him."

Matt nodded toward the darkness behind Dillon. "What's in that cage?"

"See for yourself."

"Put your hands on top of your head and back up . . . slowly."

Dillon complied. The screeching subsided and whimpering grunts came from the dark cage behind Dillon.

Matt took a lantern from the counter and motioned with the gun for Dillon to continue backing up.

"No further!" Dillon shouted, but two huge, hairy hands reached out between the bars with brute force.

Dillon's legs kicked straight out, knocking Matt to the floor and shattering the lantern. The kerosene splashed across the wooden floor igniting the room. A wall of flames blocked Matt from Dillon with his head twisted 180 degrees and his eyes bulging. The unseen creature in the cage shrieked and snorted.

Unable to penetrate the flames, and the smoke making him choke, Matt retreated to the dinghy and started the motor with his hands still cuffed.

He looked back at the cabin ablaze against the black sky. Through the crackling flames, he heard a crashing sound then saw a hulking figure silhouetted against the bright orange inferno. With a loud shriek, the simian specter stood erect and pounded its chest before lumbering on all fours and vanishing into the Glades.

When Matt reached the canal the sound of a helicopter hovered above him. When it landed on the water, Matt was glad to see Ernie peering at him from his amphibious dragonfly.

"You know how to find trouble!" Ernie shouted over the flutter of his chopper as he helped Matt aboard. "Your friend at CSI had me looking for you since ten o'clock. I had no idea where to look until I saw the fire. Feels like I'm back in Nam. Love the smell of gators cookin' in the morning."

Matt was glad he'd paid for the damage at Ernie's Eats. Seemed like a week ago, not at lunch that same day.

✳ ✳ ✳

Matt stalled his meeting with Denise Cartwright for a week, telling her that he was no longer on the clock.

Since Amy Cartwright knew only half the truth about her daughter's fate, Matt kept it that way, appealing to her softer side from that glint of hopefulness in her expression when he'd told her that Dee was truly her granddaughter.

When he returned to New York, he told Dee that her mother had been pregnant by someone no one knew. He'd say her mother, Beatrice, had died during delivery and had willed her body to cancer research at a medical clinic called the Scientific Institute of Mind Illumination and Nature. He didn't point out that the clinic's acronym was—SIMIAN—which had provided the funds for her trust. But when Matt met Dee faceto-face, with close circumspection, he couldn't help but see her in a different light.

"I have good news and bad news," Matt told her as she sat across from him in in his office, and in the same awkward, ill-fitted fashion of their first meeting.

"Please, the bad news first."

"Your father was a sperm donor for cancer research. If there were any records of his identity, they were lost in a fire."

"I suppose getting to meet my father was too much to hope for."

"What we do know about your father is clinical," Matt said. "Your father had a genetic defect which, I'm sorry to tell you, would be deadly to any child you bear. If you marry, it's essential that you never bear children."

He watched the wave of desperation cross her face, the resolve of loneliness.

"Then what good news can there possibly be?"

"You had a twin brother, born just before you, but he died shortly after your mother. You were the only one saved."

"But you said there was *good* news."

"Your *grandmother* in Florida wants to be your family now."

"Thank goodness! I can't wait to meet her."

Elated, Dee left Matt's office with a bit less awkwardness in her gait. Despite his lies, Matt was convinced that he'd done his best under the circumstances with the hope that Dee would take after her mother in the nurturing home of Amy Cartwright. Matt lost many hours of sleep over the *missing link* in this chain of events. Dee's twin brother from the same simian father haunted Matt endlessly with visions of that hulking figure lumbering through the Glades against a hellish background of black smoke and orange flames in a fetid fury. To what end, he dared not imagine.

A Free Sampling

September 29, 2016

Gwen looked like a flight attendant pulling a carry-on from her white BMW convertible to the front entrance of Lake Terrace Medical Center. Three nurses huddled outside on their smoke break. She ignored a bent woman in her eighties with a walker ascending the handicap ramp. Gwen didn't want to risk stumbling in her stiletto heels on the stairs, so she brushed by an old man wheezing belabored breaths from an oxygen tank attached to a pole on wheels. A Dial-a-Ride driver dropped off several seniors and helped them maintain their balance up the ramp.

The driver observed Gwen's shapely figure and swishing shoulder-length blond coif—like a fly fisher's lure attracting all males from boys to men. He hadn't even seen her face with a tanned complexion, turned up nose, and shimmering green eyes that couldn't be denied anything they demanded. She'd always been a daddy's girl with no siblings to compete for his attention. At twenty-eight her antennae were set in sugardaddy mode searching for a middle-aged doctor, preferably a Board Certified specialist with little time for conjugal rights to yield any offspring. Though twenty years away, she could hear her menopausal clock ticking. She intended to make the use of every second to effectively dangle her lure for the best catch.

The three nurses ignored the old woman with the walker as she tried to get passed them to the entrance, but they all greeted Gwen with her sample case on wheels as if she were their long-lost sister. The nurses commented favorably on her well-tailored designer business suit and deep tan.

"Maui," she told them as she passed through the entrance with a wink. The trip had been her company's annual promotional trip. Investment companies and bankers were prohibited such extravagances for ancillary employees in their similar cut-throat competition to become "Sales Rep of the Year." *Pharmies,* as they called themselves, had plenty of subsidies to spread around and share with each according to his or her sales production.

The three nurses flicked their cigarette butts into the sidewalk receptacle and followed Gwen into the medical center, leaving a cloud of second-hand smoke for the old man to inhale through his oxygen tube as the door closed in his face.

The medical facility's lunch break had just ended, so a line of patients were gathered at the reception window with health insurance IDs and co-pays in hand to present to the receptionist—a uniformed medical assistant.

One scoop of ice cream short of splitting her pants, Gwen thought.

At least the receptionist's pleasant manner reduced the sting on the patients' pain scale—perhaps from 8 to 6—until the next episode of whatever ailed them. In general their greatest pain was a 10—and certain that they'd lived too long in a world that they no longer recognized as home.

Gwen tilted her head so the receptionist would see her waiting behind the motley assortment of what she saw as *the walking dead.* They exchanged nods then Gwen took a seat and crossed her legs. When any of the patients caught her eye, Gwen gave them her *Cover Girl* smile with sparkling white teeth, but she didn't really see them—that could be painful as well as nonproductive. She was there to promote her goods, the only potions with any chance of easing their pains—or so she'd been programmed to accept, if not believe. Drinking the *Kool-aid* was still a matter of choice in a free society. Gwen gave in to the thirst that quenched her sense that she was above it all—the pain, the blood, and the heartache of death of someone you loved. Her life was about surpassing sales quotas.

The elderly women who left the reception line to take seats in the waiting room gave Gwen warm smiles, a reminder for them to call their granddaughters. The old men felt a twinge of renewed youth with the subtle wafting fragrance of Gwen's body wash reminding them it was time to renew their prescription for that blue pill. The men exchanged nods of mutual understanding, thinking—she's a looker, so let's enjoy this precious moment before we forget why we even came here.

All heads turned when the door leading to the doctors' examination rooms opened. The male nurse with spiked hair and a foreign accent looked right through them and nodded to Gwen, knowing the attractive sales rep was from one of the pharmaceutical companies—which one didn't matter—pharmaceutical perks for the cooperative were uniquely ubiquitous.

All the sales reps seemed to be clones from the same mold. The young men looked like Wall Street hedge fund managers and the young women, the most successful, were a combination of "flight attendants" from the sixties and runway models of today. They were Stepford pill-pushers with an MA in Business or Chemistry. No dummies, and all good looking and sharp. But like professional athletes, they had short-lived careers and knew it coming into the game.

Do the math—Gwen had often thought—I have less than fifteen years to earn enough money to retire or become a Regional Sales Director before age forty.

The patients looked blankly at one another as they had to wait for the young sales rep to finish her presentation to . . . today it would be Dr. Raymond Gelato, who was sitting at his desk making notes about a patient's medical history on an iPad as Gwen entered his office, and the nurse closed the door behind her to give them privacy.

"Hi, Gwen," he said without looking up. "Right on time as usual. How are you?"

"Swell, Dr. Ray," she said, rolling her sample case next to the chair in front of his desk and taking a seat with one leg crossed over the other and revealing more than half of her tanned athletic thigh. "I've got some hot items for you, including the one you asked about last summer, the one that will give a menopausal woman only one hot flash a year, the signal to take her annual dose, and with little side effects."

"What are the *little* side effects? For dwarves?"

"That's funny, Ray. Our test group showed one in a thousand could have uterine cancer as a result of extended usage, but eliminating the women who had any uterine cancer history in their families reduced that to one in five thousand."

"How large was your test group?"

"Ten thousand," Gwen said with a casual shrug.

"I know hot flash control is a priority for most women over fifty, but where in hell did your people find ten thousand American women to swallow that pill, knowing the potential danger? Did you even bother to tell these women there were any potential dangers?"

She gave him a twist of her head as if she couldn't believe he was asking her such a question. Who did he think he was— her father?

"First off, it's not a pill." She reached into her sample case and put a bottle on his desk. "It's an inhalant taken once a year after the first hot flash—user-friendly and economically practical for the patient."

He took the bottle in hand and broke the seal. Curious, he started to put it to his nose, but she grabbed his forearm.

"For women only." She glared. "We have no tests on men, but next appointment, I'd hate to see you with a nicer pair of boobs than mine."

He pushed the bottle aside.

"Just busting your balls, Ray," she laughed. "But we really have no stats on men for Breezerine, that's what we call it, and it's available July first.

"Who were these ten thousand women who tried it?"

"Koreans. We had over twenty thousand volunteers, but we ran out of our sample batch and had to turn away half of them."

"And they were informed about cancer as a side-effect?"

"That's not my job assignment. What's this sudden flare for social consciousness? You didn't hesitate to pass out our free samples of Scrotudum to patients when you knew it might cause seizures even though it effectively increased male potency. I thought the $25,000 bonus we paid you to distribute those free samples was enough to abate your scruples. What's it going to take *this* time?"

"What did you pay those Korean women?"

"Through the grape vine . . . I think it was a hundred bucks a pop. We had one million dollars in the budget for testing. The economy in South Korea is worse than here, where our disclosure laws for FDA compliance testing is more stringent. The Korean result was a more accurate and broader sampling. If we did the testing here, we'd have to disclose the dangers more specifically and pay an American woman twice as much. Our budget would've decreased our test group by fifty percent with a less accurate sampling."

He gave her a look like a school principal catching her smoking in the girls' room.

She didn't flinch, but her cheeks flushed, thinking—who's your daddy?

"I really don't know why I'm explaining all this to you. If you have second thoughts about taking the free-sampling bonus, I'll be back next week to see Dr. Price— and he'll take enough for my month's quota for *half* the usual bonus I'm offering you."

"I know very well why Dr. Price takes a smaller bonus," Dr. Gelato said. "We play squash together at our club."

She smirked unabashedly. "I guess sometimes *size* does count, but I'm an equal opportunity supplier. Am I getting your business today, Ray?"

"I'll pass this time, Gwen. I need to know more about it."

"It's more than that isn't it, Ray? You're a decent man in a cold world. You know you can have me any time, right here and now, or at another time and place that's more convenient— just like Dr. Price. I respect you, Doc, but let's face it, if my company can shell out a million bucks on a sample test, they'll spend a lot more to keep doctors in tow. I've seen their reports on you, Ray. They know your weaknesses and they'll use them just to keep you in line. Do yourself a favor. Take our bonus and just toss the samples in the garbage if you like. I'll still get my commission. There won't be any reason for them to be watching you unless I tell them you're becoming a problem—a potential whistle blower. I'm doing you a favor, Doc."

Dr. Gelato asked, "What will the *retail* price be for a twelve-month supply?"

"It'll be about two grand. Medicare and Health Insurance plans will pay up to half, depending on co-pays. It won't go generic until 2038."

"My wife is showing early signs of menopause at forty-four. I want her to have this kind of relief, but I also want her to be safe from harm—as in *do no harm*."

"Drugs come with no guarantees," she said putting the free samples on his desk. "If you want more, call me." She paused at the door. "I guess with hot flashes at home, you're not gettin' any. I don't have an appointment until three o'clock."

"Mrs. Stanley has been waiting out there for forty-five minutes," he said.

"Won't take more than a minute," she said, coming back toward him. She took a pair of sanitary plastic gloves from the box on his desk and blew them both open before slipping them on.

As he toyed with the curl around Gwen's diamond earring, he closed his eyes. He saw a dark void where his patients belonged to a lost world. Before Gwen got started, her iPhone vibrated in her jacket.

"One sec," she said, sliding her finger across the screen, and saw a text from her stepmother only ten years her senior: COME HOME YOUR DAD HAD A STROKE

She rose from her prayerful position and snapped off the plastic gloves.

"Got a go, Doc." Closing his office door behind her, she passed through the waiting room and saw the attentive eyes of the elderly patients admiring her good looks.

So many, she thought, wondering why she hadn't ever noticed them before.

Jetsam

"I didn't know she was missing," the estranged younger sister told him as he flashed his TPD badge, clipped it to his belt then quickly re-buttoned his blazer. With a casual shrug she continued. "Our parents died five years ago in an accident on I-4 coming back from Epcot while Jane and I were on Spring Break in Costa Rica. She was a senior and I was a freshman at USF. Jane went on to grad school in North Carolina— Duke— but I got a job here in Tampa the week after I got my Bachelor's Degree. Snow sucks. I'm—like—a *Palm*-erania."

He raised his head from his notepad as if his gesture were a question.

The strong silent type, she thought, evaluating his trim build and strong jawline. "Ya know—like—*palm* trees . . . my degree was in hotel management . . . at least that's what it came down to by the time I was a senior. I haven't seen or spoken to Jane since my parents' funeral. They were cremated and Jane and I scattered their ashes in the Gulf off Indian Rocks Beach. That final hug was my last contact with Jane. I'd sent her Christmas cards at the hospital where she was an intern in the North Carolina Triangle, but she never replied. I'd called a half dozen times, only to get her voice-mail, but she never returned my calls. I gave up trying and moved on with my life. So be it. Jane has always been *The Ice Princess,* no close friends."

"Sounds cold," he said, pushing up his sunglasses on the bridge of his sharp nose. They were at poolside on her day off at the new Plant Hotel where she was the Assistant Manager.

She remained reclined in a chaise lounge and was wearing a tangerine bikini with beads of perspiration on her tanned skin. She shaded her eyes with her hand, wondering if her wax job made her Venus mound more enticing. She sensed his stare through his dark shades, his eyes probably rolling with her exposed abdomen rising and falling as if her navel were winking at him, maybe teasing him with her intended lure of sexual provocation.

"Truth be told, Jane is a royal bitch, even to me, her little sister. But I envied her with that ice princess determination to make it in a man's world. I'm sure Jane took no hostages on her way to the top at that hospital in Cary. I understand she's become a top surgeon there."

"She was reported missing forty-eight hours ago by her boyfriend—Hank Perozzi. Do you know him?"

"Hank? Jeez, I can't believe she got back together with *him.* They broke up in college. He did show up to pay his respects at our parents' funeral, but I never thought they'd get back together . . . never."

"What can you tell me about him? He's not a suspect, but a person of interest. Was Jane seeing someone else after their break-up in college? Could there have been a love triangle? "

She cocked her head with a swish of her shoulder-length blond hair. "As I said, I haven't spoken to her, but I figured she was too intent on her career to have time for romance."

"Romantic or not, your sister was sharing an apartment in Cary with Perozzi . . ." He paused with his index finger to his lips.

"Whatever," she said with a shrug then sat up and swung both feet to the opposite side of the chaise and faced away from him. She unfastened her top and held a tube of sunblock in one hand and cradled her breasts with the other. "Could you?" she asked turning to look at him over one shoulder.

His shades allowed no clue to his feelings, but he tucked his notepad and pen in his jacket and took the tube from her hand. There was a long pause as she waited in silence until his hands touched her back, as warm from the sun as biscuits fresh out of an oven. His hands felt huge as he made circular motions on her back with both. Though warm and perspiring, her skin prickled with a chill as he kneaded her back and shoulders. His thumbs were as skilled as her masseuse at the hotel clubhouse. She wondered how skilled they'd be if she were facing him, a thought which made her nipples taut in her own embrace.

"That's enough," she said. "Thanks."

He closed the cap and handed her the tube.

"May I trouble you again?" she said. "Just a simple bow will do. I'm done for the day."

Tying her top between her shoulder blades, he said, "I have more questions."

"I live at the hotel, but I bet you already knew that, Sherlock. An entire suite of my own overlooking Tampa Bay," she said, standing and putting on a white fluffy robe that said "Plant Regency" with orange letters on the hip pocket. She took her room key and a wristwatch from that pocket. She put on the watch and jiggled her wrist in front of his face, sunrays bursting from the watch reflected in his shades.

"A gift to myself on my twenty-fifth birthday—Rolex— twelve grand." She noticed one of his eyebrows twitch above his sunglasses.

"I'm a loner, no boyfriends, so I like to treat myself right. You coming up to ask me more questions about Jane?"

"Sure. That's what I came for," he said, following her across the pool patio to the elevators.

In the elevator, instinctively, she sensed his inhaling her hairspray and body wash scent, maybe something even deeper at her core. He was a cop, a bloodhound at heart. That excited her. She hadn't been that aroused for some time. She felt a little dizzy as he followed her off the elevator on the 21st floor. In the corridor a housemaid nodded to her with recognition.

"Good morning, Ms. Travers," the housemaid said with a slight bow. "Fresh towels in the bathroom as you requested."

"Thanks, Hillary," she said. Then opening her suite with the key, she motioned for him to enter.

"Great view," he said, walking toward the balcony overlooking the bay.

"Drink?" she asked.

"Coffee," he said. "On duty."

"Whatever. It's almost noon so I'm having wine." She prepared a coffee drip, flicked on the switch, then poured herself a glass of chardonnay. "Help yourself, while I shower and change."

"Don't change too much," he said with a hint of flirtation.

She looked back over her shoulder as she let her robe drop to the bathroom floor and said with an echo to her voice before closing the door, "Creamer's in the fridge, sugar on the kitchen counter! Help yourself! Won't be long!"

She knew the hiss of her shower was muffled by the closed bathroom door as he drank the coffee. He'd see only photos of her framed on the walls or standing on side tables. No photos of her sister Jane or her parents. "Loner" called out from every corner of her luxury suite. Great management perks would buzz in the mind of anyone who entered. She wondered what this cop thought of her accommodations. He turned to her as she returned with her wine glass in hand. "You said you're the *Assistant* Manager, could the hotel 'Manager's' suite possibly be better?" He asked, sipping his coffee black.

She was dressed for Tampa's August swelter, a white cotton shift with silver-dollar-size lavender polka dots, white sandals. Around her thin neck she wore a white gold chain with a cross, a necklace purchased at the Gold and Diamond Source to match her Rolex that seemed to shout *Happy Birthday to me!*

"Last week our manager was transferred by corporate to our new Miami hotel," she said, liking his baby blues as he removed his sunglasses and took in her image head to toe with obvious mutual attraction. "I expect to receive my promotion to manager by week's end. This *is* the manager's suite."

"So it's a given . . . you'll be the manager. Congrats!" he said, clicking his coffee mug against her wine glass.

"Nothing's a given," she said with a shrug. "Life has no guarantees."

"That's a grim outlook for a young woman," he said.

"When your parents celebrate their twenty-fifth wedding anniversary at Disney World and come back in an urn, it doesn't turn you into Pollyanna. I'm not a pessimist, just a realist."

"So let's get real," he said. "You don't seem upset that your sister's missing. That makes you a person of interest . . . possibly a suspect."

"Suspected of doing what?"

"That depends on how you answer some more questions."

"Is Jane—like—*dead?*"

"For now, just missing. Today's your day off. Would you mind giving me a ride?"

"Where to?"

"A place mentioned by Hank Perozzi in my interview."

"The winter rental?"

"Yes. Where your parents came down for the winter with you and your sister until they died."

"It's across the bay in St. Pete. Jane wasn't interested and asked if I wanted it.

But even with all its benefits, the house reminded me too much of Mom and Dad. I own it, but rent it out during tourist season. I rarely go there, only when I have to."

"I'm sorry if it will be painful, but I need you to show me somethings there. Clues to Jane's whereabouts . . . or demise."

"*Demise*? That seems an old-fashioned word for a young man. What? Thirty?"

"Thirty-three."

"Three's a charm," she said with a shrug, grabbing her bag and keys. "Okay, *Marlowe*. Let's blow.

***

She drove her white BMW convertible. He seemed uncomfortable in the passenger seat as they crossed the Gandy Bridge to St. Pete. Her long blond hair fluttered in the wind and she felt exhilarated to be in control of an Alpha male of the law-and-order persuasion. So far the weather held up at 93 degrees with a breeze off the Gulf. When they arrived with the crunching sound of her tires across the circular, gravel driveway, she pointed to the rental sign.

"That's *my* number on the sign," she said, watching him take note on his pad. She expected after they'd put this *yada-da-yada-da* meeting behind them, that he'd call her for a date. She'd decline of course. Much too busy managing the hotel after her promotion. But once Jane reared her ugly head from the shadows and his case was closed, maybe a brief fling with a stone-cold cop with a hard-body would be amusing if not satisfying.

"It's late August, so not much interest in Florida until October," she said, getting out of the car. "Ya know—too fucking hot."

His expression seemed to echo that same assessment, but of her—*too fucking hot to handle.* "Isn't being the agent for your parents' rental property a conflict with your day job at the hotel?"

"I'm a multi-tasker. I've been the rental agent almost five years. Jane had no interest or the time, so it fell to me. My parents' life insurance paid off the mortgage, so after taxes, insurance and maintenance, it's all profit. Beachfront brings me ten grand a month October through April. Jane got the rest of the estate—for now, anyway."

"Do you mind telling me how much you and Jane got from your parents' estate?"

"You already know that, and you just want to see if I'm a liar," she said with a smug curl to her full lips.

"You've been watching too much TV," he said. "I'm just a flat foot, not Robert Mueller."

"Still, you must know that my parents put my inheritance in a trust with Jane as the secondary trustee if both of my parents were deceased before I turn twenty-six, which is a week from today."

"And if Jane is deceased before you turn twenty-six?" he asked as if leading her toward a confession.

"That's only a week from now, but the bank would serve as temporary trustee until my birthday . . . then it's all mine . . . no biggie—I was told it's only three million." "Nice pay lode," he said, lifting his sunglasses to prop them on top his head.

His blue-eyed stare felt like a laser. "A clear motive for murder."

"My time is recorded at work. Until today, I haven't left the hotel in the past month. You said Jane's been missing only forty-eight hours. On the hotel grounds I'm pretty much on camera 24/7 and I haven't been to North Carolina since I was a kid traveling from New Jersey to Florida on I-95."

"Then I guess that lets you off the hook," he said. "But I just need you to clarify something for me on this rental property that could help in my effort to find your sister."

Relieved to be in the clear, she said, "I have the keys. What do you need to know?"

"I want to see the backyard."

"Sure," she agreed with a shrug and led him through the front entrance. "It's a bit musty, but I keep the A/C at 78 degrees to prevent mold in the off-season because it's furnished. The heat and humidity in the summer months are *killer*."

He raised that distinctive eyebrow again when she said—*killer*. His reactive reflex gave her pause, thinking—*I am a suspect.*

The furniture was covered with plastic and the air was much cooler than outdoors in the sweltering driveway. She bent down to remove the bar on the sliding patio doors' bottom runner and unlocked the doors to lead him onto a paver patio. A round table with a granite top and a center hole for an umbrella had six chairs around it. The umbrella was down and rolled in a plastic sheath. There was a large Green Egg to barbecue on the deck. Across thirty feet of lawn was a dock with a pram to go fishing on the Intra-coastal Waterway between Tampa Bay and the Gulf.

It was very quiet except for an occasional shrill of a heron, an egret, or a pelican. The surface of the lagoon was like glass, except when a fish jumped away from a cormorant. Spanish moss hung from the trees along the banks on both sides of the lagoon.

He kept walking toward the boat slip as she said, "What—exactly—are you looking for?"

Without turning back to face her, his voice was like listening to a newscast from a distant room, and the light breeze off the lagoon was like a hairdryer set on low and blowing in her face.

"This lagoon is brackish water," he said, squatting on the dock. He skimmed his hand in the water then touched his fingers to his tongue.

His tone puzzled her. "What's *brackish*?" she asked.

"Not as salty as the Gulf, but not exactly fresh water like a lake or pond on the mainland across the bay."

She shrugged, wondering, where this line of inquiry could be going. "I guess . . . but I'm a hotel manager—not an oceanographer. Why does *that* matter?"

"Like most new Floridians who weren't born and raised here, like I was, and just got tired of ice and snow up in Yankee territory, you assume like most biologists would tell you in general, that gators make fresh water their only habitat."

"Gators? I've never seen any gators here," she said.

"That's because you're here only in the summer when there are no tenants, like now. This is when gators spend all day underwater to avoid the heat, they hunt only at night when it's cooler."

"So?"

"Unless you're on a night vigil, you'll never see their beady red eyes glowing in the dark waiting for some stupid tourist to walk her lap dog along the banks."

From the dock he looked up and down the serene lagoon. There were no neighbors' boat slips within view in either direction, north or south, or west across the lagoon. That's what her parents had always wanted in their eventual retirement retreat, solitude surrounded by protected marsh that could only be sold off after their passing. But hopefully one of their daughters would want to keep it.

"My tenants have never called me about seeing any gators in our lagoon."

"Either they were oblivious and made too much noise that kept them out of sight or they were curious enough to view them safely from a distance, maybe with the binoculars I saw hanging on a hook in the kitchen."

"Those were Jane's from when we were kids and used to look for dolphins and manatees," she said.

"I know," he said, still facing away from her where he stood on the dock. "She told me."

She felt a chill, even in the tropical heat, but asked the question she didn't want answered, "*She told you? Jane* told you?"

The serenity was shattered by the curt answer coming not from him, but from behind her, saying, "I told Jeff all he had to do was get you to drive him out here, so he could leave his car for me at the hotel."

"*Jeff?* That's your name? You know each other?" she asked, backing away from them, but she stood precariously between him on the dock and Jane coming toward her from the patio. Startled by Jane's quick advance, she stumbled back, falling onto the grass where Jeff held her down. She felt a sudden sting in her neck then watched Jane remove the hypodermic needle from her jugular. She gasped for air but felt as if she were having an out-of-body experience. She felt no pain and everything she saw seemed sharper, the colors all around her more vibrant, the words said to her so precise and curt like a spoon striking a crystal tumbler— *ting-tong-ting!*

"Why-are–you-doing-this-to me?" she asked, her own words seemed to be coming from her abdomen as if she were a cello. She was confused, wondering if it was the injection that made Jane look like her, even wearing the same polka-dot dress. She thought. *What's happening?*

"It always has to be about you," Jane said. "Now it's about me for a change."

"What are you going to do?" she asked with a tremor.

"You can scream all you like," Jane said with that same icy glare she'd had to face every day growing up.

"Scream? What do you want from me—my trust fund? It's only three million. I'll be manager next week. I won't really need it. Take it! I don't want it."

"You must have been eaves dropping on Mom and Dad talking about your trust fund years ago, but you misheard . . . it was thirty million fifteen years ago now ninety million—too much to slip through my fingers next week. I still have heavy student loans from med school. I need that money more than I need a sister."

"I always knew you were a monster, Jane. What are you going to do to me?"

"Me? Nothing but watch. That's why I needed Jeff." She nodded to the police detective.

"He's a cop! He wouldn't—" she stammered.

"You mean this?" he said opening his blazer and unclipping the badge he'd shown her earlier at the hotel pool, but now held directly in front of her face. She saw it was just a dime store toy that said: "Sheriff of Dodge."

She wondered. *How could I be such a fool?* Then she heard a chain saw start with a whir and a staccato rumble.

"No need to flinch," Jane said. "You won't feel a thing. But you'll see it all.

First your hands and feet to draw the gators."

She watched the saw sever each hand and foot with a spray of blood in her face. How could she not feel it? What was in that injection Jane had put in her neck?

Jeff threw her hands and feet into the lagoon with four light splashes then a loud heavy splash, then another, and another . . . gators coming for their appetizers. Then the saw cut off her forearms at the elbows and her calves at the knees. There was no one to hear or see the sanguine spectacle in the lagoon.

"We'll leave her forearms and thighs attached so she can watch the gators rip them off," Jane said. "The drug will keep her conscious and we'll keep her head above water with a lifejacket from the boat. She'll bleed out, but her mind won't know she's dead. It's a drug used on the Iraq battlefields to get information from our soldiers fatally wounded who could still provide field intelligence even after they were declared dead."

She could smell Jeff's nervous sweat as he dragged her to the pram and put the orange lifejacket around her remaining torso. Less than two hours ago she'd been leisurely sunning herself in a tangerine bikini. Now she couldn't wait to die Jeff's pants were soaked with her blood. He tied a rope to the lifejacket and tossed her like jetsam off the dock into the lagoon. He got into the pram and started the motor. The pram dragged her torso across the lagoon then he tied the rope to a palm tree on the opposite shore. She bobbed like a bottom-fisherman's float on the surface of the lagoon. She was beyond screaming, but totally conscious as she watched four gators, none less than nine feet long, cutting across the lagoon like submarines on the Pacific in a World War II documentary.

She called out to Jane and Jeff with her final words, "They'll be evidence! DNA! You won't get away with this! You'll pay with your lives!"

"You must have been too busy at the hotel today to watch the weather report!" Jane called back to her sister. "Category 4 Hurricane *Jennifer* will wipe out this coast in twelve hours with the next high tide and full moon. You'll just be a minor statistic of the disaster."

Jennifer? She thought as she watched them get in Jeff's car and leave her BMW behind as evidence that she'd been there. *How ironic—the hurricane is named after me.*

The alligators unhinged their sharp jaws and fought over her remains.

The sky darkened in a prelude to the approaching tempest.

There really are monsters in this world. Please, God, she thought, *let there be none in the next.*

Fractured Frontier

I was brought up to believe in God, but since that day when everything changed, I wonder—if God exists, we must have gotten it all wrong. Here we are, left with the aftermath of that misinformation. At least here *I* am, because I don't know if anyone else is left. It might be only me, who remains to witness our mistake. If so, was that intentional? Or have I just slipped through the grating of mass destruction? I must wait here to be sure, but if no one else is left, what's the point? Why delay my inevitable demise? If God was pissed off enough with mankind, what difference could my suicide make?

There are no smoking ruins or smoldering embers in sight, only soft sand as far as I can see from left to right and a tranquil turquoise sea ahead with mere ripples of surf, like a subtle memory of the cause and its effect on future existence. A salty sea breeze wafts to my tanned face with a sun-bleached, frizzled beard down to my navel. My hair drapes over my bronzed shoulders and halfway down my back. My buttocks is taut against the palm leaves used to clothe me and are held up by a kudzu vine.

The white flesh of the coconut I'd cracked open against the coral reef provides my daily bread. Though the flesh is coarse and dry, its milk quenches my parched throat. My rough hand strums the protruding grid of my ribs like a thirteen-string oud, but the only music to my ears comes from distant birds assuring me that life, though highly compromised, goes on.

Staring out at the sea with a clear blue sky above, I hesitate to turn around and face what's behind me in daylight. I've ventured into the jungle for food, also for kindling and wood to make a fire, but that's been only after dark, so I wouldn't have to see any signs of mass devastation beyond the mountain ridge. So far, the wind hasn't blown from that direction, so I'll wait until it does. And if he, like God, does exist, Satan will give me my due, and anything else that breathes. *Thy will be done.*

I've marked the days with a sharp stone against the trunk of a coconut palm tree—today is the thirty-ninth day. I must have lost more than a pound a day, maybe as much as two a day. My clothes hadn't been destroyed but, after only weeks, they no longer fit and served me better as towels, using the cloth to dry myself after a bath in a cold spring of fresh water.

So far no wildlife has come to that potential watering hole. Either I've been lucky in the event of predators, or there are no living ground creatures here, or anywhere else. I've boiled water from that spring, so I've not become dehydrated yet, as I might from solar exposure on the beach. But I have to go to the shore . . . just to look for any sign that someone else has survived. It wouldn't be a boat or a plane, no chance of that anymore, but maybe a raft with people floating toward the shoreline with the wind coming from that direction. Just one person would do, anyone. Please, God . . . if you are out there . . . if you know I'm here . . . please bring others to me soon. I may not be able to hang on for even another day. Amen.

This morning I'm gathering clams to sustain me through the day. I find three between the size of, what we'd called "top-necks" and "cherrystones," from two to three inches across. Together they make about six ounces of pure protein. I open them with a sharp piece of coral that I've tapered against a rock. I can't open them in the skillful manner I'd learned as an adolescent from my father . . .

My father, my mother, my younger sister and wife—all gone without hope of ever seeing them again.

Enough of thinking about my losses. Instead of opening clams as my father had taught me, I've learned to open them the hard way from watching seagulls. Like a bird's beak, the sharp implement will whittle at the clamshell. They spurt open with their saline juice spraying me.

I'm so tempted to eat them raw, the way I used to enjoy them best as a boy, but I won't chance it, not knowing if they will be toxic without being cooked. I've boiled the littlenecks because they still remain tender, but the only way to cook these larger clams is to grill them to perfect succulence. I pour out the remaining clam juice into an empty half of a coconut shell to make soup later with seaweed and conch, which is tough no matter how its prepared, but will slide down my dry throat better with clam broth.

Sitting in the shade at the edge of the jungle with my legs folded, I contemplate the horizon where the turquoise sea meets an azure, cloudless sky. There hasn't been a cloud from that direction since I washed up here, wherever I am, if that even matters. There are no sand fleas, mosquitoes, or flies, but I have seen a few types of bees pollenating varga bushes around the spring pool where I was bathing.

With the tip of my tongue, I feel a strand of clam stuck between two molars, but I can't floss it, so I use a bug that's trotting between my feet. I scoop it up in my hand and pop it into my mouth. The carnivorous dentic consumes the clam with a sucking hiss. Job done, I spit the bug several yards onto the sand, but a buglizard emerges from its hole and gobbles the dentic with a crunch. Not satisfied, it finds a sandworm, then a slam-worm and gobbles them up in a hurry. It blinks its black eyes at me and belches. A gull swoops down and catches the buglizard in its beak, but a crabdozer snags the gull's foot before it can take flight.

An infant troglosaur must have heard the commotion and galumphs from the jungle's edge to the beach and inhales the entire menagerie with a snort and a triumphant, trumpeting roar like a dying mammoth in the tar pits, a sound I've become used to these past weeks. On day forty, I'm awakened by a whirring sound as a spacecraft hovers above me.

Part of my conscience wants to run toward it across the beach, shouting and waving my arms, but starvation and precaution to sand predators holds me back.

A laser from the spacecraft scans the shoreline as I watch. My stomach gurgles and twitches watching a net drop to the sea and pull up a thousand stone of huge fish beyond the surf, where I dare not venture for fear of becoming some sea creature's consumption. I rely on low tide for food gathering just to survive, but seeing the silvery fish flipping within the net and lifted into the spacecraft makes my mouth water.

For fear of being left behind, I burst from the brush and run across the burning sand blistering my feet.

"Save me! Save me!" I shout without knowing what language my saviors might speak.

Instead of lifting me up with a net to safety, they toss one fish to me that bounces off the coral and lands at my feet. The spacecraft emits words from a loudspeaker in a language even my ancestors had long forgotten, but as the vessel floats upward and out of sight, I recall that language from my ancient linguistic studies at Atlantis University.

I use my sharpened bamboo pole to fight off the sand predators as I carry the huge fish over my shoulder to the edge of the jungle. The words from the spacecraft echo in my mind:

RETURN TO BASE . . . NO SIGNS OF SIGNIFICANT INTELLIGENCE.

That's when I feel so very much alone and forsaken in this frontier of mass destruction wondering who they can be and why they have come to this dying planet? To study and learn from its remains or merely to pillage its resources to better their own struggling existence?

***

I wake the next morning and hear a distant rumbling, but the cloudless sky is bright blue with no chance of rain or thunder. I feel the earth tremor beneath my feet on the sandy shore. There's a gamey scent in the breeze coming from the hinterland. I run and climb a tree with haste, looking to the distant eastern plain beneath the purple mountains. A broad cloud of dust is rolling toward me and the tree quivers in my grasp. I wonder, what terror approaches me?

I hear the crunching of distant trees crushed by the wake of the approaching onslaught. Then come the bellows of great beasts followed by high shrills in waves of what seems to be rejoicing hoots. It's a stampede, but of what? Driven by what?

With a telescope from my shoulder bag made from a bison's bladder, I peer at the distant foray of savages driving the herd of beasts toward me and the sea.

The tawny aborigines are decked in feathered garb with their faces brightly painted. They raise spears above their heads as they ride upon bird-like mounts and poke at the mammoths. Their mounts can outrun the mammoths with sudden bursts of speed, as several encircle the weaklings, tripping them with rawhide lanyards and engulfing them with nets.

Food, I think, hoping to scavenge from their catch without being seen, yet I hunger more for human discourse than mammoth flesh. Could they be amiable to a stranger? One of a different race? Dare I hope for such contact after more than a month of bitter solitude? I fear I must try regardless of any impending danger, for sanity's sake—mind over matter. Without such communication, I'm doomed, for the brain and its imagination can extend to reasoning beyond the mere gratifications of food. Nourishment of the soul has an infinite quenching over the mere sip of water or the taste of a dumb beast's entrails. The viscera of mutual understanding through brotherhood will never wither in the baking sun or fracture into crystals at the cutting edge of the great glacier.

The dust from the mammoths' stamping feet begins to make me cough, even forty feet above the shaking ground beneath this feeble tree. I clutch a branch with both arms as Mother Nature seems to cradle me like a newborn to her bosom. A hundredfold dash into to sea, some devoured by sea creatures twice their size and a thousand more are attacked by prides of saber-toothed pumas from tabby to black-hided with varied spectacled combinations in between.

The sky darkens as I look up to see swarms of pterosaurs, two at a time able to lift a mammoth's carcass and fly away with it toward the distant peaks, but not without competition from other winged flocks snatching globs of bleeding flesh from the hairy remains of what had been a proud beast upon the ground.

The mounted natives halt their huge saddled birds with serpentine necks and clawed feet that could disembowel any other fallen creature for its own nourishment. I've never seen such birds and I'm amazed what control the savages seem to have over them, feeding them with handfuls of mammoth flesh and massaging their long necks. They cluck and blink their eyes which seem to have peripheral vision from front and back with each eye having 360-degree rotation in any direction. Perhaps, even inward with near-human self-examination and calculation.

Their unique vision betrays me as the dozen saddled raptors extend their necks toward the tree I'm clutching without foliage, but enough to conceal my presence.

They flap their short emu-like wings incapable of flight and coo with a unified shrill in D-minor, which I recognize from my woodwind lessons as a boy.

One native shifts in the saddle, turning in my direction and points. Another does the same until all twelve are shouting in unique harmony unfamiliar to my acute sense of sounds. But when one native, apparently their leader, shouts a sole command, I'm aware that their language is a *Nahuatl* dialect with which I'm somewhat familiar. I shout in my best conversational *Nahuatl*, which is formal, royal court expressions that might offend these savages if they've been harassed by Montezuma's legions.

They surround the tree and look upward toward my precarious perch. I'm shocked when I look down to face their bright, toothy grins, for there is not a *man* among them. All women with wiry muscular tones, I cannot call their similar faces beautiful. Handsome would be more accurate. Despite their individual feminine auras, they exude the pride of a wolf pack. Together as a hunting party they seem like one ferocious alpha-male making me pray they are not inclined toward cannibalism.

One among the pack snarls. She points her spear at me and shakes her feathered headdress as she rasps a baritone growl that seems to mock my masculinity. The others chant as she leads them, but then she abruptly hushes them. She is surely their chief.

In broken *Nahuatl* I force a deeper tone of response to get their reaction with a smidge of hope that their huntress tribe was akin to the King of the Beasts with a male figurehead honored back at their village on his throne while they bring back their daily kill for the evening feast like lionesses in a pride. All of their full-lipped mouths drop open at the sound of my feeble utterances. I pray they will understand my best intentions as I call to them:

"Like you, I'm lost since the great cataclysm last month. I am your friend!" They begin to laugh, some almost falling from their mounts in such hysteria.

I play into their jest with self-mockery by puffing out my chest and grunting like an ape.

My gesture has frightened a few of them while others gather on their mounts around their chief as if to protect her from me.

I recall the saying of a great sage from my village when I was about eleven years old and being bullied by a teenager:

"In humility there is greater strength than arrogance," the great sage said. In kind, I let my arms drop to my sides and bow my head to their chief.

Catching only a little more than half of her words in response to my humble posture, I still understand the essence of her meaning, telling me:

"I am Ziracon, our chief's only daughter widowed by the fiery ball that plunged to our land. These are the only survivors, the widows, sisters, and daughters of our once great tribe. I honor my father by taking my husband's place as provider for the surviving children. Among them are babies born after what we have called The Great *Goolp*. It has killed so many and also has transposed the lands and waters that have fed us for millions of cycles of the moon. Where was *your* village?"

"Not far south of the southern tip of the Baja peninsula along the western coast."

"I know of this territory," she says. "What about your family?"

"My parents died long ago . . . I'm a widower," I say, creating a murmur among the women as if they are at the market shopping for the best cut of meat.

"Are you a hunter?" she asks.

"More of a trapper and a fisherman,"

"Then we can exchange our skills with each other," she says. "Come down from there, so I can take better measure of you."

I shinny down the trunk, breaking off a few branches in my descent. The women wear moccasins that give them no extra height yet they stand eye to eye with me. All of their heights exceed 3.5 cubits, a tall breed of women with tough lanky physiques, almost flat-chested, and with near childlike glimmers in their expressions. Yet, beneath their welcoming façades is an unsolved mystique that draws me to them.

"How long have you been left alone in this forsaken frontier?" she asks. "Just over forty nights."

"Join us tonight for a feast," she says. "We are celebrating the first full moon since The Great Goolp turned us back to our savage ways, which have lain dormant for centuries, but still pulse within our veins from our ancestors and noble chiefs of our tribe.

"Thank you, Ziracon."

"What may we call you?" she asks.

"Davy."

"Then join me on my mount back to our village, but hold on tight around my waist," she cautions me as the other eleven women chortle with amusement. "Hush!" she scolds her merry minions. "Pay no attention to their frivolous good cheer, Davy. These girls are young and imagine us as lovers tonight beneath the full moon, but I must mourn for my husband according the sacred laws of our forefathers for no less than sixty days. With a few more weeks ahead, I trust that you may soon find comfort with another of your choice, perhaps prettier and more affable than the daughter of a chief so hardened by the arduous course that nature has set before her."

"I have no romantic intentions," I say mounting the huge bird, which makes the young girls titter.

With my hands snug around her narrow waist I feel the hardness of her taut abdomen. Her feathered headdress tickles my nose as she turns to look at me over her bare, muscular shoulder.

"You must bathe as soon as we arrive," she says with a flare of her nostrils. "I'm sorry, with so much time alone I've become accustomed to my own fetid scent."

"Well enough for you, Davy, but I would never become accustomed to such a stench, so be grateful I don't make you walk at a distance."

"Thank you, Ziracon."

"You're welcome," she says and snaps the reins putting the giant bird into a gallop, which the others mimic with hoots and shrills like I heard when I'd first seen the stampeding mammoths from the top of the tree.

* * *

In a wooden tub, I'm scrubbed by three of the girls from the hunting party. They fluff-dry me with deer skins and set me before a fire to fully dry as night falls. Through distant trees the full orange-tinted moon reveals only half its majesty, but promises to unveil its full glory in the coming hours. Once dry, I'm clothed in shammy pants and shirt as soft as a baby's behind.

Ziracon approaches in the full regalia of a princess.

"Time to present you to my father, the Chief," she says offering her hand, which is warm but rough from her hard work.

I follow her into a teepee where I find the Chief seated on the floor with his eyes closed and his arms extended with his elbows on his folded knees.

To the Chief, Ziracon utters some guttural expression I don't understand. His eye lids flutter and blink, then his gaze turns to me. He nods for me to sit beside him. His daughter has already told him where she found me and of my story. He bids me welcome.

I nod with appreciation for his hospitality.

"There is another among us of your breed," he tells me. "May I see him?"

"*Her*," Ziracon interjects. "She refuses to see you."

"Why? I've done nothing wrong—or have I?"

"It is not your fault," the Chief tells me. "She wants desperately to see you, but it's too soon. The time is not right, at least not yet."

"You will join our tribe, just as she has," Ziracon says. "First you must take part in our ceremony before the full moon has completely risen. Join us."

One of the younger girls from the hunting party brings a tray into the teepee and sets it before us. There is some kind of fruit on the tray which glistens with the moon beams casting through the teepee's open entrance. Ziracon serves one to the Chief, and he smiles broadly. She puts the tray in front of me and nods for me to partake. I hold the bulbous plant in one hand and sniff at it. The chief bites into his with a crunch. Ziracon does the same. Their eyes blink oddly as if they are just waking up in the morning of a new day and they grin as if they are stupefied.

I shrug and bite into my portion and feel the teepee spinning. I see the full orange moon through the entrance, but colors I've never imagined dance across the sky around the moon and I feel weightless.

I hear my own voice asking in a slow, deep tone say, "I'm ready to see her now."

I hear Ziracon tell me," she is just outside the teepee, but she won't come in, and she begs you not to come out. She says, 'It's not time.'"

"Please, ask her just to stand outside the teepee where I can see her from here," I say, but everything is blurry and spinning.

"I can't, Davy," I hear a familiar voice in the distance beyond the blur and the buzzing in my ears.

"Go back," the woman's voice implores. "You've got too much left to do."

Those words echo in my mind until they blend into another voice, also familiar, but not a woman's voice. Instead it's a man's voice telling me the same thing, "You've got too much left to do."

A hand is waving in front of my face. "Come on, Davy, they're coming back.

You're wound's not so serious. Come on, Davy! Get up and fight! That bayonet missed your vitals. We stopped the bleedin', too. Those peyote that injun gave ya was powerful medicine, but you're OK. Stand up, partner. Here's ol' Bessy."

He shoves a rifle into my hands and I clutch it like a lifeline to pull me out of the whirlwind inside my head. A mission bell clangs reverberating as my eyes begin to focus. I feel a hat plopped crookedly onto my head.

"Can't fight without that coonskin cap, Davy! We gotta show them Mexicans we mean business this time."

"Georgie!" I call out and he turns back to me with a grin.

"Come on, Davy. We're gonna make that *Generali'simo* eat crow. If we don't shoot 'm all, ya can just grin 'm down like a b'ar."

"I saw, Polly, Georgie," I tell him. "She's waitin' for me to finish this skirmish and come home to stay with 'er forever."

I see the concern on my best friend's sunburnt face. He sees my wound, but I won't look at it because I'll go into shock again. Whatever that *Texican* gave me for pain sure worked, but only on my body. My mind aches with desire to see my dear wife Polly again, just one more time. I know now that I shall. Yet I wonder—on which side of this cloud is reality? What happened first, the battle for Texas or The Great Goolp and my survival in the Chihuahuan Desert on a cactus that can turn me into a time traveler?

When its effects wear off, how bad will my pain be? I see that I needn't be concerned with that, because rows and rows of troops are assaulting us in what seems like endless waves. Soon they'll be no more hunger, pain, or thirst. There will be only me and Polly. That's why I'll fight now, till I drop. Then my own voice will join with those of us left in this moment of glory. We'll rejoice in our well-fought fight to its bitter end, and those who find us dead, will shout forever:

"Remember, The Alamo!"

Vermilion

"Whatever I see, I can reproduce," the swarthy young man said to a prospective buyer at the Manhattan street fair. It was Saturday in autumn with leaves floating down from trees along the metal fence enclosing Byrant Park behind the New York Public Library.

"If you don't like anything I've already finished, tell me what you like. I'll paint it for you."

Skeptical, the elderly, well-dressed gentleman with a young woman half his age locked arm-in-arm at his elbow said, "She want's something to match our new penthouse drapes."

Penthouse, rang in the young artist's ears, thinking, wealthy and stingy with a taste for younger women. I've got you pegged. No mystery here.

Flippant, the artist asked, "What color are your daughter's drapes?" The older gentleman blustered, "She's not my daugh—"

"Vermilion," the young woman intervened. "But I see no *brilliance in* any of your paintings." She fluffed her long blonde coif from her shoulders and turned up her nose.

"By brilliance you must mean bright color," the artist said, thinking, you hussy, all of my artistry is brilliant.

"Whatever," she said with a shrug, tugging at the older man's arm to leave.

"If I paint precisely what you have in mind within the hour, what will you pay for my *brilliant* work?"

"Nothing if it's not perfect," she said.

"But if it is?" he asked, turning to the older man as his potential patron.

"I'd have to see it first," he said. "I'd have to bring you a swatch from the drapes."

"I already see it in my mind, dear sir," the artist grinned. "So if she says it's *perfect*, how much will you pay me?"

"I think a thousand dollars for an hour's work is as much as I pay my attorneys, so that's what I'd pay. But anything short of perfect is on you, and you'll have wasted your time for nothing."

"I've come from less than nothing, dear sir, so even nothing would be a fortune to me."

"Let's have lunch at The Oyster Bar below Grand Central," she said. "We'll come back in an hour to see your folly just for our amusement."

"Are you sure, darling?" the older man asked.

She sneered at the artist. "Positive."

"I must caution you," the artist said. "You are aware that the substance that yields *vermilion* is toxic from the mercurial cinnabar."

"It's you who need be cautious," she said. "You'll be rendering our painting, but we'll be observing it from a distance where it will hang above our hearth."

"May we shake on it, dear sir, that we agree that you'll pay me one thousand dollars if you return in an hour and she says that my painting is *vermilion-perfect*."

"Indeed," he agreed, taking the artists hand. "Otherwise, no payment at all."

"Yes, no payment at all," the artist nodded and took out a blank canvas as he watch the couple turn east on 42nd Street toward Grand Central Terminal.

***

When they returned an hour later, the artist stood proudly beside a 60 x 48 inch canvas with a white linen sheet draped over it on an easel for its unveiling. The older man seemed bored, and his young female companion aloof.

"Are you ready to see my masterpiece?" the artist asked them.

The older man waved with the back of his hand, impatient to get on with it and certain the artist would fail in his postured claim that his companion would say it was perfect. As the artist pulled the sheet off his painting the young woman gasped. Passersby ogled the canvas with consensus for its brilliance.

"I love it!" the young woman squealed with delight. "It's perfect!"

The older man reached for his wallet and doled out ten crisp Franklins from his gold money clip.

The artist waved off the older man. "Keep your money, dear sir. I was thrilled to accept your challenge just to satisfy your better half, but I've decided it's so exquisitely perfect in its vermilion brilliance that I'll keep it for myself. I just wanted her confirmation of its perfection."

Enraged, the young woman turned to the older man. "You shook on it. Pay him whatever he wants. I must have this exquisite work of art."

"To match your drapes," the artist qualified. "I paint to match my own brilliance, which is priceless."

The older man huffed, "Honey, it's just a fucking sunset. Let's go."

"I want it!" she shouted.

"Jeezuz. Okay. How much?"

"It's priceless, but for a *hundred* thousand, it's yours."

"What?" the old man balked.

"Pay the man," she insisted. "Write him a check."

He grumbled, pulling a checkbook from his jacket. "You'll have to accept my personal check. I'll make it out to cash."

The artist frowned, but looked to the blonde nodding her confirmation that the old man was good for it.

"Okay," the artist agreed. "Sold to the gentleman for his beautiful wife."

"This bargaining has made me weary," the old man said. "We'll unveil the painting tonight at our cocktail party." He squinted at the artist and said aside, "The Governor and Mayor will be present to see your painting tonight. You should give me a discount for displaying your art among dignitaries with great influence."

"A deal's a deal," the artist said, holding his ground. "Your guests will know that whatever I see, I can reproduce." He wrapped the framed painting and helped them put it into the trunk of a taxi. He waved farewell with a smirk as the taxi headed to the Upper Eastside of Manhattan.

***

That evening on Sutton Place overlooking the East River at the Ed Koch Queensboro Bridge on 59th Street, the dignitaries gathered with their glasses of champagne to cheer the unveiling of the painting mounted over the hearth above a crackling fire beneath a marble mantel.

The old man motioned for the guests to hush for his toast then declared, "We want our honored guests to share this special occasion of my dear wife Penny's thirtieth birthday, which I might add has cost me a pretty penny."

The guests chortled with a murmur.

"Though my dear wife commissioned this art to match these drapes," he nodded to the bright red drapes at the panoramic windows flanking the fireplace. "One of my experts at my beck and call has researched the history of this bright color called vermilion derived from the ore cinnabar, which has toxic mercurial qualities and was widely used by artists during the Roman Empire and notably by the artist Titian of the Venetian School in the Fifteen Hundreds." He paused for the notables present to acknowledge his newfound knowledge of classic art. "With no further delay, behold our modern masterpiece," he said as the painting was unveiled with a collective gasp. "My god!" the old man shouted as the mercurial qualities of the vermilion sunset ran and dripped like blood. The painting transformed, morphing from a brilliant setting sun to a classic painting by Titian, *Bacchus and Ariadne*. However, the vermilion garments at the drunken orgy highlighted the dignitaries present at this gathering, all having their intimate way with a naked blonde with a striking resemblance to his young wife Penny.

The old man began to shake and stammer without control, typical of mercury poisoning from exposure to cinnabar. Then his young wife Penny began to shake with convulsions, but her final thoughts were of what the young street artist had said, "Whatever I see, I can reproduce."

⁂

That next Monday, the New York media publicized the shocking story of the wealthy couple's strange end, but the NYPD made no report of any guests who'd been present to witness the fateful end of the couple or any mention of a painting.

The young street artist had never cashed the old man's check, so its purpose remained a mystery as did the remarkable talent of a young artist who could paint realistic portraits of any passerby though the coffee can for donations left beside his empty easel read:

PLEASE BUY MY ART, I AM BLIND

Priceless

The American couple would usually be recognized and pursued for their autographs, but in the jungles of the Yucatán where they'd escaped from the paparazzi for several weeks, no one knew any more about them than what they'd observed firsthand. They were beautiful people. She had cosmetically-enhanced full lips, a sculptured nose, and a face-lift, though she was barely forty. She was tall and lithe with dancers' legs and natural breasts of ample sway. Though her continued attractiveness would require further extensive work toward her fifties and sixties, for her, character parts would not suit her acting skills, which solely depended on her dropdead-gorgeous façade for as long as it would last.

She envied her husband, who, at forty-two had not reached his prime. Tan and ruggedly athletic, he did most of his own stunts in the series of thriller flicks that had made them financially invincible against anything but ill-health, which even if catastrophic, would not render either spouse financially inept. Her jealousy came from the attention from younger women drawn to him. The slight graying of his sideburns and the strategic character creases of his aging face made him even more attractive. In his fifties and sixties his acting would improve and his film parts would become more meaningful, enough to compete for an Oscar if properly cast.

The waning of her allure and the increase of his had begun to drive them apart.

Though they had no children of their own, they'd adopted several from Third World nations. They'd been in their early twenties back then, and those children had grown and were attending Ivy League colleges back in the States. This jaunt to the Yucatán had been a peace offering from him, a way to take time apart from Hollywood and consider no film roles, to be just the couple they thought they had been two decades ago when they were still hungry for stardom and all of its perks.

"Our guide is going to take us to a place that has been virtually unchanged for over two thousand years," he told her, knowing she loved the spirit of adventure, which was what had first drawn them together when she'd co-starred in one of his thrillers set in the Australian Outback.

"Pre-Columbian," she said piqued by the notion. "I'll bring my digital camera. Won't be any cell towers to connect with my smartphone.

"Good idea," he said. "We'll leave in an hour by mule. No vehicles can penetrate the jungles we'll be going through to get there."

She grinned unabashedly as they stared at each other silently sharing the same thought—*Maybe this can revitalize our marriage. This kind of journey together won't be enhanced by our good looks, but rather our physical fitness.*

Their trek over the mountains was difficult despite their fitness and the heat in the lowland jungle was suffocating, but they endured by encouraging each other along the way. Their guide, Pablo, told them he'd never brought tourists to this area before. They'd paid him the equivalent of five times his annual Mexican income. For them it was a lark, but to Pablo it meant the possibility of college for his oldest son in Mexico City.

Along their three-day inland trek, they'd seen a few caimans, a jaguar, and an assortment of monkeys and colorful tropical birds. The wife took numerous photos, but it was nearly dark by the time they'd arrived at a small village along a narrow tributary of a distant river. As the sun vanished behind a dense canopy, it was the darkest evening either the husband or wife had ever experienced, as if they were blinded by black ink.

As they made love in the hut provided by the village elder, the sound of insects and predators became a cacophonous symphony that seemed to swallow them like a giant anaconda. As they shuddered in mutual climax, the sounds of the jungle suddenly hushed. The last utterance was the wife's quivering sigh, which seemed to ripple through the humid night air like the wake from a stone dropped into a thick porridge.

A serenade of birds awakened them stuck together like glue in the fetid morning mist. They looked at each other in silence as if to tell the other just that one night had made their whole trip worthwhile. But as they kissed, a new sound, as if floating on the mist, entered their hut. They withdrew from their embrace and cocked their heads as if wishing to fill their minds with the melodious chords from the distant guitar.

"What the hell is *that*?" she asked.

"I've no idea, babe"

"Jesus, it sounds magical."

"Like nothing I've ever heard," he said, jumping to his feet. "Come on. Let's see where it's coming from."

She seemed reluctant, so he extended his hand to help her to her feet. "I hope we don't get our heads shrunk."

"I'll protect you, babe."

They quickly dressed and emerged from the hut.

Pablo greeted them. "We will have a light breakfast and go to the Mayan ruins. Only Mayans have ever seen this pyramid. It's sacred ground. Be respectful."

"But that music, the guitar strumming, where does it come from?" he demanded.

Pablo stared at him as if he hadn't heard it. "Oh. That's coming from the supreme elder's hut." He pointed toward the river.

"We must see this instrument."

His wife nodded, clung to his arm, then smiled at Pablo. "We simply must."

Pablo appeared conflicted, knowing his clients' foibles of assumption based on their willingness to pay whatever was required. He knew these isolated villagers and how the norms of civilization never applied here.

"These are pure Mayans, uncorrupted by the Spanish invasion which never reached this place. There had been so much gold and other spoils of the Aztecs and Mayan culture near the sea that there was no need for the Europeans to subject themselves to this harsh environment. I don't fully comprehend their language. It's *Yucatecan,* linked to other ancient languages of the Yucatán by trade."

"Try your best," the husband insisted. "I must see this guitar."

"There will be a bonus," the wife said, caressing her husband's waist where her slender arm wrapped around him like a constricting serpent. *"Comprendes?"*

"Si, señora," Pablo said with a humble bow as he backed away toward the sound of the guitar. "Please, wait here while I make your request."

Pablo disappeared for longer than the couple expected, so when he returned a half-hour later their anxiety was piqued with hope.

Pablo said, "We'll spend today exploring the ancient ruins of which I've spoken. The elder will give you his answer in the morning."

His explanation didn't sit well with the husband, but the wife stroked the back of his broad neck as if to soothe a savage beast. He'd always gotten his way, at least since his notoriety as a box office attraction. The postponement of his request soured their exploration of the ruins.

"I just want to see his goddamn instrument," he grumbled to the wife. "What's the big effing deal?"

"Easy . . . easy, baby," his wife put a long finger to his lips. "We'll see it tomorrow. Patience, love. You need to be more patient and respectful. These people have no idea who we are. Treat them kindly . . . like children."

He huffed and tried to shake off the bad mood he'd been in all day, but it lingered, hovering over him like a black thunderhead before a storm.

"What's this?" the wife asked after they'd climbed to the top of the Mayan pyramid, and Pablo had given his insight to the meanings of the relief sculptors predating Columbus and the Conquistadors by five hundred years, perhaps a thousand.

She was pointing to a deep hole, a hundred feet across and overgrown with thick jungle flora.

"I've seen this before at other Mayan ruins," Pablo said.

"It looks like a sinkhole," the husband said with a shrug.

"Whether by nature or design, this great pit was where a virgin was sacrificed annually to begin the spring season of fertility, growth and prosperity."

"Sacrificed how?" the wife asked with displeasure.

"According to studies, a young virgin, usually considered the most beautiful of her litter, was thrust alive into the deep pit. She would be blindfolded, but unbound. Some experts question if this society was that brutal, and posed the idea that she may have been drugged with no idea what was happening to her."

"Is that supposed to make me sleep at night?" the wife said with sarcasm.

The husband seemed more intrigued by the concept, perhaps thinking how the movie heroes he'd portrayed might save the innocent girl before her violent fate.

"It seems bottomless," he said to Pablo. "How deep is it?"

"Estimates have been anywhere from five hundred to a thousand feet," Pablo said, peering over the edge. "We can see the tops of trees growing from the bottom, but those types of trees can be as tall as a skyscraper. Without seeing the bottom from here, those tall trees might be rooted from the walls of the cavern, rather than from the bottom . . . if there even is a bottom. Ancient storms have eroded underground caverns that connect to the Caribbean to the east and the Pacific to the west. Earthquakes have altered these pockets over thousands of years. It is also the natural burial place for the aged, ill, and unfortunate due to accidents and diseases."

"A natural compost heap," the wife offered with a smirk. "Perhaps you'll push me over the edge when I become too wrinkled and dry to suit your needs, babe."

"Never happen, darlin'," he said with a shrug. "Even if I were tempted, you'd find a way to take me over the edge with you."

"Togetherness," she said with a smirk. "I'm in for that."

Their trek back to the village was silent and uneventful. After a light supper and a couple of ounces of tequila, the couple retired when their fire dwindled. Exhausted, neither was inclined to make love. She lay her cheek against his abdomen as they tried to sleep beneath the mosquito netting, but the haunting, almost hypnotic tones of the village elder's guitar floated to their hut like puffs of smoke from a bong altering their states of mind till dawn.

Awakened by chirping birds, they felt refreshed after being lulled to sleep by the mellow strings of the elder's guitar. The morning mist lifted, and the jungle came alive with varied creatures' shrills and roars.

"I wonder if Adam and Eve would've felt this way when they awoke each morning in the Garden of Eden?" she posed a quandary.

He grunted with amusement and nodded toward the clearing where Pablo was approaching them.

"The elder has invited you to listen to him play his guitar, but you must remain respectfully silent. His son is more versed in communication outside this remote village, but even with that, it is an effort to understand even his exact meaning when we confer."

"We'll do as you advise," the wife said. "Won't we, baby?"

He nodded and motioned Pablo to lead the way.

They sat in a circle on the ground inside the elder's hut. His wife, with bare, wrinkled breasts that hung nearly to her waist, served them a bitter porridge. They nodded and smiled, but couldn't bear more than one mouthful, which caught in the wife's throat. The liquid from a gourd that the elder's wife offered seemed to do the American more harm than good as she coughed for several minutes.

The elder remained silent, staring at nothing until her coughing subsided. He reached behind him and placed the guitar across his folded legs. He paused until even the birds outside the hut seemed suddenly to hush.

With tan hands weathered by time and the harsh jungle life, the elder struck a melodious chord that the couple couldn't recognize, though it continued to hum in their minds even after the elder put his hand across the strings to stop their vibration. He handed the guitar to the husband with a nod for him to play the instrument.

His wife was thrilled and nodded for him to try. He struck a familiar chord, but the sound was different from anything he'd ever heard. The tone was fuller and more resonant with a texture beyond his scope of understanding. He tried another chord with the same result. His wife seemed transfixed by its sound. They stared at each other.

"Tell him we want it," the husband told Pablo. Pablo shook his head, but the husband insisted.

After some guttural exchanges, the elder snatched the guitar from the husband's grasp and stood. *"N-wits-a!"* the elder said emphatically.

The husband looked to Pablo for his meaning. "He says the guitar is his."

"Tell him I'll pay him whatever he wants for it," the husband said with dismissiveness."

Pablo sighed then tried, but the elder folded his arms and shook his head, and said, "*No t-wits* !"

"He says it's not yours," Pablo said.

"Of course it isn't, but I'll pay him well for it." The husband nudged Pablo.

His wife stroked his neck with empathy, knowing how much his obtaining the guitar would mean to him.

When Pablo tried again, the elder shouted a word Pablo didn't know. The Elder's son whispered to Pablo, "It's *priceless* to my father. It can't be bought."

"That's ridiculous," the husband said. "How can anything in the godforsaken jungle be priceless? He can make another guitar when we buy this one."

The Elder's son explained that it took ten years to make this guitar and it will be a gift to his grandson when he dies.

"As you know yourself, Pablo," the husband said. "My price for his guitar could put his grandson through four years of college and a doctorate in Ivy League schools in the States."

Pablo shook his head and said, "No monetary price will be considered. That issue had been closed yesterday."

The negative result of his bargaining left a bitter taste in the husband's craw. He grumbled throughout the day spoiling the adventure for his wife. When they returned to the village at dusk after exploring another Mayan ruin, the elder and his son stood in front of their hut with their arms folded in front of their puffed out chests. After a brief exchange between Pablo and the son, Pablo returned to the American couple.

"We must leave in the morning," Pablo told them. "We are no longer welcome."

Frustrated and angry, the husband grabbed his wife by the wrist to return to their hut for the evening, but as he did, his wife caught an expression in the elder's eyes and a twist of his mouth that detected a weakness she was familiar with. She'd come to learn the darkness of men's souls in her journey toward getting her name on a marquis.

Unable to sleep with his pent-up anger, the husband took four shots of tequila, but his wife took only one. Within an hour, he was asleep and loudly snoring with occasional mumblings about the guitar in an imaginary debate with the elder over his so-called priceless guitar.

"Priceless?" The wife whispered.

In their world there was no such thing. There would always be a price that could test anyone's resistance. Their marriage had been strained before this trip, but now her husband revealed his greatest desire, to possess this guitar. The magical instrument could be what she'd use to fulfill him and seal their commitment to each other forever.

She poked her husband to be sure he was soundly sleeping. She took a deep breath and left their hut. She listened outside the elder's hut, but did not hear any snoring. There was a full moon just above the jungle canopy, so when she opened the door to the elder's hut, the moonlight cast across the elder's glaring face. His eyes were wide open and he clutched his guitar firmly to his chest as if he knew someone might try to steal it from him.

The elder's wife slept soundly in the far corner of the hut, so the American woman put her index finger to her full lips to urge him to remain silent as not to wake her. She crossed the hut like a predatory cat until she knelt before him. She opened her blouse and pressed his face against her breasts. He pulled back from her for a moment, but she nodded to the guitar and caressed its strings with her long slender fingers. She took the elder's chin in her hand and looked deep into his eyes to make him understand her proposition.

He nodded repeatedly.

She took the guitar by its neck and leaned it against the wall of the hut and fell backwards pulling the elder on top of her. She hadn't expected the elder to be so ardent or his testosterone to be so fluently aggressive at his age, but she was determined to fulfill her husband's need for the guitar. The morning birds were starting to chirp before the elder separated himself from her. She nodded to the guitar and he nodded back in agreement.

"Later," she said, though he wouldn't understand her language. She pointed to the sky, made a circle with both hands and motioned upward with her hand to indicate sunrise.

He nodded in agreement understanding that her husband couldn't know why he'd changed his mind about the selling the guitar.

She indicated with a counting gesture of her hands that the elder must accept some payment from her husband to avoid any suspicion.

He nodded, made a prayerful gesture with his hands, then she left his hut before his wife awoke. Her husband was still sleeping so she let him rest, nuzzling beside him and listening to his snoring and knowing she had done her best to make him happy, that this trip would accomplish what they had set out to do. Their possession of the guitar, she felt, would become more binding than their wedding vows. They could play it often as a reminder of their mutual dedication to each other.

When the husband awoke, he found his wife sleeping soundly beside him. Pablo called to him from outside their hut, "The elder has changed his mind!

Come and he will make an exchange for the guitar!"

Excitedly the American couple quickly dressed and came to the center of the village where they were greeted by an assembly of fifty villagers of various genders and ages. All had turned out for the exchange.

"What does this mean?" the husband asked.

"His son tells me this is an important pact between you and the elder which requires the witnessing by his entire village," Pablo said. "Come, we must follow them to their scared place."

The American couple shrugged at each other and followed. Only a ten-minute walk from the center of the village, but in the opposite direction of their recent expeditions to Mayan ruins, they came to a wide crevasse much like the one they'd seen several days ago. In full headdress and with a chorus of woodwind instruments made from hollow jungle flora, the elder, holding the guitar with outstretched arms, came to the edge of the crevasse.

With his wife at his side, the husband stood face-to-face with the elder, who uttered a chant in his ancient Mayan tongue that was echoed by the villagers surrounding them. The elder nodded to the husband, then to the wife, and bowed his head. The elder's son nodded to the husband's Rolex watch.

"He wants your watch," his wife nudged him.

The husband removed the watch and placed it in the Elder's son's outstretched hand. Then his son pointed to the husband's gold wedding band.

The husband grumbled under his breath, but his wife put a hand on his shoulder and nodded with her approval. Then she pulled off her diamond ring and placed it in the son's open hand with a gesture of personal sacrifice.

"We must have this guitar at any cost," she said under her breath.

The son nodded to the wife's digital camera, which made her hesitate, wanting her photos of this memorable trip of a lifetime. The son glared at her, so she removed the SIM card and handed the camera to him. He slung the camera over his shoulder by its strap.

"What more could he want?" the husband stammered.

The elder smiled broadly with a sallow grin of crooked teeth that gave the wife a chill, recalling last night. Before the Americans knew what hit them, the elder threw his guitar into the crevasse. The instrument made several discordant sounds as it bounced off treetops below then lay atop one tree's canopy in clear sight from above.

The villagers let out a prime-evil shrill as Pablo and the son exchanged a heated discourse.

"What the hell!" the husband gasped. His wife glared at the elder.

Pablo took the Americans aside. "He says if you can get the guitar, it's yours for the taking, and he'll return your trinkets as well."

Through the husband mind ran all the stunts he'd accomplished in his movies. The enchanting sound of the guitar echoed in his head.

"You can't!" his wife pleaded. "It's too dangerous. It's not worth it."

"It's priceless," he retorted. "I can do this. I must have it."

Over the next hour, she watched along with the villagers as her husband courageously climbed down the side of the crevasse. More than just a movie star, he was resourceful and took the chance that the tree's canopy would support him from a short height when he jumped off the side of the crevasse just ten feet above the broad leaves.

Oohs and aahs came from the villagers over his remarkable determination. When he took the guitar in hand they cheered him. He stroked a chord that rang as true as the night before, but with that strum, the branch he sat on broke. He let out a scream that gagged his wife.

She peered over the edge with hope that her heroic mate would make a remarkable escape as he always had in every film. She trembled with her back to the villagers, wondering if she had the courage to jump, joining her husband before she'd be forced over the edge.

She had to have her last say and turned toward the elder. "We had a deal!" she shouted, but he just nodded for his son to toss her husband's watch, their rings, and the camera over the side of the crevasse. Last tangible reminders of her husband.

When Pablo pleaded with the son, three villagers grabbed him, lifted him off his feet, then swung him by his hands and feet and threw him far over the edge with a scream that reverberated from the depth of the crevasse.

Horrified, the wife backed away from the edge of the bottomless pit. She felt certain of her fate, but prepared herself not to go without a fight. Having concentrated solely on her husband's efforts, she hadn't paid much attention to the other villagers gathered around her. She was sure she would be quickly grabbed and tossed over the side just like Pablo.

Then a promenade of female villagers was led by the elder's wife toward where she stood. The old woman bowed her head to the American, then the other women surrounded the elder's wife.

The movie star assumed this Mayan culture thought less of women and the elder's wife would have the lesser honor of shoving her over the side to complete the ritual . But the village women led the old woman to the edge of the crevasse where she gracefully took a long swan dive on her own. There was no scream of terror, only the sound of braking branches from her impact below.

The long silence that followed was suddenly broken with a musical chord of great volume that reverberated through the jungle. The American woman turned to the villagers and saw that each had a guitar like the elder's. All had the same unmistakable sound that she'd hoped would be the unique sound she'd share for the rest of her blissful life with her husband recalling this wonderful adventure.

My husband, she thought, *surely he isn't dead. Either I'm having a bad dream or he'll soon be back to rescue me from this nightmare.*

For the next month, she was awakened with wishful thoughts that her husband would emerge unscathed from that pit of hell and come to her rescue. But the vultures that circled the crevasse and swooped down and returned to flight with strands of carrion from their sharp beaks told her otherwise. A rancid smell of decay wafted daily from the crevasse and would until the rainy season came to wash the crevasse clean.

She thought about how this trip of a lifetime had not turned out like any of her husband's thriller flicks. Sometimes the elder would mistake her laughter as joy clutched as she would be nightly in his embrace, but she was laughing maniacally about how this wonderful vacation had turned into a bad joke that none of her Hollywood friends would get.

She laughed and blubbered simultaneous, disappointed in herself that she'd never have the courage of the old woman to jump on her own into the crevasse.

The elder cocked his head and just stared at her with curiosity when she had these daily hysterical mood swings.

She said the same thing every night, but in a language the elder couldn't understand: "It's a bad joke on us, Babe . . . truly *priceless*."

A fine line of perspective separates the degrees
of evil in our hearts.

GAW

Star Struck

Tom Larkin came out of air-conditioned Billy Munk's Pub. The heat and humidity felt like a smack in the face. He lit a cigarette with a Zippo that he flipped open and closed for the hollow, metallic click that could transport him to the past, a place where he felt guiltless over body-counts left in his wake.

Larkin waited for a let-up in the summer downpour under the pub's red canopy before crossing 45th Street. Through the raindrops, he saw the Long Island City billboard past the eastern tip of Roosevelt Island across the East River. Rush hour traffic crossed the Queensboro Bridge at a snail's pace as mist rose from the hot pavement cooled by the teaming rain.

His condo was across the street, only a chip shot from the United Nations Plaza. His business was always slow in August, so he wasn't dressed to impress. He had no boss or wife to admonish him for not wearing a suit and tie. He wore a Hawaiian shirt with green palm trees and tan surfers on blue wave crests on a black background. It was 95 degrees at 5:00 p.m. so his casual shirt, white shorts, and sandals were practical attire for a scorcher.

His iPhone buzzed in his shirt pocket. Seeing it was, Mona, on caller ID, he answered: "How much information did you get?"

"You think I'm *that* easy?" Mona said, her voice low and musical, as harmonious as a madrigal, but as unpredictable as jazz. "That's for me to know, and for you to find out. You promised to pay me upfront this time. You owe me a grand from last month."

"Stop by tonight after eight. I'll peel off fifty bucks for every meaningful piece of useful information that rolls off your sweet tender lips."

"First, you lay out the cash so I can see it all, then we'll play your game of show 'n' tell."

The rain stopped and the sun broke through. He came out from under the canopy and dashed across the street. Out of breath, he said, "Some of my contracts can become dangerous —I don't want you to become a victim on my account."

"Collateral damage?" she said with mocking timbre. "Doubt it."

"Just the same, I don't want anyone to connect you to me. You could get hurt."

"Tonight after eight—unseen, coming and going—a grand up front," she said and hung up.

Wilson, the door man, greeted Larkin in the lobby, his voice caroming off the marble walls and floor. "Have a good evening, Mr. Larkin."

He got off at the 32nd floor, his penthouse condo and office. At a wet bar, he poured three fingers of Maker's Mark into a tumbler filled with cracked ice. He took a shower and relaxed bare-chested on the sofa in his boxers with his bare feet crossed on a hassock. The doorbell rang. He slipped on a black flannel rob and let Mona in.

With no words exchanged, he poured Mona the same drink as his and brought both drinks to the sofa where she reclined.

"Cheers!" he said. "Cash," she replied.

"You're acting like a goddamn hooker," he huffed.

She tilted her head. "I prefer to think of myself as—a procurer of valuable information. I've never asked why you want the information or who gets it from you."

"It's parts to a puzzle. Without all the interlocking parts, there's nothing to *get*." Mona took a sip of her drink and rolled her big eyes, dark brown and pensive.

He got up from the sofa and went to his desk. He opened the center drawer with a key and peeled off a thousand dollars in tens and twenties. He divided the cash into piles of fifty dollars each.

"All right, Mona. Let's play twenty questions."

"What if I've got twenty good answers that will fulfill your contract?" she haggled. "Then you get the bonus prize."

She frowned. "What might that be?"

"Whatever you want behind door number one," he said, nodding toward his bedroom.

"All mouth and no go. Skip it, Lover-boy. Shoot."

"Did Consul Knowles come on to you at lunch, enough for you to confirm that he'd cheat on his wife?"

"He gave me his duplicate hotel room card. Just asked me to dinner, but he must be expecting more," she said with a shrug.

"I want fulfillment from you, not just foreplay, Babe," he said with a twist of his mouth.

"OK, tough guy," she said. "I got enough to make it a go tomorrow night and I'll know how he'll vote in the General Assembly long before dawn."

Larkin nodded and pushed two twenties and a ten across the coffee table to her.

***

Larkin woke the next morning at 7 a.m., Mona was already gone, but her scent remained on the pillows. She'd left a pot of coffee to click on with the remote. He sat up in bed with his back against the headboard and used the other remote to turn on the news. He stared at the TV, thinking about how his life had become a revolving door of brief encounters since his wife, Vera, had died. They'd only numbed him briefly without alleviating the chronic pain.

Mona was different, a valuable asset. They were associates and friends with mutual benefits. Someone to take turns with scratching each other's backs—but lately his itch had dug deeper than he'd ever expected. He cared about Mona and the idea of her in bed with anyone else had begun to get under his skin.

At 9 a.m. Larkin's iPhone buzzed on the kitchen counter. He missed the call. A cryptic text message showed *number withheld*, reading:

"URGENT – life in danger–old hangout–8 p.m. tonight. Danny R."

Larkin considered ignoring the message, but his caseload was light in August when his *marks* were on vacation with their families or back in their native countries.

✳ ✳ ✳

By 4:00 p.m., Larkin was heading in his red, '94 Camaro through the Lincoln Tunnel to avoid Manhattan's rush-hour exodus. He assumed that Danny Rampling wanted to meet him in New Jersey where they used to hang out at The Milk Barn as teenagers for burgers, ice cream, and girls—so many girls and not enough time. But The Milk Barn was demolished and replaced by a car dealership, so Larkin wasn't sure if that meeting point would work. Regardless, he had nothing more to go on.

He recalled the last information available about Daniel Rampling's illicit enterprises from his FBI dossier. When Larkin had taken the DEA's early retirement package, he'd had to relinquish all his extensive intelligence on personal friends to the agency, but his steel-trap mind had surrendered zip. Often DEA business conflicted or was tangent to FBI or CIA operations. In Danny's case it was CIA dark ops.

Danny had become a shadow figure, suspected as a CIA political informant, an outside-the-box, deeply covert specialist. He'd become an untraceable specter and a thorn in Larkin's side at the DEA. No one knew who controlled or paid Danny for his expertise, but Larkin had long ago surmised that Danny's operations were among little know government truths, warranting infinite discretion.

Larkin took precaution, by arriving two hours early. He went to Cobb's down the road from the car dealer for a couple of hotdogs and coffee. At 7:45 p.m. the sun set.

His phone buzzed in his breast pocket with no ID revealed. "Larkin speaking."

"Go to the Ford dealer on the corner of Dawes and Hamburg Turnpike. Come to the front entrance. I'll be waiting there to take you for a demo drive where we can talk," the caller said with a quiver in his voice, but he hung up before Larkin could respond.

Larkin pulled into a space away from the overhead lights to avoid being seen. He got out of the car and walked toward the entrance. His left elbow felt his 9 mm Glock shoulder holstered against his ribs. A new, white Ford Fusion pulled in front. A paunchy, middle-aged man waved to him with a dealer plate in hand. The man's swollen midriff preceded him as he tossed Larkin a set of keys.

With white wisps of hair around his ears, the dealer's neon sign reflected off the man's bald head glistening with perspiration. His thick bifocals fogged from his body heat and a stench of nervous sweat wafted from him toward Larkin seated behind the wheel.

The man slammed the door and shook Larkin's hand with a clammy grasp. "Pull ahead and make a left toward Pompton Falls."

"What's going on?" The glowing dashboard illuminated the man's left profile. "You said your life is in danger?"

"Has been for years," he said.

"How can I be sure you're Danny? You've gained forty pounds and you've gone bald."

"We ran into each other in Seoul, Korea at the Summer Olympics over thirty-three years ago. You provided personal protection for a South Korean billionaire."

Larkin said, "You told me that you were there with your family to see the Olympics, but you handed me some crap about your wife and daughter shopping." The man gave him a blank stare. "I tried to meet you and your family the next day, but you'd left. Haven't seen you since."

The man's lips made a twitch when he spoke, just like whenever Danny had been lying as a kid. Larkin knew that Danny was a pathological liar.

Larkin challenged him. "You lied to me back then—you have *no* kids, and you've *never* been married. Why should I help you now?"

"You're the only one who can."

"Can what?"

"Leave no trail," Danny said with a crooked grin. "My discretion led me to certain security operations beyond your imagination."

"Are you working for the mob . . . or is it the drug cartels?" Larkin asked.

"My client is as much a shadow as my make-believe family had been. The tobacco, pharmaceutical, and oil company lobbyist all tried to hire me as their fixer, but I've had no contact with the corporate arena or any criminal elements."

Larkin pressed, "If you've been so tidy, who'd want to kill you?"

"If I knew, I'd already be dead."

"Why contact me? Why now?"

"I trust you. You're the only one I'd considered. Now, because I have an inoperable brain tumor . . . the big C. I've got only weeks, maybe days. I'm losing my vision."

"Sorry."

"Eh! I've had a great run." He smirked. "I want to pass my legacy on to someone who'll care. I know you'll contain this situation without it spinning out of control."

"What have you been keeping under control?"

"I'm a *keeper*. I've done a great job, till now, enjoying the perks that come with the assignment. For the sake of . . . my partner, I need to pass my torch to you."

Larkin noticed spittle running down Danny's double chin. He wondered if that could be a side-effect of Danny's worsening condition, which would give credulity to his outlandish story.

"How do you mean *partner*?" Larkin asked, watching for a twitch of Dan's lip. "She has moments of clarity, but she's quickly begun to fail."

"At our age?" Jem balked.

"She's in her eighties, but could pass for sixty."

"Do you have some kind of mother complex? How did you meet?"

"At a Witness Protection Program . . . of sorts. They hired me to protect those she could harm. They gave her the choice of protection—or elimination."

"Who are these people?" Larkin shook his head, ready to pull over, walk back to the dealer, and cut loose.

"I don't know." His lip twitched, revealing a lie or a symptomatic tremor. "I inherited the position from another agent when he died back in the sixties. I took over when I was thirty-seven and she was fifty-six. It began like the Stockholm syndrome— the captured enchanted by her captor."

"You're the captured if you asked me. This is crazy, Danny. I'm out."

"You're *already* in. They recruited me the same way."

"I don't buy it."

"When you see my obituary in *The New York Times*," Danny said, you'll receive an address. Go there. If you don't go, you'll disappear. Head back to the dealer, now, before they realize one of their salesman's bound and gagged in the utility room."

"You don't work there?"

"Part-time," Danny said with a grin. "Time's up."

"That's it?"

"That's all she wrote. You're in—or you're *dead*."

"Why put this on *me*!"

"Neither of us ever allowed our emotions to interfere with duty," he said. "When you go to the address you'll understand."

Both got out of the car. Larkin handed him the keys.

"The duty is simple and controllable. You'll be able to come and go as you wish, but you can't continue your private investigator practice—too many contacts and an unpredictable schedule. The pay is high . . . very high. Here's two hundred grand. I won't be needing it."

With reluctance, Larkin took the thick envelope of cash. "Suppose I ignore this—as if tonight never happened?"

"You know better. Look after her. We won't see each other again. Good luck." Danny turned and was gone.

✳ ✳ ✳

Driving back to Manhattan, Larkin wished he could share this with someone—another reason he'd been chosen—no leaks.

Then he thought—Mona. Had they seen her coming and going to his apartment? Did Danny know he had a confidential snoop? Wilson, the doorman, was the only one who knew Mona had a key to his place. They always had come and had left separately. He could depend on Wilson, always had, but this was different. These people had their claws in Danny and weren't just two-bit thugs but a well-oiled machine. How would he keep this from Mona? If she found out, she'd be as good as dead.

* * *

Waking the next morning, Larkin wondered if the entire episode had been just a bad dream, that it was the same morning when Mona had left the pot of coffee for him. But no—his clothes from yesterday morning were strewn onto the swivel chair at his desk and his tie and socks were still left on the floor in a trail from the kitchen. An empty bottle of Maker's Mark and the caramel-colored dregs of his last drink remained in the tumbler on the night table beside his rumpled bed still redolent of Mona's scent.

He wore a pair of light-gray dress slacks and a short-sleeve cotton shirt, powder blue to go with his navy blazer. He downed one cup of strong, black coffee and noticed one cigarette left in his pack of Marlboros. He stuck it in his mouth then pulled it out again. He crumbled the empty pack and the cigarette then tossed them into the trash can. He locked his apartment door behind him and took the elevator down to the lobby, where Wilson greeted him with his usual mile. "Have yourself a fine day, Mr. Larkin."

"Anyone been asking about me? Not just today—any time?"

Wilson shook his head. "Even if someone had when I wasn't at the door, the guys on the other shifts would've called me, then I'd have called you."

Larkin nodded and headed to the newsstand on the corner. If Danny was on the level, Larkin knew this would become his morning ritual, checking *The New York Times* obituaries.

"No Marlboros today, Mr. Larkin?" the vendor at the counter asked.

"Gave 'm up for Lent."

"But it's August."

"I'm an early starter."

As Larkin headed back to his office, he unfolded the newspaper to see the obits, but his iPhone buzzed in his pocket. A text message read: 216 East 49th Street. Then he saw the four-line notice in the obits with no photo—Danny's death notice.

Only four short blocks away, the address given was among a familiar row of brownstones where some notable celebrities had resided in the past. Larkin hadn't paid much attention to that block. On the surface, the neighborhood had remained unchanged over the past fifty years. Some properties remained in the estates of old money, though the Japanese had turned a brownstone on the Second Avenue end of the block into their consulate.

There was a bagel shop at the Third Avenue end, so he had his morning coffee there and sat by a window reading the newspaper and observing number 216 across the street. It was already heating up on a bright sunny morning in August. He remained as inconspicuous as possible without ordering a third coffee as he continue to watch from the window.

At 11 a.m., a postal worker wearing shorts and pulling a three-wheeled cart stopped at 216. She took a bound handful of mail and walked slowly up the dozen steps of the front stoop. She unbound the mail, flipped through the envelopes, then slipped them, one at a time, through the mail slot in the door. She ambled slowly down the stairs to her cart then a uniformed doorman from the hotel around the corner called to her. Apparently on his coffee break, the doorman stopped to chat with her.

Larkin moved quickly while they remained preoccupied in conversation. He scribbled on the back of one of his fake business cards before coming into her view. Feigning confusion, he held his card up to several brownstones before he stood just a few feet in front of the postal worker.

"You lookin' for an address, Mister?" she asked.

"I have an address." He showed her the back of his card where it read: Daniel Rampling, Esq., Suite B, 216 East 49th Street. "But I don't see any direction on 216. Maybe it should be 216 West rather than East."

"I don't know where you got this suite number," she said, turning over his card and seeing his fake ID as an IRS agent. "Mr. Rampling receives mail here, has for the past twelve years I've had this route, but I've never seen the man."

She seemed willing to side with the IRS against someone rich enough to live in that neighborhood, so he prodded further. "Is there a *Mrs.* Rampling?"

"Couldn't say, but maybe his mother lives with him. See that open window on the third floor?" She pointed where curtains were blowing outward. "I've seen an old woman there . . . smoking and petting her dog, one of those fluffy lap dogs with a pink bow on its head to keep its hair out of its eyes. Whenever I waved, she used to wave back, but not recently. Haven't seen the dog in a while either."

"I don't want to disturb his mother by ringing the bell," Larkin said.

"No one ever comes to the door," she said. "I've tried to deliver packages that need a signature. I leave notices, but someone always comes to the post office to pick them up. I've never been there to see who did."

"If no one answers, I'll have to come back tonight. Thanks for your help."

He went up the front stoop and rang the doorbell. He pushed the doorbell three times, but couldn't hear it ring. He went down the stairs and looked up from the stoop. He saw the old woman at the window with the dog in her arms.

She was staring down at him and said with a shrill, "Got a cigarette, honey?"

He called back, "Sorry, I quit!"

"Be a good fella and bring me some?"

"What brand?"

"Slims—they make me feel elegant!"

"One pack?"

"Hell no!" she huffed. "A carton!"

He waved to assure her. "I'll be right back!"

Heading for the corner newsstand, he considered just walking away, but couldn't do it. He figured that would be like leaving a puppy in a locked car with the windows shut on a hot day. If her mind were failing, no telling what she'd do if he didn't return.

Damn you, Danny, he thought. *You knew I couldn't walk away from this.*

He wondered if the old woman had the ability to let him in. Short of pulling a Rapunzel from the third-floor window, he realized there might be no way to get the cigarettes to her.

When he returned, she was still at the window and shouted, "Door's open!"

Alone, she must have been ambulatory enough to go up and down three flights of stairs, unless there was an elevator. He turned the knob and entered, but had to step over a mound of unopened mail—according to the postmarks—for over a month. He saw that all had come to the attention of Daniel Rampling, Esq.

The old woman shrilled down the stairwell for her cigarettes.

When he came to a puffing halt on the third floor, he saw her reclining on a love seat. She was watching a movie on TV. A white Maltese was curled in her lap and licking the back of her wrinkled hand. The dog's ears perked but it didn't bark.

"Cigarette, please." She extending her arm with two fingers in a v shape, waiting like royalty to be served.

He quickly broke open one carton, then a pack. The dog sneezed, sounding like a cat coughing up a hair ball. In dog years, she and her pet were the same age.

"Either she's allergic to you, or you've excited her," she said, never taking her eyes off the flat-screen TV. She was watching the TCM channel.

Jem recognized the fifties flick, *Dial M for Murder*.

Impatient, she flexed her index and middle fingers like scissors. "Do you always keep a girl waiting?"

"I'm a loner. Women get too cloying."

"How 'bout *clawing*?" she mimicked with a purr.

She lit the cigarette with a butane lighter drawn from the cleavage exposed at the gap of her florid, satin kimono. Her head turned towards him but her eyes stayed glued to the TV screen. She puckered and blew smoke from her full, cherry-red lips. Close up, her face was pasty with a beauty mark to the left of her upper lip. Exhaling dual streams of smoke from her perfect nose, she said, "I neither scratch nor bite." Nodding toward the TV, "Neither does *Princess*." She fluffed the dog's chest. "Sit and stay a while."

He sat in a soft, recliner, no doubt Danny's favorite spot, but he sat erect with his legs crossed, keeping one foot on the floor, a habit for making a quick exit.

Her mind seemed sharp, and he figured she was nimble enough to have recently bathed herself, since her long white hair was still damp and, from an arm's length, her body smelled soapy clean. She exuded an unusual sexuality for her age, but it was a blend of nostalgia and charisma that captured his attention.

Her exhaled smoke swirled around her heavily made-up face and damp, white hair, giving her a Medusa-like pose. He imagined that, like the myth, her gaze could turn a man to stone.

She had light-brown eyes, unglazed for someone her age with no red veins in the whites. Her brownish eyebrows were well-trimmed and her shapely earlobes weren't pierced. Despite being a smoker, her teeth were like white pearls with some slight spaces. Maybe they were capped, but they weren't false.

The room hadn't been properly cleaned lately, with cobwebs in the corners of the ceilings and dust on the furniture. He saw a three-inch roach scramble across the tiled floor in the adjacent kitchen.

He couldn't be sure how tall she was, since she was reclined, but her ankles were thin with a few squiggly, blue veins. He noticed a treadmill and nautilus in the adjoining room. From Danny's out-of-shape physique, Larkin assumed the old woman had been using the exercise equipment. He wondered if she hoped to live long enough to be set free. Maybe vanity made her want to look her best in the unlikely event that she'd be seen in public again.

"Think you're up to it, kiddo?" She asked, with a high, breathy whisper.

"Up to what?" He felt like a schoolboy caught looking up the teacher's skirt.

"Up to whatever I can dish out," she said, taking a deep breath. "You remind me of Billy Holden in *Picnic*—hard as a sharp piece of steel. Are you one of those *bad* good guys, the kind who make women surrender in ways they'd never thought possible?"

"No. I'm a *good* bad guy, who won't let a woman talk him out of doing whatever is right and needs to be done."

She pouted.

"Has Danny been here since yesterday?" he asked.

She stared dreamily. "Yesterday, today, and tomorrow . . . life is but a walking shadow that struts and frets upon a stage . . ." She looked him directly in the eye. "I wouldn't have attracted you—not even in my prime—but we could've been close friends. I can see it in your eyes."

"What do you see?"

"You're *star struck*, honey. Good thing you're good, even if you're a bad guy."

"I've never thought of myself as *good*," he said.

"*Genuine* good guys never do, but the people they're good to, they do. You're like my second husband. He never let me down. He was the first guy to treat me with respect. Help yourself to a drink." She nodded to a wet bar next to the TV.

He got up and poured himself a scotch on the rocks. He sat back down and crossed his legs.

She put out her cigarette and waved both arms in the air. "Some bastards came up with *this* bright idea, making me live in a damn pumpkin shell. I'd rather be dead—all my friends are long gone."

"I'm stuck here now, too. So tell me what you know but can't tell," he said.

She turned to face him with a subtle posture that gave him a vague recollection of familiarity as she struck a pose.

"If I told you, you'd never leave this room—except feet first," she said with an expression like a mom telling her little boy not to chase a ball into the street. "I was too foolish to let anything go, things I'd seen and heard people say and do, stuff that changes everything. I was in the wrong place at the wrong time."

He shrugged with a smirk of disbelief.

"Don't mock me, *Danny*. It's true!"

Oops! He thought. *She'd been sharp so far, but now she thinks I'm Danny.* He figured she must've been playacting in some game they had established over time.

She pointed to the TV. "I auditioned for that movie, but Hitch didn't give me the part. Over-stuffed, son-of a—he hired Miss Goody-Two-Shoes instead. Look at her! A goddamn Ice Princess. That's why I named my sweet puppy *Princess*, as a reminder how I got screwed out of that part. My precious Princess is much warmer and cuddly than that cold bitch ever was."

She rubbed the dog's belly, making it groan with pleasure.

"If Grace Kelly got that part instead of you, did you *ever* get a lead part?"

Her sensuous mouth dropped open. She stared blankly and said, "Hell, yeah!"

"How about an Oscar? Ever nominated? Ever win one?"

She seemed to stop breathing. Princess whined, trying to burrow into her lap with her front paws scratching against her. Suddenly, the old woman gasped for breath. Her body convulsed.

Larkin lunged toward her and put his ear to her chest then pounded her heart with the heel of his fist repeatedly. She gasped for breath and clutched at him as if she were drowning. Her nails scratched at his face. He pushed her down on the love seat, forced her mouth open, and turned her head to see if her windpipe was blocked—all clear. He pushed his weight against her chest for CPR, counting in cadence then tried mouth-to-mouth. She gasped then puked.

Princess jumped off the love seat and scrambled with a whimper into the kitchen.

Tears ran from the old woman's dilated eyes, making her mascara run with two dark trails down her bluish cheeks. Glassy-eyed, she tried to speak. He put his ear close to her quivering lips.

She whispered, "I'm ready for my close-up, Mr. De Mille."

He wondered if she was still playing him along just for amusement.

Then she motioned him to lean closer with a limp gesture of her hand. With a singsong whisper, her words gave him a sudden jolt of recognition.

Stunned by what he heard, Larkin backed away with disbelief as her eyes rolled back in her head and her body slumped limply—lifeless.

He knelt beside the loveseat and embraced her. Her white hair felt cool and damp against his hot cheek.

He pulled back to see her face again, altered with age from the face he now recognized and had known for most of his life.

Unable to breathe, she clutched him

He reached for his cell to call 911, but realized that would be a mistake. They, whoever they were, had wanted her dead a long time ago because she knew too much. But they'd kept her alive all these years. He didn't care who they were or why they did it. He had a trail to cover, his own, which could lead to Mona.

Realizing his danger, Larkin took the glass with scotch, scrubbed it at the sink, dried it with a towel, and put it back where he got it. He wiped the bottle with the towel, then the counter. The only articles in the room he could take with him with his fingerprints on them were the cigarettes. He couldn't worry about hair follicles. He thought he'd had it covered, then

Princess whimpered and came from the next room. She scampered across the floor and licked the dead woman's hand.

He picked up Princess in his arms, and she licked his ears with a whimper. He took the carton of cigarettes, then used his pen to flip the receiver off the hook of the rotary land-line phone on the coffee table to give him more time to get away than dialing 911.

With the dog and cigarettes in hand, he took the stairs two at a time, hoping not to trip in his hurry. He wiped the front door clean with his sleeve and left before an EMS could arrived in response to the phone off the hook.

An unmarked van screeched in front of the brownstone, so quickly that Larkin barely made it to the coffee shop across the street without being seen. Within a few minutes from their arrival, a team of four was in and out, taking the body away in a black, plastic bag. They put a strip of yellow tape across the front door with a public notice condemning the building, allowing time to return later for a thorough clean-up.

For now, like an Indy 500 pit stop team, they moved so quickly that their unmarked van was gone before an EMS or any news reporters showed up.

The street remained quiet for over an hour. Neither an EMS nor the media ever came. The phone had been rerouted to alert a clean-up crew if anyone ever made a call from within the brownstone. The phone off the hook was the same. That had been a smart move, efficient, leaving no trail.

Larkin hoped no one saw him, but as he headed back to his office, his cell buzzed in his pocket making Princess bark. The untraceable text message read: "We'll never know who'll go first. I'm no longer any use to them. They'll try to get to me quickly, but I'll take care of that myself. I'm tossing my phone into the East River. I knew I could depend on you."

When Larkin came into his apartment and put Princess down, she immediately peed on the hardwood floor. He removed his jacket then cleaned up her mess. He had no dog food, so he cracked an egg into a bowl of Cheerios and stirred it with a dash of soymilk Mona had left in the fridge. That agreed with Princess.

He realized the open pack of cigarettes remained in his pocket. Pouring a splash of bourbon over three ice cubes, he swirled the tumbler and inhaled the aroma. He took a thin cigarette from the pack and leaned over the gas stove.

Plunking down in his easy chair, he watched the trail of cigarette smoke for a moment without taking a drag. After sniffing the whiskey and taking a long sip of the its dregs, he dropped the cigarette into the tumbler, extinguishing the embers on the ice cubes with the sound of a cat's hiss that made Princess bark.

Then he noticed something on his black trousers, a long strand of white hair. He figured it was from carrying Princess. Pulling the hair from his thigh and holding it up to the light, it still felt damp. "Jesus," he said, slipping the strand of hair into a plastic sandwich bag, then he put it with the envelope of cash from Danny in his wall safe concealed behind a framed photo.

* * *

The next morning, Larkin's iPhone rang. Princess jumped onto his lap and licked his face. He'd have to get those annoying pee pads because, if he was ever seen walking her, they'd both be dead. His phone buzzed and he checked caller ID.

"Hi, Mona," he said. "Come tonight for dinner . . . No, just a quiet dinner here. I'll cook. It's not about work . . . I know I never have before . . . Forget about the Knowles case. This is more important . . . I need to run something by you. You're the only one I can share this with . . . Eight o'clock is fine. On your way over, could you pick up some Kibbles 'n' Bits? . . . You'll see why when you get here."

He hung up and turned on some jazz but, try as he might, he still couldn't block out the song the old woman had whispered in his ear:

> *"Happy birthday . . . to you.*
> *Happy . . . birthday . . . to . . . you.*
> *Hap . . . py . . . birth . . . day . . . Mister . . .*
> *President.   Happy . . . birth . . . day . . . to . . . you."*

Buried Treasure

Open just a crack, the bathroom door emitted mist from a teaming, hot shower. In a fogged glass shower stall, Sally Watson slumped with a groan and leaned her aching back against the warm, wet tiles then shrieked, "Turn down the damn TV!"

Her shrill carried from the bathroom down the long hallway. She covered her ears with her rough hands to block out the blaring TV down the hall, but Tarzan's croaky call to a herd of elephants continued to echo through the corridor from the bedroom where the 1942 flick, *Tarzan's New York Adventure*, blasted from a 24-inch analog TV.

Pulsing hot water pounded the back of Sally's stiff neck. Her legs and hips ached from standing on the hard floor at work since 7 a.m. Her right shoulder and neck felt knotted from turning to the right all day to ring up groceries on the register.

After fifteen minutes, she slid open the shower door and reached for the body-length white towel. She stepped onto the fluffy bath mat then swiped the fogged mirror with the towel. Her pained grimace reflected in the mirror with new lines etched on her face. She scowled at the TV down the hall as it continued trumpeting the sound of stampeding elephants with no reply or reaction to her complaint.

"Damn it," she huffed, quickly fluffing her long, auburn locks with the towel, wrapping it around her head and swaddling her jiggling breasts with a white terrycloth robe, rough against her pert, sensitive nipples. She reached into the medicine chest for the box of tampons, but found it empty. "Crap!"

She'd left the empty box as a reminder to buy more today. She crumpled it and threw it into the waste can. She massaged the back of her thin neck knotted with stress then pulled open the bathroom door to defog the bathroom. A cool draft came down the hall carrying the crisp British lilt of Maureen O'Sullivan's swoon, "Oh, *Tah-zen*, you must put me down."

"Turn down that damn TV!" Sally shouted as she stomped down the dark hallway toward the light at the end of the corridor where the kitchenette glowed from the afternoon sun coming through the window above the sink. She pushed open the door off the kitchen from where the TV's blare vibrated dishes in the scummy sink stacked with dirty dishes as high as the window sill. From breakfast or from last night's dinner? She'd lost rack. No time with a 7 a.m. clock-in at work and just enough time to pick up her daughter from school.

She entered the room and was puzzled as she turned off the TV just as Johnny Weissmuller was about to dive off the Brooklyn Bridge into the East River. Jumping off a high bridge had crossed Sally's mind years ago with Bobbie Gentry's throaty song about the third of June echoing in her mind. She waited just to see Tarzan hit the water, surface unscathed, and swim towards Manhattan. *Unscathed*, she thought, *wouldn't that be nice.*

"What a crock!" she barked, clicking off the TV. A turntable next to the TV still wobbled with the needle scratching to a cadence of time gone by on a 78 vinyl of *Hound Dog* that kept cryin' all the time. The beige walls embraced prints of rock concerts from the '60s.

She saw a pair of madras shorts and a "Woodstock '69" psychedelic T-shirt strewn in a wad beside a pair of white sneakers with grass-stained white socks hanging over the tongues like reptilian carcasses of a world long lost. A dog-eared paperback of Kerouac's *On the Road* was spread-eagled on the unmade single bed.

Sally went to the closet where a wooden clothes hanger in an empty plastic bag from the Dry cleaners stood out prominently from all the casual wear around it, proclaiming within a red heart, "We Love Our Customers." She saw that the cleaner's receipt stapled to the bag was from two years ago and marked: 1 Men's suit–dry clean and press.

Sally's expression reflected puzzlement until she backed out of the room and turned to the kitchen table where two brown bags of fresh vegetables and fruit flanked a white plastic bag. A red apron had been draped over the back of one of the three wooden chairs around the table.

The plastic bag contained a dozen eggs and three heart medications for the next 90 days. Sally's Fendi knock-off shoulder bag hung by its brown leather strap from the back of another chair.

After hours on her feet, her long hot shower had taken priority over the mundane hurdles blocking her path to a rare fifteen minutes of serenity.

She reached into her handbag, blindly at first, then with frustration, she impatiently dumped its contents clinking and clanging onto the Formica table. She pushed the items about the table as if she were separating pieces of a jigsaw puzzle then realized that a part of the puzzle was missing—her car keys.

"Son of a bitch!" she gasped, grabbing her iPhone from the table and dialing 911.

***

Ten miles and two small Jersey towns away, the little girl sat in the front passenger seat of 2002 Saturn with food-stained seats and cigarette butts overflowing the ashtray and scattered on the floor with a hole that had often spouted water during a downpour through rim-filled potholes. An unopened pack of menthol cigarettes sat in one of the console's cup holders with a pink Bic lighter and a coffee-stained lottery ticket. The passenger-side cup holder contained loose change stuck together from sugared coffee spills ever since the car was bought used ten years and 150,000 miles ago.

"The first year I worked as a lifeguard at Pleasure Land was 1962," the old man driving the Saturn said to the little girl sitting next to him. He was dressed in a well-pressed suit and tie, though it was out of fashion with horizontal creases across the inseam of the trousers from hanging in the closet too long.

"Are you sure Mom said it was OK to pick me up from school today?" the little girl asked. Her pink backpack against the back of the passenger seat forced her to sit forward in her seatbelt, which she had to hold in her fist to keep it from choking her. Her feet didn't reach the floor.

He brushed back his white, thinning hair then reached over to pat her hand. His was liverspotted and wrinkled, like a worn baseball mitt compared to hers, small and soft. She turned hers over to feel his cool, leathery palm.

"Mom said she was going to take me clothes shopping after school today." He didn't answer right away, distracted by some faraway thought.

"Will Mom get mad again like the other time?"

Breaking out of his cloud, he shook his head. "Not this time." Then he nodded and gently squeezed her hand. "Today could make her happy . . . make you happy, too."

"Are you gonna take me to McDonald's?" She fidgeted. "Mom won't let me eat junk food unless it's a special occasion. "She said I'll become a *beast.*"

The old man chortled as he drove, not about what she'd said, but rather that he seemed to be having a good day so far . . . not really good, but at least better than some of the others. He dreaded ever losing his sense of humor.

"Your mom's not afraid you'll turn into a beast. She doesn't want you to become *obese*. That means very fat, so fat that it's unhealthy, especially for your heart. I'm sorry to disappoint you, but you're having supper at home tonight, but not until after our adventure this afternoon."

"You mean *Great Adventure . . . Six Flags* with all the rides?"

"No. It will be our personal adventure. We're going to find hidden treasure."

"Like pirates?"

"Sort of, but not from that long ago. It's as good as gold if we can find it."

She watched him staring silently ahead then she stretched in her seatbelt to see where they were headed. She saw they were getting off the highway in Oakdale, the town where her Mom had grown up. Though she enjoyed his mysterious ways, she wondered if this adventure would get them both in trouble with her mom again.

* * *

Sally got into her neighbor's car and they screeched out of the driveway with a wheelie around the corner.

"Do you think he'd hurt her? Alice asked.

Sally thought for a moment shaking her head. "Not intentionally. I'd hoped it would take longer. Now I can't be sure.

Please hurry. Maybe she's still waiting for me to pick her up. I was running late. If she isn't there, I'll have her teacher fired. I'll sue the damn school—the whole fucking town!"

Sally reached into her bag and lit a cigarette and cracked the window. "Sorry," she said fanning the smoke out the window.

"It won't kill me this one time," Alice shrugged. "It's been two years since I quit, but if Kim's not at school, I may have to grub a cigarette off you."

They grimaced with mutual concern then Sally pulled a brochure from her bag. The cover read: HOLIDAY ACRES—where we relieve all your concerns.

Sally had hoped this day would never come.

* * *

"What happened to Bugsy's hand? Kim asked as they drove through Oakdale. "Did he die?"

"No. He got a tetanus shot, and they cleaned out the puncture wound and stitched it at the ER. It was the same hospital where you were born. Bugsy still sends me Christmas cards and we laugh about the good old days. He doesn't want anybody to call him *Bugsy* anymore. I call him Dave.

Kim wrinkled her nose. "Yuk! How did they get the icepick out of his hand?""

"They gave him something for pain then the doctors yanked it out. He still has an deep scar."

"Tell me more about you and Bugsy."

He smiled, glad to have someone's interest for a change. Pleasure Land was about three acres with an Olympic-size pool, two picnic pavilions, and a dance pavilion with a jukebox."

"What's a jukebox?"

"It's what some call a nickelodeon, like the kids' TV show your mom watched when she was your age. You put a nickel in the slot to play a record," he explained as Teresa Brewer's hit song came to mind, "Put another nickel in . . . in the nickelodeon."

"Does the jukebox hold the treasure we're looking for?" she asked with a shrug.

"No, just music, but a treasure to some. On summer weekends we had about a thousand people in Pleasure Land. Lifeguards, like me and Bugsy had to clean the park between 6 a.m. and 8 a.m. Then we had to park cars tightly together, so they'd all fit inside the park, which bordered the Ramapo River on one side and the mountainside on the other off Rte. 202. There was no Rte. 287 back then, just forest and mountains with wild game, like bears and deer. The 287 freeway was just a rumor back then."

For a moment it felt like yesterday to him, seeing in his mind a steady line of cars caravanning into the park. He could see himself and Bugsy waving to cars and lining them up along the fence before the pool opened. Then at 8 a.m. they'd climb their lifeguard stands to watch for drowning swimmers, and blow their whistles to warn bathers not to rough house in the water or to run on the wet cement deck that became slippery from dripping bathers leaving the pool. On those crowded weekends, from the lifeguard stands, the pool's turquoise blue water was hidden by bathers' churning pink flesh.

"Did you ever save anyone?" Kim asked wide-eyed with curiosity.

"I had seventy rescues one summer, but not all in the pool. One toddler crawled into an open charcoal fire in the picnic pavilion. I blew my whistle for Bugsy to cover the pool so I could pull the kid away from the fire before she was seriously burned."

He saw himself running barefoot on the rough pool deck and leaping over the three-foot fence around the pool then across the lawn to the pavilion. The parents were grateful, but had to much beer and neglected to watch their child carefully enough. She suffered a few blisters on her feet which he administered to in the First Aid room.

"Life was simple back then," he said to Kim. "The greatest danger in Oakdale was a pack of Luckies, but no one even knew they were dangerous.

"What are Luckies?"

"Lucky Strike cigarettes—no filters, no warnings, and thirty-five cents a pack."

"Mom smokes. Isn't that dangerous?"

He frowned at the pack of Newports in the console. "Yes, but sometimes bad habits are hard to quit, Sally—I mean *Kim*."

Kim wrinkled her nose and stared at him as he drove.

He grinned. "I can name all the kids in my third-grade class, but don't ask me what I had for dinner last night."

"You're funny, Grandpa."

"I'll take funny. Funny is good."

"We had pizza," she said.

He nodded as if he remembered.

They turned onto Doty Road and parked outside the fence where the rusted sign read:

PLEASURE LAND PARK

The other side of the fence looked like a scene from Disney's *Sleeping Beauty* with overgrown vines, trees and weeds obscuring a clear view into the once manicured swimming attraction that had drawn thousands from the inner city for decades, but not in the past thirty years after the state had declared the property a hazard zone from annual flooding.

"This place looks scary," she said.

He just shrugged and got out of the car.

"We can't go in there," she said, pointing. "See. The gate is locked."

Seeing a fist-sized padlock and thick chains on the double gates where cars used to enter and exit, he assured her, "I know another way to get in. In 1965 the rock n roll trio, *The Shangrilas*, performed in the dance pavilion to a crowd of two thousand kids. They had a couple of big hits, "Leader of the Pack" and "Remember, Walking in the Sand." Teenagers from other towns tried to sneak in without paying and cut a hole in the barbed wire fence on the other side of the park. We'll have to walk around the fence through the woods.

Kim was frightened by the gnarled branches as she followed her grandfather along the exterior of the fence through the bramble. He had to hold back branches of briar to protect her from the thorns. He found the hole in the fence, but it was easier for Kim to duck, even with her backpack on, than it was for him, having gained forty pounds in fifty years. He regretted wearing a suit and loosened his tie. He'd had to make a good impression on Kim's teacher to distract her from looking too closely at his driver's license, which had expired two years ago. His photo and Kim's saying he was her grandpa had let it pass.

He began to sweat with wet patches at the armpits of his light gray suit. Passing through the hole in the fence with grunts, he followed Kim into the park. It was as if he'd stepped through a black hole going back in time when he was nineteen the summer after his first year in college . . .

* * *

A rusted red pickup truck sputtered and groan as it churned up a cloud of dust around the far bend of the dirt road and circled the huge turquoise swimming pool shimmering in July's bright morning sun. The pickup provided no escape from the sweltering heat. WABC's *Good Guys* blared current rock 'n' roll hits from the park's PA speakers from the folk rock *Mr. Tambourine Man* to foot-stomping *Satisfaction* to drug-enhanced *Nowhere Man*.

Louie Cavatelli, owner of Pleasure Land Park, had taken pity on the lifeguards by removing the doors from the wheezing '53 Chevy pickup with a clutch that had no friction point and a choke that did just that—choking the rattletrap inconveniently to a stalling, coughing halt. The pickup screeched on its bald tires as head lifeguard, Bugsy, jumped out of the door-less heap and waved for him to come over.

"Come on, Tom! These trash barrels weigh a ton this morning!" Bugsy shouted.

They each grabbed a turquoise-painted oil drum used as trashcans throughout the park. He followed Bugsy's lead and kicked one trashcan so the yellow jackets would swarm away from the sickening stench of yesterday's garbage. He threw a grungy beach towel over the top of the can to trap any bees still sucking the sticky empty soda bottles inside. He rolled the can on its bottom to the back of the truck, lifted its eighty pounds by the rim with both hands, and put his knee halfway up on its side as he thrust it with a crash into the pickup's corroded bed. Bees swarmed out of the trashcan when the other end of the towel remained tucked in his belt the way Bugsy had taught him.

"Jeez, this one will take both of us to lift," Bugsy said. "Damn clam shells are like lifting lead." Both grimacing, they rolled the can on its bottom then tilted it away from the back of the truck. Each with a hand on the bottom and top of the trashcan used a knee to hoist it into the truck's bed. "Bastards.

Why couldn't they eat something lighter? I'm demanding a raise after this crap."

They took their paper picks fashioned with an ice pick duct taped to a broom handle and stabbed at the loose garbage on the ground from overflowing cans.

"Hey! Look! Here come the rookies," Bugsy said. "Grab some crab apples and we'll have a fight to show them who rules this park."

Tom grabbed three apples and took aim as if throwing to home plate from center field. Bingo! He hit one of the new kids square in the back from two hundred feet away with a whap and a holler.

"Great shot!" Bugsy shouted. "Watch this!" He held his pick in his left hand with the sharp ice pick facing up, took careful aim, and threw as hard as he could to reach another kid farther away. Bugsy let out a howl when his right hand followed through with his throw and the ice pick held upright in his left hand went right through his right palm and protruded two inches from the back of his hand.

***

"Bugsy got a tetanus shot then they cleaned the puncture hole and stitched it at the ER. It was the hospital where your mom was born. We used to laugh about those good old days, but I've had no contact with him in thirty years. He didn't want anyone to call him "Bugsy" anymore. His name is Dave." When he was little his mom used to give him a raw carrot in his lunch box for school so he looked like Bugs Bunny. I used to say, "Eh, what's up, Doc?" He outgrew his nickname."

Kim stared at him silently for a moment. "You already told me about that," she said.

"I did? Was that last week?" he asked with a blank expression, unable to recall.

"Ten minutes ago," she said with a sigh. "Tell me more about being a lifeguard."

The image of Pleasure Land's owner, Louie, came to mind. He recalled seeing Louie greeting a black stretch limo at the front gate at 6 a.m. He locked the gate behind him because the park wouldn't open until 8 a.m. Her got into the backseat of the limo. The lifeguards were having coffee and doughnuts before collecting trashcans. Tom watched the limo stop in front of the snack bar where he and Bugsy sat at a picnic table. Bugsy had his back to the limo, but Tom saw Louie get out of the limo and close the door. He saw a puff of cigar smoke come from the tinted opaque window then a fist with gold rings on every finger plopped a brown paper bag into Louie's cupped hands

Louie tucked the bag into his loose shirt. Then the limo circled the park. Louie unlocked the gates and the limo left, snaking to the main road above the park. Louie locked the gates again and lit a fresh cigar. Tom had never seen him smoke a cigar before. Louie came toward the table where Tom and Bugsy were finishing their coffee.

"OK, goof balls. Quit staring and get to work," Louie said.

Tom got up from the table and turned toward the snack bar. He realized that Bugsy might have seen what he had seen, but in the reflection from the shiny metal grill inside the open snack bar. Bugsy gave him no indication that he'd seen any of it—until he opened his mouth.

"I want a raise, Louie," Bugsy said.

"You—and your mother," Louie said.

"Heaving those trashcans full of clam shells onto the truck could break a leg. I want a raise to two bucks an hour as head lifeguard and a buck-fifty for Tom."

Louie glared at both of them. "You saw something this morning you need to forget about."

Bugsy shrugged. "Don't know what you're talking about."

Louie glared at Tom, but he stared back with no expression. He was embarrassed that Bugsy was doing his bidding for him.

Louie shrugged. "A buck seventy-five for you and a buck twenty-five for Tom. If you Come back next summer, you get two bucks an hour and Tom gets a buck fifty." He glared at Tom again. "If you come back for your third summer next season, then you'll get a week off with pay like Bugsy. It may be hard work in the morning, but then you lazy asses get to sit in your chairs all day in the sun hoping one of those ripe teenies will blow your whistles on your days off. Not in my park. I don't need any attention—got it?"

"This is my fifth season as head guard," Bugsy bargained. "I want *two* weeks off with pay next summer."

Louis kept staring at Tom. "Ya gonna let this big shot fuck up your summer vacation by getting' ya both canned?"

Bugsy grinned. "You tried that a couple of years ago, Louie. You couldn't get anyone to replace me and had to close the park for a week. I was only nineteen then. I've got more friends in this little borough now that I'm over twenty-one. I'll agree to ten weekdays off with pay per season, but I get to choose them. I'll always be on weekend duty to keep the younger guards from screwing up and getting you sued. I want those ten weekdays this season and five paid weekdays for Tom."

Louie looked from one to the other and shifted his weight with the brown paper bag still tucked inside his shirt against his heart.

"OK. Ya got it," Louie said. "Now get the fuck back to work!"

When Tom came to the snack bar for lunch that afternoon, Louie's wife, Kay, cooked him a sausage sandwich on the grill, but Louie puffed on a cigar and just stared at him like an undertaker taking mental measurements for a wake.

* * *

Sally and Alice pulled in front of the school and Sally jumped out of the car. She ran to Kim's classroom, hoping her teacher would be there. She found the classroom locked, so she ran to the office. The Principal's secretary was just locking up.

"Mrs. Sarsfield!" Sally yelled down the hall.

After an excited exchange and a phone call to the Principal, Sally was permitted to call Kim's teacher at home.

On the phone, Kim's teacher said, "He said he was her grandfather and Kim confirmed that he was. He had a note signed by you saying you had to work late and had sent him instead to pick up Kim. He had your last name, Shea. Isn't your father's name Thomas. He showed me his driver's license. Is there a problem?"

"Yes, there's a problem! His driver's license has been expired for three years. Didn't you check? He's known my signature since I was a teenager."

As Sally came back to the car without Kim, Alice could see from her slumped posture and awkward gait that she had bad news.

"Take me to the police station, right now! Sally said, but reaching for her seatbelt she saw the local morning paper folded on the console between her and Alice. The front page showed a photo of Louie Cavatelli, a suspected mob capo who died yesterday. A memory flashed in her mind of when she had been Kim's age and her father had taken her on a treasure hunt. It had almost turned dark and a cop at Pleasure Land Park's gate had told them the park had been condemned and bought by the state as a drainage source to prevent floods. The cop had told her father that many had tried to enter the park for nostalgic reasons, but it was too dangerous and closed to the public. A few teenagers had been seriously injured and one had drowned after stumbling drunk into the slimy pool filled with muddy rain water.

Sally recalled how her mother had argued with her dad about that dangerous outing. It was the same kind of heated argument she'd had with him, too. First as a teenager when he hadn't approve of her boyfriend. Billy was a drunk, just as her dad had warned her. Though he'd never said, "I told you so," it was etched on his face with an expression she tried to avoid. When her mom died, she had no choice but to take him in. His pension and Social Security helped to pay monthly expenses and had kept a roof over all three of their heads. They were a family, even if disjointed by her father's unpredictability. With today's behavior, what the hell was she supposed to do?

Then she saw the other headline in the paper:

PLEASURE LAND EXCAVATION BEGINS MONDAY

"I know where he took Kim," Sally told Alice. "We'll need the police. I've got to stop him before they're both seriously hurt.

***

He remembered one skinny-dipping, after-hours pool party with Bugsy and some hot chicks from Fort Lee. He'd had too much beer and decided to sleep it off in the First Aid room. About 4 a.m. he heard a car coming into the park through the front gate. He figured it was Bugsy returning from driving the girls home. In his skivvies, he scuffled out of the First Aid room and saw someone approaching from a distance on foot. He hoisted himself onto the roof of the First Aid room for a better look. The figure approaching was too short to be Bugsy as he cut across the pool deck in his direction. He lay flat on the roof so he wouldn't be seen. Peeking over thr roofs edge, he saw it was Louie.

Louie took out his keys to unlocked the door to the First Aid room, but it pushed open without the key.

Tom used his vantage point on the roof to hang over the back of the roof to see inside the first aid room's rear window when Louie turned on the lights. Bugsy had taught him that trick so they could watch girls changing into their bathing suits at their after-hours parties.

He watched as Louie came into that backroom and pried up a floorboard with the back of a hammer. From a large brown paper shopping bag, Louie took wads of cash, all hundreds, that Tom figured was a least a hundred grand in neatly bound stacks. He put the cash into a plastic bag then slipped it into a tan leather sack. The sack fit beneath the floorboard. Louie took nails from his pocket and hammered the floorboard flat. He kicked some dirt across the floor and ground it with his foot to dull the sheen of the new nail heads.

Tom held his breath until Louie locked the First Aid room behind him and headed to the front gate. He watched from the roof as Louie locked the gate and drove his Cadillac up the hill to the main drag. Tom left through the hole cut in the fence at the back of the park and cut through the woods to the all-night diner on the main drag where he'd left his car. He broke out in a sweat driving home, but from nerves, not from the hot summer night.

Tom had hesitated for days, but bursting with excitement, he finally told Bugsy about what he'd seen. Since Bugsy had gotten him a raise, he felt indebted. At first they'd talked about stealing the cash and splitting it. Talk was all it was, especially when Bugsy gave him some practical advice.

"Forget about it, Tom. Sure, you could skip college and we could escape to the Bahamas with that much dough. We could live like beach bums for life . . . fishing all day and screwing all night. But Louie's connected—ya think he got to be a million-aire with a home in the ritzy Heights part of town by delivering ice in Jersey City when he was young and managing this park three months a year? No way. We touch that cash and we're dead. He's probably laundering it for the mob.

"What mob?"

"Like Gambino, bambino."

He'd convinced Tom that it was a dumb idea. Tom hadn't thought about that cash again for decades—not until he'd seen this morning paper with Louie's obituary and the article about Pleasure Land Park being taken over by the state. They were going to bulldoze the overgrown park tomorrow and excavate the flood zone to make a reservoir to protect future flood vic-tims downriver.

It was happening faster than Tom's mind could keep up with, but he knew he had to make an effort to retrieve that cash if it was still there after so many years. Louie had died yesterday from a stroke that had turned him into a vegetable living off tubes for decades.

The mob may have tried to keep him alive with the hope that if he ever regained consciousness, he could tell them where the cash was hidden. A hundred grand wasn't worth as much as it had been all those years ago, but it could still help Sally pay for Kim's college education. He had to give it his best shot, though the clarity of his thinking seemed to go in and out like a lighthouse beacon glowing then fading.

Louie and his wife Kay had no kids and she'd died soon after Louie had had the stroke.

Tom wondered if the cash was meant to be Louie's escape stash, or something he'd done as a favor to his Don, working numbers, prostitution, or even making a hit. Taking the rumors about Louie's connections seriously, neither Tom nor Bugsy had ever mentioned the stash again, not even in jest or after drinking a six-pack. But if Tom's hunch was right, who knew?

Maybe the cash was still there ready to be snatch today before the bulldozers leveled the park tomorrow.

***

On tippy toes, Kim stretched her neck to see over the vines entwined around the pavilion. "I don't see a First Aid room," she said.

"You can't see it through all the overgrowth. There are huge trees growing through the concrete bottom of the pool, even at the deep end with a ten-foot high diving board. I could do a one-and-ahalf off that board when I was in college."

A memory flashed in his mind—*two steps—spring—spread-eagle with toes pointed and feet together, back arched—then tuck until you see the water—open—and stick it with no splash. But now I can't even touch my toes, and my right leg from hip to ankle still aches from—*

"Did I tell you about the time I fell from the high dive with a complete flip and landed on my right heel on the concrete deck?"

"Many times," she said with a sigh of impatience.

"I did? Oh . . . but this is where it happened, and the injury had kept me out of Vietnam. That's why I have an artificial hip and knee now. These days I could sue the owners and retire to

Hawaii. No one sued anybody back then—nobody I ever knew. You got a bad break, you just took it on the chin."

"Look!" she shouted. "The diving platform is still there, but there's no diving board."

"That's so nobody will try to go up there and fall into the deep end with no water in the pool. See, they removed the ladder, too. That's a twenty-foot drop at the deep end."

"Why didn't someone fix up this place so people could swim here again?"

"It's always been a flood zone along this river. Every few years, no matter what they've tried to do about it, the river reclaims the lowland. Glaciers carved out these valleys and mountains after the Ice Age when this entire valley had been underwater. The floods have been nature's way of reminding us."

"The pool is messy and scary. Can't they build something else here instead?"

"Army Engineers have been working for decades to control Pompton Falls two miles south from here, but it's been unsolvable for the seventy years that I've lived here. They're going to tear everything down here and excavate to make a run-off reservoir. They'll start tomorrow morning. No one's sure if that will protect the homes downriver when the next flood comes, but they have to try."

She frowned. "You must feel sad about that, Grandpa."

"I guess. When I look at this pool, I can still see the crystal blue water and hear the sounds of kids splashing and playing. I can imagine their bare feet running on the wet pool deck and I'm blowing my whistle to tell them to walk, so they won't slip and fall. I had to patch up many skinned elbows and knees in the First Aid room."

Kim looked across the empty pools cracked and littered with trash. As hard as she tried, he knew she couldn't see what remained in his memories. They were only his now, nothing he could share. He'd also failed with Sally in that regard.

"It was fun in those days," he said. "I'd often close my eyes to go to sleep at night after a day of lifeguarding a big crowd. On the back of my eyelids I'd still see the pool overflowing with swimmers. On a crowded day I hardly had time to blink."

"Is *that* the First Aid room?" She pointed to a white stucco building at the deep end where weathered paint almost obliterated the words in red on the white door—FIRST AID.

"Yes, see where the letters used to be." He hesitated with a start hearing a familiar sound. The flagpole at the far end of the pool remained. On windy days the metal clasps on the ropes used to hoist the American flag every morning would chime against the tall metal pole.

It wasn't his imagination. When the breeze gusted, the metal clasps were still there chiming sharply against the pole as if to welcome him back. The speakers at the corners of the pool's fence around the pool also remained. He imagined bikini-clad teenage girls dancing in the pavilion to *Sam the Sham's* hit, "Wooly Bully."

He and Kim worked their way behind the high-dive platform at the deep end of the pool for a closer look at the First Aid room. The turquoise door was peeling. When he tried the doorknob, it wouldn't turn.

"How can we get in if it's locked, Grandpa?"

He reached into his suit jacket and took out a rusty key attached to a neck lanyard along with a rusted whistle.

"Never go on a treasure hunt unprepared," He said with a wink. But the rusted key wouldn't fit into the keyhole.

"The cops changed the lock to keep kids from coming here to drink beer and take drugs," he said nodding to the graffiti on the exterior stucco.

"What will we do now?"

He grinned and pushed his shoulder against the door. The doors hinges were screwed into rotten wood, so the door came off its hinges and crashed into the First Aid room. They heard vermin scattering into the shadows of the room.

"It's pretty spooky, Grandpa."

"If you're scared, stay right here, but the treasure could be in there."

She grimace, but followed him in anyway. Through the must and mold, he thought he could still smell chlorine. He saw a few ten-gallon canisters in the corner. When he tried to lift one the metal handle snapped off. Its contents had solidified and could be explosive.

Kim held onto the back of his belt as she followed him into the dim backroom.

He thought he could still sense the scent of suntan lotion and images of teenage girls he'd been skinny-dipping with over fifty years ago. That felt tangible in his mind, more focused than anything he'd seen or touched today, last week, or last year.

Kim's voice broke the spell with the reality of mouse droppings covering the rotted wooden floor. "It stinks in here."

"If it bothers you, hold your nose," he said.

From his jacket, he took a small hammer he'd borrowed from Sally's toolbox in the garage. From memory, he counted the floorboards from the back window. Satisfied, he pried up one of the floorboards with the back of the hammer.

"Is the treasure in there?" she asked with wide-eyed anticipation.

"Your treasure—but you need to keep it in your backpack till you get home. It's a secret for your mom to keep until you're older and ready to go to college."

He pulled out a leather sack and loosened its drawstrings to look inside. He closed it so Kim wouldn't see its contents then made her turn around so he could put the sack in her backpack and zip it closed.

"It's almost dark, so we have to get out of the park when we can still see without using my flashlight. Otherwise, someone might see us from the road,"

"The police?"

"Yes, or anyone else who wants the treasure for themselves."

A glow of excitement came to Kim's rosy cheeks. "Like Peter Pan keeping a treasure from Captain Hook?"

"Yes, something like that. Let's go. Hold my hand tight. I'll lead the way back to the hole in the fence and back to the car. Remember, don't say anything to anyone about your treasure until you're home alone with your mom. It's a *secret* treasure."

"Can I tell Mom you found it for me?"

"Yes, but only your mom. No one else, not ever."

"I'm a little scared," she said.

He held out his arms and hugged her tightly. "Don't be afraid. I'm counting on you."

She grinned and kissed his cheek, rough with stubble since that morning's shave.

Getting out of the park was harder than getting in, because the hole in the fence had been bent inward, now with the barbs against them. The sun was vanishing behind the mountain crest across the river. He stumbled against the concrete base of a picnic table where an oak tree, just an acorn fifty years ago, had grown through the wooden planks of the tabletop, lifting it so high from the ground that he hit his forehead against it.

The bramble outside the fence worked against their exit, but he held branches aside taking any injury himself so the thorns wouldn't harm Kim. When they turned the final corner of the fence, they saw Sally's Saturn forty yards away. It was dark enough for the streetlight above the car to come on. The rough ground between them and the car became a dark abyss. Fearing Kim might stumble and fall with her heavy backpack, he turned on his flashlight.

Several yards from the car, he turned off the flashlight. Just when he felt confident hey were home free, blinding headlights flashed from the shadows behind the streetlight. Red lights began to flash from the roof of a local police patrol car.

A gruff voice from the patrol car's speaker said, "Stop! Stay where you are and don't move. Put your hands on your head and stay clear of that car. You can put your hands down, little girl, but don't move."

The cop got out of the car. With his hand on the butt of his holstered gun, he walked toward them.

"Both hands against the car and spread your legs," he told Tom.

The cop tossed the hammer and flashlight onto the ground. Tom had left the lanyard with the whistle and useless key in the first aid room. He turned to Kim. "Is your name, Kimberly Watson?" he asked.

She nodded, too scared to speak.

"Your mother's been worried about you," the cop said. "She's on her way to pick you up."

"I'm OK," she said. "My grandpa picked me up at school today so we could go on a— " *Treasure hunt* had almost rolled off her lips, but she caught her grandpa's glare and stopped.

"Your mother's concerned about your grandfather, too, because he's not permitted to drive anymore and took her car without her permission. He might have had an accident that could have hurt you both." He turned to Tom. "What were you thinking? The park's condemned and dangerous, even in daylight. Your daughter will be here any minute. Just stay calm and we'll take you both home."

Another car, marked POLICE CHIEF, pulled up, then Sally came out of the car from the passenger side and burst into tears. She embraced Kim.

"I was so worried about you," she said. "I know Grandpa meant no harm, but he isn't well." With tears streaming down her face, Sally turned to him. Holding Kim's hand, she approached her father and brushed the back of her hand against his rough cheek. "We have to talk about Holiday Acres, Dad. I'm sorry, but I just can't deal with this anymore."

"It's OK, Sally," he said with a sigh. "Everything is fine now." He winked at Kim, and she winked back without Sally seeing.

The younger police officer took Tom in his patrol car. Kim waved to her grandfather and he waved back.

"We just have to take your father to the station to fill out some paperwork," the Police Chief said. "I suggest you leave your car here and let me drive you home tonight. You've had enough stress for today. Pick up your car in the morning. If you don't have a friend to drive you, I'll send a patrol car over in the morning to pick you up. We'll bring your father home within the hour."

She agreed and sat in the front seat with Kim in back.

The Police Chief made idle chatter to calm Sally's nerves, "We're just protecting public property. They're going to wreck everything in the park tomorrow morning. May have to do some blasting to break up the concrete of that old pool. I hate to think of your father and your daughter stuck somewhere in the park, maybe injured or unconscious. The demolition team would assume the park was empty. They might have been killed by accident."

Kim caught the Police Chief's eyes staring at her from the rearview mirror.

"I know some folks in town who've sent their parents to Holiday Acres," he said. "Your father would be a lot better off there.

It could be good for you and your daughter, too. You're in that sandwich generation—caretaker for young kids and old parents."

"I've probably waited too long," Sally said. "Dad started becoming delusional, unable to distinguish between past and present. He often called my daughter by my name, as if she were me still eight years old. The early signs had been there, but losing my mom didn't help. The only good part has been his forgetting how much we'd argued in the past."

"Grandpa would never hurt me, Mom," Kim said from the backseat. "I want him to stay with us. He needs us, and we need him."

The Chief's eyes beamed on Kim from the mirror. "I'll bet your grandpa took you on an exciting adventure today, but you're both lucky you didn't get hurt in that dilapidated First Aid room. I hope he didn't take you over there, That old building is ready to collapse on its own."

Kim remained silent.

"Maybe your grandpa wanted to show you the pool and the First Aid room," he said with an inquiring tone. "We had to lock it up to keep kids from shooting up in there. They liked to take souvenirs from the park after it was announced it would be demolished . . . Did you take any souvenirs?"

Kim didn't answer.

"If you did, you'll have to turn everything over to me so I can give it to the state authorities. You're just a kid, but you wouldn't want your grandpa to get in trouble."

"We didn't take anything from that rotten old park," Kim said. "Grandpa just wanted to show me the diving board he'd fallen from when he was a young lifeguard."

Sally sensed Kim's tone of fear.

"Leave her alone!" she snapped. "We've both had a rough day. Please, just take us home."

"Sorry. Just doing my duty." He waved his right hand to Kim with a friendly gesture.

Kim's eyes glared at the deep scar on the back of the Chief's right hand. She squirmed as if her backpack was on fire against her back. She held a locked grin trying to contain herself until they were safely home. Even if the sack in her backpack were empty, her grandpa had unearthed enough treasures that day that would last in her memory for a lifetime.

Treadmill

It was Tuesday morning after Thanksgiving. Heavy traffic crept through the Holland Tunnel at a snail's pace. Chuck Spingler realized he'd be late for the CEO's conference meeting. He'd forgotten the Rockefeller Plaza Christmas tree lighting ceremony would be televised that evening. Christmas shoppers would be heading into Manhattan for the full-Monty of commercial holiday exposure.

In the middle of the tunnel a delivery truck hit the car in front of it. In a chain reaction, Chuck jammed on his BMW's brakes. Though he avoided rear-ending the car ahead of him, his Starbuck's mocha grande splashed across his crisp white shirt and bright orange power necktie. He kept a box of fresh dress shirts in his trunk, and an assortment of silk ties in the backseat, never knowing when a crisis at the bank might necessitate an overnight stay in Manhattan.

Arriving a half-hour late, Chuck got a glare from the CEO's secretary, Connie, as he emerged from the men's room with a fresh shirt and tie.

"Has he started yet?" he asked, Connie.

Her response was a dismissive huff as a warning that Chuck's tardiness could cost him dearly.

She would know, because the CEO had cancelled her year-end bonus for not arriving at the office last Friday until 10:00 a.m. Her husband had been in a near fatal collision on the FDR Drive. For Connie's tardiness, CEO Woodburn had cancelled her five-grand bonus and sent a two-hundred-dollar bouquet of roses to her husband's hospital beside instead. For Connie, that floral fragrance lingered to remind her against future tardiness. That bitter-sweet scent was counterpointed by the cadence of her husband's IV drip in the ICU.

When Chuck opened the Conference Room door, seven VPs didn't acknowledge his tardy entry, but sat frozen like trained bird dogs waiting for their master's signal to retrieve the kill.

CEO Woodburn gave him an icy stare then nodded for Chuck to take the only empty seat at the long mahogany table. Its sheened surface reflected Woodburn's and the VPs images where Chuck imagined that a Bizarro Financial World existed. On the worst of days, Chuck wondered if he would prefer that adverse universe, that those reflections in the table might be a world of empathy and equity to which he could escape.

The only empty seat directly to Woodburn's left, was often referred to as "the ejector seat," and with good reason.

"The vote has been cast," Woodburn said without turning toward Chuck. Closing the folder in front of him, he added, "Unanimously, in favor of *Treadmill.*"

Chuck raised his hand for acknowledgement.

Woodburn huffed, giving Chuck a perturbed nod with permission to speak, Chuck asked, "So we're *not* taking the bail-out?"

Woodburn frowned. "Of course we're taking it."

Chuck said, "But I pointed out last week, sir, that we won't need the bail-out if we adopt my proposed plan, *Treadmill.*"

"We've just adopted Treadmill," Woodburn said with a sneer like a feral cat about to disembowel a helpless rabbit.

Thinking aloud, Chuck blurted: "Then why would we take the bail-out?"

Woodburn grinned.

"Oh, I get it," Chuck reasoned. "We'll get the jump on our competition and expand our Human Resources here and abroad with the government's money, then we can balance our books at the same time we're expanding our global operations."

Chuck's voice faded as the other seven VPs rose from their seats. With respectful nods to Woodburn, they departed, leaving Chuck in the ejector-seat.

Woodburn cleared his throat and leaned back in his high-back leather chair at the head of the table, then turned to Chuck and said, "Treadmill was brilliant . . . but what else can you offer that could justify your missing this morning's executive vote?"

"I got stuck in the Holland Tunnel and—"

"You mean your mother didn't *die, Spingler . . .* or one of your *kids*?"

"I'm not married—no kids. I just—"

"You just have no excuse. If a meeting is set for nine o'clock, then sleep over in the city if you have to, but be here on time. Only Treadmill has saved your butt, but what have you done for me lately? You came up with that plan six months ago when our home loans tumbled into an abyss of bad debt. We hadn't activated Treadmill yet, because we were waiting to see if we, too, would fit the bill: *too big fail.* We have, so now we'll have a billion dollars to play with. We're going to activate Treadmill the moment the government puts that money into our reserves."

Chuck said, "Wouldn't it be better for our public image to use Treadmill, then stand tall *without* taking the federal bail-out? We won't need it—that was Treadmill's intent."

"Treadmill's conception was yours, Spingler, and you'll be immediately gratified with a six-figure bonus—but Treadmill's *intent* is my call."

"I get it," Chuck said. "We'll use that billion to hire more people to staff our global operations and stay ahead of the competition— we'll lead the way for others to follow our example. We'll be hailed for boosting the lagging economy and putting the Great Recession behind us."

"There will be *no hiring* in the foreseeable future," Woodburn said. "On the contrary, we'll be closing five hundred domestic branches and half of our overseas operations, reducing our entire labor force by twenty thousand. We'll pay back the feds' billion dollars, but after we've doubled it in the Chinese market as they buy off our bad debt."

"But then you won't need Treadmill. It was just a failsafe plan to keep the bank from going belly-up. The depositors will be outraged if we raise their banking fees and deposit limits."

Woodburn grumbled, "De-pos-i-tors? I don't ever want to hear *the D-word* in my presence. Go soft on me, Spingler, and you won't make the next cut. I'm downsizing our executive staff from nine to seven. Don't become one of the two VPs I'll fire before Christmas."

"Isn't that cruel, sir, firing someone just before Christmas?"

Woodburn shrugged. "Crueler yet to let an employee charge his expected bonus on gifts he can't afford on Unemployment."

Chuck let that logic sink in, knowing the bills for those gifts wouldn't come in January. His plan would generate the late fees from the frozen credit piling up for thirty days. Treadmill was designed to save the bank from default, but the executive staff had voted to release his plan with a shot of speed and greed.

Woodburn said, "VPs are only two employees among the two hundred thousand we'll fire, but we'll make sure our executive staff's reduction gets *the most* publicity, just to quiet the outcry against us for taking tax-payers' money to invest. As if *they'd* ever know what to do with that much money."

Woodburn rose from his chair as a move of dismissal, but added, "We won't have to wait until January to begin your clever idea within Treadmill. You called it: 'Return to Sender.' With the holidays slowing down the mail, it will be less obvious, but the late fees for non-payments in January will make us another billion dollars just by failing to mail those credit card bills this month —we'll even save on postage. The fine print on the back of their bills will cover our butt with the few who'll lawyer up for any class-action suits. Whatever little crap slips through the grating can be easily paid for from our profits."

Woodburn led Chuck to the door then watched the doors close on his youngest, up-and-coming Vice President.

Chuck descended to the next floor where he envisioned his new corner office with a view of Battery Park—another perk in the offing for his conceiving Treadmill.

Woodburn turned with a nod to his secretary, "Send a dozen roses to Spingler's mother."

Connie's back stiffened at the mention of roses, thinking of those Woodburn had sent to her husband. But she'd still cling to Woodburn's whipping post just for her health insurance to cover her husband's mounting medical expenses.

She'd take whatever crap Woodburn would throw at her, but at least her skills had preserved her job into her fifties, despite her faded good looks since she'd been hired thirty years ago as Woodburn's convenient *grab 'n' go*.

Connie shook herself from that memory with disgust, but asked, "What's the occasion?" Thinking: *God, Spingler—what did you say in that meeting to piss off Woodburn?*

"No occasion. Make it *anonymous*," Woodburn said.

"Anonymous?" she blurted, realizing she'd posed a question—an unacceptable punctuation when addressing Woodburn.

The last time she'd posed a question was back in the '80s, asking: "You and me . . . *and* Ingrid?"

At least Connie wasn't married then, and neither was he, so the price she'd paid was a threesome in the Hamptons with Woodburn's most recently hired MBA of choice—Ingrid, a Valkyrie who'd ravished *her* more than Woodburn had. He was glad just to watch.

Connie realized Woodburn was still staring at her. She blinked and repeated with doublejeopardy defiance, "Anonymous . . . why is *that*, sir?"

Woodburn grinned. "Just a reminder to Mrs. Spingler's son, not to be late again—not unless *she croaks*."

For a moment, Connie imagined she saw a Valkyrie flying past the office windows. She wished she had wings, too. After thirty years of service, she still hadn't evolved that far and remained a lowly creature of the mire.

She wondered if there was still hope for Chuck Spingler with his defiance of authority.

Maybe . . . hmm—maybe not. There was always too much money at hand to ever say "no."

Unconscious

Commuter traffic is reporting on my car radio—accident Lincoln Tunnel helix backing up to the Meadowlands. Burning smell, my rattletrap's heat begins emitting. I unravel the green-plaid scarf from around my neck, a St. Paddy's Day remnant from two weeks ago. I open my trench coat as the windshield defrosts. A transparent porthole expands melting the ice for a clear view of our home's front bay window.

From the driveway, I see drapes at the bay window rustling, now spreading apart. Josie waves to me. She stares, holding her teddy bear under one arm. She pouts, having to endure her long day till my evening return. I try to imagine her dawn-to-dusk vigil for my return. I'll be late anyway—still enough time to kiss Josie goodbye.

I get out of the car, leaving the door open and the engine running. I open the front door with my key and pick up Josie in my arms. Holding her close, I smell her baked cookies aroma. Her feet dangle in the snugly, pink pajamas her grandma gave her for Easter last weekend. Josie won't wear the matching pink, bunny-eared hood. Impatient, my wife, Tina, had scolded her for such "willfulness." No story time for Josie before bed.

"Mommy's not awake," Josie says as I come back into the house for a good-bye kiss.

Still asleep on the sofa since nine o'clock last night, Tina, had dozed off watching VHS tapes of *General Hospital*. She's always a month behind on her favorite soap. I've put a note in my wallet— *buy a blank tape for next week's episodes.* She's promised to catch up this summer—just as she had last summer, and the summer before that. The *Luke and Laura* melodrama is our mutual connection for vicarious passion, though we're barely thirty.

Unresponsive, Tina snores with her mouth wide open when I tap her shoulder.

She hadn't heard me making a sandwich for lunch a half hour ago before when I'd slipped out to the driveway to warm up my car.

"When will you be home, Daddy?" Josie asks.

"About seven-thirty tonight."

Her expression of disappointment reminds me of Josie's sensitivity . . .

At Back-to-School Night, her first-grade teacher, Mrs. Earhart, told me and Tina that on the first day of school, Josie told her that she was sorry to hear about "*Amelia,*" and hoped they'd find her airplane soon.

"Josie is such a thoughtful child," Mrs. Earhart told us, "such a vivid imagination."

I concurred with a nod and said, "History Channel."

Tina huffed aside, "Stupid is more like it. I'll switch her to another teacher who'll *correct* her, not coddle her . . . *Amelia,* indeed . . ."

"I'll miss you, Daddy,"

Tina, stirs, sitting up with squint. "What time is it? Where are you going, Jeffrey?"

"Seven o'clock . . . going to work. "

With her back to Tina, Josie rolls her eyes at me.

Blank expression, Tina asks, "What's today?"

"Friday." Josie and I harmonize.

"I forgot," Tina says. "Meeting friends for lunch. Did you—?"

"Made a sandwich—in the car—just leaving."

"Get ready for school," Tina warns Josie. "Have a bowl of raisin bran with skim milk then get dressed—pronto!"

Josie frowns. "I want a soft-boiled egg, like Daddy makes, with toast and grape jelly."

"You're too fat." Tina bristles. "At least the bran will make you poop out some of that lard."

"Am I too fat, Daddy?"

"You're beautiful, but do what Mom asks."

"I'm not *asking* her, Jeffrey . . . I'm telling her. I'm the adult. Git!" Tina nods toward the kitchen.

Josie kisses me, then scampers to kitchen.

"Do me a favor." I motion toward the staircase where three wrinkled dress shirts hang from the banister. All were washed last week but never ironed. "If you don't have time to iron them, please drop them off at the cleaners for pressing. I'll need them for work next week. Hangers—no starch."

Tina glares, deep breath, mumbling, "Have a good day," as she heads to the kitchen and I go back out to my car.

Car still running, I get in closing the door, but it's too hot. I turn off the heat, open the vents, and crack the windows. Josie is not at the window. I drive to Park 'n' Ride.

An hour later at the North Bergen lot, a bus pulls in. I hurry, locking car, and run to the commuter queue boarding the bus to Manhattan, my same commute for ten years.

Seven years ago I'd met Tina on this bus route through the Lincoln Tunnel to Port Authority. She was reading a novel written in Italian. Though blond, she had an uncanny facial resemblance to Sophia Loren, my incentive to speak to her— smitten.

"Do you speak English?" I asked, but her eyes seemed to see me as no more than a bug to flick off her shoulder.

With an air of aristocracy, she said, "Yes, among several languages."

In the weeks following we dated—movies, dinners, dry-hump necking, manual and oral orgasms, mutual commutes.

Tina was a high-end boutique model agency receptionist where trade show spokes-persons were listed for hire. She answered the phones:

"Trade Show Productions . . . Productions . . . Tina Garland speaking."

Garland was her stage name—with no stage in sight. She was born Christina *Donkenweusser*. Since we'd met on the bus, I was dunking my *weusse*r daily. Her job was located in an East-side, midtown penthouse a few blocks from my job. She looked gorgeous answering the phones. She hoped an agent might sign her as a solo artist— acoustic guitar, singing soprano. Like *Holly Golightly,* she browses Tiffany's with eccentric, quirky charm. On our dates she purring like a cat, nuzzling—but feral— with scratching and biting. I vowed to tame her, to charm her, to have her forever.

It's an April proposal, blossoming cherry trees, as Dr. King is murdered. We make November wedding plans. We have an artsy commuter lifestyle—Jersey to Manhattan excites us daily. I have months musing from her acoustic serenades.

Writing my first novel, her crystal clear, perfect pitch rings true, striking harmonic chords with my narrative. She's pregnant the summer before our wedding. RFK dead in California, a bridge over troubled waters crumbles into oblivion.

"I've found a doctor who'll take care of it," Tina said.

"You mean the delivery costs will be minimal, since you have no insurance?"

"I'm not wearing my wedding dress with a swollen belly. My father would have a fit, such an embarrassment."

"But we're in love and we'll be married soon. You'll be moving out in November anyway. We'll build our own family. Our child is not an embarrassment, but a blessing."

"He's a Park Avenue gynecologist I found in the book. He's from Italy. I spoke to him in Italian. Don't look at me that way, Jeffrey. I'm doing this—with or without you. I have two thousand dollars saved. Dr. Visconti said that will cover everything. You could drive me home after the procedure . . ."

The word *procedure* echoed in my mind in discord with my muse. I couldn't utter the word "abortion," the procedure that would end the life of our child. I'd come to love Tina deeply, a fusion of heart and soul. Her quirkiness became a part of me something I felt that I could no longer do without. Despite my protest, I conceded to protect her that night, concealing her terminated pregnancy from her parents. Our wedding was moved up to September. We kept her secret from her father. Years later, he had a fatal heart attack and would never know. Tina's mother believed the abortion was my idea, not her angel Tina's, who would never do such a thing.

* * *

At Port Authority, inhaled bus fumes make the back of my neck prickle. Escalated down to Manhattan's bowels on the vomit and piss-stained subway platform, several, catsized rats scamper along the tracks. The train arrives with a squealing halt. Morning commuters from Queens to Manhattan burst through the sliding doors before those waiting can board, banging shoulders to get a seat or find a free hand to grasp a greasy, bacteriainfected pole.

A two-minute ride, but in winter, ice freezes track switches. In sweltering summer Con Ed's power outages trap commuters, nose-to-nose in unlighted cars. Doors slide open—push, bump, shove, curse, scowl. The platform's stench below Grand Central, is worse than a full diaper, a deathly taint on a soulless journey to hell.

Out of Grand Central through the Graybar Building, I cross Lexington to Chock full o' Nuts for a cup of joe and a doughnut.

Spring in the air, hookers are out in force—bare shoulders, cleavage, red stilettos, whispers to white-collar execs: "Ten for a blow . . . twenty for half n half . . . fifty takes you round the world."

Vice-squad roundups push business further uptown. Hookers regroup, sipping java, nodding to johns waiting for their morning a joe and a *ho* to go.

Turning east down 44th Street then crossing Third to 45th Street and up to the 16th floor at 216 East. My bag lunch goes into the refrigerator storing film, and my trench coat gets hung in the communal closet.

Studio manager, Rudy, nods slapping a mounted black-and-white photo on my drawing board.

"Bleached silhouette on the can of Coke with a soft, tight shadow. Kick up the highlights and spot for repro. Need it before eleven," Rudy says to me.

Sports jacket hung over my swivel chair, my airbrush is hissing. By noon studio windows are cranked open. From 30 to 75 degrees in three hours.

"How about a walk through U.N. Plaza along the river," Freddy, a studio oldtimer, asks. "Sandwiches on a park bench. It's like summer out there."

Just sports jackets against the East River breeze, we watch a Circle Line tour boat making a white-capped wake in brown, toxic tide past Roosevelt Island..

"I'm leaving Rio Studios," I tell Freddy. "Business is too slow. Our top salesman, Tony, reads sports pages nine-to-five, no calls to ad agencies. No salaries next week, just free-lancing for us by the hour. My commute is too expensive to sit around all day with no income. I'm going out on my own. I'll work from home."

"Whew! Big risk, Jeff." Fred's head's shaking. "Business could come back soon with no passage back across your burnt bridge with a mortgage, car payment, and a kid to feed."

"Bigger risk to stay. I need more time with Josie at home."

"Tina's OK with you quitting?"

"No time to talk about it, yet." Freddy's raises his brows.

Recalling Tina's snoring reminds me to pick up blank tape at Duane Reed's to record next week's *General Hospital* episodes.

* * *

At three o'clock, the studio bullpen phone rings—Rudy shouts: "For you, Jeff!"

Looking up from a mounted Remy Martin dye transfer on my drawing table: "For me?"

"It's a little kid."

My chest pings . . . *Josie?*

Tearful squeaks: "George was dead in his cage when I came home from school. We have to bury him in the yard? I put him in a shoebox with grass from my Easter basket. We have to bury him before dark. Can you come home early to help me?"

"What happened?" I ask, thinking—*two more hours before I can leave.*

"Mom said George was older than we thought when you bought him at Scuffy's Pet Shop . . . parakeets don't live more than five years." Bawling, "I miss George. Come home, Daddy."

My throat taut . . . then a mocking expression from Rudy with a reminder: "Need that Remy Martin job tonight."

"Sorry, Josie. Can't just leave work whenever I want. Keep George in the shoebox in the garage. We'll bury him together in the morning. On Saturday, we'll have all day together."

"Mom said parakeets don't have souls—that George is gone forever. I don't believe her. I want to make him comfortable and happy, wherever he goes."

"In the morning. I can't leave till five-thirty. It's Friday—won't get home before seven-thirty. Sorry."

"Mom wants to talk to you."

I hear Tina telling Josie to take George out to the garage in the shoe box. "You fill her head with fairy tales," Tina says. "Had all I could do not to rip the damn bird from her filthy hands to flush it down the toilet. Made her scrub her hands three times before dinner. My choir practice is tonight. Get home before eight o'clock. Don't want that stupid Smith girl in our house to watch Josie . . . Are you listening, Jeffrey?"

Waving off Rudy's daggers to get back to work, "I'm listening."

"Don't give her ice cream when you come home; she's too fat."

"I won't."

Thirty pounds gained since Josie's birth, Tina still blames the pregnancy on New Year's Eve champagne. After Tina's meticulous abortion plans, her life's other details have gone down the toilet, just as she'd wished for poor George.

Her birth control pills are often skipped. Lights on, but no one home, her mind is befuddled. Simple math: If her first pregnancy had not been aborted, and went full-term—Josie would never have been born.

My answer to that equation—Josie is our child of grace.

For Tina, Josie is another mistake to discard, not physically, but emotionally.

* * *

Watching the clock from 5:00 to 5:30, I hurry to finish Remy job, ready to bolt.

Rudy says, "Nothing more coming in tonight. Have a nice weekend."

First to the elevator, but a slow decent picking up other passengers from lower floors. I dash across Third Avenue, nearly clipped by a bicycle messenger. My mind races in my descent to the Times Square shuttle below Grand Central. The subway train rocks with ear-piecing squeal on the tracks.

Underground from Times Square to Port Authority, I feel like a gerbil on a treadmill getting nowhere fast. I dodge commuters to pass them on the escalator to the Park 'n' Ride bus. Lincoln Tunnel is jammed with theater goers into Manhattan on a Friday night. A chain of bus links are stuck on Port Authority ramp. Seven o'clock— I reach the North Bergen parking lot.

Running, reaching in my pockets for car keys—pants, shirt, sports jacket—only subway tokens. Hands cupped, peering through the car window for keys maybe left in the ignition, on the seat, fallen unto the floor—nothing.

I think, just hail a parking attendant, jack open the door, you're home free. But no—still fumbling through my pockets, sweat trickling down my face, no luck. Then it hits me—eighty degrees at lunch—trench coat and scarf—keys in trench coat pocket. Damn!

I wonder—can I gather strength, journey back to the studio— repeat those painful steps—then back to my car? Make two soulless commutes in one day—was it possible? How long will it take? On a bustling Friday night in the city—much more than an hour.

Yes—I can do it, I think, puffing, running to catch the bus back into the traffic-jammed Lincoln Tunnel.

How many times have I taken this journey in ten years? Over five thousand, but each was unconscious, my mind elsewhere—on home. My senses are alert now, not just to the downside dangers of night, but the heartbeat of Manhattan, distinct aromas of food of many nationalities and ethnicities. I'm feeling alive. Hot pretzels and vanilla-flavored, roasted peanuts from street venders—a natural high engulfs me.

Twenty minutes across town and to the freight entrance. The night watchman at the elevator knows me, sixteen floors up to the studio, dark and vacant. At the closet under a dim utility light, I fumble for my trench coat on hanger. Keys jangle in its deep pocket.

Wall clock says 7:40 p.m. as I call home on the studio phone.

The Smith girl answers: "I came over at seventy-thirty when your wife left for choir rehearsal."

"Tell Josie I had car trouble. She can stay up till I get home, unless she asks to go to sleep. I'll be home before nine o'clock. Thanks."

"Sorry about George," she says. "Josie said he was old, but when she showed him to me in the box in your garage, his neck was broken. He must've been out of his cage and flew into a window or a mirror."

Not-so-dumb this Smith girl.

I say, "I guess. See you later."

Descending in the freight elevator, I say thanks to the watchman. Night air chills me crossing Third Avenue, recalling Josie's words: "When I came home from school, George was dead *in his cage.*"

Seeing no rats in the subway to Port Authority, I'm oblivious to potential muggers after rush hour, the platforms are nearly barren with sparse passengers on subway cars.

My wrist watch says 8:20 p.m., as I'm starting my car and heading home. At 9 p.m. I'm in our drive-way. A silhouette at the bay window, Josie waves to me, smiling despite the loss of her only pet. I'll have two days to soothe her pain, answering her barrage of questions about death.

Waiting in silence, kneeling in the garden by a flashlight beam—we say farewell to George before closing the shoebox. We bury him in the sunflower garden outside Josie's bedroom window. We stomp soft earth above the shoe box to hold crossed popsicle sticks to mark the grave across the horizontal stick: "GEORGE, R.I.P."

"Did you let George out of his cage, Josie?" I ask.

"I was in school, Daddy. Will George be scared of sunflowers, like me? You know . . . they grow so tall with their big round faces peeking through my bedroom window."

Getting up from the ground and heading into the house, I tell her, "George won't be afraid of anything anymore. He's at peace now. Time for you to sleep. Big day for us tomorrow. I'm taking you on a treasure hunt in the morning, lunch at The Milk Barn— burgers and shakes. Movie in the afternoon, bring home pizza, play Candy Land."

"OK, Daddy. Come tuck me in."

Passing the staircase, my wrinkled shirts still hang from the banister.

A prayer for George before her goodnight kiss. Josie is sleeping before I leave her room. Headlights flash from the driveway through the bay window. Tina is saying goodnight to her choir friends. Their car backs out of the driveway and it's quickly gone.

Tina coming through the front door, "Couldn't wait any longer. Toby picked me up and drove me home. Josie better be asleep."

Nodding, I stare at my shirts on the banister. Tina's eyes follow the path of my stare.

"Would've ironed them, got sidetracked. No time to go to the cleaners. I'll iron them tomorrow . . . or maybe Sunday after church."

I think, I'll need fresh shirts if I give notice on Monday. I need to look my best going directly to ad agencies looking for freelance work to bring home.

"Before you get too comfortable watching your *General Hospital* tape, I have to talk to you about something important."

Snide tone, "Can't be as important as what I've got to tell you."

"What happened to George?" I ask her.

Dismissive, "George? Old, I guess. What's the point of having a bird if it can't talk or sing?"

I'm too stunned to respond.

"Me first, Jeffrey."

"What I have to tell you, Tina, is important, for all of us."

Tina's head cocked like George often had through the bars of his cage, usually nibbling at our fingertips.

Squinting, Tina says, "I'm *pregnant*."

A deep rattle in my chest, air sucked from my lungs, kaleidoscopic images from my commute racing through my mind. I'm joyful, realizing Josie will have a sibling. My response is muffled in our embrace, "That's wonderful."

Turning on the VHS to watch her tape, Tina says, "We'll need a bigger house." I nod with a grunt.

Reclining on the sofa, she asks, "What could you ever tell me that's more important than that?"

Taking my shirts off the banister and hanging them on the doorknob to take to the cleaners in the morning, I say, "Sure. Nothing I have to say is that important." Turning back toward the TV, I raise my voice so she'll hear me over *General Hospital's* theme song. "I'm taking Josie to the movies tomorrow. I was wondering—do you want to go with us?"

No response . . .

She's snoring with her mouth wide open. She's unconscious, and like George, she neither speaks nor sings.

Jersey Gal

Before he woke, Ted was dreaming about he and Sharon driving through the New Jersey Pine Barrens with baked desolation on both sides of the narrow road. He thought about how glad Sharon would be to drive to the beach that day. They'd gone to the Jersey shore together for the first time in the '60s for their Senior Prom. Sixty years later, the beach still remained a draw, even if they were too elderly to take a running dive into the exhilarating surf with a gasp from the chilled Atlantic Ocean. Still, one could dream, and so he had.

After more than five thousand days at the beach, a lifetime of joy, the first frost was predicted to come early, perhaps with mice already scrambling to find warmth within the walls of their retirement bungalow. Finally, after ten weeks of sweltering summer, no air-conditioning was needed this morning. Then the first loud *snap* of a mousetrap woke Ted and Sharon from their dead sleep.

Of all times for summer to end early, Ted thought. Just as the *Farmers' Almanac* had predicted, a short hot summer could be heading for a long, cold winter with lots of snow.

"Rise 'n' shine, darling," he said to Sharon, her eyes still closed with visions, Ted assumed, of their lazy, hazy, crazy days or summer on the Seaside boardwalk with games of chance, stuffed-animal prizes, and crackling fast food on the grills. In their teens, long make-out sessions on the beach had been piqued, like an aphrodisiac, with the essence of Coppertone emitting from their tan shoulders—as if they'd ever needed any more than a loving glance for their mutual turn-on.

Sharon's reverie before getting out of bed was shattered when Ted shouted from down the hall.

"Gotcha, ya dirty little bugger!"

"Not already, Teddy?" she called out.

"Yep! I'll get rid of 'm!" Ted shouted, holding a bloodied mousetrap at the tail end away from the flattened triangular head with its sharp teeth bared and its beady eyes glaring at nothing more than its shattered dreams of tasting peanut butter at sunrise.

As usual, Sharon screamed so shrill that Ted saw their neighbors, some still in their bathrobes, all peering toward their bungalow. They were jabbering back and forth before retreating from the brisk morning air back inside their senior housing.

One neighbor pointed at their house and all nodded in agreement—*It's just Sharon . . . must be the first mouse since last April.*

The neighbors grumbled in discourse over how they'd trap any mice that invaded their bungalows if the frigid Jersey winter predicted was starting even earlier than proclaimed by the *Farmers' Almanac*—a word Sharon could never pronounce getting all tongue-tied before spitting out "*Al-na–mac*" with a blush and embarrassed grimace of defeat.

Ted laughed, teasing Sharon about her mispronunciation going back to when they were fifteen, a time when every day at the Jersey shore, regardless of the weather, felt perfect. Today was just such day despite the early morning chill in the air. As Ted was reminded, hearing his neighbors arguing over which mouse trap worked best. Was it the old-fashion, blood 'n' guts trap like Ted used, the poison pellets, or the glue strips. Others depended on their feline companions to commit *rodentiacide* in their behalves.

Sharon ambled awkwardly from their bedroom to the bathroom, where she shielded her vulnerable nakedness by standing in the tub behind the shower curtain. She stayed locked in the bathroom until Ted had sworn that the departed rodent had been securely sealed within a plastic bag and put out in the trashcan behind the garage until Thursday's pickup. Only then did the bathroom door creak open. She made Ted hold out both empty hands before joining him for breakfast.

She gave him a sharp jab with her boney elbow as she passed him in the hall on her way to the kitchen to cook a Swiss-and-mushroom omelet with scallions, Ted's favorite.

"Wash your hands!" she shouted over her shoulder, still shuddering with images of the fuzzy varmint mixed with the soundtrack from Disney's *Cinderella* in her mind:

"Cinderelly! Cinderelly!"

They had watch the Disney DVD with their great-grand-children, reliving their own joyful childhood with so much fun and fancy free.

Her head bobbed to the tune of "Bibbity-bobbity-boo" as she flipped the omelet in the skillet, her way of blocking the bloodied critter from her mind, though Ted knew she wouldn't rest easy until the trash had been dumped into a sanitation truck on garbage day.

"Where does the garbage go?" she asked, but his offhand shrug and blank stare made her respond, "We should know these things, Teddy."

They often argued about recycling. She scolded him for not thoroughly rinsing a mayonnaise jar or a V-8 bottle before putting them at the curb in their town's recycling receptacle.

"What if everyone did that?" she challenged. "We must be responsible, do our part."

Ted's comeback: "Think of the water wasted with all that rinsing. We can't eat or drink plastic or glass. Conserving water is more important. Some day we may have none."

She stared at him that morning, the same way she always had when they had a conflict of reasoning. Once they'd turned eighty, that rift seemed to cut deeper.

She was always first to make peace, saying with a shrug, "I guess you're right, darling," but with a shadow of doubt across her expression cutting sharply through his smirk of confidence.

Ted proposed to Sharon in the fall season over sixty years ago. He had come home for the weekend from college because his older brother, Bobby, had come back safely from Vietnam. His parents had planned that celebration as a garden party with as much care as a wedding reception. Sharon had whispered in Ted's ear, hinting she wanted their wedding to be outdoors.

"How about on the beach—no shoes?" she'd said hoping he'd agree.

Ted did and knew Sharon still wanted them to be in harmony with nature. That's why they were driving to Island Beach State Park as the day got warmer, approaching 80 degrees.

As teens, even in the dead of winter when the Seaside boardwalk was like a ghost town, and the chill winds slammed the icy surf against the pilings, they'd take their four-mile walk, daring each other to remove a shoe and sock to see how painful the Atlantic's bite would be on their toes. When their throbbing ankles sent shock waves through them, it was their memories of so many summers that kindled their hearts and numbed their pain with their glow of detailed reminiscence.

"Not a cloud in the sky," he said over satellite radio's blare playing "Satisfaction" by *The Stones* on the *Classic Vinyl* station in his 2009 Saturn. The old car had over two hundred thousand miles on it. Its brand was extinct, but he kept it well-tuned. The satellite radio packet had been a gift to himself when he'd turned eighty.

Sharon had stopped remembering birthdays and anniversaries. She'd expressed her glee when their kids and grandchildren showered them with gifts on their 60th wedding anniversary, but her joy was only over the surprise, since Sharon had no idea what the gifts were for and no longer asked.

"Could be one of the ten best days of the year," Ted said over the music with a nod, knowing Sharon would agree.

She did with a subtle grin and a dimpled cheek.

Ted handed a ten dollar bill to the guard at the entrance to Island Beach State Park and wished him good day. He drove past the New Jersey Governor's grey, cedarshake shore retreat on the left then past the scrub pines and beach plum bushes. The old house had weathered Super Storm Sandy, but a few miles north, a quarter-mile of the boardwalk in Seaside Heights still remained barren without its amusement pier, fast food, and games of chance. They were attractions that Ted and Sharon had loved since their teens, but now all were gone.

"Destruction comes quick and easy," he'd told Sharon two years after the disaster when nothing had been rebuilt yet. "But reconstruction comes long and hard."

To that, Sharon concurred. When he spoke slowly with deliberation, she understood and nodded. Both of their minds were now challenged daily with memories from long ago seen so much sharper than anything recent.

There were more people on the beach surf-fishing than swimming that day.

The early chill had warned them off, but the greenish ocean, clear and sparkling, was enticing. Ted found a quiet spot by the dunes to block the brisk sea breeze. He set up two sand chairs, one with two beach towels to keep Sharon's frail body warm, but none for himself. She wore the pink sweatshirt the grandchildren had given her for her eighty-fifth birthday last month. In purple, it said across her pink sweatshirt:

JERSEY GALS DON'T PUMP GAS.

They sat quietly for hours watching the fishermen, north and south, a quarter mile away. A school of dolphin cut through the surf a hundred yards out from high-tide's peak. They were chasing bluefish that were churning whitecaps as they ate smaller fish then, in turn, the dolphins devoured the blues.

"Let's take a closer look," Ted said, lifting Sharon in his arms and carrying her to the water's edge. He recalled how he'd carry her in his arms as a teenager only to toss her into the surf. Though he had less than half the muscle tone of a teenager now, she was half her former weight. Despite a twinge in Ted's lower back, he was determined to make it through the soft sand to the wet sand before ending his trek at the water's edge.

He set Sharon down with care then clutched her close to him for support. She pointed to the eating frenzy, which had come closer to the beach. He hoped she would say something to him, anything. There had been too many long stretches of silence between them lately. The last time she'd spoken at any length was to their five greatgrandchildren when they had helped her blow out the candles on her birthday cake.

"Thank you, my darlings," she'd whispered with a wink to Ted.

Ted pointed to the surf inching closer to their shoes. From the sparkle he saw in her blue eyes, she seemed to understand, but her lips remained sealed and her countenance like stone. He eased her onto the dry sand and removed her shoes and socks. He did the same with his own. Ted helped her up again and leaned her against his hip. The seafoam gently lathered their feet. He thought he detected a grin at the corners of her lips, cracked and dry. He kissed her cheek and held her firmly as if he were holding up the world. She had always been his world.

He carried her back and they remained sitting in their beach chairs until the sun began to set with an evening chill. Mesmerized by the lapping surf and the brilliant sunset they turned to each other with knowing looks. They each saw themselves as they clung together, but with the perspective from the vast ocean, as if they were watching themselves on the beach, like actors in a romantic film from their youth.

"This is where we go home for the last time," Ted heard his conscience say. Apart from himself, like an out-of-body sensation, Ted wasn't surprised when Sharon said knowingly, "Yes, Ted. Our long life together will be wonderful."

Ted smiled and nodded, both from where they sat on the beach and where their youthful selves paddled in the surf on an inflated raft, the surf's foam rolling over their tan shoulders, giving them that euphoric sensation of young, painless bodies with the carefree minds of teenagers in love.

They watched from the ocean and pointed as Ted carried Sharon to their car. Then Ted came back to get the two sand chairs. They drove outside the park's gate and parked along the bay on the west side of the narrow land strip in Seaside Park. They watched the sunset cast a crimson glow that lit up Sharon's face. Ted thought she looked like a pharaoh's queen with exotic, ancient beauty. The two teenagers agreed feeling weightless, like two soap bubbles from a blow pipe as their youthful spirits drifted above the old couple.

"She was his first and only love," the teenage girl said to the boy.

"And he was hers," he agreed.

"How magical," they said in harmony.

"How eternal love is compared to war," he said.

As the sky turned mauve, Ted patted Sharon's boney hand, and said, "It's time to go home."

He thought he had heard her mutter something, but it was just gurgling from her empty stomach.

He drove slowly back to their village in utter darkness with no streetlights after the Garden State Parkway through the Pine Barrens, where a wrong turn could put them in a labyrinth of confusion. Maybe no one would find them for weeks, out of gas and starved to death, a frightening journey, but the two teens grinned knowing they'd be safe and soon would be home.

Ted pulled the Saturn into their garage and carried Sharon into the house. He set her gently on the sofa then turned on the TV so she could watch *Jeopardy*. She used to know all the answers, but now she just stared glassy-eyed at the screen. He brought out two cups of mint tea, the leaves fresh from their garden, and set them on a folding tray in front of her. He held a cup to her lips and she sipped, but continued to stare at the TV. He took a few sips from his cup, but saw that she didn't want any more to drink, her eyes half-closed.

He turned up the volume on the TV then carried her to their bedroom and eased her onto the same queen-size bed they had slept in for the past twenty-years. The bedroom set they'd received as a wedding gift from Sharon's parents hadn't made the move from the larger house where they'd raised their children. She'd cried, realizing their king-size bed and the huge dressers wouldn't fit into to their down-sized bungalow after retirement.

"Can you hear the TV?" he asked over the volume blasting down the hallway from the living room to their bedroom.

She used to shout, "Louder!" He assumed she had, his memory on auto pilot, so he turned it up a notch.

He fluffed her pillow and rested her head back onto it then tucked in her side of the bed. The memory of their youthful lovemaking still lingered in his mind like the shadow of bird in flight. He slid into bed beside her and kissed her cool, wrinkled cheek.

"It was a perfect day at the beach," he said, staring at the ceiling with his hands folded behind his head on a pillow. He waited a minute in silence hoping—praying— for any reply from Sharon. Their outing must have exhausted her. The only sound he could decipher under the blare of Alex Trebek's voice was a rattling in Sharon's chest.

Ted felt restless, his face still warm from exposure to the sun and sea breezes all day. His lips tasted salty. He reached over and took Sharon's hand firmly in his, then lifted it to his lips and kissed it. Her diamond ring and wedding band felt cold against his flushed cheek.

He was certain he had heard her whisper, "Thank you, darling, for a perfect day at the beach." But before he could sit up and look her in the eye with wonder and joy, a loud *snap* echoed down the hallway from the kitchen.

Sharon didn't shriek, but the rattling in her chest had stopped. He nestled close to her with her head beneath his chin. Set at 55 degrees, he heard the thermostat click on. The baseboards clunked with heat for the first time since mid-April.

The mice must have known it was coming, he thought.

"It's going to be an early winter," he said, hoping for a response from Sharon.

Ted heard Sharon reply in two voices, one from his memory when she was sixteen, asking "Did you read that in the *Farmer's Al-na-mac.*" The other voice asked the same question but in harmony from who he now knew for certain, was his first and only love.

The teenage Sharon kissed young Ted as they'd kicked and paddled on the raft in the surf then she said, "Promise me, Teddy, that's exactly how our life will be."

Seeing the old couple clearly in his young mind, he nodded with a grin, confident that's exactly how it would be. For their generation's battles in Vietnam and for their children's and grandchildren's wars in Iraq and Afghanistan, the scars would fade with time, but love of family would always reignite, even from the embers of deadly wars.

The Last Gulag

The Soaring Sixties had begun with a bright outlook for American youth.

The new president, John F. Kennedy, promised a hopeful future for the United States. On the contrary, while JFK promised the moon, Soviet youth saw their future as colorless, like an old black-and-white movie from the Thirties. Russian leaders lined up like hogs at the trough every first of May, peering down at the crowd of loyal comrades from the Kremlin's balcony above a military parade to demonstrate Soviet power.

At thirteen, I envied those in high positions, like Khrushchev and Malenkov, because they had great power, enough to put my father in a gulag for twenty years for printing flyers opposed to Stalin during World War II. Papa wrote to me once a month, but his script had been redacted to the point of sounding like drivel. I imagined my letters of encouragement to Papa had been reduced to much the same. The KGB could put my father into a gulag, but had no power to get him out. That knowledge sparked an idea in my head that I concentrated on for the next three years of my adolescence.

At sixteen, I was chosen for a special youth program that opened new doors for me with the chance to join an elite group of teenage boys and girls who were trained in unique, long-term espionage tactics. Spying on America meant little to me at the time, despite my daily indoctrination to worship the Communist State of Mother Russia emboldened by her Soviet minions throughout Europe and her Communist allies in China, North Korea, Cuba, and North Vietnam. My underlying goal was merely to free my father from the last gulag, but without my dedication to this elite comradery of spies, I saw no other hope to save him.

Though I never mentioned my father to my KGB trainer, it was his business to know every detail about his trainees' lives from when we farted to when we masturbated. Of course Ivan knew my father was in a work camp, a fancy name for prison that suited the Soviet image of service to The State. So I used a tip from one of my espionage lessons to bait Ivan into a personal conversation, a way to earn his trust and put him off guard. I let him catch me writing poetry. I was the spider. Ivan was the fly.

Ivan snatched the poem from my grasp and made me stand at attention beside my bunk as an example to the others should they ever do the same.

"Are you writing to your papa again, Otto?" Ivan asked. "That's a pointless effort on both your parts. You'll never see him again."

"If that's what serves The State, sir, I agree," I said, perhaps too cocky for my own good.

"It's not for you to agree or disagree. Only to obey!" Ivan snapped.

Ivan had tried to come on to trainee, Olga, a blue-eyed blonde with pendulous breasts. As the best skilled trainee in our class, she was having none of that.

Ivan needed to jerk off and move on before he had a heart attack from his lust for Olga. I kept my feelings for Olga in abeyance.

My nonchalance about Olga had gotten me a quickie one night on a trainee stakeout, but my greater lust was for my father's freedom, even if life in Moscow outside the gulag wasn't really freedom, not in the American sense.

I had to know the enemy, which first was America and next was China, a difficult concept for Western logic with their cowboy mentality. Americans assume that China is our ally because we are both vast Communist nations. America hadn't realized yet that China, by its population alone, would eventually take over the world, East and West. All the Caucasian world can do, is stall against the inevitable.

Our ultimate plan was to overpower America first, but then make them our ally against China. That's what we teenagers were being trained for, to become moles in The United States and fully accepted as red-blooded Americans by the Nineties, when we were middle-aged and trusted as upper-middle-class capitalist. Our only hope against the Yellow Peril would be to rule America from within without ever firing a shot. Only then could Western culture survive against China with the key to success being Russia's cold determination and America's wealth to finance our mutual destiny.

The fluke of electing a movie actor for president in America created a great opportunity. Many of my fellow cohorts, including Olga, had been strategically placed in East Germany since 1961, where we watched the great wall rise between East and West Germany. But by the Eighties, others of our cohort were close enough to whisper subliminal ideas into President Reagan's ear—"Mr. Gorbachev, tear down that wall."

That was our moment thirty years ago, when the Berlin Wall collapsed and many of us flowed into The United States as East German refugees to become implanted in American Society. Well trained, we Russians passed as Germans filtered through the immigration system in America and were welcomed with open arms.

By the end of the Millennium we were well-placed to do the bidding of our former KGB hero, Vlad, who'd cried crocodile tears over the Soviet Union's collapse as symbolized by the fall of the Berlin Wall. Putin would be the executor of our final plan to control The United States at its highest level—the White House.

What was believed to be the collapse of the Soviet Union, was merely a feint—one step back, before two steps forward. Thinking they were freeing Europe of Soviet strongholds, the Americans let the worst of our worst infiltrate their entire economic and political system, and made America our potential political puppet. That's how Security Prefect Beria had first explained Russia's plan to us as teenagers.

Now, thanks to Beria's reforms, with my papa free to live out his old age in peace, I had to fulfill my mission to prepare our target for what would come after America elected their first Black president for a second term in 2012. Obama was too Liberal, but still hawkish against Russia, especially with Secretary of State Clinton as his strong arm against us. We'd have to make them appear foolish to the American public. That would require a flag bearer, our influential American target.

We all laughed at a secret cell meeting in Louisville, Kentucky when we watched President Putin asked on BBC, "Do you ever have a bad day?"

In response, our hero, Vlad, asked the reporter, "Do I look like a *woman*?" He had used a more vulgar term equivalent to the American C-word for Secretary Clinton, but his interpreter, stammered a moment before changing the translation to "woman."

We liked how Putin's eyelids seemed to roll back like a crocodile's before it snaps. We've been so happy since Yeltsin died—couldn't hold his vodka, such a disgrace. But Putin, bare-chested and riding a stallion is what we stood for as our plan neared fruition.

My key talent was always subtlety, to get our target alone so we could speak man-to-man, a Russian and an American the same age, with similar thirsts and billions of dollars, he a real estate mogul, and me an oil and mineral oligarch. My mission was to make the American see things our way, to make our plan his, not just personally, but in a way that would make him feel like an American hero. Better than using force, flattery can bring a conceited man more easily into the fold.

* * *

It was a cold November night, and I could see the venue with its domed roof a quarter-kilometer ahead. The building's sign usually said "Крокус-Сити-холл" on the roof's logo, but for this event it read: "Crocus City Hall" for the thousands of international guests. The owner of the pageant was our codename *Agent Orange*.

His propaganda would poison American morale internally by tearing down the fiber of their belief in American institutions and the Rule of Law, road blocks in our journey to victory.

My target didn't drink, so I appealed to his greatest vice, lust for beautiful women. It wasn't enough just to have them, he needed to own them, so he could control them. Another vice, one I didn't share, was his love for fast food, so his penthouse suite at the Five Star Radisson Blu Olympiyskiy Hotel was stacked with Big Macs, buckets of KFC, and pizza.

He had a high class image, but with unsophisticated eating habits. It's a wonder his flashy ties never got stained, but if they had, he probably had them shredded to destroy the evidence. I heard tell that he ate pizza with a knife and fork. I felt that our highest risk was that he'd have a heart attack before he ever became president. Lenin forbid, that he should choke on a French fry before ever taking the oath of office.

When I entered his suite, he was alone with just his longtime bodyguard. I approached to shake his hand, but his bodyguard frisked me first. I envisioned him with several bodyguards within the next few years, Secret Service, but of course, they'd be our own people to protect our asset, though none would guess.

We've all been here ingrained in American society for decades, we new Americans replacing even the Italian Mafia with our own, as well as Congress year by year. We're like Trojans concealed within a gift horse, and with no one having the good sense to look that horse in the mouth.

Our greatest enemies are Liberal Democrats because they propose a similar message to the Communist ideology with a Socialist point of view that benefits the mass population. Instead of the Left, we'd recruit Right-wing Christians, especially in America's soft underbelly in the South. Historically, "hate" has thrived there against anyone unlike themselves. As Russians, we feel the same, but know how to use these fools to attain our own ethnic symmetry. We'll replace them all eventually with our own people, "*Nostrovia!* Y'all!"

Though his grip was tight, his hand felt small in mine. His breath, though Tic-tac tainted, concealed the stench of a deep cavity from which his foul breath flowed like a reptile with sharp, infectious teeth after devouring some helpless rodent.

"I hope the accommodations suit you, sir, though I thought you might have preferred Hotel Ukraina." I said, testing his sensitivity. "It's our tallest building among other skyscrapers, which combined you Americans call 'The Seven Sisters.' Don't use that moniker talking to Russians. They'll smile then spit in your food when you're distracted."

I'd thought he would prefer the tallest building since he always wants to be the tallest man in any room, which could be a problem for Director Comey of the FBI.

Our target responded, "Though our current administration seems to like all things Ukrainian, I prefer Mother Russia for its long history and culture. I'm a city boy, so Moscow suits me well. I picked this hotel for its high tower. You know how much I love towers."

"Perhaps we can arrange for one of your towers to bless the Moscow skyline, sooner rather than later," I bribed him with subtlety.

He grinned boyishly, perhaps something that appeals to some women as much as his wealth. He was like a teenager, just told he could drive his dad's Maserati to the prom. I'd struck a well-tuned chord. We were on the same wave-length, but to his credit, he knew it as well as I did. We'd soon begin to make sweet music together, he for himself, me for Mother Russia for releasing my father from the gulag years ago—*quid pro quo*—an oligarch's motto.

"A Moscow tower with my name on it . . . sounds great. It will look great, too. What's *my* side of the deal? What do *I* need to do for your side?"

"Start implanting ideas in people's heads," I said, sipping my vodka. "Many think you're a Democrat, a woman's right to choose, contributing to Bill Clinton's campaign twice in the Nineties. You've made some positive public statements about Hillary, too. That must change, but slowly, with subtlety."

"I don't do subtle very well."

"Don't just go along with extreme right-wing belief that Obama had no right to run for president, that his presidency is illegitimate. Just be our spokesman by demanding his birth certificate. He's an elitist Black and won't humble himself by offering to show it to the public. Use that against him. We can dance to that tune before the next election. Though he can't run again, we'll make Americans believe you'll be the legitimate American presidential prototype to make America White again, and Obama will be seen as just an aberration."

"More of an abomination. But me, as president? Hillary's in line after Obama. She's got the pussy vote hands down."

"We'll change that. We'll expose things about her that will make her unelectable."

"How?"

"We have our ways."

"The Republicans will want another Bush . . . Jeb's in line for that."

"Not a chance, not after you make mince-meat of him in debates."

"How will I do that?"

"Be yourself—just like on your realty TV show. Just be 'The Donald.'"

"That's what my first wife called me, but now we're divorced, so it's a tag I avoid with respect for my current wife and our son."

"Had you not divorced your first wife, you'd have been all in by now. She wasn't trained like us, but an informant whose strings we could pull. I selected her myself during the 1968 Warsaw Pact to put down the Czech rebellion. Now, your children by her are just as compromised. They'll need you to lead them and all of America against the force that threatens your country and ours—China."

He nodded with pursed lips.

"I want you to meet someone now, who'll confirm all I've promised."

"Sure, I'm all ears."

Flanked by two bodyguards, an older woman with a veiled hat entered.

My target showed his curiosity, but with displeasure because our prior communication had promised him a night of debauchery with a bevy of Russian high-end prostitutes willing to comply with demands decent societies, even ours, would not allow. The woman removed her hat and veil.

"Jesus!" our target bellowed seeing it was Putin.

Vlad spoke in slow, but well-practiced English. "It is folly for Russia and American to be adversaries when we can both gain so much as allies."

Agent Orange nodded and exchanged a lingering hand-shake that was more like an arm wrestling match that ended in a draw of mutual respect.

"We must be friends, AO," Putin said.

"AO?"

"The *Alpha* and *Omega* of our plan," Putin lied, knowing our contact would not be pleased by the tag—*Agent Orange*—a moniker of destruction and death. "You will be the beginning of our mutual ascent and the end of China."

"Nukes? I know everything there is to know about mass destruction."

"More subtle than that, but it's the only way our people can survive in our grandchildren's lifetimes against the Yellow Peril.

Even Czar Nicholas II had the good sense to understand that threat from the Japanese when China was still just a disarray of tribal provinces. But it was Communism that made the Chinese strong like the Soviet Union. Back then, China just had the most people."

"A shit lode of people," AO agreed.

"But soon, they could have the most money. If we join forces against China, we'll be hailed in the West forever by crushing that threat."

Agent Orange nodded with a grimace, then asked, "What's in it for me?"

"The American presidency of course," Putin said with a grin, but not like any former American leader, because you'll have Russia's full support."

"What exactly does that mean?"

"We'll make certain you'll win in 2016."

"Against Hillary?"

"She's been a thorn in my side, but better she's disgraced with a loss to you than assassinated. American politics has too many martyrs. That's why we worked with the politicians who agreed with our point of view against China to block Obama's agenda rather than eliminating him, which would have been easy—acute lung cancer undetected—a natural death for a smoker. A Stage Four coup d'etat."

"I've dealt with the Mafia in my real estate business. Is this an offer I can't refuse?"

"You can do whatever you wish, but it would be a shame to have your beautiful daughter vanish to the benefit of the highest bidder in the dark realm of Muslim brothels."

Agent Orange turned red and clenched his fists.

"Don't be upset," Putin said with a glare. "I'm offering you the highest power in the world. We'll protect you and guide you through all of it for this noble cause, the preservation of the White race against the Yellow."

"What about the Blacks?"

"As said in my favorite American movie, *The Godfather*: They're just animals."

"What about the women's vote? Hillary will have them in her pocket."

"Hillary? Русский!"

Agent Orange turned from Putin to me for interpretation. I said," She's the bitchiest."

"But she has power and she'll get Obama's endorsement."

"You'll have something greater, *my* endorsement as your silent partner, and all the power behind it. You could become as powerful in America as I am in Russia, as Xi is in China. But together we'll be more powerful than Xi. By 2020, you'll put an end to the two-term limit as president, and die in office at age one hundred. You'll rule the Western hemisphere and I Europe. Together, we'll share the East, two great Caucasian empires. By then, Africa will literally be our *booty*."

"And I thought *I* was a great deal maker. Where do I sign?"

"We'll shake hands, then there will be no trace beyond this meeting." Putin nodded to me. "Otto will be the only contact with your trusted people, so choose your administration carefully. We can recommend some who are already with us, but the choice, of course, is yours. You will be the power in America that saves our race for future generations."

They shook hands. Putin replaced his veiled hat then left.

Agent Orange turned to me and asked, "Was I just dreaming? This is unbelievably beautiful. I love it."

*** *** ***

Like clockwork, in this case, Clockwork *Orange*, all had come to pass as promised, despite a variety of snags. Ultimate success would depend on the 2020 election, but the American institutions, despite their cracked foundations had kept their structures erect through the turmoil. Our campaign of alternate truths had been most effective, but weaknesses in Agent Orange had come to the fore. His need for daily praise and loyalty, two things so lacking in his youth because his father treated him like a bastard, then paid him off to get out of his sight. AO was stripped of the tenacity needed to succeed, by running off-script, behaving as Vlad described, "like a fool."

Putin instructed me to reinforce our position against Ukraine's independence.

"From his lips to my ears and my lips to yours," I said to Agent Orange. "Putin wants you to think of the Ukraine as Texas or California, rich states among your fifty.

"Why?"

"How would you feel if Russia sent in troops against your federal government to protect a state's sovereignty ? Think of your response, verbally and militarily. You'd attack with all your might to keep the United States' unity. Ukraine isn't Poland, Hungary, or Romania. It's part of Mother Russia. We want it back. You must help us get it back."

He agreed to work with us and recommitted to his obligation to us for getting him elected. But when a new, unsuspected Democratic candidate arose from the 2020 chaos brought about by the coronavirus pandemic, I was given the signal to abort my long-term mission and cover our trail in America. COVID-19 left our network too vulnerable. Forty years work, all lost because of this idiot, Agent Orange.

Believing he had our full support for re-election, Agent Orange imploded with his self-importance undermining our goal more than the opposition itself.

He was supposed to meet privately with me in the men's room at The Russian Tea Room with just his, or I should say "our" Secret Service agents assigned to him. Though I'd asked if we should use our usual subtle means of undetectable elimination, Putin had said, "*Nyet!*"

Instead, we'd let Agent Orange turn slowly in the wind from the gallows of his conceit and would continue to work on the next generation, perhaps his daughter would make a good president rather than a Saudi's concubine.

My life's work done in my seventies, and as the sole source for this pipeline between the Kremlin and the Oval Office, it was my duty to close down my network, and myself along with it. I had always known that would come.

When Agent Orange straightened his tie and left the rest room at The Russian Tea Room, I ran hot water in a sink until the steam from the faucet clouded the mirror. With my index finger, I printed my name, which I'd chosen myself sixty years ago at age thirteen when I'd entered the program. It was a moniker that read the same from both perspectives, from two opposing worlds. Both sides of a mirror is where inner space and outer space intersect as one, itself and its reflection always reading the same from both angles.

As the poison took hold of me, life drained from my face, just like my name with each letter dripping down the mirror into obscurity until my dual identity, O T TO V I H I H I V, was lost and forgotten forever. . . .

A 30% Chance of Tomorrow

Spectrum News 9 shows the seven-day forecast with daily highs of 95 degrees and evening lows 85, unchanged for fourteen weeks from last May 13th through this Sunday, October 7th. My 60-inch HD TV screen might as well be a storyboard with no digital electronics. The prediction shows no changes in the foreseeable future. The station's meteorologist with her straw-like, platinum blond, shoulder-length coif, and burnished leathery skin, might as well be a feather-brained "weather girl" from the '50s when T&A mattered more to network CEOs than the THI.

In High Definition, I see her crêpe paper skin fold and unfold with each stretch of her electronic pointer. She notes the Bermuda High's vortex over Virginia Beach expanding over a thousand miles in all directions. Not a Low or cold front appears in the Western Hemisphere, only dead air. Despite her makeup, on the close-ups, blond menopausal hairs feather her upper lip. I turn off the TV to spare energy, watching only morning and evening weather reports. What's the point?

The monotonous 10-degree sunlight differential has created a diurnal dew point on Florida palm trees, keeping lizards alive with morning condensation during the drought, but without a drop of rain in five months. By 9 a.m. each morning, the dew that's not consumed by wildlife has evaporated in the heat. Less fortunate lizards lay dead, dried like unsealed raisins on my deck in the blistering sun.

The gators don't seem to care about the heat yet. I wish I had our local 12-footer's seemingly blase attitude about the weather. Laid back in this swelter, he lets a snowy egret hitch a ride on his scaly back across our pond. The spindle-legged water fowl doesn't exert itself by taking flight, and the gator is too lethargic to open his jaws, even for such an easy meal—a two-gulper at best. Perhaps he's patently waiting for people to die, as they surely will.

I've been working on my novel to meet the publisher's deadline on final revisions due October 1st, which came and went last week. The Tampa Bay heatwave and drought have had only a 5-degree daily temperature differential from New York City, with no rain there as well. My editor, Fred, and agent, Sally, have empathetically compromised by giving me a deadline extension till the weekend.

"I understand," Sally, says to me on Skype. "We've had brown-outs daily since September in Manhattan. The A/C in office buildings, retail stores, and hotels in the city has essentially failed with daily excuses from Con Ed about outdated power grids. To make his point, the mayor has appeared every morning on all the news stations in a sleeveless wife-beater. He sips water from a plastic bottle twisted from the heat and assures us the A/C will come back on in a matter of days rather than weeks. The governor has sent water bottles down here in a caravan from Canada to keep the stock market open. Yesterday, the mayor fried an egg on the steps of Town Hall. The death toll is over five hundred in Manhattan. All the steel and brick holds the heat like a sauna."

I tell Sally, "I used to tell my friends in Manhattan that they'd hate Florida's heat, with our bugs and snakes, but it was an intended lie so my favorite bars wouldn't get more crowded than they already are during Spring Break. I've loved it here on the Gulf Coast with its sea breezes despite the heat. Now, with no rain for months, that breeze feels like a blow torch. I write only at night but, with power failures, mostly by candlelight. I use a generator to charge my laptop, smartphone, and TV when I watch the news just for fifteen minutes in the morning and again at eleven p.m. But don't worry, Sally . . . I've got only another day's work before I send you the revisions. I think you and Fred will be pleased with the final draft, and my novel will make it to the shelves for the Christmas rush."

"Great! I can't wait," she says. "Call me to say you've sent it."

"Will do."

"Ciao!"

"Bye," I say as her image fades from my phone's screen though, with the heat, it seems more like Sally's face is melting.

It's 7 p.m. and the sun is setting on the rear balcony over-looking the pond from the second floor of my condo. The edge of the pond's shoreline has receded by twenty feet during the drought. Last year at this time, I looked forward to a cocktail on my rear balcony before dinner. Occasionally, a bull gator declares his territory with a brazen, wakeless cruise from one end of the pond to the other. The pond comes from a natural spring, so it's still ten feet deep in the middle drawing gators from other ponds that have dried up completely.

I light three scented candles and arranged them on the balcony's table so I can see my laptop's keyboard. I scan my notes from my last conference call with Sally and Fred. I sip a bourbon neat, figuring when the Pinellas County power grid comes back on, I'll celebrate with a mint julip over crushed ice from Publix. I've rationed one bag of ice in the freezer of my fridge and try to stretch it over three-day intervals with the power off. I'll run out by tomorrow, but don't look forward to the zoo at Publix or Walmart with lines for ice backed up in a queue around the block.

The warmth of the honey-hued whiskey passes smoothly over my tongue and down my throat and settles in my gut with a radiating glow like the hot-water bottle that my mom used to put on my belly for a tummy ache. I wipe my lips with the back of my hand and feel the roughness of my beard and moustache gone wild since the water shortage. I tried shaving gel, but with no water to rinse it off after a shave, I broke out in a rash. Staring at my image in the bathroom mirror, my reflection makes me look like a cross between *Mr. Hyde* and a caveman from a GEICO insurance commercial—hairy and scary.

More alarming than my appearance are the tricks the heat and thirst play on my mind. That moment each night before I extinguish the candles, I wonder if I'll see the light of day ever again. My thoughts have drifted nightly to crevasses of uncertainty much darker than the night itself. Tonight I feel somewhat blessed with a full moon on a clear night, but only until the frogs begin their Pavlovian chorus stirring the appetites of many gators. The huge bull gators grunt and hiss staking their claims in the evaporating pond's miasmic hell below my balcony.

It's too hot to sleep inside with no A/C or fans, because I'm preserving the fuel for my generator for the sake of finishing my final draft to send to Sally tomorrow. I can only hope for relief with a possible evening breeze from the Gulf or Tampa Bay, each five miles away respectively to the east and west. I have a cushioned chaise lounge with a pillow on the screened balcony, but just a beach towel for a cover should a wind pick up during the night. It's been so dry that we've had the least amount of lightning this season than ever recorded. Good thing, or the glades would surely be aflame to add to this misery.

The full moon casts a bluish hue across the pond, silhouetting huge black gator heads with red eyes aglow. A female must be in heat with two bulls raising their scaly tales above the surface in an arc and lashing at each other in their premating ritual, whereby, to the victor goes the spoils of crocodilian propagation of the species.

"I hope she's worth the excursion," I say aloud, my voice echoing across the steamy, primeval pond.

I hear a cough from the adjacent screen porch with just a ten-foot wide alley between our condo quads. In such heat the A/C units below would drown out other sounds, but the units are all as silent as tombstones still in wait for Duke Energy to power our grid. It's a smoker's cough, which I haven't heard in some time. I confirm with a nod to myself, affirmed by the glow of a lit cigarette across the alley. Even by moonlight, only the cigarette's lit end is apparent, moving back and forth from lips to ashtray, like the invisible man in the old black-and-white, SciFi Horror flick from the '30s. But it's a woman. Like the bull gators, even in the dark, I sense her presence, her hair flowing to her shoulders, full lips puckering around the filter tip, her bosom inhaling then exhaling. With a tingling at the base of my spine, I imagine my scaly tail in its mating arc.

"Hi!" she calls out, I suppose to me, since I see no one else in view. "Hi!" I return, but my voice feels like a driving range golf ball. No matter how far and straight it's driven, it will never come back to me.

Through the moon glow, I see her silhouette backlit by the rippling pond agitated by horny gators. I figure that's it, my thrill for today with maybe just a 30 % chance of tomorrow. She stands up, probably to return through her sliding glass doors to go back inside. We've never met, and I have no idea what she looks like. I hear the doors slide open, but there's a long, silent pause.

"Fucking hot, huh?" she calls out, standing and facing me with her breasts pressed against her screen. I can't tell what she's wearing, if anything at all, just her nose and nipples indicate she's really there, but like a phantom of every woman I've ever known. She shakes me from my pondering with, "You got any ice?"

"A little left in my freezer! I've been stretching it out till tomorrow's weekly delivery at Publix."

"Enough for two?"

"You have a husband . . . or a friend with you?"

"I meant two—like you and me."

"Well, I—"

"I'm off tomorrow. I'll bring you back your two-bag ration, so you won't have to wait in line tomorrow. Been there—done that. You'll just have to give me your driver's license to prove to the regulators that we're neighbors. Maybe you could do the same for me next time."

"OK, should I bring you some ice now?"

"I'll come over to you," she says. "Gimme ten to freshen up and get dressed."

"OK. What do you drink?"

"Gin 'n' tonic, but I'll bring my own. I just need some ice, 'kay?"

"Sure," I agree, sensing a nod from her. Then I see her naked figure leaving her porch, her buttocks tinted blue from moonlight reflected off the pond.

I haven't showered since this morning, just a splash or two with bottled water and rubbing alcohol. I quickly repeat that ritual and put on some deodorant with a dab of cologne for my beard. I grab a pair of scissors and try to create some adorning order to my facial follicles. It's a hack job by candlelight, but will have to do in a pinch. Who knows what she looks like after enduring these same dreadful conditions? All I have to connect the dots are her throaty voice, a nose, two nipples, and an enticing derriere.

I carry a candle to the kitchen and set it on the counter to see into the freezer above the fridge. Maybe enough ice cubes for three drinks each. I've already begun drinking my bourbon neat, so I'll save all the ice for my guest, reminding me of my favorite line from *Who's Afraid of Virginia Woolf?* "Let's play get the guests!"

Ten minutes have past, fifteen . . . twenty. Candle in hand, I go to my front door and open it. Of course, with no power, the guiding lights of the condo are out, so the wooden stairs that lead from my garage to my front balcony are hazardous in the dark. The moonlight doesn't help yet, because the full moon is still low in the night sky on the other side of the condo by the pond. The corridor between the condo quads seems to echo with guttural gator snarls, and the garden of the unit beneath mine is alive with slithering serpents of varying sizes and venomous toxicities. I imagine the Jurassic Era ended much like this with dinosaurs hissing and squirming till their final sighs of extinction. I wonder if the bitter end will be the same for humans.

I hear light footsteps ascending the stairs.

"Sorry I took so long," her voice emits from the black abyss below. "Using bottled water to bathe is no picnic."

"I know," I respond to the inky void, but don't mention the rubbing alcohol I've used to conserve water while washing up. Then I make out two floating lights ascending toward me as her steps quicken—her eyes, not red like the gators', shimmer brightly, then a flash of white defines the arc of her smile. Still not tangible, more like a shadowy spirit, her scent cuts through the dark heat of night, making my nose twitch as if from the first waft of my favorite childhood soup . . . Campbell's "cream of potato."

When I hear my lips smack together, I hope the sound is just in my subconscious, but then my stomach gurgles in real time.

"I brought some chips," she says. "You *sound* hungry."

Great—a comedian. My libido envisions Rita Haworth, instead I get Carol Burnette I put my palm to my belly and feel the hunger pangs vibrating, but wonder, is my appetite piqued as much for food as for passion? My only sense of how long the weather has remained so hot and dry are the red circle indications on my wall calendar. May 13th had been circled, but in retrospect, after the first month of drought and 90-degree temperature each day since. The nights give little relief, but it wasn't until June when the power outages began and fireworks on the Fourth of July at Clearwater Beach marked the beginning of the water shortage. The rockets' red glare faded that night along with traffic lights on Ulmerton Road between Route 275 and Indian Rocks Beach out ever since. I haven't been more than two miles from home in the past ten weeks. High tide in Tampa Bay has been two feet below the norm since August. The Major League Baseball Season was cancelled after the All-Star Game and the NFL never got started. George M. Steinbrenner Field and Raymond James Stadium across the street have been used as centers to feed refugees from their own homes, which have become uninhabitable with no power since Labor Day.

She brushes past me so briskly in the dim candlelight that I don't see her face, and now, with her back to me as she faces the kitchen cabinets, she's found a bowl to fill with the potato chips she's brought. The colors of her clothes are muted by the dim light, but she wears light shorts, perhaps white, and a dark, florid top tied in the center of her slim back with a bow. From her, the creamy essence of potato soup flares in my nostril.

"Sorry I've got no dip to go with the chips," I tell her. Her shoulders shrug as she says, "No biggie."

Waiting for her to turn and face me is like stalling an orgasm, anticipation trumping ejaculation. My breathing is shallow as I wait . . . and wait. I hear her pouring from the bottle she's brought, 1.75 Liters of Bombay Sapphire, 94 Proof, vapor infused gin, which, in the moon glow, is bluer than The Star of India. The crackle and pop of the warm gin over the ice cubes in the tall glass makes me regret having started with bourbon neat. The sound of fizzing Schweppes tonic over the ice to fill her glass makes my mouth feel dry, my forehead feverish.

I catch my breath when she reaches into a drawer and finds a sharp knife, but she giggles, showing me a lime she must have had nestled in her cleavage.

"Bought it three days ago when it was still hard," she says. "Now it's squishy."

Hard . . . I think, the word hanging out there to dry with my innocence like Bambi caught in the headlights, saying, "Bird!"

Just her hand reaches out from the shadow, her face striped with shadows from the blinds where the direct moonlight filters through. I take her hand, cold from handling the ice, and say, "I'm Dion."

"I know," she says. "Your mail has been mistakenly delivered to my box . . . but I've always put yours back in your box, not to embarrass the postman. He's kind, so I leave him cookies for the holidays."

"I've neither met him, nor received your mail by mistake. So . . . you are—?"

"My family calls me 'Ari' but that's short for *Ariadne*. We're Greek so my papa wanted his daughter to be a goddess. Do I make the grade?" she asks, moving into the candlelight where her sculptured features and dark eyes draw me closer. "Cheers, Dion?"

"Cheers! To our new friendship." Our glasses click as she glares at me.

"You don't recognize me, do you?" she says. "Look closer, Dion. My friend Mary said you told her you had a crush on me."

"Mary? Mary who?"

"Mary Dendy."

That name swims in my head like a tropical fish dropped into a strange bowl and trying to get out by banging its head against the sides of the tank. Then it comes, first, with the smell of newly sharpened pencils, then a lunchbox with the Sulphur taint of hardboiled eggs and mayonnaise, then chalk dust from blackboard erasers clapped together, and vanilla cookies and milk, all jumbled with the lavender scent of my kindergarten teacher, Mrs. Hughes, back in Queens at P.S. 137.

We both sip our drinks, just our eyes over the rims of our cocktail glasses, but the heat from my bourbon makes me feverish as Ari's face morphs into a five-year-old's, the face of the first girl I'd ever had a crush on. But from her lips comes the voice of my mother, terse, unforgiving, and scolding.

"I told you never to walk a girl home from school! You're just five years old. Serves you right, walking home that little troublemaker, Mary Dendy. That whole family has been quarantined with measles. That's what you've got now, too. See, God punishes you if you don't obey your parents."

"Ma! What about the power?"

"What power are you talking about? Lie back down there and take your next dose of sulpha. Open wide for Mama. Tastes just like chocolate milk. There you go. Now take a nap. You need the rest. You've already missed two weeks of school. If your throat feels sore, I'll crush an aspirin and mix it with honey and lemon juice to swallow, so your tonsils won't hurt. Promise me you won't walk Mary Dendy home again, or any other girls.

"What about the pythons, Ma? The drought is driving them north. They could reach Tampa Bay soon."

"Tampa? Whatcha talkin' about, Dion? We've never been to Florida. Hmm. doctor said these sulpha drugs could have side effects, maybe hallucination with the fever. You just lie back and rest now. You'll feel better after some sleep."

'No, Ma! I don't wanna go back there with the gators and snakes."

"Oh, dear, you are having one of those spells, huh?"

As she pulls my patterned quilt up to my chin, the swirling designs turn into thick snakes constricting me as I break into a sweat. I wonder if I would be better off dying now or, as I've been imagining, waiting till I'm a grownup. The weight of the world and all its horrors has been choking the life out of me over time. But I must consider what lies between my earliest recollections and final breath to know how to end my novel. The past and present will give me at least a thirty percent chance of tomorrow.

As Mom turns to leave my room, she stoops to pick up something from the floor and puts it on my dresser beside my bed. As she closes my door, I stretch to see what she'd picked up off the floor. I look at it with disbelief, but quickly fading from the sulpha drug's side effects, my Florida driver's license vanishes from my memory. Where shall I awaken? In kindergarten with all my life waiting ahead? Or in Florida with everyone left behind and dead?

Flowers on the Wall

When I turn my car's ignition, it sputters for a moment then the engine stops cold. I turn the key again—utter silence. Crap! I have my first Unemployment Bureau interview tomorrow morning after two months without a job since the restaurant I managed closed during the coronavirus pandemic.

My COVID-19 federal stimulus check still hasn't come two months after it was promised. Unemployment applications and benefits have been clogged up like a septic tank from the inept Florida website.

My wife threatened to leave me after the first four weeks of Pinellas County's stay-at-home order. I tried to calm her nerves by watching old classic movies together, some from our childhood, but there was nothing romantic in it for her, not even in a Forties nightclub called "Rick's." To make her laugh, there were Laurel & Hardy shorts, *Francis the Talking Mule* with Donald O'Connor, and *Animal House* to recall our college days.

For exercise, I played *The Beatles* and *The Rolling Stones* albums to get my wife up off the sofa, where she'd been *languishing*—a verb I'd learned watching the animated film of *Charlotte's Web* three times. I identified with the rat in the barn more than with a spider lip-synced by Debbie Reynolds.

My objective was to get some safe indoor exercise together by dancing to Sixties hits, but the tunes only reminded her of another guy she dated in college and always thought she should've married instead of me.

Apparently that guy is a hedge fund manager and makes eight figures on Wall Street, but the pandemic reduced his income to only seven figures. My own connections, as few as they are, informed me that he'd been divorced four times, but that only made my wife cry and wail, "That's because he should've married *me!*"

Whaah! Whaah! Whaah! Heading into week eight of stay-at-home orders, I wish he had married her. She still has the corsage he'd given her at their Senior Prom.

I'd come across it in our attic in a carton marked: NOSTALGIA. Tucked between her yearbook pages, the corsage was now flat, brown and, like our marriage, its petals were crumbling into minute particles of dust.

We've been sleeping in separate bedrooms. She said it was to protect each other from COVID-19, but I knew better. Her mother has been feeding her a steady stream of vindictive assaults on my character, which was passed through my wife's more gentle filter as: "If your best friend didn't own a chain of restaurants, no one else would ever hire your lazy ass! Without a handout, you're effing unemployable!"

I slept on that proclamation—at least I tried to sleep—but I knew I'd have to be up at the crack of dawn to take a bus for my interview in St. Pete, because my car wasn't going to start in the morning, and I had neither time nor the means to repair it. Besides, the auto repair shop was backed up for thirty days to keep customers and mechanics a safe distance apart. COVID-19 = Catch-22 on speed.

It's still dark as I awaken. I'd taken a muscle relaxing pill I'd rarely used, but when I was still wide awake at midnight, I'd given in. Five hours after taking the pill, I was still feel the palsy-effect in my limbs with only three hours before a cup of black coffee could make me semi-conscious for my Unemployment interview.

After I completed the three-S ritual of morning preparation for work, I don't even bother to say goodbye to my wife, still snoring deeply on the sofa with the morning news blaring loud enough for our dog, Missy, to bury her head under the covers on my bed.

Missy has never caught on to her name, because she answers only to my wife's repetitive monikers—"Bitch! Mutt! Filthy, goddamn—effing—dog!"

Any one of those cheerful tags would get Missy's tail wagging with appreciation. Our cat, however, would just lie in the sun on the window sill with a smirk of agreement with my wife's assessment of the canine species. The cat, "Smokey," was usually docile, but the climate of confinement in our home has made him bite me, drawing blood, which made me qualify for a new Olympic contest in track-and-field, in which I felt certain I'd win the Gold Medal—the classic *cat-put* event.

With a spinning turn and a thrust, I sent Smokey flying out the backdoor, but even with a record-breaking thirty-foot cat-put, he still landed on his feet, confirming that long espoused wives' tale. Perhaps another eight kitty lives will be my punishment for this futile *catatonic* exercise.

After walking to the bus stop on the next corner, for twenty minutes I stand six feet apart from the dozen commuters as they do from one another, all in silence.

Finally, I ask in general, "When's the next bus?" *Anyone? Anyone? Anyone?*

After grunting shrugs and blank stares, one elderly gentleman says, "There's no definite schedule. The morning news said they'll run about an hour apart, depending on how many passengers. A bus passed here almost two hours ago, but it said FULL."

I take a deep breath, look at my watch with discouragement, and start to walk toward the address I put into my car's GPS yesterday which said: 10 miles and 25 minutes. Those stats convert to a sweat-drenched walk of over two hours, maybe just less than two hours with alternate jogging. I'm in no shape for that ordeal, having broken a sweat the other night just dancing for two minutes to "I Saw Her Standing There."

I changed the lyrics to "I Saw Her Lying There," which got me the middle finger from my sweet, sweat-less wife reclined on the sofa.

I'd be late for my interview. Regardless, my wife's shriek still echoes in my mind to drive me forward: "*Effing*-unemployable!"

There isn't much traffic in this pandemic, but I decide, hopefully, that I should try hitchhiking. Maybe I could ride in the back of a pickup, or in the backseat of a sedan wearing my homemade mask. My wife refused to make me a mask, so I just pulled a pair of her panties over my head and used a sanitary napkin taped securely at the crotch and the leg holes to see where I was going.

If nothing else, the mask draws the attention of passersby, but the first two offers to give me a lift are a buxom blonde in a red convertible, with no mask, and a masked redhead with piercings and tattoos wearing a thong bikini and driving a doorless yellow jeep.

"No thanks," I tell them both. "I'm meeting my wife."

Then a white Lincoln town-car pulls up. The driver's window rolls down and a cloud of cigar smoke billows in my face, with the question: "Where to?"

Coughing I say, "I'm going to St. Pete."

The burly red-face man with a broad grin says, "You're already in St. Pete."

I look around realizing that, after a couple of hours of walking, I've almost reached my destination. Funny games the mind can play when you're preoccupied with survival.

When I show him the address I'd written on a piece of paper, he shrugs and says, "Hop in."

The backseat is spacious, easily six feet from the driver, whose face I see in his rearview mirror when he comments, "Nice face mask."

I shift the panties on my head to make my make-do mask tighter around my ears with the elastic waistband, and say with my voice muffled by the sanitary pad, "*Thumpsk.*"

Dropped off at the Unemployment Bureau, I thank the driver again, and he says he'd be driving by this way later if I need a ride home. I neither agree nor turn him down, uncertain how long my interview will go, or if I'll be sent directly to a new place of employment.

The woman at the desk I was directed toward, with a hard wooden chair placed six feet in front of her, has the aura of a prison matron in a black-and-white B-movie from the late Forties or early Fifties. She's stern, judgmental, with with penis-envy written all over her craggy face. She makes no comment about my face mask, but there's a lot of graffiti scribbled across her face, and her glare, like an ocean wave in April, gives me instant shrinkage, even without a drop of cold water in sight for my parched throat. The only comforting effect is the flower pattern of her dress with red and white roses.

"What kind of work are you looking for?" she asks with a growl.

"Well . . . I'm not really looking. You see, I'm a restaurant manager, and with the pandemic regulations, no restaurants are hiring. I put in my Unemployment application almost two months ago under the COVID-19 Cares Act to keep me afloat till the restaurant I've managed can reopen."

Her look reminds me of my dad when he asked me how I got the dented fender in his car and had told him everything but the truth.

"My wife and I haven't received our federal stimulus check either, and her employer is a small local business that also hasn't received any benefits yet."

I feel like I'm talking to a brick wall. She stamps my application with "Under Further Consideration" and gives me another appointment in two weeks.

Disheartened to return empty-handed, I'm glad to see the white Lincoln town-car waiting to take me home. Our conversation for the fifteen-minute drive is about our favorite film noir classics from the 1940s. He preferred blond, Lana Turner, while redhead, Rita Hayworth, was my favorite femme fatale of that era.

When I arrive home, I see the red flag is down on my mailbox, which means the last mortgage payment we can afford to make has been sent. I wave goodbye to my voluntary chauffeur and sift through our junk mail.

Wedged between the pages of a local shopper is an envelope from the U.S. Treasury. I tear open the envelope, which contains a federal stimulus check for $2,400 with that distinctive signature.

I feel a jolt of relief, but it's more physical than psychological with lightning striking very close and the sky opening up with a downpour and a roar of thunder. I clutch the mail to my chest and run toward my front door, but it's locked. I realize that, when the car wouldn't start this morning, I left my keys in the ignition.

I bang on the door, but my wife doesn't answer. I see her through the bay window. She's still lying on the sofa. The rain is too heavy to make a run for my car, so I ring the doorbell several times. I see her get up to come to the door.

"Where the hell have you been?" my wife whines with squinting eyes as I brush past her to get out of the pouring rain.

"Unemployment Bureau."

"Did ya get a job?" she asks, yawning and stretching like our feline, Smokey.

"Not yet, but look what finally came in the mail."

I hold the check with two hands in front of her face as raindrops drip off my elbows

She squints and wrinkles her nose, asking, "What is it?"

"The stimulus check!"

"Yeah, right," she says and flops back down on the sofa.

"No, really!" I shout, but when I shake the rain water from my hands and look at the check, all the ink has run and the only word that's even barely readable is "Tr%&p." When I run my thumb across that name, even it vanishes before my eyes.

I just stare out the bay window, watching it pour as lizards and toads seek higher ground. Blue herons and snowy egrets wait patiently to gobble them up as the reptiles and amphibians hop and leap to no avail with repeated gulps of the raptors' serpentine necks.

Then I see the white Lincoln town-car backing up slowly to the apron of my driveway. The rain suddenly stops with mist rising from the macadam street. The Lincoln's horn beeps, and I pay no attention to my wife asking me from behind, "Who the hell's that?"

"A friend," I say, going out the front door without looking back.

The front passenger window slides down and the driver is wearing a mask, not the improvised type like mine, but a professional medical mask. "Get in front with me this time," he says, his words muffled through his mask.

I do, and like the soothing music he's playing on the radio, woodwinds and oboes with occasional clunks of percussion on hollow logs. I would've appreciated a Tahitian dancer wearing a grass skirt and a flowered lei around her neck and a crown of lilies on her head. I could almost smell the lilies for want of her warm body next to mine after shivering in the rain.

"Where to?" the masked driver asks. I shrug. "Does it matter?"

"Sure it does," he says. "Would you like to drive this time?"

"Really? You don't mind?"

"Nah. Come on. Let's switch."

He turns off the motor and tosses me the keys as we pass each other in front of the Lincoln. But he doesn't get in, Instead, he helps my wife into the passenger seat. She's wearing a mask as well. I get behind the wheel and feel her hand touch mine. I lift her hand to my lips. It smells fresh, like spring lilies.

I adjust the electronic seat and the mirrors, put my foot on the brake pedal, then turn the key.

The radio comes on playing a song from my youth:

> "And the flowers on the wall,
> they don't bother me at all . . ."

Rather than the sound of the engine's purr, the clunk and hiss of compressed air engulfs me. The masked man standing beside my window rubs away the condensation on the fogged glass and motions for me to open the window.

When I do, my wife squeezes my hand tightly as the masked man says: "Welcome back, fella. We've just taken you off the ventilator . . ."

After weeks unable to breathe on my own, I feel my foot tapping to that old song:

> "I'm smokin' ci-ga-rettes and watchin'
> Captain Kang-ga-roo,
> So don't tell me,
> I've got nothin' to do . . ."

The Aviary

A scent hovered around Sara's face as she stirred. She recalled canaries and parakeets from her childhood—chirping, fluttering—and their distinct, near-sweet aroma that still made her light-headed, even in memory. The old hermit on the ridge had converted a 1940s motel into an aviary for his hundreds of multicolored minstrels. Each ten-by-twelve cabin had been a separate chamber for their morning symphony. Her mind began to fill with their many songs, like hymns she'd memorized from Sunday school.

That bright spring morning from long ago lit her mind. She'd been listening to the subtle sounds of spring's thaw. Melting snow from the mountains poured over the jagged rocks, now barely exposed beneath the rapids. By summer's drought she'd be able to cross the creek from rock to rock and run through the open field of wildflowers with bees humming. At the sound of her steps, deer would scatter, bound for forest cover.

Trying to catch a monarch butterfly that morning, she'd wandered off the dirt road that ran behind her home. She followed the orange-and-black beauty along the brook. She picked a wild daisy and put it to her nose, but it had no sweet scent, more like damp sneakers. With her eyes still on the monarch, she picked off the daisy's petals one-by-one. As she came to "he loves me not," that petal fluttered away and the daisy slipped from her hand. Wanting to know her romantic destiny, she wandered down the hill after the limp, near petal-less wildflower.

The brook's rush was swallowed up by the melodic twitter of the flock when the old hermit emerged from his den across the stream. His matted white beard was yellowed by thousands of dribbled egg-yokes after decades of soft-boiled breakfasts, all partaken in solitude—except for the accompaniment of his high-pitched throng needing to be fed.

An intruder, she felt his stare like a laser of midday sunlight through a magnifying glass. The "Bird Man of McCoy Hollow," as he was called in town, took unkindly to trespassers, even one in a blue sun dress with auburn pigtails and a pert, freckled nose.

It was rumored in town that his winged colony was sacred, not to be shared, not even with the innocent.

"Get!" he shouted, but she held her ground, determined not to retreat without whatever remained of her precious daisy. "Are ya deaf? I said get!" he threatened again, but noticed her gaze toward the muddy bank on his side of the brook. "What the hell ya lookin' at, girl?" He stretched his thin, wrinkled neck and cocked his head to peer over the tall grass along the bank above where her gaze seemed affixed. "Lose somethin'?"

She nodded then pointed to the bank where her daisy clung to a branch with the stream's rapid current making it quiver.

The old man grumbled as he pushed the chest-high reeds aside with his gnarled, wooden cane. "Ya want me to get bit by a cotton mouth?"

"There's no moccasins in this brook." she sassed him. " 'Cept maybe a fat ol' water snake with a bite big as a dog's. My Uncle Teddy got bit by one a them, but he didn't clean it out till he caught his limit of big-mouthed bass . . . Got infected so bad he died a week later."

"Hmm . . . I remember 'm . . . Teddy Fraiser," he said, then aside to himself, "What a jerk."

"Whatcha say?" she shouted.

"I got whiskey in my aviary to take care of infections, so I ain't scared," he assured her. "Medicinal spirits!"

"My boyfriend says you're an alco . . . holic."

"Boyfriend! Jeezus, girl. Your momma know ya got a boy-friend?"

"Nobody knows but me," she said, brow furrowed, lips pouting.

"So ya ain't told this boy ya love 'm yet?"

"I'm waitin' for him to tell me . . . He doesn't know he loves me yet."

"How old's this feller?"

"Don't matter," she huffed. "My daddy's ten years older than my mom."

"You Sally Fraiser's little gal?"

"You know my mom?"

He hesitated before answering, his expression from ten yards across the stream curious about this trespasser. "Use to go to yer church."

"Why'd ya stop comin'?"

"Well . . . I lost my son in Vietnam," he said with a sigh and a scratch of his protruding Adam's apple. "Just got mad as hell at everyone and everything . . . 'cept my birds . . . my little angels. They give me peace and light up my days . . . somethin' I can't get sittin' on a hard bench every Sunday, listenin' to a bunch of . . . lad-dee-da."

"Is that what made you an al-co-ho-lic?"

"Who's this boy tellin' ya that?"

"My boyfriend?"

"Ain't he got a name?"

"Billy."

"Billy who?"

"You're not gonna hurt 'm, are ya?" She wrinkled her nose like a dog about to snarl.

"Nah! He prob'ly heard it from one of them hoity-toity church women who ain't got nothin' better to do than talk others down. Losin' my boy didn't make me an alcoholic. Either ya are one or ya ain't. When you find out ya are one, ya got a choice— drink . . . or don't drink. Ya think I could take care of my birds if I was a drunk?"

"I dunno." She shrugged. "Bible says God takes care of birds, so folks don't need to."

"Tell that to a pelican," he huffed. "Soon they'll be extinct just like the dodo bird. Damn folks screwin' up nature with pollution. Birds are like people, some need carin' for and some don't. You're just like my birds; ya need lookin' after. What if I wasn't around to see ya runnin' along the brook chasin' after somethin' ya lost. Prob'ly end up in the drink, drowned and washed away."

"Would not! I can swim."

"Maybe so, but it's April and that spring water is about forty-five degrees, 'nough to give ya hyper-thermy. Your mom would never know how it happened."

"You gonna help me find my daisy or just keep squawkin' like your birds?" she said.

"My birds don't *squawk*! That's for crows. My angels sing . . . Some of 'em even talk."

"No way!" she said with a grimace.

"I'll prove it to ya . . . once I find yer flower," he said with a groan. Supported by the cane wedged under his armpit, he ambled down the slope to the water's edge. "Ya see it?" he asked.

"There, hanging on that branch."

"Call *that* a flower?" he wheezed with amusement. "Nothin' left of it."

"Please, get it for me?"

As he bent down to reach the flower, his shoes sank into the black humus and his pants cuffs got muddied. He nearly lost his balance when he retrieved the limp daisy. He tucked it into his breast pocket and waved to her, but muttered indistinguishable obscenities as he used his cane to steady his trek back up the bank.

"Ya know the cross-bridge about a hundred yards downstream?" he asked. She nodded.

"Come across and I'll show you my aviary of *talkers*."

She watched him walk back toward the former motel with white shakes and red shutters on each cabin. He was already entering the door before she started toward the bridge.

The clunking of her shoes across the old wooden bridge ceased with her steps across the soft field. Now she could hear her pulse pounding in her ears as she approached the hermit's aviary. She noticed her hand was trembling, reaching for the doorknob, but then the chirping, fluttering, and the sweet taint of birds draped across her face again like heavenly light . . .

* * *

Her cheek felt wet against the damp pillow as her pulse, in cadence with her recollection of the old hermit, pounded in her ear. The scent came from her bed, from the lump beneath the sheets beside her. She heard a wheezing breath, but wasn't sure if it was her own or coming from the heaving mound beside her. She held her breath to listen, but the sound stopped.

Perhaps her imagination was getting the best of her. What time was it anyway?

Not daybreak yet. If only she could get back to sleep.

She did, but the bird man crept back into her mind, refreshingly, like a drink of sweet ice tea from a frosty glass on a humid summer afternoon . . .

* * *

"Ya ain't scared of birds, are ya?" the old hermit asked as he opened the door to let her in. To her amazement, the interior lit up brighter than the bright sunny day outside.

"Maybe owls," she confided with a shrug. "Owls can be creepy."

"Yeah. Know what ya mean . . . the way they can turn their heads all the way around and hoot on a windy night. No owls in here. An owl would eat my angels . . . pop their pretty heads right off and swallow 'em whole."

"Really?"

"I'm no liar—nor an alky neither. Ya got a name?"

"Sara . . . you already know my last name. How about you? My boyfriend calls you "The Birdman of McCoy Hollow.""

"Would that be this Billy ya mentioned."

"You said you wouldn't hurt him."

"I never hurt anybody . . . too busy to care about anything but my flock. This is my canary house, birds from pure white to almost orange, some speckled, and others with dark wings. These are my singers. When I whistle, they sing to me." Demonstrating, the canaries high-pitch trill made her lightheaded. "Whaddaya think?" he asked.

"Makes me dizzy," she said, reaching for the arm of a rocking chair beside her and wilting into its cushioned seat . . .

The chair's swaying made her stir for a moment, aware she was deep into her recollection. The birds, their singing, and the old man's amusement over the overwhelming effect they had on her were all intangible—nothing to fear or dread. She was safe

270

now . . . at home in her own bed . . . where she'd always thought nothing could harm her.

Still—there was a tangible presence with her, right there within her reach— emitting an intoxicating fragrance, just like the birds . . . not the *singers* so much as the *talkers*.

She'd told the old man, "That's singing—not *talking*."

"I was saving the best for last." He grinned, sallow teeth with dark stains like the rows of Indian corn her mom hung on the door for Thanksgiving. "My singers are my *angels*. Now I'll show you my *clowns*."

She rose from the rocker, maintained her balance, and followed him into the next cabin. Upon her entry, a feathered rainbow of chattering parakeets startled her, but the veil draped over her face again, the sweet scent of their droppings that calmed and slowed her pulse, taking her deeper into her memory. It felt as if she were truly there, so much that her adult self, waiting for sunrise, seemed more the dream.

The parakeets chortled and snickered, running back and forth on their perches, bobbing their heads and vying for the old man's attention. He opened the cage of a bright blue parakeet, and nudged it with his bent index finger to hop on.. He held the bird close to his face and it pecked gently at his pursed lips.

Probably attracted to the dried egg yolk on his beard, she figured.

"This is Mikey," he said. "Say hello to Sara."

Mikey bent down from the old man's finger and spread one wing aside as if to bow, then said with a voice like a crackling telephone connection, "Hello. . . I'm Mikey . . . Have a good day." He ruffled his head feathers and chortled.

Sara became entranced by Mikey. "Do they all talk like that?"

Mikey answered for the old man, "Some do, some don't, so what. Mikey's the best . . . Mikey's the best."

The old man let several other parakeets out intermittently, never more than three at a time, and Sara spent most of the afternoon with parakeets on her head and shoulders, even letting some peck at her lips as they perched on her finger. By late afternoon, she felt hungry and realized she'd have to go home before her mom got worried.

She thanked the old man for sharing his angels and clowns with her and headed for the door.

"Aren't you forgettin' something?" he asked. When she gave him a puzzled stare, he reached into his breast pocket and cradled in his palm what remained of her rescued daisy. "Hardly anything left of it."

Dejected, she came close to see, but a bright smile quickly spread on her face. "What're ya so happy about?" he asked. "There's only one petal left."

"That's my secret," she said, gently scooping it into her hand and bolting for the door.

"If you want to visit my angels, you're always welcome!" He called after her, but she was too excited to answer.

Mikey twittered behind the old man, "You're welcome . . . You're welcome . . . Have a good day."

As she headed for the cross-bridge over the stream, she saw the old man still standing in the doorway and waving to her. She waved back with her free hand, but cupped her daisy in the other. When the old man's aviary was out of sight and her own home was just ahead, she took her daisy and plucked off the last petal with a sigh whispering, "He *loves* me . . ."

***

A warm glow came over Sara, realizing in her reverie that she was reliving what must have been the happiest day of her life. She hadn't thought about the old hermit and his birds since that day twenty years ago. But then her elation plunged, like the first drop on a roller coaster, to the realty of now . . . so the *then*, and the *what was* could never be again, engulfing her in desperation and sorrow.

A part of her wanted to return to that day with the old hermit at his aviary when she was innocent and curious. Although that day had foretold her future—*he loves me*—Billy wasn't coming back. She'd thought it was her neighbor returning her baking pan when she'd answered the door this morning, but it was a U.S. Marine with the message that her husband, Billy, had died in a roadside bombing on his second tour in Iraq.

She shivered under the covers where she'd retreated to their bedroom with the message from President Bush still clutched in her hand. Numb with shock, she realized she'd already called her mother. Mom was coming to be with her. Sara remembered going through the motions of making the call . . . but none of that conversation.

Sara wanted so much to go back to the aviary, so she could relive every day until now, savoring every moment she'd shared with Billy. She struggled to picture the old hermit's face again, but in her sorrow she drew a blank. She wanted to reach her arm to the other side of the bed, grasping for a straw, hoping Billy would be there beneath the covers, that the telegram this morning was just a bad dream.

She reached over, but was startled when the lump beneath the covers stirred with a flutter. Then she saw her mother coming into the bedroom toward her with open arms of comfort for her grief.

They embraced and wept without words for some time, not knowing how to express their feelings. Then her mother shared something with Sara that she'd kept from her.

"Sara, I know you think I can't possibly know how you feel . . . but I do. I had a boyfriend when I was in college. We'd been engaged before I met your dad. His name was Tim and he was my first love. He was killed in Vietnam the week before he was coming home for our wedding. Remember the old man who lived across the brook, The Birdman. He was Tim's dad . . ."

Sara felt faint from this revelation, but steadied herself to listen and learn.

"I could never look Tim's dad in the in the eye again because of my grief. It would've brought back all the pain. I couldn't bear it. He'd probably felt the same way and had kept to himself so he wouldn't have to see me again, especially in church.

"It was selfish in a way . . . but we had been unable to share our feelings of grief.

He'd died before we could. I met your dad a few years later and started over. I don't want us to keep our feelings to ourselves. Tim's dad died alone, a recluse talking to a bunch of birds in that old motel he'd converted into an aviary. His life must have been miserable with the loss of his only son."

"No, Mom, the old man's life was good." She told her of that special day at the aviary and how kind the old hermit had been to her, saving her daisy and letting her play with his birds: his angels and his clowns.

"I don't know how to comfort you, Sara," her mother said. "But the sorrow is too much for either of us to bear alone."

"I know . . . but sometimes we can be messengers, like I was to Tim's father. He must have seen *you* in my face, Mom, when I spoke to him that day. I don't know why a memory of that one day in my life came back to me so vividly, maybe because it was the day I knew I'd love Billy forever . . . but I think the old hermit had a message for me, too. Before you came into the room, I felt Billy right here beside me. I reached over to touch him but he was gone."

As Sara spoke, the sweet scent of birds wafted to her. She reached to the other side of the bed again. The bed felt warm and, as often happened, several small white feathers from the down pillow lay on the sheet. But nestled on the concave pillow was another feather—a finger's length and bright blue. Then she saw a blue bird, a parakeet on her open window's sill.

"Look! Billy was here," Sara told her mother, but the bird took flight.

Sara felt the warm glow of new light as she heard the old hermit's parakeet, Mikey, speaking to her from afar, telling her that Billy would be waiting for her return to the aviary.

Vaccine Nation

Another decade has passed since the third wave of COVID-27 took its lethal, mutant course in autumn 2049 when mandatory vaccinations for newborns was passed by the Americana Federation and signed into law by President Dolores Fatima Paz. Her election victory with Ching Lau Nguyen, her gay VP running mate, was overwhelming with an unprecedented Electoral victory of 509 to 29, losing only the state of Florida.

President Paz's landslide victory mandated the mass inoculation of every Americana Citizen against all potential diseases, successfully classifying "racism" as one of the Federation's Top Ten lethal ailments to be eradicated by vaccination since there had been no other recourse since the 2021 uprising that had destroyed the former United States of America.

"We can no longer depend on contemporaneous outcries of Federation victims," Paz proclaimed in her inaugural speech. "We have the cure at hand so it would be unconscionable not to use it to our full extent."

With the ratified Popular Vote Amendment, President Paz was reelected to her second term after the dissolution of the Electoral College with a landslide popular victory of 654,125,019 to 1,391,267. The greater conundrum wasn't the overwhelming lopsided Paz victory, but rather how her opposition managed to get any votes at all in what had become a unitary electorate for the past twenty-four years. All of the contrary votes were write-ins by mail ballots, and all for a candidate unknown to the national media. Who "Jason McClellan Davis" was to over 1.3 million Florida residents was still a mystery well into President Paz's second term.

In retrospect, many editorial opinions and history pundits pointed to a combination of the Mandatory Inoculations Act of 2049 and the dismantling of the Electoral College as the turning point in the empowerment of the Populist Party with its 99.9% mandate to do whatever their platform desired in the restructuring of the Americana Federation's populace future.

If the United States' technical innovations had increased three-hundredfold between 1970 and 2020, the advancements in the next four decades increased exponentially to the 10th power. Any opposition to President Paz's platform was minimal and limited to *Frequency 76*, which spouted patriotic propaganda from the Founding Fathers via the hacking of the FCC's Cerebral Implant system, referred to in the media as "CI." That FCC program had been signed into law by President Paz's predecessor, President Vladimir Dystruski of the GOP, a naturalized Russian oligarch who'd taken advantage of the 2033 Article 39 allowing naturalized citizens to become President of the Americana Federation. He'd won by the Electoral vote despite getting only 42% of the popular vote.

"Foul play!" the media's outcry reverberated throughout the Western Hemisphere, unanimously renamed "Americana" by the Federation Supreme Council's 9-0 edict in 2040.

The Popular Vote Mandate literally cut the head off the Gerrymander, now an extinct amphibian by land and sea alike. The shift in popular sentiment under President Paz coincided with the Mandatory Inoculations Act as a means of preserving

"Americana," the 54-state union, which included, Puerto Rico, Cuba, Mexico, and Canada. These shifts in boundaries, occurred under President Dystruski in 2037. He referred to this land grab as a necessary "chess" maneuver. The purpose was to shore up non-Asiatic territories against "Chindia," which had overrun Australia, and stretched eastward to "Europa" as far as the Alps. Southward, Chindia expanded its borders as far as the northern fringes of The Great Desert, formally the Saudi Republic before its oil fields went dry in 2035. As a result, the scarce Saudi survivors were encamped in former Pakistan. Their enslavement there by the Chindian Federation was as an emergency food source for the next Ice Age predicted to commence by 2080 with the expected complete melting of the north and south polar regions, already reduced by 75% of what glacial ice had remained back in the 2020s.

Soon there were only three world powers with South Americana, Africana, and Australiana used solely as sources of food, natural resources, and pharmana, formerly known as "pharmaceuticals," a term stricken from the Federation Dictionary ever since the CEO's of all such corporations had been publically beheaded, and corporations were outlawed by the Supreme Council in a narrow 5-4 decision in 2038. These three supply sources now supported the three world Federations of Americana, Europa, and Chindia.

The Mandatory Inoculations Act of 2049, led to an underground movement within the Americana Justice Department to find out how President Paz had become so popular with virtually no public opinion against her in any metropolitan news media. There were only rare public demonstrations in opposition to her personally or to her Populist policies. At no time had any more than a band of less than a thousand demonstrators assemble in the streets, waving the antiquated Confederate flag as a symbol of rebellion against what they called ANA—"Abundant National Apathy."

"Let's try inoculated citizens against that!" was a common rebel yell.

Rarely had a social marauder on a motorcycle or in a pickup attempted to penetrate the Whitehouse compound at high speed waving the Confederacy's racist banner. The only coverage such intrusions were given in the media were as an item in the Humor Section of the news media or on the Laugh Sequences of social media, often with a punchline beneath the photo or video such as:

"Rebels—We can't live with 'em and can't *effing* live with 'em."

The word "fuck" had also been stricken from all Federation language along with "pharmaceutical" and six other words once referred to by an ancient orator simply referred to as "Carlin." Both Carlin and "Merlin" were deemed as myths by the Federation Evaluation Bureau. The penalty for possessing any recordings of this "Carlin" menace to the Federation was expulsion to Amazonia for life, and if Carlin's words were spoken by a citizen, public decapitation. *Frequency 76*, in addition to espousing antiquated patriotic propaganda, also played on the rebel network, what was known as Carlin's "stand-up routines," though the Federation proclaimed: "This Carlin character stands for nothing worthwhile."

To protest was to offend the sensibilities of the middleclass, which composed 90% of Americana's population with 9.9% in utter poverty and .1% ultra-rich owning 99.9% of all property, both tangible and intellectual. To rid the Federation of this rebel cancer, lethal to Americana's way of life, policing was needed, a special law enforcement unit to assure success, the ABI.

Agent Steve Slocum's assignment as an Americana Bureau of Investigtion agent was to find a way to join this underground group of rebel vigilantes and report their means and manifesto to his ABI Group Leader, Jessica Chavez.

"If exposed, your assignment won't be acknowledged as an approved mission," Group Leader Chavez told Slocum as they lay entwined on her king-sized bed in her zero-gravity boudoir.

Her 80th-floor penthouse in Alexandria, Virginia was a frequent nest for Slocum in an affair beyond its third year. In all Americana districts, cohabitation for five years was ruled a "Common Law Marriage," regardless of sexual persuasion. The jury was still out for Slocum on his commitment to Jessica. He was ambivalent about the next two years, because he wasn't sure if his going into deep cover would be considered just a temporary time-out, or his final severance with "Jess," as he preferred to call her when they were alone and unjudged by their ABI peers.

At the agency, with the outward appearance of a nerd, Slocum was riffed with physical attributes that matched his superior intelligence. His bookworm façade at work was a ruse to stave off any suspicion of his unacceptable cohabitation with his ABI superior. He'd begun as a musical theater major at Syracuse University before the ABI got their hooks into him. He had a minor drug arrest so, with a guaranteed expungement and a variety of perks, he agreed to take freelance undercover assignments for ABI as an informant on campus.

When his ABI handler became impatient over Steve's slow process of intelligence gathering, Steve would refer to the still frequent bursts of frigid winter weather on the Syracuse campus with the stall: "When the snow melts, the shit shows."

Slocum's success on his first mission resulted in a concerted effort by the agency to recruit him full-time. The bennies and perks offered to infuse himself in the program were further enhanced by his attraction to his cadet classmate, Jessica

Chavez, a crack shot with a brilliant mind and a face, in Slocum's mind, to die for. Though her body was in superb physical shape with skills to match any man's, Slocum was in perpetual orgasm over Jessica's mind more than the gymnastics they performed suspended weightless between silk sheets—and her athletic, vice-gripping thighs.

The night before Slocum's scheduled infiltration into the subculture of *Frequency 76*'s underground headquarters, Jessica told Steve, "This marauder, Jason McClellan Davis, is hiding somewhere in south Florida, a Federation District ABI agents refer to as the former '*Gun* Shine State.' You'll notice the map of that district is even shaped like a goddamn pistol. Careful, Steve. These rebels have undetectable hardware."

"Why haven't our satellite tracing probes pinpointed their position by their weaponry?" Steve asked, running the back of his hand down her naked thigh.

"I expect you to bring back that intelligence to me," she said. "Even if their illegal guns are outdated, this mission won't be a walk in the park. I'm concerned for your safety if they find out who you are before you find out where they are."

"If they have any women recruits I may have to seduce one to obtain her confidence."

"Whatever," she shrugged with a smirk."

"That's only if they have any women there, Jess."

"It's not only a bed of potential usurpers against the Americana Federation. Our intelligence tells us it also serves as a breeding farm for dissidents. So there will be female rebels there reproducing the old-fashioned way."

"I'll take my monthly pill to be sure my informant doesn't pop out any more of those rebels on my account."

"Aside from *this* weapon," she said, grabbing his crotch, "you'll be unarmed.

Otherwise, they'll suspect you're one of us."

"That's my initial ploy, Jess, seeking an illegal weapon."

"You're the best man for this mission, Steve. Don't disappoint me."

"Are those mutually exclusive statements?"

"You've never disappointed me."

"Likewise, Jess."

Only Federation Law Enforcement agents were permitted to own or carry lethal weapons. A satellite tracking system in 2036 had been able to locate any firearm outside of law enforcement. Unless turned in to Federation authorities by year-end of 2036, a laser system tracked and melted any lethal hardware wherever stored or carried. Federation Law Enforcement weapons were made of a Tungsten compound with no effect by the satellite lasers.

After making love for hours that night, as Steve dressed before his early morning flight from Arlington to Miami, Jessica said nervously, "Remember, it's the only district where guns outside the military and police have been shielded from our satellite laser, mostly in the Everglades. It was the last Americana district to relinquish its firearms to the Populist Federation movement. A fringe element of the defunct GOP still runs guns, whiskey, and drugs from the swamps as their means of financing their insurgency."

"Hmm. Guns, whiskey, drugs, and female breeders— reminds me of the Good Ole Days described in our ABI Service Manual about a place called 'Disney World.' I think it was located smack dab in the middle of Florida and families came from everywhere to amuse themselves in fantasy. Of course it was COVID-24 that killed hundreds of thousands there, which stopped cold any further tourism."

"That's what led to the concentration of dissidents there, hoping to bring it back, but with no success." She shrugged. "I prefer our virtual tourism now. No cancellations, mosquitos, or fellow travelers to annoy us. This backward ideology in Florida has to be snuffed out quickly before it spreads like a coronavirus. At least we've rid Americana of football and basketball as illegal forms of sport. Only FASCAR competition to the death and baseball have been permitted by petition, but only viewed on the CI network in our minds. All wasted on these rebels who have no minds for anything but disruption."

"I miss the Federation fries at stadiums most," he admitted.

"The Saturated fats interfered with cerebral implants causing fatal strokes."

"To be sure, Jess. So, are we on track with our FCCI communications?" Steve asked, referring to their Federation Certified Cerebral Implants, which could be coordinated for a variety purposes from virtual coitus to a Federation mission, which would provide shared thoughts without conversation or visual body language.

"Yes, Steve. I verified our program this morning with ABI Headquarters. You and I are in sync. It's a go. Bye, Love."

"Give me a long one, sweet and sloppy, Jess. Then I can clone it for nights when I miss you."

Their tongues swirled and both became breathless the old fashioned way.

"See you when you get back," she said, abruptly breaking away from his embrace. "Clones are great, but I think I'll be looking forward to the real thing on my return." One last clutch with Jess then Steve was out the door. Jessica waved to him as the ABI transit hover-sled took him to the airport. She shed her first tear since she was three years old when the Populists arrested her father for hiding a collectors' 9mm pistol from the Pre-Americana Dark Decade in 2025. She never saw him again, and before she was ten years old, her mother had died of COVID-34.

Jessica was adopted by her single aunt, a staunch Populist against the corrupt twelve-year Dystruski administration of Russian influence and connected at the hip to the pervasive Europa Federation under the military dictatorship of ninety-year-old Vladimir Putin. Overthrown, the entire Dystruski family from the elderly to infants were publically executed by cerebral laser infraction, which was then, and still is, the instant meltdown of the guilty parties' cerebral implants. Once found guilty of treason against the Americana Federation, an entire bloodline would be eradicated for the preservation of the Populist Movement in Americana.

Since Jessica's father's offense was considered a "misdemeanor" at the time, she and her mother had been spared. Had her father's weapon been anything more than a collector's pistol encased in a frame without a firing pin, he would have been charged with treason in Federation Court. Jessica and her mother would have been publically executed with her father.

Instead, his misdemeanor involving a formerly lethal firearm, gave him twenty-five years hard labor at Amazonia foresting the main source of both food and legal drugs in Americana.

However, interment there was as lethal as a death sentence since no one had ever returned from Amazonia to any Americana Federation district. Her father became a persona non grata along with hundreds of thousands of Americanians deported to the Amazonia work camps to produce food and pharma for over six hundred million loyal Populists.

* * *

Steve sat in a window seat on his flight to Miami. On take-off, he watched the DC monuments below, only meaningful to the Federation, like the Pyramids of Egypt, of an ancient civilization without any relevance to the present.

He puts on headphones and turns on TV news.

The anchor says: "As expected, President Paz has announced her bid for a third term as Americana Federation President. It's hard to believe anyone will consider opposing her. Just seven years ago she won the last recorded Electoral by 509 to 29 with Florida the only Federation District lost. In her incumbent bid for a second term, the Electorate had been abolished, but President Fatima Paz took the popular vote 654,125,019 to 1,391,267.

The greater conundrum wasn't her overwhelming victory, but rather why would anyone bother to vote against her.

Steve grumbled to himself, " Indeed, why?"

He noticed the passenger in the seat beside him, a burly man with red beard, watching the same news. The man motioned for Steve to remove his headphones. He did.

The passenger said, "Because Fatima Paz has blood-washed all of Americana but Florida."

"*Blood*-washed?"

"Y'know. All that vaccination bullshit to rid the Federation of COVID pandemics."

Annoyed, Steve said, "So what? That's what the Mandatory Inoculation Act of 2049 achieved. We wouldn't be sitting this close without face masks if we hadn't rid the Federation of all illness."

"That super serum brainwashed everyone in the Federation but Florida. You don't believe that spic bitch in the White House got all those votes without adding something to that last COVID-49 serum to brainwash everyone into voting for her do you?"

"I believe the Americana Federation system of the popular vote."

"Sannie Claus, too, I bet. When they'd get to you, bud? Prenatal? Or Preschool inoculation? Don't matter. Unlike me, you no longer know when to call a spade, *a spade.*"

Steve put his headphones back on, and mumbled, "I'm not into conspiracy theories."

The passenger beside him made a devil's horns gesture with index fingers beside his head and wagged his tongue at Steve.

Steve sighed, pressing the control that slides a plastic shield between them. He watched a news clip of a speech President Paz made at her first inaugural address ten years ago.

President Fatima Paz was just forty, stunningly charismatic as she'd spoken:

"We can no longer depend on contemporaneous outcries of Federation victims. We have the cure at hand to prevent all pandemics and we must use it at any cost. But our greater threat is racism, bigotry, and lack of empathy for others. Given the power with my re-election, I'll stop at nothing to eradicate that curse on Americana. Nothing!"

The passenger beside Steve tapped on the clear plastic between them. "What I tell ya? Goddamn blood-washed!" he shouted.

***

Steve stood at curbside arrivals in Miami feeling the heat and humidity.

A beat-up pickup pulled up to the curb and the driver waved to Steve. He opened the door and got in beside driver in his sixties. Missing front teeth, the driver chewed on a straw of sugar cane. He wore torn jeans, a stained wife-beater, and a crooked straw hat with a stained sweatband. Sweat dampened his sleeveless T-shirt.

Steve wrinkled his nose at the man's odor as the pickup pulled into airport traffic.

With a drawl, the driver said, "I know I ain't purty, but I do like ta dance. What's yer churse?"

Steve replied, "The cha-cha, but only if I can lead."

Extending his rough hand to Steve, he said, "Welcome to the last hell hole in the Federation, Steve."

"Sam, right?"

Sam nodded.

"You got my watercraft ready to embark, Sam?"

"Set and rarin' to go, boy. Might as well take a nap. We got a long drive to Key West and its hotter 'n hell. After this A/C, when ya step out a my pickup, it'll hitcha like a Louisville Slugger to the back of yer head.

Steve nodded, pulled his baseball cap over his eyes, and slumped down for a nap.

* * *

Steve woke and shook his head as the pickup crossed a bridge on US Highway 1. "We there yet, Sam?"

"Almost. Case yer wonderin', I'm retired ABI. Medical—burnt out. When my Daddy couldn't drink no more, he just enjoyed watchin' me drink. That's how the ABI is for me now. I just like to watch."

"How's that workin', Sam?"

"Beats a sharp stick in the eye."

"I guess."

"Well, ya know, I got security clearance. So I'm wonderin', what they 'spect ya to do in this hell hole of rebels?"

Wary in unchartered territory, Steve hesitated to say.

"Shit, Stevie, we both got our Cerebral Implants, so we're being monitored by Central Control. We didn't have to do the code words at the airport.

We both already knew who each of us was, and so did yer Group Leader Chavez.

"You know Jessica?"

"Sure. Back when I still had my front teef. She was green and I was ready to retire, but we passed like ships in the night at DC Headquarters. Was her idea to put me here as a liaison. Got no family, so stayin' connected to the ABI for the perks ain't bad. Did Jess arm ya?"

"No. If I got caught by the rebels with an ABI tungsten pistol, they'd kill me on first contact."

"Sure would, but with no weapon they'll know fer sure you're ABI undercover. I got a piece for ya, right thar in the glove compartment."

Steve opened the glove compartment, took out a pistol, and whistled.

"Ain't she purty, Stevie?"

"A classic from the twenties, a 9 mm Glock, standard law enforcement carry forty years ago till the Federation outlawed them with repeal of the Second Amendment."

"It's standard rebel issue in Florida. Without it, you'll be gator food b'fore sunrise."

"Thanks, Sam. I assume the rebs think you're one of them."

Sam said with a wink, "In the 'Gunshine State' it would be your mistake to think I ain't." Steve grinned and they exchanged Federation nods of *—it's what it is.*

"I'll take that under advisement, Sam. Once I establish my presence with my treasure trawler, what's my best direction?

Barney's Stone Crabs is walkin' distance from the marina. Work it till you're trusted. Be patient. Rebels 're as deadly as swamp rattlers. Don't blow it."

* * *

At the bustling Sigbee Marina on Dredgers Key, Steve boarded his 40-foot trawler and gave his thumbs up to Sam as his retired ABI connection departed.

Steve took his trawler out into the Gulf. He fished and scuba dived off the boat as the sun went from midday to dusk He docked his trawler named "Raging Storm," showered, and applied instant tanning lotion to look like a native. He dressed casually, white shorts, a colorful Hawaiian shirt, and sandals, even on deck because sneakers were only for tourists.

He quickly saw his target on a neon sign a block away: BARNEY'S STONE CRABS – EST. 2049

* * *

Steve established a presence in the Florida Keys for several months. Using ABI's flash credit for easy maneuverability, Steve created an identity as an adventuring soldier of fortune in Key West, seeking rare relics and sunken treasures. His aim was to fit the profile of a loner, which the rebels might be seeking to join them.

Slocum's manner was subtle, so it took longer than expected, almost two years, but with patience and persistence, he felt certain his approach would be like sticking a firm hook into a marlin's jaw for a sure catch.

He knew his instincts were right when he sensed that his encounter with a young native Floridian at a clam bar could become his "soft contact." The young woman called "Bonita" was just a feeler, and probably not from the main source. Still, that hookup could help Steve ease into Bonita's daily routine as her bar customer where she worked at *Barney's Stone Crab's* shanty on the Gulf with a patronage of locals off the tourist beaten track. Sam's direction had been on the mark.

"Hard contact" directly with a rebel would come only after he'd given Bonita enough slack to swim freely away with his lure, even to dive deep to avoid his questions. He'd been well-trained with this approach in the field, even just as an informant long before.

That had been prior to any of his intense ABI indoctrination as a cadet. He then served as an F-14 field agent for five years with one year stints in five different Americana districts: Montana, Hawaii, Alaska, Mexico, and Cuba—now Florida.

According to other employees at *Barney's*, his mark, Bonita, had been tending bar there for years.

"Bonita on the night shift makes the best mojitos I've ever had—and I've had quite a few," Steve remarked to the waitress at his table tucked in a corner by an open bay window where he could peer out at the marina and see his docked 40-foot trawler-style motor craft and feel the Gulf's breezes. In a pinch, his utility fishing vessel slept two.

"Bonita? She's been here since Barney's opened," his waitress remarked. "So she can make a perfect mojito better than any of us."

He saw on the restaurant's wooden sign with the stone crab logo: *Established 2049.*

He tipped his waitress and walked over to the bar. He knew Bonita's schedule from habit: 7 p.m. to 2 a.m. Bonita checked in ten minutes early as usual. He was reading *The Miami Herald* the old fashioned way on paper, still part of the charm in Key West. He sat at the bar as if unaware of her entrance. She waited behind Joey, the daytime barkeep, as he cashed out, then she filled the antique register with her leather sack of cash and change.

Monroe County, FL had been granted a special Federation permit to use cash in Key West as a tourist attraction with a feeling of history and tradition from bygone days. Tourists bought a certain amount of cash for their Key West vacation, which was charged digitally to their Cerebral Implants. All unspent cash had to be returned upon leaving Key West, but with no refunded credit. Tourists accepted this courtesy loss, encouraged to spend every dime before departing for home. The loss by tourists amounted to millions in annual surpluses for Key West—the cost of doing business for visitors. But Steve saw the financial system as a legal means to create a slush fund for the rebels suspected of hiding in the swamps a hundred miles or so north on the mainland of Florida.

With his head literally buried in the newspaper, Steve knew nearly two years of bating Bonita had succeeded when he was startled by her snapping her finger against the front page of *The Miami Herald* spread open to the sports section, showing last night's digital baseball scores.

"Hey, handsome! How 'bout a mojito—on me," she said with pursed lips and sparkling green eyes. Her platinum pixie coif gave her an elfish presence as did her personality, glib and curt. She was like a female leprechaun, petite, with a hidden pot of golden information about a secret rebel encampment.

"On you? What's the occasion?" Steve asked.

"Birthday."

"Not mine."

"Mine.

"Really. Wow!"

"Bet you can't guess my age?" she challenged.

"Bet? If I get it right, what's in it for me?"

"Jeez! Men! How 'bout nothin' but a free mojito?"

"Not worth the risk," he said.

"Why?

"If I guess too old, I might never get another perfect mojito from you."

"You think I'd give up my reputation here by wasting my temper on the likes of you—a soldier of fortune in the tropics with no woman? Not that there's anything wrong with it, but I've heard rumors that you're gay."

He joked, "As the day is long—NOT!"

The other regular bar patrons laughed enjoying Steve's volley with their favorite bartender, all in favor of seeing Bonita get the best of Steve.

"There's a good reason for not having a woman," he said. "When *you're* free, I'm at sea. You're the only woman I've seen worth passing up a day of scavenging or fishing. But I'm up for that loss if you are."

She blushed at his flattery and the night shift bar patrons howled.

"So . . . if I guess you're age right, we take the same day off together. Deal?"

"And if you're wrong—even by one year—what do *I* get?" she asked.

Steve reached in his pocket for a pearl necklace and put it on the bar. The patrons began to *ooh* and *ah*. Bonita was street-smart and water-wise enough to know that the pearls were genuine, probably scavenged from a shipwreck.

Actually, the pearls served as a "flash roll" to lure a suspected rebel and gain trust. The necklace was the real deal passed to Steve on a scavenger dive from another ABI undercover agent, and underwater in case Steve was being watched, always the best assumption to make on any ABI mission.

Bonita took the pearl necklace in one hand as if she were weighing it, then held it close. Her eyes reflected in the pearls with a greenish shimmer.

"You're on, Stevo," she said, addressing him by the moniker she'd chosen for him months ago. She'd nicknamed all of her regulars.

Steve slid off his barstool and said, "This is like sizing up a thoroughbred. Let me check your teeth? Say, *ah!*"

"I'm a gift horse, Stevo, so you don't get to look me in mouth. C'mon. How old?"

"It's a matter of deduction, Bonita darlin'."

"How so?"

"You've been tending bar here since Barney's opened, so you had to be at least twenty-one ten years ago. An obvious guess would be thirty-one, but I think you might've gotten away with tending bar with fake ID, maybe at eighteen."

"So you're guessing twenty-eight?"

"No. I'm allowing one year as a fudge factor and assuming you wouldn't offer to buy me a drink if you were turning thirty, you'd be home crying about it. You're celebrating your last birthday before turning thirty. My guess is you're twenty-nine."

"You lucky son of a bitch!" she shrieked.

"I won that date with you, Bonita. When—that's your call. Regardless, the pearls are yours. Happy Birthday!"

Across the bar, he swung her around and fastened the pearls at the base of her long, thin neck. She turned around and leaned across the bar to nuzzle Steve's nose with hers before giving him a kiss. They were heralded with applause from Barney's regulars.

His hook was sunk deep into the marlin's jaw.

* * *

Steve urged Bonita to join him on his trawler for her next day off. On a perfect day in April with the college Spring Breakers come and gone, she seemed thrilled to spend the day on his boat. With a cloudless azure sky and the turquoise Gulf clear enough to see the bottom forty feet below, they headed out to sea.

Three hours into their leisurely cruise heading northwest, Steve anchored a mile north of Cape Sable and the mouth of Shark River, but south of The Thousand Islands.

"You seem to know this area well," Bonita remarked, handing Steve a mojito, made from the ingredients she'd brought in a cooler at his request.

He nodded as he took his first sip, his throat parched from shouting to be heard over the trawler's engine for the past three hours.

"Yeah, I've been coming to this secluded area for the past two years. Before that I docked my boat at Boca Chica Key. "

"I thought that was a Federation Naval Station?"

"Naval Air. I'm a pilot. Served my six years then decided I wanted to go freelance. I kept my watercraft docked there for my days off away from all that spit 'n' shine bullshit," he said with his own bull shit sliding off his tongue like the slime of a slug.

"Can you make a good living at this scavenging business?"

"Enough for one. I'm not greedy and easily pleased. However, you've spoiled me with your mojitos. They're addictive."

"So am I, once you get to know me. Then there's no going back."

"Hmm. Sounds like a plan. How about a scuba dive for starters. Then we can talk more about my potential addiction over drinks and the stone crab sandwiches you brought us from Barney's."

"I'm in," she agreed, then they suited up to see if there was anything worth spearfishing between the reefs and the mangroves for a late dinner.

* * *

Their shared day-off routine continued for two months well into the hurricane season. A Cat-2 storm, kept them from the Gulf for one week in October, so they agreed to go to her place that day since his boat, where he also lived, would be too dangerous where it was docked and subject to high winds and tide surges. Since going to her place was Bonita's idea, Steve's assertion into her private life was subtle, his MO.

He'd had no interference from Jessica via their coordinated cerebral implants, mostly because he'd been following her ABI orders to a tee from his CI. Since Bonita was a native Floridian going back to the Post-Trumpian collapse of the United States as a capitalist democracy, her parents had avoided the newborn inoculation and cerebral implant mandates under the Populist movement since the election of President Paz.

Steve had learned this from Bonita over long conversations on their shared days off with their intimacy finding solid ground with mutual outlooks on life, even if false or feigned, surely by Steve, but perhaps by Bonita as well. No inference about rebels ever came up.

His only shared thoughts with Jessica to date had been the nightly: Miss you. Plan going well. I've made soft contact. 😊 👌 💋 😎 💌

Though Steve and Bonita had shared nothing physically intimate beyond long passionate kissing, entrance into her bed in her space was a first. He didn't worry about what Jess would think regarding his sexual intimacy with his soft contact, because Jess was a dedicated ABI Group Director who had done likewise in the early stages of her own career. The mission always came first. Field assignments would eventually terminate, but his mutually vested feelings with Jess, hopefully, would not.

The first time Steve had made love with Jess was much different than with Bonita, which he assessed must be Bonita's free-thinking, un-implanted mind, and his showing no visible scar from a newborn or Federation Academy entrance vaccination. Jess had been a methodical lover, right out of procreation and recreation training. There were no tags from Black Market films or books, like BJ, 69, doggy, or cowgirl style. Jessica had asked him the first time if he'd preferred Program 3, Article 7. Page 11, from the ABI Training Manual. He'd preferred Program 5, Article 8, Page 9 and wasn't shy about it.

Though to some, this academic approach might have seemed dispassionate, the cerebral implants' projected visuals were similar to what people back in the earlier 21ˢᵗ Century, would have tagged as "porn."

Though there had been a rough learning curve in the early stages of cerebral implanting, by 2040 it had evolved into a smooth process that excited all participants. Unlike Jess, Bonita came at him like a savage, an animal hungry for fresh meat. There was a control for his CI to be put into "sleep mode," which Steve quickly applied so Jess would not be sharing his passion for Bonita. Fortunately, because Bonita sunk her teeth into Steve's shoulder and mounted him with her tongue thrust deeply into his open mouth. He gasped at how her green eyes seemed to glow in the dark like a panther in heat or about to devour its prey.

To bring her fervor down a notch, he teased her with, "My, what big eyes you've got, Grandma."

"Grandma? My eyes are young and beautiful?" she balked.

"Indeed. But so-o-o big, Bonita."

For sure," she said, taking his member in both hands and shouting, "So-o-o big! Like this, but the eyes have it! Aye-yiyi-yi yi!" she shrilled with laughter, something Jess had never done, with sex being an activity for them to enjoy with great precision, but never with any shared amusement. The lighthearted simmer of their mutual passion over time forged an inseparable match of their minds as well.

"I'm a virgin," she said, to his surprise and disbelief. "But don't tell me this is gonna hurt you more than it will hurt me."

"I'll be gentle, Bonita. I promise."

"No way! I want to remember tonight forever. Slam my head against the headboard, Stevo, and give me all you've got."

To the benefit of the mission, Steve's physical aplomb met her challenge. By morning, as far as convincing Bonita of his rebel recruitment was concerned, Steve felt sure he was in—like Flynn.

* * *

Having won over Bonita's confidence, Steve was poised for hard contact with the Floridian marauders that he felt sure were pulling her strings. Still, he waited with patience for her to make the first move in that direction. An opportunity arose on the long Winter Holiday weekend in late December with the hurricane season behind them.

"Listen, Stevo, if I ask you to meet my family this weekend, are you gonna blow my suggestion out of the water with all that solo forever lingo you keep spouting? I'm not looking for marriage, just for someone with mutual trust. That's what rattles my cage, something I can sink my teeth into."

"You've never talked about your family, *Bonbon*," he said giving her an affectionate tag of his own.

"Sort of, I was taken in by strangers, left on their doorstep during the COVID-29 surge. I have a big family with twenty brothers and forty sisters . . . an adopted family of course. We're having an old fashion Christmas party. You know, from the olden days when they were still permitted."

"You're not afraid of a Federation raid and arrest?" he asked.

"No chance of that."

"How come?"

"Trust me. You'll see. C'mon. Let's pack a few things and take your boat."

"My boat? Where to?"

"Can't say, and when we're close, I need to surprise you by blindfolding you for the last ten miles of our cruise."

He wondered. *Could I have played her any better? Or is her trust in me too good to be true?*

* * *

"OK, Stevo. Time for your blindfold."

Bonita didn't know that Steve had the special ABI GPS tracker in his implant, which was technically a "cerebral" implant, but not standard issue for the public. It was an *anal* implant impossible to detect by any current systems, not even by Chindia's pervasive hacking technology ever since the Eastern Federation landed on Mars and set up an inter-planetary tracking system of American's population. Some ABI agents joked that Chindia's Chairman Hu Bong Yu new when President Paz was having her "mense" as the Chindians called it. Bonita never asked outright, but must have assumed that, if Steve was a native Floridian like her, he'd neither been implanted nor vaccinated as required elsewhere.

Though relinquished by the other fifty-three Americana districts, Florida was the only district to maintain the anti-quated "State's Rights" referendum, whereby cerebral implants and newborn inoculations were voluntary, rather than manda-tory as was the law throughout Americana. The enticement for Floridians to voluntarily be implanted and vaccinated was their greater employment opportunities, Federation benefits, and a guaranteed 75% retirement income at their highest annual salary by age sixty.

An hour after he'd been blindfolded, Steve was disturbed by the sound of Bonita lowering the dinghy off the side of his trawler. When he tugged at his blindfold, Bonita shouted, "No! Not, yet, Stevo! Don't spoil your surprise!"

He was surprised, but mostly to find that his GPS was scrambled and dysfunctional, a hindrance he hadn't counted on, figuring Federation technology could outmaneuver any rebel defense.

She helped him into the dinghy and she began to row. Not until he felt dense foliage brushing against him from both sides did he insist, "Come on! I want to see where you're taking me."

"Just a few more minutes."

With his anal GPS scrambled, he was confused.

When she removed his blindfold, his CI went into 360-mode allowing him to scan his surroundings in every direction, even in X-Ray or MRI modes, which only ABI agents were equipped with, and even then, only in limited distribution to the most esteemed cream of the ABI crop. Jessica had pulled strings to get Steve the most recent update on those CI features for this crucial mission to round up the last cohort of rebels and dispose of *Frequency 76* for good. She hadn't foreseen that, though the Federation could see through Steve's eyes, the scrambled GPS couldn't pinpoint the rebels' location where he was with Bonita. "Just don't get caught as a spy by the marauders," Jess had warned him. "As your Group Leader, I can hit my central control to liquidate you rather than let our technology get into the hands of the enemy."

"Enemy?" Steve had questioned her terminology for the rebels. "They're neither Chindians nor Europeans, but Amercanians who've gone astray. I see my mission as an attempt to win their hearts and minds over to the Americana Federation, to make them understand and appreciate all the benefits to them and their offspring if they fully embrace the future as we see it, disease, virus, and racist free."

"I guess that's why I love you, Steve—always empathetic. However, anyone you can't win over will either be publically executed or sentenced to hard labor in Amazonia, depending on the degree or their crimes against the Federation."

Steve thought of those words from Jess as he tossed his blindfold aside and sensed a heat mass coming their way, but no weapons were detected in the group of a dozen, seven male and five female, one among them, as shown from Steve's updated CI scan, was in her third trimester carrying a baby boy.

"Who's that with you, Bonita?" the tallest among the men shouted.

"A friend!" she called back.

"With benefits," Steve whispered, so she prodded him with her foot.

"A friend to whom?" the tall man shouted.

"To us and what we stand for!" she proclaimed.

"State the oath then!"

"Stand up and lock arms with me," she told Steve.

The dinghy bobbed in the water as they locked arms and tried to steady their balance. "We join together in peace and harmony with nature and with gratitude to the creator who made us all intricately different from one another, but with acceptance and love, as taught to us by his only son, our beloved redeemer, now incarnate within the shell of our great leader, Jason!"

"Does your friend agree?" the man shouted as the eleven others stood like totem poles at his flanks. All were dressed in white, with shorts on the men, mid-thigh level skirts on the women, and all with loose-fitting smocks with bared shoulders. All wore straw hats of various designs meant to keep them more comfortable in the steamy swamp with Spanish moss dangling from higher growth and the water, brown and rippling with snakes and gators.

"You must answer for yourself," Bonita whispered to him.

Aside he asked her, "And if I don't?"

She rolled her eyes toward a passing bull gator longer than the dinghy.

"Yes!" Steve shouted. "I agree wholeheartedly!"

"We accept your pledge on face value, but if we find that your faith is a sham," the tall man said, "our sentence of hard labor here is no less painful and deadly than in Amazonia, and you will never leave here."

"Judge *me*, too. If I've been misled by my friend, I offer myself to be sentenced instead of him if I'm wrong about his soul."

"You speak as if betrothed," the man challenged. "If so, your father will be disappointed that you've not first asked for his approval."

"Though that may be our custom, I've found this man to be exceptional, and trust that my father will agree,"

"Then come forth, and we shall see!"

Steve whispered, "Your father."

"Jason is father to all of us—in spirit."

Each member of the greeting party carried a machete, and as Steve and Bonita passed between their flanks. Each man grasped Steve's forearm by the elbow and each woman kissed him on each cheek as he responded to all in kind, much to Bonita's unfiltered glee.

Walking briskly, the trek along the narrow path took half an hour including a two-minute pause to allow a twenty-foot python to pass without incident.

Bonita said aside to Steve, "We kill nothing that breathes."

* * *

When the greeting party brought Steve to an open clearing, he saw a village with families sheltered in lean-tos suspended above the jungle floor by thick vines. There was a central cooking area to boil drinking water and make soups from various vegetation. A member of the greater assembly blew a horn made from a kudzu vine. The sound drew many others concealed in the swamp all chanting: "Ja-son! Ja-son! Ja-son!"

An old man, taller than any of the others, came out of what was the largest and highest hut in the village with a rope ladder ascending to its open porch. With long white hair tied in a ponytail, and a white, braided beard that dangled below his waist, he raised both hands above his head, palms to the sky.

All took a knee with respect. Steve followed suit, watching the final knot with a metal cross at the end of the tall man's braided beard swinging back and forth hypnotically.

Lowering his arms, their leader turned to Bonita and asked, "Who is this man you've brought to us, dear daughter?"

"The man I love," she declared as the crowd murmured, but the leader raised one hand to quiet them."

"To what purpose?" he asked Bonita.

"To learn our ways and accept them as we do."

"Is this true, my son?" the old man asked.

"Yes, sir," Steve said with a nod.

"Do you love, Bonita, enough to share her dedication and responsibility to us, her family? To keep our secrets from the Federation?"

Steve was trained not to quiver and quirk undercover with many missions requiring lies and behavior that, outside the ABI, would appall him. He'd become fond of Bonita, surely attracted to her physically, but he'd have to set aside all feelings for Jess on this potentially deadly mission to infiltrate and destroy this minority rebellion before it could take hold beyond Florida. He was confident that Jess believed that was true from the moment she'd chosen him for this dangerous assignment.

He wondered. Was it a test of his loyalty to Jess as much as to the ABI and the entire Americana Federation?

He recalled his training motto: *To catch them, one must run as they do. To terminate them, one must be willing to be terminated with them for the future of Americana.*

Steve quickly learned within a day among these rebels that their cause was as vital to them as his was to Americana. They revealed how *Frequency 76* could function in a primeval swamp with little physical connection to the outside realms of Americana. They'd made a pact with Chindia to gain access to some of their high-tech systems from Mars, which enabled them to broadcast anti-federation propaganda throughout Americana without revealing its source. They used a system referred to as "laser ricochet" that made tracing its original source impossible for the ABI. The communication was based on the antiquated WiFi systems of the 2020s, but enhanced with the lasers that were generated from an energy source found only on Mars. The simplicity of the system boggled Steve's mind, but even if he were prone to disclosing this information to the ABI, the rebels would surely kill him if he tried to leave their hideaway.

He stalled for time waiting for a possible chance to escape with what he'd learned about the rebels. It was nearly two years since he'd been with Jess. He no longer thought about the comforts and pleasures of his secret affair with his ABI superior. It was Bonita on his mind daily, making him wonder if what he felt for her was deeper, less fleeting than what was waiting with Jess for him back in Virginia.

* * *

A week later a feast was prepared to welcome Steve into "the tribe," as they referred to themselves. Musical instruments were made from vines and animal skins, never from a killing, but salvaged from confrontations between species, gators vs. pythons and the like, for clothes, shoes, and entertainment. Most revered in the Glades, was the—believed to be extinct—panther of the swamps. For this celebration of tribal matrimony, Jason wore a headdress with a panther's head, his eyes glaring from the jungle cat's sharp open jaws.

"I thought—?" Steve started to challenge Bonita about the killing of the panther for tribal pageantry.

She put a finger to her pursed lips, shook her head, then whispered, "A road kill on I-75. They're elusive, but not yet extinct, much like our tribe."

They exchanged smirks, which electrified a mutual communication that blocked out everything around them. For Steve, that look from Bonita's green eyes seemed to erase all intimate connections with Jess. He would marry Bonita in this tribal ritual without guilt. Though it was his duty to ABI to do so, just to get information, it felt like more than that. His mutual attraction to Bonita was like a natural stream seeking its level as it flowed toward a high waterfall then poured over into a calm pool of infinite depth below.

The words of clarification from Chief Jason resonated in Steve's mind. Like their livelihood their rebel cause was simple: "To vaccinate against disease is for the greater good of all humankind, but to inoculate against prejudice is to kill the soul by removing that free choice, which has the power to condemn us to hell or raise us to the heights of our redeemer."

Jason explained his condemnation of the Populist movement that gave President Paz a 99.9% majority.

"Her mass constituency has let her combine the cure for disease with the blindness to any differences among us. We need to accept our differences as they are, not create a shield between us and truth with the guise of healing. In so doing, we lose the gift of empathy God has given us with our free will."

Steve wondered, had he found a firm foundation to build a better life, not for Americana, but for himself with Bonita? Not in comfort with the Federation, but here in the miasma of swamp life and always on the run with the constant fear of discovery and punishment.

Steve felt that this was the happiest day of his life, because Bonita had fulfilled his yearning to belong to something greater than himself. The ABI may have lured him to believe his loyalty to the Americana Federation could satisfy that need, but something had been lost in translation along that path. He belonged here, but knew he'd have to tell Bonita everything about himself on this, their honeymoon night in the Glades among the same marauders he was trained to track down, then imprison or kill.

As Jason brought Steve and Bonita before his Council of Elders encircled by the entire tribe, Steve felt elated to be making this commitment to Bonita and to her people.

Jason held them by their joined wrists and asked the tribe, "If any tribe member objects to this sacred union, speak now, or forever hold your peace!"

A loud voice came from the entrance path to the village, "I've been holdin' my *piece*, but it's a 9mm pistol. I'm gonna shoot this Federation spy for messin' with my betrothed!"

Steve saw two men standing side by side. The younger man had shouted. He was tall, brawny, and in his mid-thirties. By his manner and tone, Steve recognized him, confirmed from his CI which showed the same man giving him the finger and devil horns on his flight from DC to Miami two years ago. The other man was old and emaciated, seventy or older. Steve looked to Bonita biting her lower lip.

"Zach!" Bonita shouted. "We thought you were dead."

"There's a first for everything, and I'm the first rebel to ever escape from Amazonia. My friend here is the second. It took us five years to make it here, but we ain't dead, and I've come back for my darlin' bride."

* * *

Bonita clutched Steve's hand tightly and looked to Jason for judgment.

"Honorable Council," Jason called to his elders. "What says the Good Book of the Glades on this matter?"

"Death challenge!" one shouted, echoed by the elders.

Bonita gasped. "Have I no say in this?"

"Not according to the Good Book, daughter," Jason proclaimed. "We have your first suitor back from the dead, surely a miracle to ponder. We have your second suitor, chosen by you. But would you have chosen him if Zach had never left us on his assignment to protect us from the Federation's wrath? This is a choice which only these two men can resolve in a challenge to the death."

"No! Please, father, not to the death," she pleaded, but to no avail.

"A tribe with no adherence to its own code isn't worthy of allegiance." The elders nodded and murmured in agreement.

"Let me warn you"" Jason proclaimed. "Even if Zach dies and the interloper kills him, Steve will still face trial by Council to prove his innocence of the charge Zach has made against him. If Steve is a Federation spy, and possibly the worst kind, an ABI agent equipped with their latest technology to destroy us, he must die despite his victory in this challenge."

"I've admitted my guilt," Steve argued his case. "I've been converted and stand by the rebel cause. I'll show my loyalty by taking Bonita as my wife swearing to rear more rebels for the future."

"How can you be sure Zach is still loyal," Bonita challenged. "No one has ever escaped from the Amazonia work camps. Have you made a deal with the Federation for your release? And who is this elderly stranger with you? Maybe he's your ABI handler tagging along to reveal the location of our secret encampment to the federation."

Zach sneered at her accusation. "The old man helped me escape. He'd been a prisoner in the pharma fields for twenty-five years long than me. Together we served the last two years daily planning our escape, he with inside information about security and me knowing where to go once we'd found our way out. We were in Mexico for a year, but then we worked as fishermen and island-hopped the Caribbean. We made here to Florida where the Federation is a curse word. Let me introduce my friend, Carlos Chavez, an Amazonian inmate for thirty years. He served half a lifetime for a misdemeanor when the Federation was just starting its strict ground rules against the now defunct Second Amendment. Back then we had the right to defend ourselves against tyrants."

"Your friend's fate is in your hands, Zach. If you die in this competition, The Good Book says he must die with you. To outsiders loyal to the Federation, our ways seem harsh, but maintaining strict accountability has preserved us."

The old man with Zack shook with terror, perhaps wondering if his escape had been worth it. Steve felt sorry for him, but also sensed something familiar about him. He was certain he'd never seen him before, but there was an itch in Steve mind about this old man that he couldn't scratch.

Before Steve could think about it more, he and Zach were led to a long table encircled by the villagers.

"Choose your weapon wisely, my sons!" Jason called to them from his balcony above. "You will depart in opposite directions for as long as it takes to bring back a Glades trophy, a living animal for our judgment. The two animals will be caged together. The animal chosen that kills the other will then be enclosed with the dead animal's captor. If the animal kills that man, the other will marry Bonita. But if he kills that stronger animal, only then will two men face each other in a final death challenge because, according to the Good Book of the Glades, no man shall take the life of another without losing his soul to the devil, lest it be in self-defense."

Zach nodded for Steve to choose his weapon first. These were handmade weapons which all the tribe were familiar with. When Steve chose a machete, Zach laughed and those in the tribe who were his friends did likewise. Zack chose a bamboo pole with a sharp stone honed and attached to one end for a spear and the other end with a sharp bamboo point.

Zach mocked Steve. "A bull gator in these parts will have your arm clean off before you can get close enough to swing that machete, let alone catch 'm. My weapon is a twofer, death at both ends and enough distance to give me leverage to tie up a gator without gettin' chopped up in his jaws. Good luck. You'll need it, Federation loser."

Both men turned to Bonita for confidence, but she seemed distressed over losing either of them, Zach because he had been good for the tribe, her Stevo because she loved their shared intimacy.

The horn sounded and the men took off in opposite directions. Steve knew he was at a disadvantage because, despite his five-year absence, Zach knew these swamps. Steve used his CI to track Zach, which enabled him to circle the village's outskirts and observe Zach from a distance to learn from his methods and find an animal that wouldn't become easy prey to Zach's catch. The game was afoot in the sweltering swamp, with a miasmic pool of death at every turn.

***

Though Steve was a superb physical specimen at 6' 2" and 190 pounds, barrel-chested Zack was four inches taller and out-weighed Steve by sixty pounds. *Brains over brawn* fluttered in Steve's conscience tainted by Jessica's thoughts from afar. *Out think him,* her voice penetrated his mind as he focused on Zach's heat image, waist deep in the swamp with his spear held over-head. Zach's quick pace made Steve feel sure that his nemesis knew exactly where he was headed and what his trophy would be. He could neutralize that advantage by countering Zach's catch with his own catch better equipped to kill it. Better yet, Steve needed to catch something that, in turn, could kill Zach so he wouldn't need to.

He didn't want his killing Zach to scar his future with Bonita.

Though in the rebel's den only a short time, so many things that Bonita shared about her tribe, made Steve respect their courage despite the odds against their ever bringing down the Federation. Steve was posing as an adventurer inadver-tently dragged into this lethal conflict. He was not a killer, and didn't see Bonita's people as killers either. They were different from what he'd become accustomed to since he was a boy. His CI from birth and pre-school vaccination made him see no adversity from others. In the Americana Federation, all saw each other as equals without question, not as a choice, but as the result of the serum that killed prejudice along with lethal viruses.

Neither Bonita nor any of her tribe had uttered an expression of violence toward those outside their tribe. All any of them had ever expressed, until just before Zach's return, was defense, protection against the outside forcing them to conform to the ways of the Federation defined by mandatory prenatal vaccination and cerebral implantation.

Steve had never thought about either, because his conscience had told him ever since he could remember that both were best for 99.9% of Americana's population. A sacrifice of all individual freedom to decide for themselves, but for the greater good.

Who would ever want to depose President Paz? Except for these rebels and those few willing to listen to their *Frequency 76* propaganda, everyone else loved Paz like their sister, daughter, or mother. She was the essence of all that was good and she should be cherished by everyone. If only Steve could make Bonita believe that doctrine the way he did, maybe he could save her.

Suddenly, his CI sensors detected a struggle in the water. It was Zach for sure, but what had he caught? Or what had caught him?

* * *

Steve saw, in his mind, that Zach was having an exhausting struggle with a twelvefoot bull gator, its raised head on the bank was the size of the engine panel door on Steve's trawler, a deadly brute. Steve's instinct was to help him, but he held back. An impulse from his CI came like a whisper from Jess telling him that Zach could be in line to succeed Jason as the rebels' leader—*Zach must die.*

After an hour battle with the gator, Zach escaped and retreated to find another prize to bring back to the village. Rather than wasting energy looking for his own trophy, Steve tracked Zach for several hours. After an encounter with a deadly creature, Zach emerged from a thicket with a fifteen-foot Burmese python. The snake wasn't nearly as long as many found in the Everglades, a recent record was twenty-three feet, but it was still a lethal threat as evidenced by severe bites still bleeding from Zach's calf and forearm Zach had brought a burlap bag in his backpack, his Glades experience giving him the edge to know the huge snake's most likely habitat, how to find its trail, and the best way to bag it. He'd bring it back alive to face Steve's catch, and possibly in the end, to face Steve. Now with a taste of human blood, the python's appetite for humans was piqued.

So his own choice would best match its opponent, Steve followed Zach to be sure he didn't decide to scrub his first catch and replace it with another. When Zach appeared resigned to return to camp with the python, Steve used his CI to scan the swamp for possible choices to meet the tribal challenge against the huge snake. Though physically capable of killing most anything the Glades could provide, Steve's mental prowess made him what Jess had called a "double-threat" with a sharp brain backed by brawn.

He matched what his heat sensors detected with a CI image in a burrow along the banks of the mangroves. Hearing his steps, the creature retreated into its burrow, but not before Steve got hold of its tail. In a tug o' war, Steve won and dragged the creature's five-foot length from its den. Though its best defense was playing dead, it had a secret offensive weapon to use as a last straw. Aware of that danger, Steve bound its hard shell with kudzu vines and proceeded to drag its 120-pound weight back to the village. He was careful not to touch the creature, which his CI warned could infect him with a dreaded lethal disease, not adversely affected by Federation serums contained in prenatal inoculations because of its rare habitation in highly populated districts.

***

Nearing dusk, the rebels were in loud celebration over the ensuing contest to the death. Jason raised his hands high to quiet the rebels to an immediate hush. Steve stood at the village entrance, his proud figure backlit and silhouetted by a vermillion sunset.

"What have you brought to the fray?" Jason called to him.

Steve tugged on the vine to bring his creature into the light of the festive bonfire centered in the village. Many expressions of amusement, confusion, and mockery flowed through the village in a wave of insults like the squawks of fleeing magpies.

"What were you thinking, Stevo?" Bonita asked, certain this odd creature stood no chance against the python, which was already agitated by the villagers' raucous shouting for the match to begin.

With confidence, Steve told her, "Trust me, Bonbon."

Steve's creature entered the cage first, nervously running from corner to corner for somewhere to burrow and hide.

With a grin of satisfaction, Zach dragged the heavy sack containing the python and unfastened its tie to release the huge snake into the cage. The tribe cheered.

Both predator and prey sensed the other, the snake coiling for its first strike, but the nine-banded armadillo Steve had captured cowered in a far corner of the cage.

The villagers jeered and Bonita huffed with disappointment, obviously wishing Steve had brought back a more worthy opponent to face Zach's python. Her apparent disappointment hurt Steve more than his leaving Jess behind in Virginia. Bonita had broken through his hardened ABI exterior, which he'd thought was as firm as an armadillo's shell.

He'd thought his ABI training and preschool vaccination had given him immunity to the rebel yell on the pirated airwaves emitted from the Glades. Instead, he'd absorbed all of their treasonous rhetoric through his intimacy with Bonita. His thoughts empathized with the marauder's manifesto against the Federation. He hadn't fully acquiesced to ABI's sole prejudicial discriminatory bias against these rebels. Through intimacy with Bonita, he felt a new awareness, foreign to his upbringing. He saw what these marauders possessed, an allegiance to a greater spiritual judgment from beyond their material world—something lost, but once sacred to humanity.

It didn't matter to the rebels whether their assessment of others came from an omniscient God or merely from infinite empty outer space. They believed the human condition itself demanded their acceptance of all humankind as equals from their heart and conscience alone. Imposing empathy within anyone by violating their bloodstream, or with the electronic impulses from a CI into their grey matter was unacceptable to these pariahs hiding in the swamps.

These backward folk opposed Federation Cerebral Implants monitored from Americana Central Control, the ever pervasive ACC. These rebels would have none of that, but with the risk of possibly returning to a life of rampant racism and intolerance of anyone different from themselves. They were willing to take that risk by depending only on their natural consciences and adopting the ancient Patrick Henry soliloquy by blasting that slogan over *Frequency 76* airwaves: "Give *us* liberty, or give *us* death."

Steve recalled Jessica's condemnation of the rebels: "We'll give them what they want—death. Much worse than death would be to keep on living outside Americana's protection. We'd end up like Europa or Chindia, shitholes whose constitutions are sealed with no more than traitors' excrement."

Bonita had argued with Steve, "Our citizens can see others as our equals without vaccinations or CIs to monitor our thoughts and behavior."

Steve couldn't admit outright to Bonita that he was an ABI spy, which would result in his execution by her people. If implicated by Steve's mission as his accomplice, she'd be killed by her own. With compassion for her, Steve preferred she lived with Zach as his mate than have any harm come to her.

He asked himself, "Is that love?"

He supposed it was, and what he admittedly enjoyed and missed with Jess was what? Mere recreation? Or was it a comfortable by-product of his vaccination to accept his partner, his family, his friends, his job, everyone in Americana, all who were ever born there, all who would ever be born there ? If so, what intrinsic value could a predetermined life have? A life without personal choices?

"Equality by all and any means!" had been the outcry of supporters of President Paz to win in her first term. She'd achieved that by her second term. Why would anyone want to argue against no disease or racist bigotry? Only this unruly cohort of vagabonds protested against her ideology of a flawless Americana Federation with each empathetic to one another and to the whole of Americana society.

Challenging Americana's discrimination against the Europeans and the Chindians, Steve had asked Jessica, "Why can't we vaccinate our enemies as well, so they'll respect and honor us as equals, just as we'd respect them? Wouldn't that serve a greater global ideology of equity for all humanity?"

Jessica's answer had been direct and concise: "Because only Americana is blessed by God. Europeans and Chindians wish to destroy us because they're jealous of our biotechnological advancements that have cured all illness and wiped adversity from all Americana citizens' minds. That belongs to us alone, never to be shared outside Americana."

These thoughts gave Steve an intense headache—unless it was Jess trying to reach him by his CI. She was so honed into his mission that she made him envisioned its outcome as if it were already successfully completed. That was a special CI upgrade for ABI agents to keep them focused enough to predetermine all outcomes.

The crowd's shrieks shook him from his thoughts as the python struck at the armadillo's shell with no ill effect to the weird-looking, scaly mammal. The snake seemed to feign retreat, but in so doing, lured the curious armadillo closer where perhaps a strike could penetrate its natural armor.

A sudden strike broke several of the python's teeth, much to Steve's satisfaction and Zach's dismay. The villagers were placing bets on the outcome, declared illegal back in 2041 by the Americana Federation Council and unanimously signed into law forbidding gambling, football, and basketball. Though virtual baseball remained, betting on the sport was punishable by banishment to Amazonia work camps for life. Offenders were tattooed on their backs with a life-size image of the notorious offender, Pete Rose, from seventy years ago.

Smuggled out of Key West, Steve had a few dollars to bet on his armadillo, a diversion to take his mind off Bonita, and his concern for her safety by her association with him. The tribe's energy peaked when the snake was about to coil around the armadillo and squeeze the breath out of it. Instead, the shelled mammal sprung projecting its armored body with the force of a cannonball fired at close range, killing the snake.

Steve grinned and said to Zach, " Your snake's death grin looks like an item for the Chindian wet market."

He's learned about an armadillos secret weapon when his land vehicle couldn't avoid an armadillo on I-75. Projecting its shell caused five thousand Americana trade units worth of damage under the hood.

Still agitated by its near death, the armadillo curled up in a ball in a far corner of the cage. One animal had killed another animal, so the villagers had no qualms about chopping up the dead python to make shoes from its skin. The meat was fed to gators, and their domesticated dogs, assuming they would acquire a taste for python at the top of the Glades' food chain. Pythons had extended their northern migration as far as Pennsylvania with year-round the daily average temperature at 70 degrees since the northern and southern poles had been reduced to no more than a local snow storm, now a phenomenon that had not occurred in the past thirty years of recorded meteorology.

Zach said to Steve, "I'm going to spear your ugly beast and feed it to the gators, then I'll do the same to you."

"I'd stay as far away from that armadillo as possible and let it wander off on its own," Steve said.

"Hell I will!"

Before Steve could stop Zach from throwing his spear at the armadillo. It wriggled, impaled by the spear as Zach mocked the dying creature in its death throws. He lifted it by its tail and held it up to kiss its head as it faded into death's slumber. Saliva from the armadillo dripped from its death grin down Zach's arm and into the blood still streaming from his python bite when he'd wrestled with it before its capture.

"There's no point in challenging me now," Steve said. "You're a dead man walking. Neither you nor any of this tribe will live another week, for some, not even another day."

"More bull shit!" Zach laughed.

"Though my vaccination makes me immune, without that, you're all vulnerable to the deadly disease armadillos carry. Those of you who aren't lucky enough to die quickly will suffer with the horrors of disfigurement from leprosy. In this environment, without Federation inoculation, the disease will spread through your village like wildfire."

"There must be some way to save us!" Bonita pleaded.

"My dinghy holds only two, so Bonita will leave with me." Steve said, turning to her. "I'll take you with me back to the Federation for inoculation, which can cure you." He turned to the tribe. "Bonita is your only hope to preserve your beliefs and carry your rebel cry into the future. If you let us leave unharmed, I'll join her in that effort. If any of you want to be saved, we'll return to rescue you if you're willing to surrender to the Federation and be vaccinated. Only Bonita can lead us back to you in that effort. So it's up to her."

"What does Jason say!" the crowd demanded.

"I'm old," he responded to their cries. "Too late to change my ways. I wish to die here with my people, but each of you must decide for yourself. That's our creed, self-determination—no inflicted Federation programs for the so-called—greater good."

Steve said to the villagers, "Those with young children may wish to be saved upon Bonita's return with a Federation medical team to vaccinate you."

The elderly gathered around Jason in allegiance to their leader and his wisdom from a lost world of innate spiritual empathy before it was artificially imposed by the Federation with a vaccination. The Americana population had been told its vaccinations were meant only to end all viral pandemics forever. Americana citizens outside of Florida had no idea they'd been inoculated against all bigotry. More than just brainwashing it amounted to what Zach had claimed, *blood* washing.

With Jason's blessing, Bonita clung to Steve in their departure. They left the Glades in his dinghy and returned to his trawler to contact a Federation medical team in the Gulf.

"I love you, Stevo, even if you've been an enemy to my people and our natural ways."

"I love you, too, Bonita. We'll get through this mess and figure it all out later, once I'm sure you're safe."

They embraced and kissed then he rowed the dinghy toward his trawler. He didn't need to contact Jess for confirmation, as he saw by the sky sleds surrounding his boat.

Agents and first responders were ready to be led back into the Glades to destroy the rebel encampment and *Frequency 76* from any further broadcasts.

Steve's biggest surprise wasn't the speed at which the team had come to his rescue, but that his Group Leader, Jess, was leading them. The vibrations in his head told him he was glad to see her, but when he didn't give in to that sensation, he felt nauseous and puked over the side of his trawler.

Nodding toward Bonita, Jess asked Steve, "Is this their dirty little spy?"

"I've promised her immunity and inoculation. She's been exposed to leprosy."

"Hmm. We'll see. I've missed you, darling."

"Either you give her a vaccination now, or she won't disclose the rebels' location."

"Don't be foolish, Steve. I could torcher that information out of her right now if I wanted to."

"She'd never tell you that way. She'd gladly die first."

"He's right, bitch," Bonita said. "I wouldn't tell you shit."

"It seems you've let yourself get too close to the enemy, Steve. I'll have to request a review board to see if you require reprogramming when we return to Headquarters in Virginia."

"Do what you like to me, just give her a vaccination so she won't die of a disease she was exposed to in the Everglades."

"Are you sure that's what you want, Steve."

"Goddamn it! Yes!"

"Roll up your shirt above your shoulder," Jess said to Bonita. Jessica swiped Bonita's shoulder with disinfectant and injected her. "Satisfied?" Jess asked him.

He nodded. "For now."

"You're next," she said. "You've been undercover almost two years, darling. Since I last saw you, we've developed a booster shot. With so much exposure to the enemy and all their diseases and propaganda, the best of us must receive ultra-care. Roll up your sleeve, Steve."

As he did, Bonita frowned at him then looked away with disgust.

"Go with my agents," Jess said to Bonita. "Lead them back to your hideout while I debrief Agent Slocum. We'll decide what to do with you later."

Bonita huffed and shook her head. She followed the other ABI agents to their sky-sleds then led them back into the Everglades. Once they were out of sight, Jess tried to embrace Steve, but he stiffened and withdrew.

"Come on, baby," she said. "We're just days away from our fifth anniversary together. You know what that means."

"I'm not coming back to you, Jess. I love her."

"You can't be serious. She's like a feral cat. She'll bite, scratch, and piss on your floor."

"Sure, Floridians are backward compared to our Federation sophistication, but they still have something we've lost along the way to our perfect world without dissent, disease, or discrimination."

"I can't imagine what? Unless they enjoy their rotten teeth, cancer, and arthritis."

"*Choice*, Jess. They're able to make their own choice to empathize with anyone who's not exactly like them. A free choice. Nothing imposed by vaccination."

"The Americana's population approved it by more than ninety-nine percent twenty years ago, Steve. The few marauders should have known better than to rebel."

"But Jess, only because of our apathy, *we the people* chose not do that on our own. Not without the serum to make us see everyone as we see ourselves. Without that, to most Americanians anyone outside their own family would be just niggers, spics, chinks, honkies, Karens, guineas, Micks, wops, wetbacks, ragheads, whatever derisive tags that hate had espoused up to the 2030s."

"It's progress, Steve. We can't go back to those tribal divisions of hate. If we did, how could we avoid civil war? Wouldn't Europa and Chindia love *that*."

"But, Jess, that popular vote came after two generations were fully vaccinated, like a self-fulfilling prophecy. In so doing, we've lost our humanity. We're just like machines."

"If that's the free choice I could have had at birth, I sure don't want it back. Do you, Steve? You don't really believe you could love that disgusting swamp tramp if you hadn't been vaccinated?"

"It's too late, Jess. I already love her."

"I can't let you leave me, Steve. In two days we'll become a Common Law couple. It's time for us to have children, to propagate the Federation."

"We've been apart for two years, Jess. That broke the five-year Common Law chain."

"With my rank—I've pulled Federation strings for the Council to look the other way. I've already had the contract drawn up by a Federation Judge who owes me. Done deal."

But Bonita loves me."

"How sad for her, truly, especially since you'll no longer want her when she returns to us."

"How can you know that?"

"That wasn't a booster shot I gave you, Steve."

"What? Did you poison me?"

"Just your mind, with the old ways. You've been de-vaccinated, Steve. Now you'll see her as she really is."

As Jess laughed, he felt strange and feverish. He ran to the sink on his yacht to drink fresh water, but as he chugalugged the water to quell his fever, he saw his reflection in a mirror. He put his hands to his face in horror seeing a human race that had vanished almost three decades ago. Vanished, yes, but only from the perception of differences between races and ethnicities. Such distinctions had been eradicated by vaccination in the trade-off with the same serum that ended the plague of coronaviruses in Americana.

The Federation kept its miraculous serum from the other two thirds of world's population in the enemy Federations of Europa and Chindia.

President Paz had proclaimed: "Without definitive enemies, societies will implode upon themselves with the self-absorption of their own ideologies."

Steve had been educated in college to fear impending socio-economical cannibalism.

He argued, "But you've injected Bonita with the serum, so she can't perceived me as I am. She'll perceive me the same way she perceives herself, with no racial or ethnic distinction. By vaccination, you've made Bonita one of us."

"I gave that little wench a placebo. She'll see you just as you are, and now you'll see her just as she's always been. Then you'll come back to me, and I'll reinject you as a wedding gift so we'll both see each other as we had before this terrible mission that almost took you from me."

He felt sure Jess was just bluffing, that when Bonita returned to his trawler, they could resume what they had started in Key West together. He imagined how they'd celebrate the New Year 2060 in New York's Times Square together, an Americana tradition that had been suspended until the serum was fool-proof against all pandemics from a resurgence of measles to the last coronavirus, COVID-49.

* * *

Hours later, Steve saw from his trawler, the returning ABI agents, medical team, and rebels who'd agreed to succumb to vaccination. Jess grinned at him with resolve, a look that had always alerted him that she knew so much more than he did. He looked for Bonita among the group heading toward him, but didn't see her.

"What have you done to her!" he demanded, but Jess just shook her head and went below deck waiting for him to join her in his bed."

"Bonita!" he shouted to the crowd as the hovering sky-sleds came close.

One young woman turned her head toward him with sad, sunken eyes, but she didn't seem to know him.

"Bonita! Where are you, Bon-bon? It's me, Stevo."

She stood up at the sound of her familiar nickname, but when she saw who was calling to her, she gasped in horror seeing how pale he was, the mark of a race that had been erased from Americana before she was born, and thought to be extinct—a much dreaded Caucasian.

Trying not to look at him, Bonita put her arm around the old man that Zack had brought back from Amazonia with him. Emaciated, and his eyes glazed with cataracts, the old man's lips quivered as he called out with a gravelly voice, "Jessie baby! Where's my baby girl?"

Bonita shouted to Steve, "His name is Carlos Chavez, he won't be vaccinated and expects to die, but he wants to see his daughter one last time."

Hearing the commotion from below deck, Jessica appeared beside Steve. "Daddy?" she called to him, but before she could say more, he pulled a tungsten pistol from the ABI agent's holster beside him and shot his daughter in the head.

"What has my baby daughter become?" he asked with his final breath as an ABI agent grabbed back his pistol and shot the old man in back of the head.

Chaos broke out between the surrendering rebels and the ABI agents, but the rebels outnumbered and outflanked them, quickly taking over the hover sleds and the tungsten weapons.

The placebo Bonita had been given by Jessica couldn't shield her actual perception of Steve as he watched her wrench the pearl necklace from her neck with disgust and throw it overboard.

"I'm their new leader!" she proclaimed. "I'm the blood daughter of Chief Jason."

She flipped her middle finger at Steve in defiance as he watched the pearls in the aquamarine Gulf sliding off the chain in their slow decent to the sandy bottom from whence they'd come. The rebels took control of the hover sleds and motioned for Bonita to join them in their return to their tribal lair in the swamps.

Steve hoped this had all been a hallucination. Maybe from the drugs Jess had given him for a good night's sleep before he left on his mission against the rebels hiding in Florida and broadcasting propaganda 24/7 on *Frequency 76* against the Federation.

"I still love you, Bonita," he said, watching her vanish in flight with the others.

Then he dove off his yacht to retrieve the pearls discarded in anger by Bonita. The cool rush of the crystal clear water showed the pearls glistening brightly at the bottom with just a fading hint of Bonita's green eyes sparkling from their deep dispersion.

"Inclusion and empathy are two legs of a three-legged stool. The third leg, which allows that stool to support the weight of the world, is love."

Gerald Arthur Winter

Acknowledgements

Buried Treasure – *Connotation Press* – 2-25-14

Star Struck–*The Creativity Webzine* – 3-07-16–Hollywood River Rats–*The Creativity Webzine* - 7-08-16 – Stories We Tell

A Free Sampling–*NY Literary Magazine* – 9-29-16 – 5-Star Award for Meaningful Fiction Treadmill–*The Creativity Webzine* - 1-22-17 – Behind the Scenes

Priceless–*The Creativity Webzine* - 4-16-17 – Languages of the World Menagerie (titled "Simian")–*The Creativity Webzine* 8-27-17 – Sci-Fi Meets Horror Vermillion–*The Creativity Webzine* 11-26-17–Art

Fractured Frontier – *Gremlin Creative* – 4-13-18 – Mixed Genre

The Catch–*The Creativity Webzine* 5-04-18 – The Net

Afterglow–*The Creativity Webzine* 9-25-18 – Music of the Night

Jetsam–*The Creativity Webzine* 1-31-19 – Gods and Monsters Hand to Hand–*The Creativity Webzine* 8-31-19–The Quantum Reality

The Last Gulag–*The Creativity Webzine* 11-30-19 – Outer Space vs. Inner Space The Aviary–The Creativity Webzine 5-31-16–Faith

Visuals

Leonardo Da Vinci–The *Vitruvian Man* (c. 1485) Academia, Venice

Chicago Tribune–Election Day 1948

Michelangelo di Lodovico Buonarroti Simoni–*Volta della Cappella Sistina*), painted between 1508 and 1512 Detail from *The Creation of Adam*, portraying the creation of mankind by God. josef-stalin-gulag100-v-gseapremiumxl_orig

"Flowers on the Wall" – The Statler Brothers Columbia Records © 1965

About the Author

Gerald Arthur Winter has a BA in Journalism from Rutgers University and an MFA in Creative Writing from University of Tampa. His short stories have been published by The *Connotation Press, The Creativity Webzine, 2 Elizabeths, Gremlin Creative, Hardboiled, Writer Fairies,* and *NY Literary Magazine* which published his story, "A Free Sampling," with a 5 Star Award for Meaningful Fiction in September 2016. He has published over 80 literary stories since 2014.

His mystery novel, *Hemingway's Trunk*, is serialized in twelve monthly episodes from March 2020 through February 2021 online at:

https://moultoniancreativity.weebly.com/hemingways-trunk.html
Read more about the author: www.geraldarthurwinter.com

Many thanks to . . .

Charles Moulton at *The Creativity Webzine* for his continued acceptance of every aspect of my work including many of the stories contained in this collection and for his generous serialization of my novel, *Hemingway's Trunk.*

Stevan V. Nikolic at *Adelaide Books* for his acceptance and publication of this collection.

Elise Holland at *2 Elizabeths* for her acceptance of my story "Auld Lang Syne," and my sixword story in the *Love and Romance* anthology.

Michael Fromm at *Gremlin Creative* for his appreciation of my multi-genre, difficult to place story, "Fractured Frontier," also included in this collection.

Meg Tuite for her acceptance of two stories at *The Connotation Press,* including "Buried Treasure" also included in this collection.

Gary Lovisi for his acceptance of two stories at *Hardboiled.*

Steve Kistulentz, Director of the graduate creative writing program at Saint Leo University, for reading my collection with genuine enthusiasm and appreciation for its worth.

Donna Koros Stramella, author of *Coffee Killed My Mother,* for her appreciation of my advice and her enthusiasm for my work.

Brook T. Amos, coauthor of *Iron Horses & Paintbrushes: My Life as a Railroad Man & Artist,* for reading and appreciating each story in this collection.

All my mentors and alumni from the MFA in Creative Writing program at the University of Tampa, especially Directors, Steve Kistulentz and Erica Dawson, and my personal mentors: Tony D'Souza, Mikhail Iossel, and Jeff Parker.

My daughter, Kim Winter Mako, fellow author and my toughest, but loving, critic.

Ms. Messenger, my 5th grade teacher in Oakland, New Jersey, who encouraged me at age eleven to become a writer.